E. HOFFMANN PRICE'S
WAR & WESTERN ACTION
MEGAPACK®

ALSO BY E. HOFFMANN PRICE

E. HOFFMANN PRICE'S
WAR & WESTERN ACTION MEGAPACK®

WILDSIDE PRESS

COPYRIGHT INFO

Contents

INTRODUCTION, by Shawn Garrett

Welcome to *E. Hoffmann Price's War & Western Action MEGAPACK®*! Wildside Press, in association with Mr. Price's heirs, are dedicated to making the extensive body of work of this pulpsmith extraordinaire accessible once again to the public through their line of MEGAPACK® collections.

Edgar Hoffmann Price (July 3, 1898 – June 18, 1988) was born in Fowler, California. A graduate of West Point, he served in World War (followed by military duty in Mexico and the Philippines) and was a champion fencer and boxer —fellow pulp author Jack Williamson referred to him as "a real-life soldier of fortune." Hoffmann was also something of a polymath—a Republican and a Buddhist, he was also an amateur Orientalist, and a student of the Arabic language.

Price's first fiction sale was in 1924 to *Droll Stories* magazine and over the years he befriended, corresponded with, and personally met many authors of the pulp era including Robert E. Howard, Clark Ashton Smith and H.P. Lovecraft. He wrote hundreds of stories for many pulp magazines (including *Weird Tales*) in varied genres like horror, detective, adventure, fantasy and science fiction. Wildside Press is proud to make his work available to readers again. Due to the inaccessibility of much of Price's work (he kept no manuscript archive and so we must resort to those original publication copies we can track down) we have decided to package the material into themed MEGAPACK®s, highlighting specific genres he worked in. Later volumes will be released as we gather further material (any collectors interested in aiding our endeavors by supplying photocopies from their collections are urged to contact Wildside at our website: http://wildsidepress.com/).

The *E. Hoffmann Price War & Western Action MEGAPACK®* contains 20 stories—11 war stories and 9 tales of the old west. The war stories begin with 3 pieces featuring Price's tough-guy series character Dan Slade, before moving on to various theaters of conflict around the globe. The western stories begin with 4 tales about series character Simon Bolivar Grimes, followed by others to round out the set. All these stories were published between 1936 to 1945.

We hope you enjoy these thrilling tales of crime and detection.

TRIANGLE WITH VARIATIONS

Originally published in *Spicy Detective Stories*, Aug. 1935.

Everything was strictly kosher until Valene invited Dan Slade to stick around for a drink, and headed for her bedroom instead of toward the refrigerator. And then Slade took a tumble.

While it was private stock she was breaking out, it wasn't anything kept in a bottle. He didn't actually see her slip out of the gown that for the better part of the evening had kept him wishing she had put it on backwards, but he might as well have, for while her negligee, when she reappeared in the doorway, could have covered everything a lady keeps concealed from all but two or three very dear friends, the edges of the filmy substitute for nudity weren't on speaking terms...

There's an infallible way of losing one's memory and Valene's formula did the job in an instant. One eyeful—Slade forgot that she was Jim Tilford's wife, and that Tilford wasn't chained to the roulette wheel at Coppa's.

That eyeful was something like eating nine hundred dollars worth of pep tablets and then getting kicked into the Sultan's harem. Valene's silken legs were perfect from her dainty ankles to the guard stripe on her hosiery, and from there on the view became really good.

The white roundness of her thighs found refuge in a froth of lace just in time to give Slade a chance to observe that Valene's sighing inhalation threw her breasts in dazzling relief against the chiffon that caressed them like a lover's hand; and her scarlet smile was as inviting as her warm curves.

Then she remembered that the negligee had revealed everything but her wisdom teeth, but before she could do anything about it, Slade had an armful of Valene and a carload of plans for the evening.

"Oh... Dan! You're hurting me!" she protested, trying to withdraw from his embrace. Slade's crushing kiss cut her short, but her retreat was highly successful: it brought them a pace closer to a divan that was an acre of invitation—though it might have been the courthouse steps for all Slade now cared.

Her struggles suddenly relaxed. A shudder rippled down her body and her breath came in quick, short gasps. Valene's protests were becoming inarticulate murmurings, but she was doing her best to say no—in sign language, since his fierce kisses again stifled her objections.

Then the edge of the lounge made her knees buckle; and treachery from the rear was too much, with persistence from the front. A flurry of silken legs and chiffon—and then her arms closed about him to make the best of it...

Bit by bit, Dan Slade's failing memory responded to treatment. He began to recollect that she was Jim Tilford's wife. Valene laughed softly at his tardy penitence. With feminine wisdom, she had repented in advance. And it was his fault anyway, and if she'd screamed, it'd have caused an awful scandal.

"Don't be stupid, Dan," she murmured. "Jim and I have all been all washed up for ages."

Which was true, and earlier that very evening, the Jim Valene armistice had flared into open warfare at Coppa's place. Tilford, sourly drunk, and as usual, bucking the roulette wheel. Valene, sweetly reminding him that he had lost a play after ignoring her winning suggestion.

That was always good for a fight, and it ended in an appeal to Caesar:

"Dan, for God's sake take her home! She's a hoodoo!"

And here they were: Slade and Valene.

"He's wild about Nancy Forrest," she added. "And he wasn't as drunk as he pretended. That quarrel was just a stall so he could ask you to bring me home so he could hang up with Nancy tonight—weekends aren't enough for them any more."

That was more than half probable; but Slade and Tilford were passably good friends and it was a rotten situation, All the more so, since an hour or so with Valene was enough to make it a habit with anyone—anyone but Tilford, and he'd in some way gotten out of the habit, as Slade had just deduced from one thing and another.

"Jim's drunker'n hell, and what's more," he countered, jerking away from her embrace, "he began winning as soon as you stepped to the check room for your coat. I'm going back to pilot him home. Been too damn' many holdups of gambling house customers lately, and—"

"Dan, don't be silly!" Valene was on her feet at a bound, but Slade, resolutely ignoring the ankle-to-collar-bone view, stalked to the door.

He stepped on the starter and tramped on the gas, driving wrathfully and recklessly, sending the *coupé* screaming to the outer fringe of the city and then hurling it out the highway.

It was going to be hell from now on, keeping away from Valene; and facing Tilford would be worse.

And then, three miles from Coppa's, Slade jammed his brakes to a screaming, smoking halt as he rounded the sharp curve. In the moonlight he saw a car that had smashed headlong into an oak that would telescope a battleship: Jim Tilford's canary yellow Packard. On the far side of the wreck Tilford lay sprawled on the ground. You could see with half an eye that he was dead.

Slade stepped to the running board of the sunburn special, and noted that Tilford, though drunk, had snapped the switch as he left the road.

And then, glancing back toward town, Slade saw the cause of the crackup; the self-luminous marker that indicated a sharp turn in the highway had been moved from the left to the right of the road. It would fool a sober driver.

"Accident, hell! It's murder."

Murder—and robbery. He had beaten Joe Coppa's wheel, but Death's roulette stopped at double zero.

Slade, as he reached for Tilford's wallet to verify his conclusion, saw a scrap of paper, hastily crumpled and half thrust into a vest pocket. He withdrew it. It was a penciled note, in crudely printed letters:

Tilford:
Better go home early tonight. You might see something worth looking at.

A friend.

"Good God..." muttered Slade. Robbery was bad enough; but this was fairly putrid! No wonder Tilford had left Coppa's, driving like the hammers of hell. But who had given him that damning note, that tip-off which but for Slade's belated qualms of conscience would have brought Tilford to his house before Valene could remember that the refrigerator was in the kitchen and not the bedroom!

"But maybe it's just a gag—it'll work with any married man." Slade assured himself. Still, it didn't quite stick, and he was hoping that robbery was the motive. Somehow, that would make him feel a bit better about it; better than thinking that somebody really had been wise and had in good faith sent Tilford to check up on his wife.

He reached for Tilford's wallet and the long, legal size envelope that peeped from the inside coat pocket; but his fingers did not quite make it. Something crackled behind him.

He started, heard a tense, short gasp, and from the corner of his eye saw a dark form lunging toward him. And as he whirled, he was knocked headlong across Tilford's body.

Something hard and swiftly moving crashed against his head and shoulder. His brain roared into a burst of flame, and then blackness blotted out all sensation...

When Slade's consciousness finally returned, he struggled dizzily to his knees, rubbed the egg-sized lump on the side of his head, and resumed his search of Tilford's pockets. The envelope and wallet were now gone.

But in a side pocket of Tilford's coat, Slade found three small blocks of wood wrapped in paper. Odd baggage to carry to a gambling resort. They must mean something—but what? He took them, then picked up the penciled note which lay in the grass, near the head-bolt wrench which had felled him.

The ache of his shoulder told him why his skull had not been crushed as Tilford's had been. He had started just in time to rob the blow of a portion of its force.

As nearly as he could estimate from a glance at his watch, Slade had been out for about half an hour. He looked back toward town and saw that during

11

that time the self-luminous highway marker had been moved back to the proper side of the road.

"Anyway, it was robbery—that note was just a stall," he concluded. "I happened along before they could roll Jim. And got cold-cocked."

But the fact remained that Tilford had headed home on a hot tip. And as Slade drove to Coppa's to phone the police, his thoughts were none too pleasant.

"That note may be evidence, but I'm keeping it under cover. Even if it's a fake, it'd sound like hell...or was Valene in back of this job..."

Self-made widows aren't unheard of; and that spat at Coppa's began to seem tailor-made. Slade and Tilford had snapped at the bait. And for the last mile he suddenly hated Valene and himself.

* * * *

Slade found Joe Coppa circulating among his patrons, his sharp black eyes missing nothing as his gold and ivory smile salved the losers and greeted the newly arriving optimists.

"Joe, how much did Tilford win?" he demanded.

Coppa shrugged and guessed it might be four-five grand; which was a trifle at his place.

"Any strangers? Any tough mugs hanging around?" snapped Slade.

Coppa's beady eyes contracted as he saw the sallowness of Slade's grim face.

"'Smatter, Dan? What the hell—maybe some of the crowd ain't social register, but I don't allow no rough stuff—"

"Jim Tilford's been run into the ditch and robbed. He was pie-eyed, and I came back to get him."

Slade touched only the high spots, and said nothing about having had his own brains well shaken up. Neither did he mention the three wooden blocks.

"Come to think of it," said Coppa, "there was a coupla hard-looking mugs eyin' Jim while he was taking us down the road, and then they parked themselves along the sidelines and begun reading a paper. I sort of think they did leave right after he did."

He indicated a now vacant row of chairs not far from the wheel Tilford had been bucking. A Chicago *Tribune* lay on the floor.

"That's it, lyin' there now," added Coppa.

"Nail it," snapped Slade. "May have finger-prints. There's not many stands that carry out-of-town papers. People don't come out here to read the news— unless they're damn' well interested in checking up on the hometown and don't care to write or wire. Get it!"

"Uhuh," agreed Coppa. "And by watching the down-town newsstands, you might grab 'em when they come for their next number. Particularly since we got good descriptions of 'em."

Slade phoned headquarters, then drove back to Tilford's wrecked car, to await the arrival of the police. He detailed his finding Tilford, and mentioned everything but the penciled note. He had forgotten the three blocks.

"And now that you've got something to work on," he concluded, "I'm going home—my damn head's about ready to bust."

But Slade returned to the city, he was certain that no out-of-town hangers-on at Coppa's had written that note to advise Tilford to come home early. And for the looters to take the long, white envelope from Tilford's pocket was distinctly a false note.

"And finally," demanded Slade, "why was Jim carrying a business size letter around with him to Coppa's? Also, what's he been so damn' worried about the past three-four days! That's what made him flare up and ask me to get Valene the hell out of there—that's what made him pile out, hell-bent, when he got that crackpot note."

He did not want to go home, nor did he want to see Valene. Valene last of all. He feared that he might read guilt in her smouldering eyes. Amorous—and spiteful—she might have done anything.

Spiteful—

And that reminded Slade of Tilford's secretary, and Valene's remarks. If anyone could give him the inside track, Nancy Forrest could. When Jim wasn't battling with his wife he was at Nancy's apartment. Slade stepped into a drug store and dialed her number.

"Dan Slade speaking. I want to see you. Right now. About Jim. Never mind why."

He hung up before she could argue. Ten minutes later he was punching the doorbell; and then he began to understand Jim's choice in sweethearts. He could hardly believe that this could be the trim, self-effacing piece of office equipment he had called an armful of nothing at all.

She was taller than Valene, and just as shapely; but unlike Valene, hers was a cool and restful loveliness. Her eyes were star sapphires, veiled by heavy lashes, and her smile was refreshing instead of inflaming. Yet the severe simplicity of her dressing gown could not quite conceal the fluent sweetness of her body.

They eyed each other for an instant. Slade knew he could not tactfully edge up to the subject.

"Jim just got cracked off," he blurted in a dry, hard voice, "Murder, sure as God made little apples."

Nancy's breasts for an instant swelled the silk of her gown. Then she froze —still lovely in her wide eyed, rigid incredulity.

"How?"

Slade told her. Everything—except the color of Valene's step-ins.

She listened in dry-eyed silence. Slade knew she was too hard hit to weep.

"All right, Nancy—you sing yours," he concluded. "What kind of letter would Jim be packing around in his pocket, even out to Coppa's? Why'd he

13

want to mail it personally? And what's he been telling you about Valene?"

Nancy Forrest forced a pallid smile.

"He told me," she finally said, "that Valene was nutty about you, and he wished to God you'd take a tumble and get her off his hands—only, he'd kind of hate to have you tangle up with a hell-cat like her."

"Then he couldn't have been so damn' wrathful on his way home tonight."

Nancy agreed and then queried, "But why would the person who beaned you take the wallet *and* letter?"

"A guy in a hurry would grab the works. But what the hell was in that letter! You ought to know."

"Nothing but routine for the past few days. But he has been awfully up in the air about something."

Which got nowhere. And Nancy was beginning to crack under the shock. She'd be weeping all over his shirtfront in another moment. He could tell from the nervous twist of her fingers as they knotted the edge of her dressing gown.

Slade reached for his hat.

"Don't go," she said. "God—I feel—so damn' lost—"

She looked it. He wondered what Valene would say when she heard the news.

"Get a drink," he said. "You need it. So do I."

Murder or no murder, if that gorgeous armful draped herself all over him, and they began swapping condolences—

"Anyway," he grimly reflected as she turned to head for the kitchen, "Nancy still remembers the refrigerator isn't in her bedroom."

Which gave her the edge on Valene. And so did the bright lights as she crossed the threshold from the kitchen, playing the devil with Nancy's transparent gown.

But Slade's resurrected conscience balked at making the evening a study in comparative anatomy.

He resolutely ground a half-smoked cigarette into the ashtray, and fumbled in his pocket for a fresh one.

He found more than the smoke. With it he drew out the three small blocks of pine.

"What the hell are these?" he asked Nancy, catching her wrist just in time to keep her from depressing the lever of the siphon.

As he swallowed the straight Scotch, he watched her examine the odd cargo Tilford had carried to Coppa's—after he'd wrenched his glance from points of interest not far south of Nancy's shoulders.

In the bright light of the living room, he noted a red stain on the center of the cross section of the pieces. There was an unstained border not more than a sixteenth of an inch wide. It was perceptibly yellow—a decided lemon tint, and not the natural color of pine.

Nancy frowned, then answered, "Why—these are samples of *Wolmanized* wood."

14

"Which?"

"Wood," explained Nancy, "that's been treated with Wolman solution so ter-mites—tropical wood-eating ants—won't touch it. Jim was shipping over five million feet of treated lumber down to a big job in Belize—"

"Fancy coloring," observed Slade, still a bit cross-eyed from noting that Jim's secretary was really stacked up.

"That red stain," she explained, "indicates the parts that weren't touched when the wood was put under pressure. The chemical in the wood bleaches that red testing dye. Good Lord, how Jim tore the office to pieces when some of the samples didn't come up to specifications!"

Nancy reached for a handkerchief. Slade reached for his hat. He wanted to think.

"Be seeing you," he said, striding toward the door. "And if the police ask you things, *forget about that screwy note*. Get it?"

Nancy sobbed an inarticulate yes. But Slade did not look back to catch the sudden narrowing of her eyes, and the tensity of her lovely face.

He had something on his mind; and as he took the wheel of his car, he won-dered at Nancy's ignorance of the letter Tilford had carried with him in his pocket instead of including it in the outgoing mail.

"Something is cock-eyed," he summarized. "She ought to know about that letter. It was important enough to steal—then how could she have skipped it?"

Nancy might be holding out. Maybe she suspected him of having teamed up with Valene. In which case Slade would have the police on his neck for palm-ing a few scraps of evidence. Slade wiped the sudden rush of sweat from his forehead. Nancy was business-like enough to be dangerous. It had the makings of a damn' nice jam.

He drove to police headquarters. The news he got there hit him squarely on the chin. It was too good to be true.

"Hell, yes," said the sergeant. "We got 'em. Two mugs with Tilford's roll. A packet of fifties, with the original bank wrapping band about them. Dated, and initialed by Coppa's cashier. They claim they found him dead, and frisked his pockets, that they didn't gum up the highway marker.

"They were going to knock him off, but someone beat 'em to it—only, they'll fry in a hurry. Nothing to do but give 'em cigars and chicken, and watch the lights blink."

"Let me talk to them," demanded Slade.

The two mugs were sweating and desperate. Caught with the plunder, there had been no need of sapping a confession out of them.

"Listen, Jack," said Slade, addressing the Italian. "Tell me something and maybe I can get you a break."

They eyed each other. The red headed ex-pug grunted; Pichetti answered, "Hell of a lot you can do."

"Take it easy, fellow," grinned Slade. "Just because you sapped me on the nut don't mean I got any grudge. I think someone else did it, and you birds are

15

taking the rap. That's the guy I want. Now talk fast—or smoke, later."

"Damn it, Mac, how the hell can I talk?" muttered the wop. "We found him and his bus all cracked up. Which saved us the job. So we grabbed the roll. And we didn't sap you nor him."

"Oh, all right," grinned Slade. "Just stick to it then. The smell of roasting meat won't bother you, though the young news hounds'll park their lunches at their first execution."

"Listen," countered Pichetti, "whatta ya trying to work on us? You ain't no dick. We seen ya check out with the black-eyed broad. So what the hell can you do for us—and why'd you want to?"

"I have my reasons," retorted Slade. "Who talked to Tilford after his wife and I left?"

"Him and some short, stocky fellow with a red face chinned a couple minutes. Your buddy gave him a growl and a dirty look and told him something that made him madder'n hell. He reached for his coat pocket, and I ducked, figuring he was goin' to pull a gat—your buddy, I mean. Then he shoved some more chips on the layout, and the other guy walked off. How would I know where? Me and Red was tendin' to business."

Slade handed the prisoners the remains of his pack of cigarettes. But when he reached the entrance, he retraced his steps and asked the sergeant if they had Tilford's key ring.

"So his secretary can get into his private office in the morning," Slade explained. "He had a stack of important stuff to get out, first thing. I work with Jim on a few deals."

"Better look somewhere else, Mr. Slade," said the sergeant. "We found nothing but his car keys in the ignition lock."

And that left Slade with but one play: go to the house, and ask Valene to find Jim's key ring. Somewhere in that office, despite Nancy Forrest's insistence to the contrary, there must be a clue to that letter for which someone had killed Tilford.

Slade was certain that Tilford had had words with a person who was interested in that envelope. If he could prove that, he would have an out for Valene —and himself—just in case Nancy began thinking things.

"Damn it," he growled as he headed his car to Tilford's apartment, "short, red faced fellows in a town this size are thicker'n bum tips on the races! But she couldn't have been screwy enough to team up with anyone to run Jim off the road!"

Valene answered Slade's ring. She was surprised and a bit incredulous. He was certain that she couldn't have heard the news. Her dark eyes widened as Slade broke it out.

"God, Dan..." She swayed, caught the table for support. Slade wondered what she would say if he mentioned the warning note which had driven Jim into a trap. Then she recovered, and soberly added, "We did battle an awful lot, but that does leave me wobbly."

She looked it. Then he wondered if it was from the strain of waiting, or whether it was a spark of friendliness that had survived the Jim versus Valene skirmishes for several weary years. That remained to be seen. She had the good grace not to paw him.

"The two thugs are nailed," he concluded. "See if you can find Jim's keys. He's got some blue prints of mine in his office, and some papers I don't want his successor to get in on."

He heard her stirring around in the bedroom. He stalked up and down the Chinese rug, clenching and opening his fists. Valene couldn't be messed up with that missing letter. There was a false note.

And then, just as he convinced himself that Valene was strictly on the level, and that the red faced man had turned the trick on his own account, Slade's glance shifted toward the telephone pad. The line of advertising printed on it matched the heading on the slip which was in his pocket. His heart stopped as he bent over to scrutinize the top sheet.

There were marks which had cut through from the sheet which had been torn off. He cocked his head, and saw the unmistakable trace of words shaped with a sharp pencil. And the signature was plain: *A Friend*. That note had originated in Tilford's house! Valene was it—

"Dan, I can't find his keys," she said as she reentered the living room. Then, eyeing him: "Good Lord! You're white as a sheet. Why—what's wrong—"

"You know what's wrong!" he rasped, tearing the sheet from the telephone pad and thrusting it before her eyes. "You wrote the message that sent him tearing home hell-bent to find out whose boots were beneath the bed—after that highway marker was gummed up to lead him into the ditch. You—"

"Dan—" She recoiled as from a blow. "That note—wait—I can explain—"

But if she could, it was to vacancy. The door slammed and Slade was heading for his car. He drove aimlessly. Valene was up to her neck, but despite the evidence against her, there must be other factors.

Why had Tilford's keys vanished? Why had that envelope disappeared? To cover Valene's trail was to share her guilt—and yet, after what had happened, he couldn't sell her out. The only way of finding out where he stood was to go through Tilford's desk. And Nancy Forrest would have a set of keys.

* * * *

A quarter of an hour later he was jabbing her doorbell.

Her eyes were reddened, but she wore her grief well. Her cool, fragrant beauty subdued the wrathful surging in Slade's corroded brain.

"I'm so glad you came back," she murmured. "I've been thinking…and…"

"So have I," he said with a grim brusqueness that startled her, "And I'm damn' near ready to crack it wide open."

Her blue eyes suddenly became almost as dark as Valene's. Her fingers sank into his arm.

17

"How did *you* guess—it just dawned on me, and I've been following his work—know it almost as well as he did—"

She was leaning forward, her eyes blazing into his. Slade did not answer her question. The fragrance of her body intoxicated him, and the curved whiteness of her breasts dazzled him.

"I was shocked stupid," she continued. "But after you left, I caught the point of those samples. Those bits of wood prove that—"

And then she cracked. Too much poise to start, then giving away all at once. She was half laughing, half crying, calling him Jim and Dan alternately, and clinging to him as the one remaining link to the past.

"Steady—pull yourself together!" Which wasn't the most appropriate thing to say, but Slade couldn't think of anything else.

A full-blown case of hysteria was a new one on him. Plumb loco, and getting worse every minute. Not a chance to break away and get her a drink or souse her with ice water, or whatever you do to snap them out of it.

Jim was gone, and Nancy suddenly needed someone or something to hang on to. But as soon as she calmed down, she'd give him the missing kink she had doped out. Only, it didn't quite work out that way.

Slade gathered her in his arms, ignoring her clinging curves, the long, fine sweep of her legs, and the tantalizing pressure of breasts that every racking sob and its alternate laugh forced against him. He stroked the disarrayed, gold bronze ringlets as he tried to coax her back to balance. But things began to get complicated.

Valene had tricked him into a rotten situation—and the tighter Nancy clung the more sincere his indignation became. By the time his shirtfront was fairly soaked with tears and his ears jangled with bursts of laughter, he and Nancy were companions in misery.

And since whispered consolation had no effect, a shock might snap her out of it.

One hand slipped from her waist to the warm white curves that smiled through her filmy gown; but it was Slade who got that shock. Nancy shuddered and snuggled closer. It might have been hysteria, but it reminded him of something else—though the two are after all pretty much the same.

His next exploring caress made her breath come in short, quick gasps that weren't a bit like sobs. Then they were lip to lip, and Nancy's sighing murmur was quite rational.

As she sank back among the cushions, drawing him toward her, Slade told himself that if he broke away now, there was no telling what she might do. As it was, she did nothing more outrageous than snap out the floor lamp...

* * * *

For an engineer, Slade had it figured out well enough. And when he finally extricated himself from Nancy's arms, they were both closer to rational thought.

18

"…You must think I'm perfectly awful…" she whispered. "But… Oh, for the time, I just didn't…"

"Forget it—" interrupted Slade. "But what was your hunch? According to those test blocks, there must have been a shipment of five million feet of phony lumber about to go to Belize—"

"About? It's already gone. And with that faked wood—which'd rot overnight—costing the manufacturer about half as much as the real article, you can figure the profit someone would have taken if Jim hadn't cracked down on them."

"Get dressed and we'll follow it up."

A few minutes later, Nancy Forrest stepped into Slade's car and they drove downtown to the Federal Indemnity building. The janitor recognized Nancy and admitted them. He took them to the eleventh floor, and turned back to his rooms. Nancy unlocked the front office door and followed Slade to Tilford's private suite. They set to work searching Tilford's desk.

"Here it is!" exclaimed Slade, after five minutes of digging. He jerked a carbon copy from the center drawer. "A letter to the surety company that bonded the contract, telling them to pay off on account of the fraud. In other words, Union Wood Products is sunk—the bonding company'll burn 'em alive and—"

And then things happened in a dizzying blur of split second action. A click, and the faint screech of a hinge. Nancy's scream. Slade whirling. The blast of a pistol, and the searing scorch of lead. A stocky, red faced man, automatic in hand, standing in the threshold. *The killer had come back for the carbon copy of Jim's report.*

Slade ducked as the pistol again jetted flame. Something hit him in the shoulder like a sledgehammer. Nancy hurled a filing basket.

As the third shot blasted the plaster from the wall, Slade recovered and crashed home, driving the enemy into a corner. But he was dizzy from pain and the loss of blood, and the red-faced man was desperate. He felt his strength slipping.

Another pistol blast. As Slade forced himself to a final effort, he saw Nancy sink into a chair, clutching the red stain that blossomed from her side.

Slade's fingers closed on the armed wrist just in time to deflect the descending barrel He wrenched, and hammered home with his free fist. Red Face's head snapped back. He was out cold.

"Oh, Dan—!"

Valene's voice. She had arrived at the height of the party.

Slade staggered to his feet. Valene's face was pale and her eyes blazing. She dropped the smoking stand which she had picked up just too late to brain Red Face.

"I'm all right," said Nancy, pulling herself out of her chair. "That shot just raked me—Oh, you're bleeding!"

"Nuts!" grumbled Slade. He picked up the keys that Red Face had dropped at the threshold: *Tilford's missing ring.* And then the police followed the janitor

19

into the office. Slade eyed Valene, and concentrated on Wolmanized wood.

"Damn' near a hundred thousand graft. This buzzard tried to beg off, but Jim couldn't give him a break. Finally he sat down and wrote the letter to the bonding company himself, to keep the mess strictly private in case he relented. Put off mailing it, hating to sink the fellow, even though he had pulled a fast one. And that cost Jim his life. That's what I make of it," he concluded.

"Now if you want to check his finger-prints and see if he tinkered with that self luminous highway marker, go to it. But his coming up here with Jim's missing keys is enough."

And that held the police. Before Red Face recovered, he was getting more from the cops.

There was a three cornered exchange of glances as Tilford's friend and two widows stepped to the hall.

"I guess we'd better get patched up a bit," was Slade's suggestion.

Nancy's glance was curious as she said, "I'll call a cab, Dan. It was only a scratch. You take care of Mrs. Tilford."

Then a brief, deadly crossfire as blue eyes clashed with black.

"What the hell are you doing here?" asked Slade, as Valene caught his arm.

"I knew you'd end up here, probably with her keys," said Valene. "So I came up—to tell you—you wouldn't listen—that Jim and I wrote that note. He knew he couldn't give me to you. Even if we broke, you'd steer clear of me, just for the looks of things. So he faked that message to catch us at it and make you like it. And to give Nancy a break. Jim knew you really liked me a lot."

And that was a lot for Slade to digest at one bite. He shot a long look at Nancy, then said to Valene, "Once the doc picks the lead out of my frame, you and I are going home—to give me a chance to find out what it's like with a clear conscience!"

NIGHT IN MANILA

Originally published in *Spicy-Adventure Stories*, Oct. 1935.

The broad-shouldered American who lolled in his chair and stared somberly at the colorful whirl of dancers in the ballroom of Chow Kit's cabaret was still sober, though he had spent all evening challenging native liquor to do its worst. His white duck suit was still neat, and he was clean-shaven, but his craggy, bronzed face was drawn and deeply lined, and his blue eyes were haggard.

Lieutenant Dan Slade, posing as a dishonorably discharged soldier, had come to Manila to find out how Datu Ali, the Moro rebel down in Jolo, was getting United States government ammunition.

Chow Kit was the answer: but try and prove it. His fleet of inter-island trading boats had a dozen times been searched for contraband, but in vain. The only remaining move was to get the low down on that crafty Chinaman by a flank attack directed through the chain of dance halls and bawdy houses that made him wealthier every day.

Slade spat disgustedly as he saw Chow Kit emerge from the private office of the cabaret. Suave, immaculate in a shantung suit, his slanted eyes inscrutable as the moonstones that gleamed in the only ring that adorned his long-nailed, thin hands. The Chinaman was sizing up the colorful whirl of *bailarinas* whisked about the pavilion by dancing soldiers, sailors, and white civilians.

Exotic girls of every shade from walnut to old ivory. Malay, Japanese, Chinese; Eurasians, and *mestizas* whose touch of Spanish blood gave them an inflaming glamour that no white woman can have. Those girls had the inside rumors of Manila—but try to get at the truth behind their dance hall smiles!

Chow Kit, seeing that business was good, turned back to his office, leaving Slade to continue pondering on a bedroom and bottle approach to of government ammunition.

Presently the office door again opened. The gift who emerged could have no more than a drop of Malay blood. The slant of her dark eyes was scarcely perceptible, and the faint flare of her delicate nostrils was just enough to be exotic. And as she picked her way to a table near Slade's, the American sensed that he was getting a break. She had the run of Chow Kit's office, and she might warm up to a white man, and tell him things.

Bell shaped sleeves, and a scarf of incredibly fine *piña* cloth about her shapely shoulders, and the tall, glistening combs that adorned her high piled, blue black hair gave an oddly foreign touch to the apricot satin of an evening gown, cut low in front, and lower in back. And the *piña* scarf cast a tantalizing mist about the warm, firm curves that smiled at Slade as she reached across her table for a match.

His glance shifted from the pert breasts that rounded out the shimmering bodice, lingered along the inviting curve of her waist and the blossoming richness of her sleek hips.

"Let's dance, *chiquita*," he proposed as he caught her hand.

Agata Moreno's clinging, supple curves aroused more than Slade's hope of information. At the end of the dance, as she headed for her table, he countered, "Nuts on that notion! Let's go home and talk—"

"About how nice a shack we can keep on thirty *pesos* a month?" mocked Agata in English almost devoid of accent. "Don't be stupid, Dan."

"Thirty *pesos*, hell! Wait till I fell you who I am, and then we'll get your suitcase and spend a week or two in Baguio."

Slade, short circuiting all arguments, headed Agata toward one of the square, bamboo houses on the main street of the village just off Paranaque Road. They're primitive things, these *nipa* shacks, with floors of split bamboo. The cracks between the slats made plumbing unnecessary, and they're high enough up on stilts to give a free range to the scavenging pigs and chickens. Agata's shack, however, was ritzy. She had wicker furniture, and an American style bed instead of a grass mat.

Agata's eyes narrowed speculatively as she regarded him for a moment. Then she said, "Let's not talk about Baguio. Why don't you go back to the States?"

His story had spread. She was sorry for him.

"To hell with the States! Not after the deal I got. Just pure luck I didn't get three years and a kick, instead of a straight bobtail. So I'm staying. From now on."

In the Islands, jobs for white men are as scarce as *bailarinas* who can say no. A *nipa* shack and a Tagalog girl to hustle the groceries is the only career left to a white drifter. Slade was paving the way for someone to hint that a rebellious Moro *datu* down in Jolo could use desperate American renegades as well as stolen ammunition.

Agata's dark eyes were troubled. She was white enough to sympathize with the American outcast in a way no native woman could. Which made her valuable.

"Don't be stupid," she whispered as she seated herself on the arm of his chair. "Go back. While you can."

"Go back with me?" proposed Slade.

Her brows rose, but her smile contradicted the shake of her head.

"Sure you'll go," Slade urged. "As soon as I can raise enough money for the two of us to travel."

And that was an offer that few *mestizas* can decline, coming from a white man, even if he is a renegade.

Agata's smile was becoming more personal, but she hesitated.

"We'll get married," he added. That was the ultimate bait. And the only way a bobtailed soldier could raise transportation across the Pacific would be in some illicit enterprise. She'd talk to Chow Kit, now. "How about it?"

And before Agata could answer, Slade's arms closed about her. Despite her parrying gesture, he found her unwilling lips. Unwilling—but only for a moment. She broke away, but only to be drawn closer, to have her mouth seared anew by that savage kiss.

Agata was a fragrant armful, and as Slade's embrace tightened about her, he forgot that he was searching for information. Her slender hands clawed at his face, but he evaded their attack, kissing her throat and shapely shoulders; and as he shifted back again to her crimson lips, she no longer struggled, but clung to him. Each supple, rounded curve was quivering, and as one hand probed the sleek folds of the apricot satin skirt that was working its way over her knees, Agata shuddered, and sighed luxuriously.

Slade broke away long enough to catch a fresh breath, but her questing lips followed his.

"Don't! Not tonight," she begged; but her dark eyes were misty with promise. "*And not here*. Stay away from here, Dan! It's dangerous."

Still holding Agata in his arms, Slade emerged from the wicker chair and headed for the further room, where a whirring electric fan was spraying a cool breeze across an acre of white counterpane.

"What are you afraid of?" Slade retorted, striding towards the threshold.

"Chow Kit," she tremulously whispered. "He's been making a play for me ever since I came here. I just about convinced him that I do nothing but dance —but if he suspects—oh, don't you see, I won't be able to stall him off any longer—I'll have to leave here—he'll kill me—and you—"

That rang true; which made Agata all the more worth a play. But as Slade barged across the threshold with his clinging, quivering armful, the munitions situation in Jolo became quite unimportant.

"Don't...you'll get my dress all rumpled up..."

Well, that might arouse Chow Kit's suspicions. Slade's embrace relaxed.

And then Agata let out a yeep that shook the *nipa* thatch. The sudden flurry of arms and legs caught Slade off balance and the treacherous footing of bamboo slats did the rest. He clutched at empty air and crashed to the floor. As he gained his knees, he saw the cause of Agata's sudden alarm: not Chow Kit but a bronzed American with shoulders as broad as a box car and a face like Gibraltar on a stormy night.

One glimpse of Agata's dismayed recognition and the newcomer's wrathful amazement told Slade that Granite Face was very much at home in that shack. Nor was there any time to spring the one about waiting for a street car; not after the ankle-to-hip display of ivory tinted flesh that had greeted him as he reached the threshold.

23

Granite Face crossed the room like a *carabao* charging through a cane brake. Slade escaped utter demolition by flinging himself clear of a devastating fist that would have lifted him through the roof.

Sock!—Slade's return bombardment. The explosion caught Granite Face like a pile driver, but it was like spraying a roman candle against the side of a battleship. They closed in as Agata, getting her legs, the counterpane, her streaming hair and other odds and ends untangled, gained the floor on the far side of her bed.

It looked as though she was screaming, but Slade couldn't hear. A sizzling hook had turned his head into something that sounded like a dozen cathedral bells shaken up in a basket; and the stranger's wrathful words were like thunder out beyond Corregidor, only louder and dirtier. Slade, lighter, was quicker on his feet; but his efforts were as useful as assault and battery against a locomotive.

The *nipa* shack now resembled the center of a China Sea typhoon, a roaring confusion with sound effects by Agata and the splintering furniture. They clashed in a savage clinch that ended in a power dive that carried them both under the table. They emerged, whirling. Then Slade broke clear, bounded back, side stepped, and gained enough space to time the *bailarina's* jealous lover.

Smack! Granite Face took it, but it knocked him boarey-eyed and loop-legged. Slade followed through, fists hammering. Another concussion. For an instant the iron man looked silly. Slade's guard lowered. And that was a mistake. The refreshing pause was just long enough to let the enemy decide that swapping punches was an error. He recovered and flashed from a crouch. It was like feeding time at the zoo, with Slade at the receiving end.

The world became a blurr of bamboo slats, overturned furniture, *nipa* thatched ceiling, and Agata's bare legs viewed from the oddest angles...and then the room began blackening; but Slade's muscles still worked, though with a blind, instinctive stubbornness. He relaxed, absorbed a crushing punch, then got his hold. It was good. Granite Face catapulted half way across the room. Slade followed through—but so did Agata.

The three met in one spot Something sizzled past Slade's ear as he plunged forward to finish Granite Face. It smashed down on his shoulder, numbing him to his ankles. Agata, swinging the standard of a floor lamp, had missed her aim —and her boyfriend got the works.

The *bailarina* knelt for a moment beside her victim in error, then dashed into the other room to get water. Slade retrieved a cigarette case and wallet, automatically thrust them into his pocket.

Then he saw the fun was just beginning.

Half a dozen brown men came swarming up the veranda stairs and into the living room. Tagalog bouncers, drawn from the dance hall by the riot. At their heels was Chow Kit, narrowed eyes flashing from Slade's battered face and torn tropicals to Agata's streaming hair and rumpled gown. He chuckled silkily as she started, yeeped, and dropped the tumbler she was filling. The shock troops charged, clubs and bolos flailing.

Slade snatched a chair and slashed out at the advance guard, but the short, broad blades and pounding staves were too much for one man so near the end of his strength. He was forced back, raked and battered. They were now flanking him right and left. From the corner of his eye, he caught a glimpse of Agata's hand—but he had no time to wonder what her contribution would be this time.

It looked like payday on Paranaque Road—

And then the lights flickered out. Slade, milling the splintered remains of the chair, ploughed through the enemy's line. A long bound carried him to the veranda; and another flung him clear of the pack. He landed in a heap at the foot of the compound palisade, stumbled over a stray pig, and headed east. Native legs were not long enough to break his lead. As he reached the highway that led toward the Walled City, a grin crinkled his battered face.

For some reason, Agata had given him a break.

Nearing Cuartel d'Espana, he hailed a Red Diamond. As he boarded the cab, he fumbled for his wallet. He drew two from his pocket. For a moment he was perplexed; then he understood.

The extra item was Granite Face's roll.

Slade went through the contents. The wallet belonged to Captain Rupert Dwyer, Post Quartermaster at Fort McKinley. He had charge of enough ammunition to equip a *datu's* army. Lord knows how many thousand rounds were stored at McKinley for the coming target season.

It *proved* nothing, but it was a strong hint.

And one card among the others that filled a compartment of that wallet upholstered with five hundred *peso* notes seconded the growing conviction that Captain Dwyer was not entirely what a well-regulated officer should be. *"Nomura-ro"* was engraved across the center of the card. Beneath it was a street address. At one end was a column of Japanese, and in a corner were the words, *"Shigashi San—O Shoku Kabu."*

Nomura-ro was the name of the last word in aristocratic brothels; and Shigashi San was the lady who had given the captain that card. The words that followed her name indicated that she was the reigning beauty of the house.

Such luxury might not be beyond the means of a captain, but Slade's suspicions became more pointed as he recollected that the Nomura-ro belonged to Chow Kit; that it catered to the wealthiest sports of Manila; *and that a patron who had established himself followed the oriental custom of running a charge account.*

What an officer does with his spare time is his own business; but once his taste for Asiatic diversions became noised about in the somewhat strait-laced military circles, it would be somewhat too bad. Evidence of indebtedness to Chow Kit would be more than enough to finish his career.

Chow Kit could thus demand government munitions as the price of discretion.

All this flashed through Slade's mind as he stepped into his room and set to work obliterating the marks of battle.

An hour later he was presentable. And Shigashi San's card, being unmarked by any handwriting, would get him an audience with the lady without arousing suspicion as to his right to be received. She wouldn't scratch or scream, and she'd know plenty about Captain Dwyer.

A hired car took him toward the lights of Sampoloc.

Nomura-ro was a rambling, two-story bungalow a block from the blazing lights of the quarter where the proletariat played with ladies whose greetings depended on their race. Crude places for crude people; whereas an evening in Nomura-ro was like being presented at the Court of Saint James, except a lot more entertaining.

Slade presented his card to the gray-haired, leather-faced *obasan* who managed the palace.

"Irrasshai," she greeted, "You are very welcome."

The *obasan* consulted a register, nodded, pressed a bell button; and oriental courtesy somewhat lightened the ensuing shock as Slade's expense account for the evening was jacked up to astronomical figures.

No mere captain playing the Nomura-ro could be on the level!

A tiny, black-eyed *kamuro*—one of the several maids who attend a high class Japanese *oiran* to serve a seven year apprenticeship in the intricate art of becoming a courtesan—conducted Slade down a hallway and into a reception room.

Shigashi San, her slender body ablaze with brocaded silks gathered about her waist with an eighteen inch sash that one flip of her fingers and Lord knows how many silver *pesos* would unwind, sat in the sacred seclusion of her *zashiki* to receive her guest. Her glistening black hair, towering pagoda-high, was rayed with long fade pins and garnished with jewel-frosted tortoise shell combs.

Her gesture and bow and voice were the artistry of an ancient tradition; yet her smile was alluring, and her dark, oblique eyes animated the ivory and carmine painted mask of her face.

Shigashi San, famed from Singapore to Tokyo—and Slade saw how genius escaped the bonds of formal ritual and made that feminine toy a vibrant fascination, an infinite promise lurking behind screens of studied artificiality.

One of the *kamuros* knelt at Slade's feet to remove his shoes. Another prepared to serve tea. A third set a low table with trays and platters of Japanese hors d'oeuvres; the "august repast" itemized in the two yard long bill.

Three geishas entered the reception room to twang their three stringed samisens, dance and entertain Slade with Japanese ballads. And he had to like it. He tossed the chief *geisha* a fifty-*peso* note. She scooped up the extravagant

26

tip, clicked her fan shut, and utterly ignoring Slade, turned to Shigashi San to say, *"Oiran maido arigato!"*—"Thank you, Madam, for your constant favors!"

Yoshiwara courtesy: entertainers don't thank the patron of the house for his liberality; they thank the courtesan whose fascinations have dazzled him. And Slade, though he did not know it, was to see an ironic play on those words before the evening was over!

Twice at long intervals during the *saki* sipping, Shigashi San retired to one of the further rooms of her suite, each time returning in lighter, more informal robes. And at last when the three bright eyed *kamuros* finally left their mistress, Slade, head buzzing from rice wine, followed her into an inner room whose ceiling was painted with an enormous phoenix.

A single subdued light cast the shadow of a six-fold screen across a foot-deep pile of silken quilts. At the head of which was a curious little cylinder of wood supported on carved legs: Shigashi San's pillow, which supporting the nape of her neck, preserved her mountainous coiffure.

Slade, thinking of Agata's passion-pulsing breasts and disheveled hair, suppressed an urge to dive for the door; but only for an instant: Shigashi San's artificiality was contradicted by the invitation of her eyes, the tantalizing, slow deftness of fingers plucking the bow of the *obi* that gathered the crepe gown about her waist.

Skill there, and the artistry of a thousand year old tradition. Figured silk caressed and shadowed and hinted unexplored delights in old ivory. One brusque hand could part the veil—but Slade, kneeling beside that gracious creature half sunk in the yielding quilts, hypnotized by studied ritual, could not make that impatient gesture.

His heart began rising into his throat, eagerness flamed in his blood; and as his eyes became accustomed to the scented dimness of the alcove, the gauzy gown seemed almost to melt before his hungry gaze.

Bought. Paid for. But through sheer artistry become infinitely more alluring than any woman won in a flare of passion. His brain was a surge of fire before that silken cincture finally yielded, and Shigashi San's mellow ivory body smiled from ambush...

Miraculously, it seemed, the lights dimmed to a fantastic twilight as her arms closed about him. Artistry that needed no mockery of ardor to make it perfect. And for a long time Slade was not worried about Datu Ali and the Christian dogs he was slaying with government ammunition, down in far off Jolo...

Shigashi San finally rang for *saki*. Time now for matching wits with that exotic toy imported from Japan; but a buzzer whirred, and one of the little *kamuros* entered.

A murmur of Japanese that Slade could not understand; and then Shigashi San apologized, in sweet voiced, stilted English, "August friend, the unexpectedness of your visit forbids me the pleasure of your company for the remainder of the night."

27

Heavy feet invaded the outer *zashiki*. Some guest with a previous engagement was entitled to her time. Slade would be ushered out a side door so that new arrival and departing playmate would not meet. He had to check the rush act, or the evening was wasted.

But Slade's knowledge of Yoshiwara traditions saved the night. He had but to follow the ancient precedent of many an infatuated Japanese *samurai*.

"I am going to my lonely plantation in Mindanao in the morning. Go with me. I will buy your contract and debts to the house."

As he spoke, he flashed a roll that fortunately was fronted with a five hundred-*peso* note. He replaced it before she could see that it was far from enough to withdraw a *de luxe* courtesan from her river of debt.

And if Slade met her terms, she would be well established for life. For a long moment she regarded him. Slade returned her gaze, and her loveliness put a convincing glow in his eyes.

Finally she beckoned to the little *kamuro*; but before she could tell her to cancel the newcomer's engagement, Slade interposed.

"Is there no *naki* leaf in your mirror?" The subtle question was to remind her that Hakone Gongen, the Japanese god of pledges between men and women, forbade her breaking her promise to the waiting guest. More than that, it told her that he knew the old traditions.

She smiled and murmured a few words to the *kamuro*, who conducted Slade to a further room of the suite. He could now wait for Shigashi San's visitor to leave. He could postpone the trip to Mindanao; and with the promised liberation ever dangled before her eyes, she would try to spur him to haste by hinting at another who wanted to buy her contract.

She might mention Captain Dwyer...

Slade listened to the murmur of voices. He opened his penknife and set to work on the partition that separated him from Shigashi San's bedroom...

The *oiran's* guest wore quartermaster collar ornaments; but he was not Captain Dwyer. Sergeant's chevrons were on his sleeves.

Yet that twilight shrouded meeting was more than it seemed. One of the sergeant's arms slipped clear of Shigashi San's embrace. He was reaching toward a low cabinet. Toward a small brazen Buddha that adorned its top.

The move was stealthy, not swift. The sergeant was placing a second image on the cabinet. Then he palmed its identical duplicate, the one that had originally been there.

The exchange could mean but one thing: the sergeant had either received or delivered a message or token of identification. All in one move which Shigashi San could scarcely have perceived.

Having seen as much as he had, Slade could not afford the risk of missing anything that took place in that room. This was more than the meeting of a soldier and an *oiran*; it must be the subtle hand of Chow Kit. But Slade gritted his teeth as he watched...

Clear thinking became difficult...it all hinged on whether the Sergeant had delivered or received a message. If the former, wait and see who came to Shigashi San's room to get it; if the latter, follow the quartermaster man. But which?

An insurrection in Jolo depended on the right guess.

Finally the sergeant prepared to leave. Such haste confirmed Slade's growing certainty. Shigashi San accompanied him to the *zashiki*. That gave Slade his chance. He tiptoed into her bedroom, snatched the brazen Buddha, and turned to the exit. Ducking into an alley, he paused to scrutinize the tiny image by the glow of a distant streetlight.

A fine line indicated that it could be removed from its pedestal; but there was no time to seek the combination. He pocketed the effigy, rounded the corner, lurking in the shadows, where he could command a view of all approaches to the Nomura-ro.

Presently the sergeant emerged. Neither car nor *caromata* awaited him. He had trusted no one with his destination.

Slade followed. Ahead of him was a *tienda* from whose window a light gleamed. He reached for a handful of silver, stepped into the store and in a moment emerged with a pair of coarse socks and a cake of soap. Then, stretching long, legs, he narrowed the gap between him and his quarry.

Another block. The sergeant entered a saloon. Slade caught a glimpse of him as he stepped to a telephone booth. Aside from a bartender, and a few Chinese and Filippino loafers the place was deserted. Slade ordered a beer and edged toward the booth.

"Two-one six-nine six."

He recognized the number: Red Diamond Cab. Slade drained his beer, and stepped to the street. He slipped one sock into the other, then thrust the cake of soap into the foot of the inner one. Silent, effective, and harmless.

A moment later, the sergeant ploughed through the swinging doors. His tropic tanned face was tense, and his eyes instinctively flashed right and left as he cleared the threshold. Slade swooped from cover; but some sixth sense warned his victim. He jerked his head. The soap cake bludgeon missed by a hair, instead of laying him out for a long count; and for the second time that evening, Slade had his hands full.

Before he could drop his now useless weapon, the Manila night blazed into a carnival glow. Groggy and with legs limp as macaroni, Slade tried to block the sergeant's rush, but it was like boxing with a kangaroo. One more charge—

But before it connected, the sergeant, over reaching himself, tripped and sprawled headlong into the gutter. That gave Slade an instant's respite. When the noncom regained his feet, the mill began in earnest. It was touch and go for a moment, reckless, wrathful slugging; and then Slade blasted home with one that popped like a boiler explosion.

The sergeant was frozen before he hit the ground. Slade settled back on his heels and drew a long breath; but that was cut short in mid gasp. A brazen gleam from the darkness caught his eye. He made a dive for his pocket as he recognized the little Buddha lying in the dust. His own was still in place; it was the sergeant's that had rolled from cover.

Slade stooped to pick it up. The hidden springs of the trick pedestal had responded to the impact against the corner of the saloon! The Buddha's body contained a slip of paper. He struck a match.

"Sin Ban Fong is waiting," he read, which was damn little to learn for his trouble!

He stuffed the paper and the halves of the image into his pocket, regarded the prostrate sergeant, then used his victim's shirt and belt to improvise gag and bonds. That done, Slade stepped into the saloon, slid ten *pesos* across the bar, and struck a, bargain with the proprietor.

"Keep him on ice until morning," Slade concluded. "If he's here when I come back, it's five more for you; if he's gone, you'll get some of what he got. And when the taxi gets here, tell him it's the wrong number. *Sabe, hombre?"*

He did; and Slade dashed back toward the Nomura-ro.

The next play was to put the *empty* Buddha on Shigashi San's cabinet, and wait for someone to call for the one the sergeant had left.

"Sin Ban Fong," he muttered as he slipped in through the back door. Then, with a bleak grin, "I hope the bastard enjoys waiting!"

Shigashi San, hearing him enter the further room of her suite, appeared from her bedroom. Her smile was cryptic.

He wondered if she suspected. She might not even know that the Buddha swapping had taken place in her room. The smile became alluring…it began to seem not such a bad idea after all to have the exalted blossom shed a few more petals.

All of which he worked into the discussion of his estates in Mindanao. But as Shigashi San luxuriously settled back into her heap of silken quilts, and reached for the bow of her *obi,* Slade put the empty bronze Buddha back on the lacquered cabinet.

And then the *oiran's* draperies parted and her arms closed about him.

But that embrace was checked by the faint whine of a sliding panel. Slade was on his feet at a bound. Shigashi San, outraged at the invasion of her privacy, shed half a dozen hairpins as she snatched for the edges of her robe.

Chow Kit was in the doorway! Sallow, evilly smiling Chow Kit behind the muzzle of an automatic that yawned like a siege gun. He also had come by the back door; and at his heels were half a dozen Chinese and Gugus; murderous riff-raff, armed and leering and spitting *betel* juice on the mats as they waited for action. And two at the further edge of the cluster between them supported a woman in apricot silk. She was bound, and a gag masked half her face, but Slade recognized Agata Moreno.

All in an instant. *"Sin Ban Fong,* my dear sir," murmured Chow Kit, "is waiting with the patience known only to a ship. A Chinese junk whose concealed engines have fooled the revenue cutters. You and *Señorita* Agata will both take a long ride down the China Sea, where the sharks are hungry—don't make any false moves, please, or Shigashi San joins the party."

"Why wait for a junk ride?" snarled Slade, fighting for time, "Do it now—"

Chow Kit chuckled and explained, "Disposing of corpses on land is awkward and betraying, whereas the sharks are discreet."

Then he added, "One of my men works for the cab company which the sergeant called. The bartender was wise enough to ignore your warning. He phoned to inquire about his prisoner. The news reached me. And in the meanwhile, Agata's collection of American sweethearts had aroused my suspicions —so, we all go for a cruise in the *Sin Ban Fong*. With things turning out as they did, I really do not need the message the sergeant left here for me. I liberated him. He's getting the ammunition now."

Though Chow Kit was safe behind a pistol and Slade was empty-handed, the Chinaman's eyes did not shift as he purred a phrase in Tagalog, ordering his retainers to bind the American. Steady pistol, and unwavering eyes—

But Chow Kit's watchfulness worked against him. In watching the desperate American, he overlooked Shigashi San, and the *saki* jug she had stealthily plucked from a shelf.

A flash of white. A spattering of porcelain shards. The blast of Chow Kit's widely fired pistol. Slade's flying tackle carried him clear of the *oiran's* bed as the Chinaman's weapon clattered into a corner. Flinging Chow Kit aside, Slade scooped up the six-fold screen and hurled it athwart the headlong charge of the Chinaman's armed retainers.

Wadding a silken quilt about his left arm, he parried a sweeping bolo slash, and hammered home with a blasting fist that knocked a Gugu smashing into an alcove. He shifted as the attack swerved to envelop him, seized a lacquered washbasin and crashed it about the ears of the flank guard. He ducked a hurled bolo, flung out the folds of the silken quilt to parry another, side stepped and snatched the first weapon by the hilt.

Slade now armed; but his breath was coming in jerking gasps, and the odds were heavy. Chow Kit, once more on his feet, was urging his shaken retainers to the attack. He had recovered his pistol and hovered on the fringe of the battle, watching Slade's blade dance in and out, steel striking fire from steel. The Chinaman feared to risk another shot; but as Slade's desperate charge swept the pack a yard to the rear, the weapon rose into line.

Shigashi San's voice shrilled high above the cursing confusion. Slade caught the warning, and his brain blazed red. The heavy bolo zipped point on, a streak of steel that ended at the Chinaman's chest as the automatic spurted flame. Slade won the exchange. Hot lead seared his ribs, but the bolo split Chow Kit's chest like a chicken for the grille.

Slade was empty-handed. Another saki jug, hurled from the sidelines by Shigashi San, bowled the foremost enemy end for end; and then the charge broke. They saw Chow Kit crumpled up on the matting, a red, twitching hud-

31

dle. They scrambled madly for the door. No chief, no fight. Slade's reckless wrath had succeeded where caution would have been overwhelmed.

He bounded from his corner. As he snatched Chow Kit's weapon, he heard a pounding of feet, and a polyglot chatter that was submerged by a voice like a typhoon. An unpleasantly familiar voice—Captain Rupert Dwyer!

Slade's salvaged pistol jerked into line as the granite faced renegade burst into the room.

"Drop it, you rat!" Slade commanded.

Dwyer's hands rose. He recognized death when it stared him in the eye. But Slade's weapon dropped the next instant: behind Dwyer was a squad of military police, and the Provost Marshal.

"What the hell?" boomed Dwyer, eyeing the gory wreckage.

Then a cross-fire of questions, and Slade identified himself.

"And cut that girl loose—over there in the corner. That *mestiza*, with the gag in her mouth—"

Dwyer followed Slade's gesture.

"*Mestiza*, my eye! That's my sister!"

And Agata, when she was liberated, explained, "Dad was a colonel. And years ago, we were in the Islands, so it was easy—"

"But why that *bailarina* gag at Chow Kit's?" demanded Slade.

"When the old colonel died in the States, she came over to see me. And landed just in time to find me in a rotten jam," interposed Captain Dwyer. "Ammunition being lost by the case. And me responsible. You know what that would mean. I had to clear it up. We suspected Chow Kit. And Agata, damned little idiot, insisted on getting a job as a *bailarina* to do a bit of spying—"

"*Agata?*" echoed Slade. "But what's her real name?"

"Named after my stepmother: Agata Moreno Dwyer."

That simplified it.

"Anyway," resumed Dwyer, "I went out to Chow Kit's place to check up on Agata's hazardous game, and when I saw you two—"

"Rupert, you idiot!" interposed Agata, "you didn't see a thing! As if I couldn't take care of myself!"

"Listen, Dwyer," intervened Slade, "honest to God, I didn't mean a thing—and anyway, it was in the line of duty, getting evidence."

Dwyer snorted, and Agata's Spanish eyes glowed in fond reminiscence. Slade changed the subject to ammunition.

"Chow Kit was so busy with you, there in Agata's shack," resumed Dwyer, "that he overlooked me. And when I recovered from that crack on the bean, she was gone, and I checked up. That card of admission you took from my wallet was one the sergeant had dropped. That gave me a hunch as to his connections. I'd suspected him for some time anyway. And in trailing Agata, we tangled up with him, all beaten up, and hell bent for the warehouse.

"He explained plenty when I bluffed him about no honest enlisted man being able to hang out at the Nomura-ro. So don't bother trying to open the other

32

bronze Buddha. That crook had arranged to have a tunnel dug to open into the warehouse, so he could load the whole works on a barge, in spite of the doubled sentries we'd posted about the place. That was the big raid—the earlier thefts were just petty larceny in comparison."

And then Slade remembered that Shigashi San's *saki* jug had given his chance to hang on until the M.P.s arrived.

"Sorry about that plantation," he said, "but I'll buy up your contract."

"Death has canceled it," she answered, gesturing toward Chow Kit's body.

Slade dug out his wallet and handed the *oiran* the contents.

"Anyway, here's a ticket home."

Shigashi San had not missed the glow in Agata's dark eyes, and the glances she and Slade had exchanged. She accepted the present, then, utterly ignoring Slade, she turned to Agata to bow and say: "*Oiran maido arigato!*—Thank you, madam, for your constant favors."

Shigashi San, now a free woman, used Japanese courtesy as a harpoon; but only Slade caught the point.

"What did she say?" wondered Agata, sensing her mockery.

"She said," Slade falsified, "that you're a damn lucky girl to get a chance to carry on where we left off, in that *nipa* shack."

FOOL'S EPITAPH

Originally appeared in *Short Stories*, February 10, 1947.

CHAPTER I

The coffin-shaped face, the straight mouth, and Mr. Bowley's years on the Northwest Frontier, where ideas have to be few, simple, and strong, had prepared Slade for a wrangle. Mr. Bowley, however, outdid himself by saying, as soon as Slade had given reasons for not being in uniform, "Get Captain Kellam out of Peshawar, and his men with him, the entire detachment. We're afraid of incidents."

"Hmmm—incidents. Such as?"

"Purely by the grace of God and our own small efforts," the gray-haired commissioner elaborated, "none of Kellam's men has been murdered for such tricks as herding pigs into mosques, assaulting policemen, and accosting the women of Moslem dignitaries. Or did your superior tell you it was merely a matter of curbing boyish pranks?"

"The chief told me there was a problem. I'm here to handle it, instead of agreeing with you that nothing can be done."

"I've given you a neat solution, Major Slade. Recommend to your superior that the entire detachment be transferred. We have riots enough as it is, between Hindus and Moslems, without having your military cause trouble. With the natives still quite unable to see a bit of difference between the British and you American chaps, that detachment reflects on us—right when we are having troubles of our own! Get them out.

"Your recommendation can do it. If you didn't have your superior's entire confidence, he'd not've sent you here."

This last was all too close to the truth for Slade's comfort. He protested, "I can't recommend anything of the sort. Once I get Captain Kellam straightened out, he'll get his men in line. Relieving the entire detachment would give ideas to all the others who are crying to go home."

Bowley fingered his chin. "To be sure, to be sure, that'd create a precedent, an unfortunate one," he admitted, grudgingly. "Unfortunate for your service. What I mean is, this is for you to solve at your expense, not ours!"

"I can't condemn without having seen, and I don't intend to. My duty is to get the facts, and that's what I propose to do, with your help, or without it."

"I can simplify matters," Bowley said. There was a gleam in his eyes, a gleam which revealed more humor than Slade relished. "Since you insist on your own way, you'll have to assume full responsibility. I'll withdraw the undercover nursemaids who've kept things from getting entirely out of hand. No more police protection, no paying of indemnities to soothe ruffled natives. I'll declare open season, and let nature take its course. How'd you like that?"

"If that's the way you want to cooperate, I'll play it that way, sir!"

Having accepted the challenge, Slade got up and took his hat.

The commissioner said, affably, "Any time you change your mind, look in and tell me. Pleasure to have met you. Come in again."

* * * *

Slade left, and without slamming the door. While he would hardly blame the commissioner, he resented the idea of summarily having Captain Steve Kellam relieved and probably dismissed for gross incompetence when there was nothing wrong with the man except that, not being a career soldier, his morale had buckled the moment the shooting was over.

Kellam had done well in Africa, only to go to the devil once he'd been shipped to Peshawar to take charge of a supply depot set up in anticipation of a need which had never materialized. Unable to accept uselessness as one of the by-products of an attempt to forestall the most remote emergencies, Kellam had sulked, with his outfit following his example. Like their captain, they wanted to go home, and expressed their craving by swilling arrack, and by brawling.

All wrong; but give the man a chance to get himself and his men straightened out instead of condemning him out of hand. So Slade turned his back on Mr. Bowley, to do things his own way, and at his own risk.

And Slade set to work that very evening. He wasn't handsome to begin with, having a large nose, and a face apparently assembled of spare parts which hadn't been precision fitted. Squinting into the tarnished mirror gave him a ferocious aspect. A hot wind, heavy with hashish reek and the garbage stench of Peshawar, made the sickly flame of two tapers waver, so that the angles of his face cast deceptive shadows; "Allah curse the wind, Allah curse its religion!" he growled in the guttural Kurdish which he'd learned in the oil fields of Iraq, before the war. He cocked his head, to get a fresh start on darkening his eyelids with collyrium; and as the job progressed; he cursed Allah, and with fine impartiality, Satan also. Being a thorough man, Slade included Peshawar town, and especially the Pathans who insisted on painted eyelids.

In the corner of the tiny room squatted a white bearded man whose belt bristled with daggers, and whose deeply lined face contained evidence of all qualities except pity, benevolence, and candor. As he stirred the aromatic mixture in a wooden bowl and added ingredients, he watched Slade's progress, and found it good.

When Slade had finished his cosmetic task, he smoothed out his gold laced vest, and patted his gold fringed turban.

"Now the roses!" he grumbled. "And Satan fly away with all men who wear roses behind the ears!"

The old man grinned, being a Pathan himself. He got up and offered Slade the bowl, which was dirty from many campfires.

"What's this?"

"*Post.* To make your breath smell like a Pathan gentleman's."

"*Post?*" Slade's nose crinkled. "Isn't being doused with attar of roses bad enough?"

"Very good, drink it, your Excellency."

Slade scooped the bowl from the other's fingers. He drained it so quickly that the pause at his lips was no longer than an eye-wink. He choked, coughed, and demanded, "What're you trying to do, poison me?"

"Friend of Allah—"

"Being anyone's friend is a fool notion! What is *post*?"

"Verily, your Excellency, *post* is a drink."

Strong white teeth gnashed audibly. "Listen, Shir Dil," Slade said, very slowly. "I know it is a drink. Allah and my guts bear witness to that. What I want to know is this—suppose I wanted another drink, what'd I put into the bowl?"

Shir Dil stroked his beard and said, impressively, "I, thy friend, and the least of the slaves, I would mix it for thee. With my own hands!"

Slade, praying for patience, achieved it. "Shir Dil, thou Lion Hearted friend," he said, making a play on the old man's name. "Thou block-headed friend, thou dung-brained friend, if I, thy friend, were to mix thee a bowl of *post*, what should I put into the bowl?"

"Verily, there are several ways."

"There always are!" Slade raised his voice till it was somewhat like thunder in the Khyber Pass. "But one way is enough, one way is always enough for anything, O Friend! One way of settling that fool of a Kellam is enough."

"A certain amount of arrack, some cardamoms, some rose water, some opium," Shir Dil enumerated. "And a little sugar, and some milk."

"Sure there weren't any crankcase draining or high-octane?" Slade demanded in English.

"No, by God! Only palm brandy and opium and—"

"Skip the rest, I won't be mixing any tonight."

"It is good when you get used to it," Shir Dil declared. "Captain Kellam drinks it all the time."

"I'd not be surprised. But how do *you* know? We just got here a couple of hours ago."

Shir Dil regarded Kim with condescension. "It started when I went to buy those magnificent clothes. But it was in the coopersmith's bazaar where I heard of Captain Kellam, verily, the father and the grandfather of fools! He has a house in the Dabgari Quarters."

"In the *which*?"

"The Dabgari Quarters."

This was an unusual spot for an American officer to live when not on duty. Slade groaned and demanded, "You mean to tell me he's living in a house of ill fame?"

"Oh, no, your Excellency! Not in one. Just close to maybe three-four. Where he spends his time is in the home of Yasmini—" Shir Dil bunched his fingertips, kissed them, rolled his eyes so that craft and evil and greed gleamed in them more than ever. "A Kashmiri lady, very beautiful."

"You saw her?"

"No, but everyone knows her."

Slade frowned, and groped, "Trust—trust a Kashmiri—"

Shir Dil quoted, *"Trust a snake, and then a Kashmiri—"*

Slade got up, dusted his baggy pants, hitched his belt, and adjusted his silver hafted dagger. He pulled down his vest, scowled as he fingered the roses behind his ears. The peak of the felt cap about which his ponderous turban was wrapped grazed the smoke-stained ceiling. "Best we can do for Kellam," he observed, sourly, "is to kill the poor devil before he gets into trouble."

Shir Dil, chuckling appreciatively, said in English, "Captain Kellam is a skillet-headed, dim-wit and a chump."

Slade regarded the old man with envy. "I wish I could talk Pushtu the way you do Americanese."

"Keep your shirt on, pal. You're not bad, and these jerks in Peshawar will say you make mistakes like a Kurd, so no one knows you are an infidel."

"And, everyone'll live happy ever after, if I get away with it."

"Like in the cinema," Shir Dil remarked. "And there is a new American woman, a new one, I tell you, at McLean's hotel. Very beautiful!"

"Malish!" was what Slade said, to cut short the eye-rolling and the leer wasted on the dirty walls. "Let's find the captain."

"In the name of Allah," Shir Dil exclaimed, piously, and led the way into the courtyard of the caravanserai, which was crowded with camels and donkeys, with bales of rugs from Boukhara, with stinking bundles of sheepskins, and with bags of dried apricots from Kandahar. Bearded men squatted about fires of burning dung, over which they cooked rice. Others baked bread on heated rocks. None of them gave Slade a second look as he went with his guide to find out what made Captain Kellam tick.

CHAPTER II

There was music in Peshawar that night: querulous flutes, and the wail of bagpipes. Hillmen droned through their beaked noses the stanzas of border ballads whose theme was looting, ambush, and feuds; homely tales of the untired Pathan businessman's daily life, except when spring ploughing kept him busy. Already, Slade realized that impersonating a Pathan would be even more strenuous than learning Pushtu, which those wild men spoke.

Shir Dil nudged him into a narrow and odorous alley. From there they slipped through a doorway so low that both had to stoop.

"This way, there be stairs, only a few treads are missing," the old man whispered. "Then to the roof—Allah willing, it won't cave in."

Allah was willing, for presently, the two crouched in the shadow of the parapet which guarded the flat roof. Lights winked behind the lattice-work of windows overhanging the street. On further roofs, charcoal laid on the tobacco of bubble-pipes glowed and subsided, giving momentary glimpses of turbans, and the gilt embroidery of vests.

"Now the wall, and then Yasmini's roof," Shir Dil directed, as he dropped cat-like, landing on all fours.

Slade, not quite as agile, had the breath knocked out of him, though he stayed on the wall. After a moment of crawling, he crouched, balanced himself, and sprang straight up after Shir Dil, to catch the parapet of Yasmini's roof.

The attempt had been timed so that the moon would be at precisely the height required for concealing shadows; but then, had Shir Dil not been an accomplished horse thief before wandering to Iraq to work in the oil fields, he'd not lived long enough for his beard to whiten.

The two looked down into the small court in the center of Yasmini's house. Moonlight gave a clear view of jeweled lady, and a man in civilian clothes. They sat in a tiny garden. Moonlight reflected from white stucco and softened the shadows. Yasmini's guest was Captain Kellam; and Slade wondered, as he watched his old friend, whether Mr. Bowley's shortcut might not, after all, be the sensible thing.

But he told himself, stubbornly, "Poor guy doesn't realize what he's got himself into, hanging around this part of town, with a wench like that! And drunk as a hoot-owl."

"Somebody's been following me," Kellam complained, thickly, "ever since I stowed that baggage of yours in the supply depot warehouse." He caught her arm, but nearly pulled himself off balance; bracelets jingled; "I want the truth of it, has some money lender got a claim on your things?"

Yasmini laughed softly, whimsically, as though humoring a peevish child. "Don't be silly, darling! Who'd be following you?"

She lifted a bottle from a pail of ice, refilled the hollow stem glasses, and laced the champagne with brandy. "You're homesick, impatient," she went on, as she handed him a "Royal Peg."

"Always impatient! Suppose your government has forgotten all about you and that depot of supplies that nobody wants?"

Silk rippled and shimmered as she gestured to dispose of his qualms. Kellam coughed, swayed a little, spilled some wine. "Here's to nothing! Here's to amnesia!"

Yasmini's laughter tinkled. "Oh, but then you'd forget who I am, if you forgot who you are."

She picked the *sitar* from the carpet spread on the tiles and plucked a few notes. Kellam got up. The music stopped. "You're going to move that stuff," he told Yasmini. "I'll move it right back here. I'm sick of mystery and hedging and fooling around."

"But I'll be robbed," Yasmini protested. "Nobody'd dare break into your depot, it's guarded by barbed-wire and machine-guns." She got up, and caught him by the shoulders. "Every time there's rioting, a few houses are looted. Surely you can help me protect my few valuables. Even if someone remembered you and sent an officer to inspect the depot, you could always say the things are yours—in a way, they are, aren't they, being mine?"

"I've been trailed," he repeated. "And a couple times, someone's tried to cut the barbed-wire."

"Pathans are born thieves."

"They didn't pay any attention to the depot till I took your things out there," he declared, stubbornly.

"Oh, you're afraid?" she taunted.

Because of her move, Slade got a better view of Yasmini, and saw that Shir Dil had not been misled by the rumors of her loveliness. Her low forehead, and small, almost straight nose, her chin and throat were exquisite in profile as she looked up to mock the drunken captain. A velvet hood all agleam with jewels set off the shapeliness and fine carriage of her head. Her skirt, very full, and striped in light and dark, swelled and billowed and then clung to her legs when a breath of breeze made the jasmines rustle.

But she was too clever to wait for the jibe to register. His face had scarcely twisted in wrath when she went on, "Of course you're not, you're just impatient." Then, catching him by the shoulders, Yasmini pleaded, "Do be patient, Steve, you'll be transferred before long, and then we'll both leave this terrible town, oh, how I hate Peshawar! I'd've left long before now, but I can't, I won't go till you can leave."

Slade was thinking, *"I'd pretty nearly fall for that myself,"* when Yasmini screamed. Three turbaned men, tall and bearded, came from the darkness of the passageway which led from the front. Whether they'd got in by bribery, or trickery, or breaking the lock, it made no difference: they were there, and moving without speech. Knives would speak for them. If these were the men who had been trailing Kellam, their mission seemed as good as accomplished.

Danger, however, tightened Kellam and sobered him. Warned, he whirled, and so quickly that his response knocked Yasmini sprawling into the shrubbery along the wall. He was big, and quick, and now that he faced only men and not boredom, he was himself again.

He got one good swing with the chair he had snatched in turning. His weapon, however, was too heavy, and while he knocked one of the raiders rolling across the flagstones, the others bored in, since his guard was open. He let go the chair, and would have darted back to grab the wine bottle, a far handier bludgeon; but the edge of the garden rug tripped him enough to break his stride, so that now he had to face the enemy empty handed. Desperate, he lunged, getting under, and tricking the blades before they could shift.

All this happened in the sliver of time which Slade needed to hurdle the parapet, and drop into the court. He rolled, scrambled to regain his balance. His yell startled the raiders, giving Kellam an instant's respite, which was prolonged by Shir Dil's shout. Slade drew his curved dagger and darted in.

The blade bit a long trace. A back hand jab of the pommel knocked out a handful of teeth. In the snarling scuffle, he kicked someone in the stomach. And then Shir Dil, calling on Allah to witness the folly of fools, pounced into the fray.

The intruders, being quick thinkers, ran before they could be whittled down. The one Kellam had flattened was able to join the scramble. Yasmini, making the most of the confusion, raced for the inner rooms. A bar slammed into place, and then another. In a matter of seconds, Slade and Shir Dil faced each other, with Captain Kellam lying between them.

Slade bent over the unconscious officer. "Not cut much. Bet I kicked him by mistake."

Shir Dil was interested mainly in a wallet lying on the tiles. The initials, S.K., in saw-pierced gold letters, identified it; and as the old Pathan reached for the loot, Slade caught his wrist. "Not this time, my friend! I'm looking into it."

He struck a match, and flipped the wallet open. One of the cellophane windows protected a color photo of a red-haired girl wearing a green play suit. "Lucky she couldn't see him tonight," Slade grumbled, and for a moment considered himself several sorts of a fool for going out of his way to get Kellam back in line. Slade knew the red-haired girl, and liked her. He always had.

Shir Dil exclaimed, "By God! That's the new American woman, the one at McLeans Hotel."

"The devil it is! You sure?"

"*Aywah!* The way she shows the teeth when smiling." Shir Dil struck a match, squinted, and added, triumphantly, "Yes, and she came from the cinema wearing one of those dresses with the top cut off." He rolled his eyes. "Clearly the same woman!"

Slade had no further hope that the observing Shir Dil could be wrong. Then he was glad that Diane Crawford had come to Peshawar. She'd be a valuable ally in getting Kellam back on the beam. Second thought gave him time to decide that she'd stick, instead of making things worse by turning against Kellam because of the scandalous yarns she couldn't have helped hearing in the Cantonment, that bit of old England, two miles west of the native city.

"Let's hustle this fellow out of here before those monkeys get help and come back to finish it," Slade said to Shir Dil. "Give a hand."

In front, they found an army sedan, with an enlisted man asleep at the wheel. After bundling Kellam into the back seat, Slade shook the soldier. "Wake up, dope!" he commanded. "Your skipper's out cold, and cut up a bit, damn lucky he's not finished."

"Uh—um—what—"

"Get rolling, soldier!" Slade commanded, and the man obeyed, though still too groggy to realize that he was apparently taking orders from a native.

As the car roared out of the quarter, Shir Dil said, "Now go back to talk to Yasmini; she will talk, she got hell scared out of her."

Slade shook his head. "Kellam's the guy I'm talking to, as soon as I get shed of the fancy clothes. You know, a turban has its points, Kellam'd've cracked that fellow's skull if it hadn't been wrapped up so carefully."

"Talk to Yasmini," Shir Dil persisted.

"Help yourself, then! I can find my way alone."

He watched Shir Dil swagger back to the Kashmiri girl's house. After a moment of wondering how reliable the old man was, he decided that whether bent on business or sociability, Shir Dil's notions could not do any damage. The brief masquerade had given him such a start that he needed no further undercover tricks; he now knew all he needed to know about Steve Kellam. It was all too clear why there was no discipline in the captain's outfit; the officer was to blame, not the men.

CHAPTER III

Slade, deciding against seeing Kellam that night, had postponed his visit until the following day; but once inside the barbed-wire enclosure of the depot, he lost no time in cornering Kellam in the orderly room and giving the substance of Mr. Bowley's remarks. The captain flared up, "So I'm condemned on hearsay! I'd like to see *him* keep these hoodlums in line."

"G.I.s," Slade contended dryly, "are pretty much like their officers."

Kellam's sandy brows bristled, and his ruddy face darkened. He was red-eyed from not enough sleep, and too much drink. He'd become puffy about the jaws; his cheeks twitched perceptibly. And, having the shakes, he took the aggressive by thrusting his chair back and getting on his feet. "I'd like to see *you* keep this outfit in line!" he challenged. "*You* try it!"

"Steady, fellow." Slade wagged his hand, palm toward the square-faced captain. "You're lucky I asked for this, instead of letting someone else handle the chore."

"You asked for the chance?"

"Sure I did. To give you whatever breaks I could."

Kellam relaxed, and quit fingering his desk pen. But after a moment of scowling at the blotter, he looked up to say, "I'm not asking favors."

"Way you've been cutting up, you'll need some!" Slade told him, and sharply. "You're lucky not to be under arrest right now. Fooling around with native women is all right if you simply must, but you had to pick the most notorious one in the lousiest quarter of Peshawar, and on top of it, you had to have one of your men drive you out to her dump, and leave a government car parked in front to advertise that that's where officers play. Yasmini's dynamite —break away from her."

Kellam's mouth sagged, making him look slack and stupid for a moment. Then he retorted, "Nobody's business how I spend my time off duty! They've left me to rot in this hell's hole, guarding, inventorying, reporting in quadruplicate, quintuplicate, sextuplicate and ad infinitumcate that truck and airplane parts are available in such and such quantity. God in heaven, they've always been available, and what for? But they remember I'm alive the minute I find— find—"

"Find the girl of your dreams! She's made you famous all over the native town."

"So what?"

"You're an officer and a gentleman. Which is to say, you're not supposed to make a public spectacle of yourself. Anyway, Yasmini is a side-line. Bowley's gripe about the way your company cuts up is what I've come to settle. Have you sent Yasmini's baggage back to her, or is it still stored with government equipment?"

Kellam's eyes widened. "See all, hear all, know all!"

"That's only the half of it. You and she had a wrangle last night as soon as you showed you had sense enough to want to get her junk out of this depot. You nearly got your gizzard sliced out by three Pathans that got into her house, somehow or other. Your doings aren't as private and personal as you think they are."

This set Kellam frowning and groping for a new line of defense. "Check my accounts," he demanded. "Take inventory. Discipline—all right, that's all shot, and maybe I've not been such a fine example, though they're all fed up and no example would do any good."

"If you were suspected of dishonesty," Slade retorted, evenly, "I'd not be here talking. You'd be relieved of command, and maybe under arrest to boot. Let's look around the depot."

"Why?"

"Because I said so."

The captain changed his mind about protesting. They went out to inspect the blocks of warehouses crammed with supplies which no one needed. After an hour of the dreary business, Slade said, "This makes a chump of the needle in the haystack. Where is Yasmini's stuff?"

"In Warehouse No. 12. Why?"

"I want to look at it. Get a pinch bar." Kellam eyed him. "What makes you think we'll need one?"

Slade chuckled. "You must be pretty groggy from the going over you got last night! Only way to hide the stuff would be in an arms chest or the like, or those chaps who cut the wire would've made it good and grabbed the loot. But in chests—well, try and pick which one!"

Kellam got a pinch bar, and regarded it so thoughtfully that Slade began to wonder. He'd seen homesick soldiers do some odd things. But all Kellam said, when he finally spoke, was, "Funny she'd tell you all about it."

"Nothing's funny in Peshawar."

In Warehouse No. 12, Slade watched Kellam set to work.. Wood splintered. Nails squealed. Lifting the lid uncovered a layer of compactly folded Kashmir shawls the like of which had not been woven for many years.

There was a small Boukhara camel-bag whose fine weave and garnet-red made it fit for a Mogul prince. The scent of jasmine and rose and sandalwood billowed into the superheated air of the tin-roofed building.

"Let's see some more."

Kellam obeyed. He took out a rug perhaps five by nine. Slade had once seen its like, in a dignitary's palace in Kurdistan. There was no mistaking that deep red from the dye-pots of Herat, nor the tawny gold, nor the solemn green, nor that Persian blue whose secret had died three centuries ago. Slade almost exclaimed, but restrained himself, and remarked, "Neat, but thread-bare. Jewelry, eh?"

"Dancing girl's junk," Kellam said, sourly, as he took out a few pieces.

The anklets and the bracelets, the collars, the pendants, they were massive enough to be just what the captain had called them; but there was something unusual about the stones set in the trinkets. The cutting was the work of ancient lapidaries; the colors caught Slade's eye.

He began to understand Yasmini's fear of looters, and he was no longer puzzled by the raid on her house. He licked the dust and the spicy scent from his lips, and then said, "Ok, pack it up."

Kellam fingered a velvet hood solidly embroidered with pearls too large not to be genuine; but they had lost their "orient," though they might still come back to life if the right woman wore them, rethreaded, and against her skin.

"She'd rattle like a junk wagon if she put on half of this at one time," Slade remarked, and Kellam agreed.

"There's another chest," he added.

"Skip it. My throat's so dusty you could plant spuds in it. Let's get a drink while we talk about your next move."

"Can do." Kellam looked better. He asked, hopefully, "If you put in a high powered report, I'd be relieved from duty and sent home?"

Slade, remembering the red-haired girl who had come all the way to Peshawar, wanted to wrap Kellam around one of the warehouse columns.

"You stay here, and do your job. You mean to say you don't know Diane Crawford's in town?"

"Good God! You mean that? How long?"

"Saw her, didn't speak to her. Didn't want to, not with this chore on my hands. Lucky, she didn't recognize me," Slade improvised. "Damn odd she didn't get in touch with you before now."

Kellam gulped. "Maybe she tried. I—ah—"

43

"Skip it, I don't give a hoot where you were the past couple days, and I'm not guessing aloud. Cook up a yarn she can swallow and stick around white man's quarters. Ten to one, she knows you're on the pan, and she's all for you. Or else she'd not come to this hell's hole."

Kellam groaned. "With her father military attaché in Kabul, she'd hear about me almost as soon as you!"

"Sooner," Slade answered, grimly. "War's been over too long for people to keep their traps shut. And people like to peddle dirt to anyone who'd be hurt from hearing it. One of my superiors in Washington tells his wife the juicy story about the cockeyed captain, she tells a girlfriend, the girlfriend needles Diane to make her squirm. So, Diane wangles transportation somehow or other, regardless of conditions in India."

Kellam spent some moments staring at the floor. Slade turned his back, to let him think things out. These were important minutes. He hoped he'd use them to the best advantage.

Kellam finally said, "Before I get in touch with Diane, let's get that junk off the reservation."

"Good idea. And then sell your men discipline. They'll stand to heel as soon as they see that you're settling down to business."

Kellam, however, was still troubled. "How about joining me and Diane at dinner at the hotel, tonight?"

"I'd be butting in. After all, she may not have come to Peshawar to snap you out of it."

"But if she has," Kellam argued, "your being there would convince her that everything is under control."

"Do it that way, then," Slade agreed. "See you for cocktails. And here's luck."

CHAPTER IV

"He'll be here any minute now," Slade told Diane Crawford for the twentieth time, and tried to keep from glancing over his shoulder to get a glimpse of Kellam. When she didn't answer, he beckoned for a waiter to bring another round of Martinis to join those which were on the table, warm and untasted.

"It's an hour after retreat," she said, finally. "What in the world, Dave!"

Her upper lip was drawn tight enough to hide the three teeth which usually showed just enough to make her seem always on the point of smiling. Diane's eyes, striking because they were brown instead of the blue or green which her white skin and copper colored hair made one expect, had become so intense that Slade borrowed not only her impatience, but also a premonition of trouble.

"I'll phone," he suggested, uneasily.

She caught his arm. "No, no, don't! He'll be here any minute."

They studied each other; and whatever she read in Slade's face, it made her say, "Then it's worse than I heard."

"He was all right when I saw him this morning."

Weighing his words, she sensed the evasion. "How long've you actually been in Peshawar?"

"Probably as long as you have—"

Without another word, he got up to phone the depot. When he came back, she said, "No answer?"

He shook his head. "Man on duty said Steve drove to Malakand to pick up an AWOL. You'd better go to your room and relax," he advised, "and have dinner sent up later."

But he didn't get rid of her so easily. Before he could make his break, she had him by the arm. "You're a liar, Dave," she said, in a fierce whisper. "Something's wrong! Where's Malakand?"

"Gateway to the Wali of Swat's territory."

"Please! Skip the gags! Something is wrong, badly wrong, or he'd not keep me waiting this way."

She was twisting the diamond on her finger; Kellam's ring. Slade had wondered how many times she'd mentally taken it off, during the past two hours, "There is a Wali of Swat," he told her. "He isn't a gag. He gets a cash allowance for not raising hell or letting anyone else kick the gong around in the Chitral country. The Wali—"

"Stop or I'll scream! You're trying to hide something."

He plucked vainly at the fingers which dug into his arm. "I'm looking into this. You sit tight."

"I'm going, too. You can't pry me loose."

His quick move caught her off guard. He broke free. From twice arm's length he said, "I'm going where you can't possibly go. Be a good girl, it's bad enough as it is."

He darted into and across the lobby. Once in his hired car, he let out a sigh and mopped his forehead. Then, to Shir Dil, "Out to the supply depot, and step on it."

Shir Dil had booted enough trucks across the rocky deserts of Iraq to make short work of the Peshwar plain. As they neared the sprawl of warehouses enclosed in barbed-wire outlined by electric lights, Slade shouted above the roar and rattle of the car, "Ease up! There may be a sentry tending to business."

A spotlight blazed.

"Take it easy!" Slade repeated.

Shir Dil grinned, but didn't finish his wisecrack. A rifle whacked. A star-shaped pattern rayed the windshield. He cut the wheel, and jammed the brakes, kicking up a protective screen of dust. Before the sedan was fairly halted, the old fellow was diving for the dirt, and cursing in several languages.

"Halt! Who's there?"

"Friend."

"Advance one, to be recognized."

Slade went forward with his hands in the air. The spotlight blinded him. He could not see the sentry, but judging from the second "Halt!" given at six paces, the man was strictly military.

"Hold it till I call the corporal." This after some seconds of study. "Why the hell didn't you pull up when I sounded off? Who the hell you think you are? You Limeys are getting too high ranking."

A corporal showed up, and then the sergeant of the guard. The latter, after looking at Slade's identification papers, was skeptical. "Major, my hat! Where's your uniform?"

"Captain Kellam will identify me."

"The commanding officer isn't in."

"Where is he?"

"That's his business."

Then one of the men exclaimed, "Say, that is a major! I heard the captain call him that."

The guns were lowered. The sergeant reddened and stood at attention to pop his buttons. Slade chuckled, acknowledged the salute. "Carry on, you're doing well. Since you tell me Captain Kellam is not here, I don't want to come in to check up on you or on him."

"Sir, I'm not covering for the captain."

"Very well, Sergeant. You'd be dead wrong to cover for him, but you'd be a poor excuse of a soldier if you didn't go the limit. How come you're standing such a strict guard? I'd heard you fellows were a bit slack."

"Captain Kellam gave us a bucking up, sir."

"Sergeant, is there anything beyond that fence that would hurt your commanding officer if I saw it? Don't answer if you don't want to."

"No, sir," the noncom answered, without hesitation. "I'm just standing a strict guard."

"Then take me to Warehouse No. 12. I'll put it in writing if you want."

"Does the major think it's necessary?"

"It might be, it depends entirely on your orders. I'll write it anyway."

Slade followed Sergeant Warren to the orderly room, and wrote a few lines. Then they went to Warehouse No. 12. Yasmini's treasure hoard was gone. Slade gestured to a chest. "Sit down. Red tape and regulations are putting us both on the spot. Whatever your private thoughts are or used to be, you're making a good show of loyalty and respect for the skipper. Don't spoil it. I'm trying to play square with you, with Captain Kellam, and with myself. My hunch is that something has happened to Captain Kellam, something connected with a couple of chests that were here this morning and aren't here now."

The sergeant plucked at his stripes and gave a yank. Slade shook his head. "It's the man, not the insignia, you can't dodge that way. If Captain Kellam has taken a couple too many, I don't want to hear of it from you, either man to man, or otherwise. If he is in real danger, it's up to you to sound off. Use your judgment and don't waste time."

46

"The captain drove off with a light truck, sir. Alone. He wore civvies. That was about four o'clock. He was expecting a message, and he said he'd be back in an hour."

"Anything about Malakand Pass?"

"No, sir. I cooked that one up. He'd given us a jerking up like I'd never heard before. Said we were a disgrace to the uniform. That the same applied to him. That'd he'd set the wrong example, so he didn't blame us. But that the next man caught off base would find out in a hurry that this post was a military establishment, as of even date. He was sober and not hopped up."

"So you fellows tightened up?"

"Yes, sir. Don't know how long it'd lasted, but he sold us something. Forgetting rank, and being honest about things."

"Did you think he was going south with government property?"

"No, sir. He brought a lot of native stuff in one day, and I detailed a man to box it up."

"Why did you take it so much as a matter of fact when I said Captain Kellam might be in serious danger?"

"Last night when he came in, he was cut up a bit, I helped him use a first aid kit."

Slade got up. "That's all, sergeant."

"Sir, there's one thing more."

"You mean you have an idea where he took those chests, and you think I ought to know where to look for him?"

"Yes, sir."

"Thank you, sergeant. But I know already. Oh, one more point. When was the last time he did drive to Malakand?"

"About a month ago, with—uh—"

"With a native lady name Yasmini, and I'm not interested in how you happen to know. How'd you like the Wali of Swat?" The sergeant's mouth clamped tight. Slade nodded, smiled a little, and said, "That's right, don't answer. Until your commanding officer is accounted for or another officer ordered to take his place, you'll continue in command."

The sergeant's face showed that being left in command was an old story. Slade, as he put the depot behind him to rejoin Shir Dil, wondered whether the strictness of the guard had been the noncom's reaction to responsibility, or whether it had come from Kellam's pep-talk.

Shir Dil made short work of the distance to Yasmini's house. Like most of those facing the court, hers had window openings at the second floor level. These were hidden by screened balconies, whose carved and fretted panels gave the occupants perfect cover and an equally perfect view of the street. When Slade stepped up to hammer at the door, Shir Dil glanced toward the inner panels, which often were moveable. But nothing was thrown down at the visitors; and no one answered.

47

Shir Dil took a turn, beating with the haft of his dagger, and shouting, "O thou father of pigs! Thou brother of lewd sisters! Open, O thou Black-of-Face!" Finally, breathless, he turned to Slade: "Nobody home, no porter or he answers back, not so?"

"He'd've at least told you you're another."

"You wait, one second, I fix something quick."

Slade studied the ground. The headlights revealed the prints and the impression of hard soled shoes, and of native style shoes. Someone had helped Kellam unload heavy cargo. Ahead were tracks showing that the truck had left the court.

"Don't prove that Kellam was in it," he told himself, uneasily.

Shir Dil quickly came back. Two soot-smeared men followed him. He explained, "What you call him, smith-locks, they fix keys et cetera."

The two set to work, but neither with probe nor pick. Instead of wasting time to outwit the massive lock, they used a sledge. No one peeped from the panel openings across the way; if at all interested or occupied, the other residents of the vicinity were tending to their own defenses. Also, none of Peshawar's Sikh policemen appeared. The invisible neighbors knew something was wrong, and the law wanted to know nothing.

With the lock shattered, it was easy to slide the bolt. Shir Dil paid the smiths, who went away happy from a day's wages earned in a few minutes. Slade followed the old Pathan to the end of the shadowed passageway, and into the court.

The dark splashes on the flagstones were from blood spilled the previous night. In the trampled foliage, Slade saw a "hand of Fat'ma," in blue enamel. A bit of dirty string which had hung the good luck charm about the wearer's neck was nearby. The Five Holy Persons of Islam, symbolized by the fingers, had apparently justified the faith of the wearer, since he had escaped the kick-back of the raid which might have finished Kellam.

"O thou without-a-nose, thou sister of Satan, thou mother of little pigs!" Shir Dil bawled, and added further insults to meet the echoes of his opening remarks. "Come out before we come in and get you!"

"Someone laughed," Slade said, cocking his head.

Shir Dil spat. "Is across the court. You know what, I bet she is flew the coop, is not so?"

As the search progressed, Slade began to fear that he would find Kellam. Stairs led to the second floor. Others descended from there to the ground floor rooms in the rear. Some, just for variety, were directly connected. But long before he had gone through the characteristic hodge-podge of additions and extensions, he had to admit that Yasmini was not using her hide-and-seek facilities.

The walls were bare. Nothing remained but the sooty hearth, several cracked pots, two string cots, a quilted pallet, and a cosmetic odor considerably modified by the smell of ginger, garlic, sesame oil, mustard oil, and cloves.

Shir Dil's nostrils flared. "Also brandy—" He kicked a litter of bottles. "Hashish, and American cigarette. Lipstick, but not on the smoke."

Slade played his flashlight almost parallel to the floor. He noted a man's heel prints, and those of a woman's bare feet, and others of a woman's small feet shod with soft shoes.

"She's gone—he's gone—no new signs of a fight—"

Slade's face lengthened. There was one conclusion to draw, and he hated to draw it. Instead, he said to himself, "They could have conked him or covered him with a gun, to steal the truck. Last night's riot scared her, and she wouldn't stay here."

Then Shir Dil spoiled it with bitter realism. The old man twisted his wrinkles into an evil and knowing mask and said, "You know something, that captain is a smart man, he don't want to get kick out of the army, so he runs away with Yasmini. Like my cousin, Gul Mast, he takes Ahmad Khan's wife, Ahmad Khan's money, everything—only, they don't live happy ever after. Ahmed Khan ride like hell, he shoots Gul Mast and then he cuts off the lady's nose."

"That's nothing to what I'll cut off of Yasmini if I ever get hold of her," Slade growled. "That damn dizzy blockhead—good God, what'll I tell Diane!"

CHAPTER V

Slade got Diane on the house phone. "Can't give you any details, from here," he said. "I'll be up soon as you're dressed for a huddle."

"How do you know I'm not?"

"From the way you sound, darling. Pull yourself together and—hold it! I'm being paged—it's official. Can't see you till this is settled—top official, the Commissioner. Yes, Mr. Bowley's orderly. With orders." He followed the bearded Sikh to the official car which was waiting at the curb. But for the crisp salute of the driver, who held the door open, Slade would have felt that he was under arrest. And during the short drive, he was wondering what new atrocity Kellam's recently bucked-up soldiers had committed.

Slade found Mr. Bowley in dinner clothes, which made him all the more severe; and the presence of the sharp-faced native was an added omen of evil.

"Good evening, Major Slade. Thank you for coming." A bow so formal that it was insulting; and then, indicating the dark man, "May I present Colonel Sir Pratap Singh Bahadur?"

Sir Pratap's boots had the gleam of onyx. His knee length white tunic was gathered at the waist by a gilt sash with golden tassels. As he bowed, he made courteous pretense of offering the pommel of the curved tulwar, whose scabbard was of gold inlaid ivory. The medals which made a solid bank on his chest tinkled; the aiguillettes of the *jouragere* draped from right shoulder to cross-belt made a golden tinkling.

"Mr. Bowley exaggerates," the Rajput said, pleasantly. "I am only an honorary colonel."

Black brows shadowed his deep set eyes, which were falcon sharp; a lean cheeked man, with deep lines setting off the curved nose and straight mouth. His wiry hand found a natural stance on the *tulwar's* hilt. Though he had measured Slade, there was no guessing his appraisal. Mr. Bowley's opinion, on the other hand, was all too clear. "You're from Rajputana, Sir Pratap?"

"Yes, Major Slade. On urgent business. Unhappily, it concerns you."

Mr. Bowley took over. "It concerns you all too much, Major Slade! Put Captain Kellam under arrest at once or I shall go over your head and make demands on your superior!"

"On what charge?"

"Receiving stolen property. Accessory after the fact in the matter of the looting of Sir Pratap's villa near Jaipur."

"Jaipur! Good God, sir! Do you mean to tell me—how far is Jaipur from Peshawar?"

Mr. Bowley smiled frostily. "It is not alleged that Captain Kellam himself pillaged the villa. However, the loot has been traced to Peshawar. To a clique of *budmashes*, border ruffians. A lady named Yasmini is one of the group. Do you begin to understand?"

"Aren't you carrying birds-of-a-feather logic too far?"

"Sir Pratap has uncovered the fact that Captain Kellam was storing the loot in an United States government depot."

"May I ask for a list of the articles Sir Pratap lost?"

Mr. Bowley picked a paper from the desk, and offered it to Slade. At a glance, he recognized several items. "This is a carbon. May I keep it?"

"I'm sure you're quite welcome! Meanwhile, I demand immediate action."

"You're welcome to search the depot."

Mr. Bowley's fury subsided, only to surge anew when Sir Pratap's glance shifted and caught his eye. "First, I demand that you bring Captain Kellam to this office."

"Pardon me, sir, you are not dealing with me, or with Captain Kellam, but with the United States Army."

From the corner of his eye, Slade noted a smile twitching the corners of the Rajput's mouth, and the tips of his upturned black mustaches.

Mr. Bowley retorted, "In a criminal matter, we have jurisdiction. You will either oblige me, or else I shall immediately and forthwith communicate with your superior, who'll not thank you for making an incident."

Sir Pratap's hidden smile showed now in his hawk-eyes, and in the sharpening curvature of his nose.

As Slade figured it out, his defense of Kellam, at the first meeting with the commissioner, had made him an accomplice in Mr. Bowley's eyes. Also, Sir Pratap Singh Bahadur, whoever and whatever he might be, must know or suspect a good deal more than had come into the open. Ten to one, he had been behind the raid of the previous night; and, failing at direct action, he was using the commissioner as a stooge while he, Sir Pratap, used the old, infallible methods of his people.

Kellam, that is, must be alive, and for the moment beyond the Rajput's reach.

Once more, Slade accepted Mr. Bowley's challenge:

"If you have a warrant, please serve it. Get in touch with my superior if you care to." He bowed to both commissioner and Rajput. "Good evening, gentlemen. Call on me when I can serve you."Mr. Bowley's teeth clamped like a bear trap. Sir Pratap said, pleasantly, "Thank you for calling, Major Slade."

When he left, Slade knew that he had bitten off a big one; whether he could chew fast enough depended on keeping ahead of Sir Pratap. Worse yet, he sensed that he'd played squarely into the Rajput's hand by defying Mr. Bowley.

As the official car took him back to the hotel, Slade studied the inventory of loot. That hood sewed with pearls—that elephant driver's *ankhus,* studded with gems—that Herati rug—there wasn't a shred of doubt as to the origin of the hoard which Slade had seen.

Before calling to give Diane the official score, Slade located Shir Dil and said to the old man, "We may have to get out of here faster than we came. And a lot more quietly."

"Toward the Malakand Pass and Bajaur?"

"How do you figure *that?*"

"Yasmini, she can't get out of India other way."

"Take a message to Sergeant Warren, at the depot. When we leave, I'll have paint on my eyes and a rose behind each ear."

The old man grinned. "That will fool Sir Pratap."

Slade didn't bother to ask how Shir Dil had got on the inside track. And if Shir Dil knew that the Rajput dignitary had come to town to turn things inside out, everyone else in native Peshawar must know.

Some minutes later, Slade was explaining the situation to Diane, whose eyes were now dry and much too bright. He offered a story which left Yasmini out of the picture.

"He's either a prisoner—a hostage to check pursuit, though if Sir Pratap takes a hand, the answer would be, Cut his throat, we're still grabbing our trinkets. Or else—"

"If he'd been killed, you'd've found—"

"Snap out of it!" Slade broke in, harshly. "He might've deserted."

"He'd never do that!" she exclaimed. "Foolish, rash, impatient—but not—Oh, don't be ridiculous! Or nasty!"

He came near telling her about Yasmini, but backed down. Slade liked Diane too well, and he also remembered that no one ever got thanks for bringing an unsavory story. She'd not believe him anyway.

"The native friend whose plunder he'd stored might've murdered him to shut him up. Or else, he'd be on the loose. A native, I mean, would either go panicky or else, silly-reckless."

51

His conviction, rather than his logic, made Diane weaken. As though dazed by a blow, she said, "He might—in panic—"

Then her voice went shrill, and she cried, "Panic! With you coming here, snooping and threatening! Making him so ashamed he couldn't face me! Oh, you blundering fool, you drove him to desertion—get out of here—I'll—"

She snatched and hurled an ash tray. She followed with most of the tea service.

Slade dodged, ducked, danced about till he caught her empty handed. Then he got a hold and squeezed her so tightly she could neither kick nor claw. "I'll slap your ears till your head rings like a church bell! I'm so far out on a limb on account of that damned fool that if I don't make the grade, I'll have to do a bit of deserting myself!"

She quit struggling. Her eyes widened. She clung to Slade, and sobbed against his shirt front. "M-m-maybe it's my fault, coming here."

"You did your best. I'll do mine."

"But I've got to help undo my mistake. Dad's fixed it for me to go all the way to Kabul."

"You're crazy! No military attaché ever had that much pull!"

"Oh, but he could. I'm to be head nurse in the new woman's hospital in Kabul. Not really, of course not. But I *am* qualified, and—well—I didn't see any harm in applying, coming as far as Peshawar, then getting Steve straightened out—"

"And then to hell with the ailing Afghan females?"

"Well, of course! Steve's lots more important, isn't he?"

"Get this: You're not going to Kabul. I'm heading for the Malakand Pass and the Wali of Swat's territory, to overhaul that idiot and get the loot from his buddies. Get it settled before Sir Pratap takes a hand. That Rajput hard-case would rather there weren't survivors to tell what happened."

"That gives me all the more reason for going to Kabul! Get Dad to help, from the inside."

"You're not funny, darling, you're not even amusing. A dozen M.A.s couldn't make an impression."

She eyed him for a moment. "You're so afraid of your career. You're bent on overtaking him, for the honor of bringing him back. I'm going to Kabul. I don't care where you go, but I hope you roast!"

CHAPTER VI

Instead of quitting Peshawar as a Pathan, and afoot, Slade left in uniform, and driving a jeep. These, as well as other necessities had come from the supply depot. The fugitives, he reasoned, would not risk entering Afghanistan either by the Khyber or by any of the southern passes, since, despite century-old animosities, the British and the Afghans had a species of cooperation. Likewise, if Kellam and Yasmini were rash enough to risk the southern trails, they'd be captured, which would put them beyond Slade's efforts. It simmered down to a painful simplicity which he summed up by saying to Shir Dil, "Unless they've headed for Swat Valley, there's no use taking out after them."

They followed the railroad to its terminus at Dargai, on the frontier. Once more, Slade had gambled because he had no other choice.

Shir Dil said, "Try the Malakand Pass, or try the Shahkot Pass, or try some others, they all lead to the same valley."

At Dargai, there were questions. Slade's well prepared answers left the officer in command of the guard with no reason for making him stand further examination by the local political officer. Slade gestured to the bales lashed to the jeep, and said to the Indian Army captain, "Presents for the Wali of Swat. Field telephones, and walkie-talkie outfits."

The captain nodded. "The Wali is very fond of telephones. Thank you, don't bother to show me. Pleasant trip, sir."

"Just one moment, Captain!"

"Yes, sir?"

"How far ahead is the Wali's first inspection station?"

"Perhaps ten miles. I doubt if it's manned."

"I'm glad to hear that! The man who left ahead of me, late yesterday afternoon didn't have instructions on that matter and might've been squeamish about pulling up for inspection, which'd cause trouble." Slade offered another cigarette, and flicked his lighter.

The captain for a moment ignored the flame. "He's not as careless as you fear. He asked."

"Eccentric chap. Unpredictable. Quite a chance he'd gone by Shahkot, just to have his own way about something. Wonder if we're thinking of the same man?"

The Indian officer took a deep drag, flared his nostrils, exhaled slowly; he liked American cigarettes, and watched Slade's groping for a carton of Luckies which projected from the dunnage. "This man," he told Slade, "drove an army truck. A light one. A big man, red faced."

"You inspected his orders?"

"They were correct in every detail."

"How many men with him?"

"He was alone."

Slade cursed. "Helper probably was dead drunk and riding the load! Well, thanks a lot. Let me offer you a carton of smokes for the guard."

As they cleared the frontier station, Shir Dil wagged his beard and said, "Nice work! I bet you was born with a horseshoe in each hand, picking up Kellam the first crack."

Slade grinned and mopped the sudden rush of sweat from his face. "About time I got the breaks. Though if we'd tried Shahkot, and got no news, we'd'd've then guessed he must've come through this way."

By the time the jeep reached the summit, steam plumed from the radiator. Once a quarter of a mile down the reverse slope, Slade pulled up to look at the valley, whose upper end, narrow and rocky, was gripped between spurs of the Hindu Kush range. The left wall, nearly as high and sterile and foreboding, skirted the Afghan frontier. Far ahead, Slade saw a ridge along which ran a straggling row of poles. Insulators gleamed. "Telephone line," Shir Dil explained. "Like I said."

"I was thinking of that. No matter where he goes, or we go, someone'll give the Wali a buzz and tell him he's got visitors. And if the Wali grabs Kellam and the loot we're sunk!"

"Buck up, major! You bet she got phony papers, everything fix up ahead of time, Yasmini is one smart girl."

Ahead, the road narrowed and became rutted. It branched into tracks which lost themselves in the sun-baked upper slopes. This was one of the ways by which invaders had come from Turkestan and High Asia to loot the plains of Hindustan, but since it was not suited to vehicular traffic it had in modern times lost its ancient military importance.

After pulling into the shadow of a ledge, Slade put on Pathan finery. That done, he took binoculars and studied the country. "Couldn't go far with a truck. He'll have to find pack animals, and soon."

"Maybe wait till Yasmini's friends help her. That means, she is hide some place. Not too far from where the truck can't go no more."

They lacked any plan more definite than getting into the hills, where Shir Dil would question Pathan farmers. With each crest capped by a walled sheep fold, and a watch tower, no stranger could go far without being observed. How Yasmini expected to keep the mountaineers from sharing the wealth was beyond Slade's reckoning; but since that fascinating lady had made the attempt, she and her clique must have devised a way.

"Suppose the Wali is getting a cut of the loot?"

Shir Dil shrugged. "Can be."

"If I knew the Wali, I could talk it over."

"Very bad! Suppose the Wali has got a present from Yasmini? He sends you back, quick. Suppose the Wali has not got a present from Yasmini? Then he helps you hunt, and he keeps every damn all!"

Slade grimaced ruefully. "You think I'll get by as a visiting Kurd wearing Peshawar finery?"

The old Pathan sized him up from hobnailed shoes to turban. "Very nice, only don't talk too much."

Shir Dil took the wheel. Steam began to spout from the radiator. The jeep jounced and pitched, wove and skittered, as the wiry mountaineer picked a course between boulders. Presently, the rock and baked clay ended. The stretch ahead was dusty. "Wheel tracks!" Slade shouted, "Pull up!"

They got down to study the prints. Shir Dil said, "The Wali has one car. Each year, he makes one-two mile of road."

"Modern, eh?"

"Damn right. Got one very nice hospital, all the time full of fellows shot up with feuds."

"Quail tracks cross the wheel prints," Slade observed; after they had idled along for several hundred yards.

Shir Dil frowned and squinted. "Quail run this early morning, but the wind don't blow in too much dust. The wheels, she run last night, you understand?"

At the end of another mile, Slade got further evidence. Crankcase drippings showed where the truck had halted. The dust recorded a the change. Shir Dil said, "One man, American style shoe. One lady, small feets. One woman, big feets. She help the man, the lady sits there, she don't do nothing only smoke the cigarette."

Further on, rainfall had cut a deep slash athwart the trail. The fugitives had stopped to bridge this bad gash with boulders. "Step on it!" Slade urged, "Every bit of road building they do, it gives us a break!"

His exultation did not last long. Shir Dil, twisting the jeep around a hairpin curve, forgot his English and yelled, "Allah curse their religion!" A wall of rocks blocked the trail. He booted the brakes and went into a spin which brought the car broadside against the obstacle.

"What the billy-hell?"

From behind boulders on the upper slope, and out of dry washes on the downgrade side, men with weather-beaten faces popped up. Their baggy pants were ragged and greasy. Their sheepskin jackets had a mangy look. However, they leveled Enfields whose stocks and barrels were groomed as though for inspection. Slade muttered, "Talk, and talk fast! That old buzzard with the red beard has a trigger-happy face if I ever saw one."

He got out of the jeep, hoping that Shir Dil had the right answers. The delegation from the adjoining hills, however, ignored the old Pathan, and concentrated on Slade. They fingered his vest and his turban. They admired his shoes. One drew the silver-hafted dagger. Another found the wrist-watch a thing of intense interest.

They reeked of garlic, asafetida, and sheep. Their hands were gnarled and grimy. Their belts sagged from daggers and cartridges. One finally questioned Slade, who tapped his chest, and answered, grandly, *"Min kurdim!"*

Shir Dil sounded off. His remarks aroused interest and approval. Finally, he said to Slade, "I tell these fellow we take the jeep from two soldiers. Now they say, we go to the *khelat*, that stone place up on the hill."

"What for?"

"Meet the *khan*, he is boss, his name is Akbar, very nice fellow."

Half a dozen of the tribesmen packed themselves into the vehicle. The others broke the road block. Shir Dil said, "They say, go ahead, is a road to the *khelat*."

Slade took the wheel. Beyond the trail fork, the ascent made the rough spots previously covered seem smooth as a boulevard. In compound low, the jeep required man-handling to make the final quarter of a mile.

The *khelat* commanded watered slopes on the further side of the ridge. Dogs the size of Shetland ponies came bounding out. Armed men followed the snarling brutes. But despite the interest aroused by the arrival of strangers in a car, the two men stationed in the high watch tower remained at their post. However much the Wali of Swat had gone modern, the hillmen still felt that only a fool trusted his neighbors.

Children, and unveiled women joined the crowd. They came out of the mud-walled houses which hugged the stone wall of the *khelat*. And before he was herded into the gloom of the central building, from whose corner rose the watch tower, Slade decided that while a telephone network to keep the Wali in touch with the headmen of the principle villages was a splendid idea, modern plumbing and a garbage disposal system were what the valley most urgently needed.

Mustering up his first lessons in Pushtu, Slade asked the red-bearded man, "Where is Akbar Khan?"

"He comes back soon. You tell me how to steal cars. Where are the presents?" Slade gestured to Shir Dil, and spoke a few words in Kurdish. The old mad went to the jeep to get cigarettes and K-rations. When he came back, he said, "No telephone line to this place."

"I noticed that," was the glum reply. "But we'll be staying here long enough for the news to get to the Wali."

CHAPTER VII

Shir Dil, having wolfed the last bits of cheese and the leathery bread which the red-bearded second in command had offered them, was not a bit impatient. He squatted in his corner, and nodded as he smoked. Slade finally asked, "How do you figure that road block? They couldn't've seen us from far enough way to have had time to build it. No matter how much dust we kicked up."

Shir Dil left the answer to Allah.

Slade however continued to grapple with his query. "The captain at Dargai had lots of information for us. Then, just to make it nice, Kellam changed a tire. Next, there's a road-block and a reception committee. Nothing missing but the smell of Yasmini's perfume, and a gallon of that wouldn't hurt this place at all!"

Shir Dil grinned. Seeing that the old man would not bother to deny the possibility that they had been trapped by allies of the fugitives, Slade got up from his sheepskin mat and made for the entrance of the watch tower. The men who dozed at the other side of the hearth looked up, but offered no objections when Slade stepped in, and began to climb the ladder of poplar trunks to which rungs had been lashed.

The sound of his ascent warned the two who stood guard. They were blue-eyed, and sun-tanned rather than swarthy. Welcoming a close look at the visitor they had spied from a distance, the sentries made room for Slade on the small platform, and greeted him amiably.

"And the peace upon you, and the blessing of Allah," he answered. "*Min kurdim*. A Kurd from Kurdistan. These mountains, they are like my own home. But you have more grass here."

He offered them smokes. The more he studied their thin lips and straight noses, the greater became his confidence in his disguise. Since, as far as their features were concerned, these mountaineers did not look foreign to him, he could hardly seem outlandish to them.

They asked questions, many of which he understood, though he answered only a few, and some of those, absurdly, to make his ignorance of Pushtu seem even greater than it actually was.

At last Slade produced the field glasses. Neither of the guards objected; and both were interested. After carefully focusing the eye pieces, he scanned the hills.

"Over there," he said, gesturing. "Those sheep. Count the ewes, the rams, the lambs."

With vision about twice as keen as the air corps required, the naked eye had a chance of classifying the animals grazing on the distant slope. The man wearing the felt jacket answered, "There are no rams. Of the ten ewes, two have two lambs each, the others, one each."

"*Shabash!*" Slade exclaimed, admiringly. "But there is something else, O Brother! Too small for any man's eye."

The guards accepted the challenge. That gave Slade his chance at details more important than the age and sex of mutton. Far off, almost at the furthest reach of binoculars, he noted ancient ruins, half buried in rubble. He studied these, and the neighboring country until one of the sentries shouted, "By Allah, you're right! A child asleep under a juniper. Well away from the sheep."

Slade shifted the binoculars. "By Allah, what eyes! The grandfather of eyes!"

"Let me try the glasses," one demanded.

Slade thumbed the eyepiece adjustment. "Welcome, O Brother!"

There was muttering and frowning. Then, "Satan fly away with them, they make us blind."

"These be for poor eyes, not for good ones like yours."

After wishing them a peaceful watch, Slade went down the ladder. Shir Dil came out of his cat-nap. The man who had been lounging in the dusky room where Akbar Khan and his men assembled of an evening were gone. Outside, horses switched flies, and made chains jingle. Two big dogs lay just beyond the entrance.

"Those devils," Slade said, "will keep us from sneaking out. Even if the jeep didn't wake everyone up."

"No good to go too soon," Shir Dil objected. "Stay to find out why these fellows make a road block before they see our dust come up on the wind."

"I got a look from the watch tower." He tapped the binoculars. "I saw something to look into. Suppose Akbar Khan's men saw a truck roll by, or heard one pass during the night. They knew it can't go very far."

Shir Dil straightened. "*Hai!* The man drives, they say, then he got to come back, to try another road, this time they block him."

"Right! They thought we were Kellam, that we'd come back for a fresh try, along another branch. They'd heard Kellam roll past the first time. They didn't bother to wonder why they didn't hear him go back for a fresh start. Seeing us made them think they'd missed something. Something that doesn't count because they've got us finally."

After a moment of finger combing his beard, Shir Dil agreed. Then, "I fix something for the dogs. We got no arrack, no cardamoms, nothing for making post. I use the opium with—"

"Use K-rations," Slade told him. "These dogs'll eat anything."

Shir Dil went to the jeep. When he came back with all the ingredients for a canine Mickey Finn, Slade asked, "Anyone snoop around enough to find our guns?"

"That is one thing not yet snafu. You watch me fraternize with the dogs."

But the first move was interrupted before it could begin. The sleeping brutes raised their heads. They bristled, they sniffed the air, they snarled; then the monsters raced for the gate. Human voices joined in the racket. Hooves clattered up the trail. Horses in the courtyard snorted, and whinnied. There were answers from outside.

Shir Dil thrust bait and opium into his pocket. After listening to the voices, he said, "Akbar Khan is come home quick, now we say something nice, give him presents, and tomorrow, we go. I told you better keep the pants on, too much hurry, he is bad."

They went out to greet the returning chieftain, who was followed by a dozen men. The Khan rode a long-legged bay Turkoman, the biggest horse Slade had seen on the frontier; no smaller animal could have carried such a burden.

Akbar loomed up like a mountain. His beard flamed red in the wind. Little blue eyes squinted from a face which seemed to have been hewn, and crudely, from a block of teak. Grooms led two weary horses almost as big as the khan's exhausted mount.

Had the *khelat* been on the next ridge, the last of Akbar's horses would have given out.

When the khan dismounted, cat-nimble, Slade wondered which was the heaviest, horse or rider. Then Shir Dil stepped forward to greet the master of the fortress.

"I am one of your own people, and this is my blood brother, Ayyub Khan, a Kurd from Kurdistan. He does not speak our speech, but he learns fast and rides hard." Slade made his salaam. After returning the compliment, and with little ceremony, Akbar stalked over to the jeep, which he sized up as he would a horse.

Having completed his inspection, Akbar faced Slade. "If you're a Kurd," he said, in English which, despite its thick accent, was dismayingly easy to understand, "then I'm a bloody Englishman."

"I speak a little English, your Excellency, I went to a mission school in Iraq."

Akbar Khan's eyes began to twinkle. "You don't walk like a mountain man, and your eyes don't look like a mountain man's. That car is no good to you, so I am keeping it. The road gets worse the further you go."

"That's gospel," Slade answered. "I was about to tell you that we're in a hurry to move on, but we've waited to offer it to you. On the roads around your place, it's pretty good."

"I've always needed a car," Akbar continued. "I can't find horses big enough for me."

"There's not much gas left."

"I'll tend to that, Mister—never mind what the name is, Ayyub is good enough."

"Do you know how to drive a jeep, Akbar Khan?"

"I don't have to know how. You are staying to be my chauffeur. Whatever you've done on the other side of the border, I don't care but stealing a car is reason for not going back. You're crazy if you want to go ahead. A lot of people in this valley, they don't like foreigners."

"Look here," Slade protested, "I've got business in Afghanistan."

"Then I'm saving your life by keeping you here. Those chaps over there—" He pointed toward the further wall of the valley. "—are cut-throats, they murder each other when there aren't any strangers. You stay. You're under my protection. Even the Wali would think twice before he tried to send you back to Peshawar. Go in there and wait for me!"

Akbar turned to his followers. Slade and Shir Dil went into the assembly room of the fortress.

"Chauffeur by special appointment to his majesty! You did a fine job fixing me up to look like a mountaineer."

Presently, Akbar came in. The young man who trailed after him had that same rough-hewn facial expression, though he was not as heavy as the khan. Akbar said to Slade, "Very nice clothes. They make me look foolish, I am not dressed so good as my chauffeur."

Shir Dil intervened. "*Huzoor*, his are too small for you."

Akbar smiled. "That is why I bring my son, my little son, Daoud. With letting out some seams, he can wear those things. Be pleased to change, Mr. Ayyub-whoever-you-are."

When the swap was complete, Akbar wagged a heavy finger. "You should be pleased, Mr. Ayyub. You give my little boy one suit too small, he gives you the same as two suits."

Stately and incredible, the human mountain stalked out. His son, a mere hill, followed at a respectful distance. Slade eyed Shir Dil; the old man said, "Look, some guards go over to watch the car, like he told them to."

"How come he skipped my watch and binoculars?"

"Not polite, taking everything too quick."

"You better start studying the dogs again. We've got to get out of here. The more I think it over, the more I'm sure that Kellam has to be within a few miles. He couldn't have gone much further."

"Where you think he hides?"

"Some place where a truck won't show. Looking west from the watch tower, I saw some tumbled down buildings. Half buried. Big, lots bigger than anything these hill people build."

"Two thousand, maybe three thousand years, the King of Roum, Iskander Dhulkarnayn—" Shir Dil gestured. "Iskander with the two horns."

"Alexander the Great?"

"Yes, he is king of all this country. Plenty of cities. Today, under the ground, from earth shakings, from, hill slidings, from armies busting down the walls."

"That's where I'm going. He might have made it in the truck. If we lose each other in the scramble, head for that place."

Though the shadow of the watch tower now reached far beyond the wall, Akbar Khan, sitting under a striped awning, was still busy settling the disputes which had come up during his absence. As he listened, he studied the jeep; but the *durbar*, public audience, was an obligation he could not evade for any private purpose. Slade went out and seated himself on the ground near the others who listened.

If the disputed horse trade took too long Slade would have to depend on Shir Dil's devices. If the argument ended too early he would be equally handicapped.

Finally, Akbar gave his decision. When he got up, and gave the audience permission to leave, Slade accosted him, saying, "I'd like to borrow a horse."

"Why?"

Slade pointed to the jeep. "I lost a can of gas. We were going to go back after it when your men held us up. Someboy's likely to find it and cut it in half for a cooking pot."

The khan's glance shifted to the animals stabled along the wall. For a moment, Slade feared that he would get exactly what he'd asked for. Then Akbar said, "You're fool enough to try to get away."

"Send a man with me."

"We'll be eating soon." Akbar eyed the guards, who had not yet tired of taking turns at the wheel of the jeep, "But we'll go in that."

"We?"

"Of course! I want an idea of what the thing is good for."

Akbar welcomed an excuse; his dignity had thus far kept him from the joy ride which his followers would have taken immediately upon getting possession of the vehicle. Several of those who had lingered after the *durbar* now came up, earnestly discussing the jeep and its possibility. Akbar ignored them, and their hints. He wasn't interested in finding out how many passengers the devil-wagon could haul.

Slade took the wheel, and watched Akbar Khan perform the miracle of wedging himself into the other scat.

"This is the starter—" The engine roared to life. "This is the gear shift. You can drive with all four wheels, in rough places, or you can drive with the hind wheels, to go fast on good roads."

"Two wheels are faster than four? Don't lie to me!"

"This is the clutch—now watch—"

Slade cut the wheel sharply and goosed the throttle. Accelerating on a small radius made the top heavy *khan* sway as though an agile horse had almost unseated him. Then, straightened out, the jeep swooped for the gate. The cheering of mountaineers for a moment drowned the voice of the engine. They made a rush for the picket line, to get horses and give the devil wagon a race.

"Faster!" Akbar commanded, as he looked over his shoulder.

"Too steep and too rough."

The clattering of hooves and the shouts of riders mocked the khan, who demanded more speed; but Slade answered, "Wait till we get to the road, then I'll show them."

The sun barely peeped over the peaks which rimmed the valley. The floor was already dark. Long shadows and ruddy bands of light marched along the upper slopes. Slade blasted the horn; the laughing horsemen who had overhauled the jeep made way, as further evidence of their triumph. Horses tossing their heads sprayed passenger and chauffeur with foam and sweat. Slade booted the throttle to the floorboard.

Gravel rattled like hail on a tin roof as he swung into the road. Dust hid the horsemen. Now that he was clear of them, he raced into the rapidly deepening dusk, trusting the headlights to pick out the worst ruts and boulders.

"They'll never catch up!" he yelled.

Between jarring and jouncing, Akbar Khan contrived to grin. Finally, on a stretch that forced the jeep to a crawl, he said, "Now go back."

"Can't turn till the next wide spot. How do you like it?"

"Very nice."

Akbar had forgotten all about the spare gas can. He'd been too busy to wonder why Slade had driven in the wrong direction. And then the widening of the road, and Slade's next maneuver combined to keep the khan's mind on the moment at hand.

Slade cut the wheel, and as the whiplash spin began, he kicked the brake. There were two possible destinations for the top-heavy khan: over the side, or over the windshield. Akbar took the former. Knocked breathless, he rolled, all the while clawing gravel to keep himself from going over the shoulder and into the ravine. Slade came out of the spin and raced on.

While he didn't hear what Akbar Khan was saying, he heard the three shots which smacked overhead. The fourth pistol slug thumped into the luggage.

Then a curve blacked out the tail-light.

Slade pulled up. He got his field kit, as well as the carefully concealed pistols and carbine whose existence Akbar Khan's people had not yet suspected. Next, he uncapped the remaining can of gas and set it afire. As the flames shot up, he pushed the jeep over the shoulder.

When the gas tank, almost empty, let go with a roar and a geyser of fire, Slade shouldered his pack and set out afoot. Akbar Khan, reasonably assuming that his shots had taken effect, would be hoofing in the opposite direction.

CHAPTER VIII

During his march along the rutted track, Slade heard the barking of dogs but neither farmer nor shepherd challenged him. When moonrise made for easier going, he at times fancied that he could distinguish his goal, the far off ruins. Most of the time, as he plodded through silence broken only by the whine of the wind, he debated whether to hike only by night, or to risk daylight, and being sighted by suspicious mountain men.

At dawn, he scanned the crests, and was tempted by the nearness of the ruins heaped on a broad shelf jutting from a mountainside. Cornices and the stumps of decapitated columns jutted from the debris of landslide and earthquake. The slope of the approach was comparatively gentle. His goal was too near to permit rest. He resolved to press on. And at the same time, he scanned the steep grades below the trail, half fearing that he might see the wreckage of Kellam's truck.

Vultures wheeled black against the sky. Recklessly, and wooden from weariness, he lurched on until, from the opposite crest, a puff of smoke blossomed. Perhaps a second later, a high velocity slug popped past, to glance from an outcropping rock. He rolled for cover. Then came a second bullet, raking up dirt, and moving so slowly that it did not whine. Two reports followed: the dry whack of cordite, and the boom of a muzzle loader charged with black powder.

"Bum shot with good gun misses, or I'd not have ducked the musket—wonder if she's a Tonk *jezail?*"

For a quarter of an hour, he lay in the shadow of a ledge. The slope from which the shot had come showed no further trace of life. He tried to puzzle it out: the watchers might have mistaken him for an enemy they had hoped to ambush; they might have fired on the general principle that a stranger is a menace, or that a man plodding alone was a fool to be put out of his misery. Or, bored by watching, the two had welcomed any moving target.

Lying motionless gave fatigue a chance to grip. When Slade awakened, the sun was half past the meridian. Mirage danced over the rocky slopes. Except from close range, not even the best marksman would have a chance. He took a pull at his canteen, ate part of a K-ration, and risked coming from cover.

The vultures no longer circled. After an hour he rounded a sharp curve. Two bearded men squatted in the shade, their heads drooping to their chests. On the rock between them was half a cake of bread, part of an onion, and a scrap of granite-like cheese.

Slade halted. For moments, he waited, carbine ready, until, finally, he moved on. Whether from weariness, or from too much opium, they did not awaken. The encounter gave him a new problem; that of meeting people who might pass through Akbar Khan's territory and chatter about a stranger who mangled the language.

"Can't cold caulk 'em, can't shoot 'em in their tracks," he summed it up. "So—hole up, and dodge the issue."

This was a hard decision. However Kellam might be traveling, each hour of Slade's hiding out would get the other just so much nearer Afghanistan.

From his perch, he watched two mountain men trudging along the trail below him. They plied their long barreled rifles as walking sticks. He studied their slow, swinging stride, and the way they carried their shoulders.

"Looks like hell on the parade ground, but it eats the miles."

He waited until nightfall to practice what he had observed.

Finally, the trail skirted the slope leading to the shelf which held the ruin. When Slade climbed to the level stretch, he was surprised by its expanse. From somewhere in the gloom below him came the trickle of water. He wondered why there were neither villages nor sheepcotes in the vicinity.

Iskander, he remembered, had once proposed hewing a granite mountain into the image of a god whose extended hand would hold an entire city; Iskander, ploughing the earth with war, had sown cities as a farmer scatters grain, though with more of whimsy than of purpose. The fallen heads of columns picked out by moonrise were Grecian. Who but Iskander of the Two Horns would have built a marble city for no reason except that a shelf was there to hold one? Though this place, whatever its name had been, might once have guarded the Valley of Suastos, now called Swat.

The ground shivered under his feet. At first he thought this to be a trick played by tired legs until, irritated, he stopped and stamped the earth. There was a hollow sound, separate from that made by his hobnailed shoes; and the yielding was unmistakable. This place had more than met the eye. No wonder herdsmen didn't like such ground.

Slade began to think of a name for the place. Iskanderville...no good...cold as billy-be-damned—no, I'm so tired I'm shivering in this louse-ridden jacket... Swat...that's Babe Ruth... Suat... Soo-at, that's better...not pretty, not funny either... Welcome to Suat, Major Slade, be one of the ghosts of the Suat Rotary Club...

He stopped a moment. From the shadows came a rumbling, a *vocal* sound. He forced a grin and thought, "Heck, it's not Rotary, it's the Lions Club, and they're saying, *'Oooooo-Wahhhh'!'*"

He sniffed the air, and nearly laughed aloud. The smell was that of a bat colony; the vocalizing, a trick of the wind which forced air from out of the buried houses of Suastos. Bat-wings kissed his cheeks and made him shudder.

63

Tiny claws hooked his turban; elfin piping twittered in his ears as the bats rushed out.

But no gust of air should frighten the creatures.

Slade stepped into the gloom which gaped from the base of the column-riddled mound. The opening was wide, and its ceiling high over his head. Once more there was a roar. Air compression struck his ear drums, as from the blast of a shell exploding a long way off.

Feeling his way, he went further, until he noted light which at first seemed the trick of tired eyes; but when it did not flash or dance, he knew it was not inside his head. He sniffed again. The scent of wood prevailed over the stench of bat-droppings, and there was still another smell.

"Gas, by God! Lube, and rubber."

Now the light was strong enough to show deeply rutted flagstones; the wear of Iskander's chariot wheels, or those of Kanishka, the Tartar who had ruled a Graeco-Buddhist kingdom.

He crouched to take off his shoes. After tying them to his belt, he walked on, avoiding slabs of fallen masonry, and earth which had pushed through the wall he skirted.

The lion-roar kept him from hearing whoever waited by the fire around the corner, so that when he at last turned the angle to step from penumbra to full glow, he had his carbine leveled.

He stood looking at the man and the woman until he could lick his lips, swallow the dust in his throat, and gulp the cramp which gripped it. His presence aroused the two, but not until Slade was able to say, "Hello, Steve. Never mind the gun. It's me, not a hill-billy."

"Dave, for heck's sake!" Steve Kellam exclaimed, as he hitched about, putting himself between Yasmini and the man who had found life in the bones of Suastos.

Yasmini sat unveiled, and unafraid.

Something stirred in the shadow of the truck. Slade's carbine shifted. "Come out or I'll let you have it!" he warned, and fired at the figure; anyone but the captain was fair game.

"Take it easy!" Kellam shouted above the clash of the carbine's bolt as a fresh cartridge went home.

A grizzled hag, big-footed and barefooted, came out screeching.

Yasmini's reassurance bit deep: "Don't worry, it's just Halima, my maid."

"Don't be trigger happy," Kellam protested. "How'd you get here?"

Slade answered, "You might've known that Peshawar spills top-secrets in no time. How could you possibly *not* be found?"

"Who's with you?"

"More than are with you. But none within hearing distance. I've sold them the idea that this is between you and me. Nothing you say can be held against you."

Kellam became thoughtful. Yasmini smiled seductively, and rearranged the tunic which she wore in place of dancing girl's skirt. With no jewelry, and without even a stud to disfigure her nose, Yasmini filled the eye as she had never before.

Slade squatted in the angle of a pilaster which gave flank protection. "Let's go back."

"I can't." The captain drew a deep breath, glanced at the truck. "All snafu."

Yasmini's inward smile lighted her face; it made her look like a goddess who contemplates her work, without either loving or hating it.

Slade's hands tightened on his carbine. Then he relaxed, resigning himself to chicken heartedness that forbade knocking her over with a bullet. After all, he wasn't sure what such a decisive move would do to Kellam. Then sanity came back to Slade. Yasmini smiled understandingly. She nodded, as though she had weighed him and found him to be worthy of her respect, for having appraised the merits of blotting her out, if need be, for quicker victory.

"The mountaineers don't know you're here," Slade went on. "They didn't tell me. I learned in other ways."

"My friends," Yasmini said, "haven't arrived, and Steve doesn't want to leave me here alone. Do you understand him now?"

"A bit too well."

"Just as I understand you."

"That loot," Slade resumed, "belongs to Pratap Singh Bahadur. While you were heading for the frontier, I was catching hell from all sides for not bringing you up before the commissioner, Mr. Bowley. I knew by then you were gone, and who with, so I told him to find you and serve a warrant if he felt he had enough to make it stick."

"You came to bring me back?"

"No, to tell you, so you'd want to come back. You were dumped on from the start. Guarding her so-called belongings was well, not too smart, but I can understand. Conniving to get a million in loot across the border, using U. S. Army as the front, that's something you can't do, Steve."

"I've done it."

Kellam's voice told far more than he realized; it explained that something other than fatigue and tension had marked him. Wrath made the base of Slade's brain ache intolerably; pain compressed his temples. Once again, Yasmini's life depended on a trigger finger. There'd be no complications. In the Valley of Suastos, a Kashmiri dancing girl counted even less than the woman of a True Believer.

But anger wouldn't save Kellam, so he said, "Go back and put your cards on the table. I'm your witness."

"I'm A.W.O.L."

"I radioed and got you a thirty day leave. You're out of bounds, but not A.W.O.L."

Kellam got up. Yasmini remained cross-legged on the Boukhara carpet whose shining nape had caged the soul of many embers. Slade arose. He was not as steady as he should have been. Swallowing his fury had poisoned him with a venom worse than that of weariness. When he went to the truck he saw there was no cargo.

"Where is the stuff?"

Kellam gestured. "Here and there, there's no end to this nest of caved-in buildings."

Slade mounted to the cab. The key was in the ignition. He prodded the starter. The engine spun merrily, but would not fire. Kellam told him, "The spark plugs are gone."

"Sounded odd." Slade got down and lifted the hood. "Who took them out?"

Kellam reddened and lowered his eyes.

"Where are they?" Slade demanded, "Tell me or I'll knock your damned head off and—where are they?"

"I don't know."

"I'm afraid I have to believe you. Come outside. I give you my word that there's no one who can understand a word of English."

"Go with him," Yasmini said.

Kellam went with Slade to the mouth of the passageway. There, seating himself in an angle sheltered from the wind, the deserter said, "I didn't have guts enough to face Diane."

"So she thought, and nearly clawed my eyes out, and said it was my fault, the way I'd cracked down," Slade told him. "Go back and face it out."

"When a man makes a mess that smells to Washington, and a girl comes all the way to Peshawar to save him," Kellam explained, "he can't face her."

"Quit beating around the bush! You're so dizzy about that fancy shape you can't break loose. You want to break away, but you can't."

Kellam coughed, fidgeted, and stared at his toes. This was answer enough for Slade. "You heel," he said, quietly, "I could have told Diane about Yasmini, I could have fixed it for someone else to tell her, a neater way of playing my own hand. All right, I have always liked Diane a lot."

"You have to bring me back alive, so she can be a hundred percent fed up with me, and you'll have a clean chance at her!"

"I'd like such a chance, but that wouldn't get it for me. My job is to put you back on the beam. I want to do it man to man, not in military style."

"Meaning, you don't want to put me under arrest. Because you know there's hardly a chance of our getting back?"

"It's not *quite* that bad."

Kellam pondered for a long time. "On your word as an officer, is that stuff stolen property?"

"Sir Pratap Singh Bahardur had an inventory. I read it. Too many items checked for there to be any chance of funny business. What'd she tell you when you hauled the things to her house?"

Kellam eased up as though talking it out was a relief. Slade hunched forward to grasp at victory.

"I was—am—fond of her. She wasn't a public character—not in my time—we'd made plans—"

Slade kept his teeth from gritting audibly.

Kellam continued, "The story rang true. She could damn well have been in danger of robbery in times like these. I met you all the way in taking the stuff to her house. I knew I was giving her a slap in the face. Seeing Diane would clinch it. I didn't know what to do, which way to turn—what could I tell Diane?"

Slade, seeing the man's face in the moonlight, threw off his contempt; he was merely sorry that this was the real thing. He could not deny that Yasmini had, in her way, planned on a new life with Kellam. A fatally foolish plan, but if they both meant it, then out of common humanity, he had to accept and understand. Slade had to swallow anything that he had to swallow if by doing so, he could redeem the poor devil.

Kellam had given his men a bucking up that had snapped them to their feet with a jerk. Only a soldier and a good one could have towered above his own bad example and got response from such poorly disciplined G.I.s. Marching Kellam back a prisoner would be like the surgeon's reporting that the patient had died after a successful operation.

Slade said, "If I'd been in your fix, it'd had me biting ten-penny nails in half. Then what happened?"

"Yasmini was afraid. She wasn't pretending. She begged me to drive her to the frontier. She'd been prepared, she had everything but a truck and a front."

"Papers, you mean, to flash at Malakand?"

"Right. And I had a spare uniform at her house. She hid under the load. That battle-axe of a Halima, we made her up as a man, she has nearly enough mustache. She faked being drunk, out cold, to explain my being at the wheel. It all went so fast I hadn't time to think of how I'd get back."

Silence, until Slade prompted, "You didn't plan *not* to come back?"

"Didn't plan. Period."

"I've been that way about a woman, only I was lucky. Then what?"

"She knew of this place. I didn't know that a truck couldn't get through to Afghanistan. She told me then that she'd prepared for everything. That a letter to relatives in Kashmir would—had already—started them on the way to here. With pack animals to carry the goods. We'd not dare try to buy horses around here, or we'd be looted in five minutes."

"I see how you got into, deeper and deeper," Slade admitted. "You balked and threatened to leave her, unless she left the loot hidden here and came back with you?"

"Something like that. I'd done my share. I told her she could go back to India, and wait safely, far away from Peshawar, till I got out."

"And with Diane in the picture, Yasmini knows better than to risk that?"

Kellam groaned, and buried his face in his hands.

Slade caught him by the shoulder. "On your feet, soldier! We're finding those spark plugs. We'll shoot our way past Akbar Khan's place if we have to. I'll drive, and you hose them if they try to make us pull up."

Kellam looked less harassed, less confused. He said, "You're about ready to fold, what in God's name've you been doing to get here? You need some chow, we have coffee, and brandy, and—"

Slade shook the hand from his arm. "No go. I'm risking nothing from any commissary Yasmini is running. I'll hit the sack in a corner I pick for myself where she can't knife me. And you could do with some rest. Then find the plugs."

After watching Kellam fade into the gloom, Slade told himself, "That jeep's got enough plugs to get us out, and to hell with Yasmini's foxiness."

CHAPTER IX

When Slade came back with the spark plugs of the jeep, he showed them to Yasmini and said, "You were right when you told me that if I tried to make you find the plugs, Kellam'd turn against me. You're right saying I'd not be tough enough to force a woman to talk. You're right in everything—*except this*."

Yasmini looked worried. Slade turned to Kellam. "You won't lift a hand to stop me."

When he would not answer, Yasmini and her woman went down a cross passage whose right-angled reach from the main entrance extended far through the rubbish and ruin. Daylight came in, though faintly. Kellam did not follow them. "Get the stuff," he finally said, pointing. "I can't stop you."

"Do you want to?"

"Anyway I turn, I'm wrong."

"Sit tight, I'll get busy."

Enough light came in through overhead crevices for Slade to catch the glint and gleam of jewel and silk and metal. Shir Dil's absence worried him until he stopped to reason it out: the old man must have been convinced by the wrathful khan's account of how a handful of pistol slugs had settled the fugitive chauffeur. And Shir Dil was among his own people.

After loading the loot, Slade told Kellam, "Checking out by daylight can't be done. Akbar Khan would see our dust and build a road-block we couldn't break through. So it's a night march."

He checked the spare gas cans, and found more than enough to make the Malakand summit.

"Give me your gun and the knives," Slade went on. "We need all the shut-eye we can get before dark. I don't trust Yasmini—*what the devil've you been drinking?*"

Kellam was definitely owl-eyed. He reddened, but wouldn't answer. Slade caught the smell, and exclaimed, "*Post*, by God! Isn't honest liquor bad enough?"

"What's wrong with *post*?"

Slade eyed him, and shrugged. "I believe you don't actually know what that girl has been feeding you—well it explains a lot."

"What's in it beside brandy and flavoring? She called it *panj*, anyway."

"*Panj*, my eye! *Panj*, in case you've been too busy to study Urdu, means five: brandy plus rose water plus citron juice plus sugar plus arrack—one-two-three-four-five, *panj*, hence the English 'punch'."

"Interesting," Kellam said caustically, "but what of it?"

Slade eyed his own hand, and the fingers thereof. "Five equals *panj*, which you'll get and in English, brother, if you drink any more of that stuff she's mixed. It's doped with opium or hashish, and with you out cold, where'd I be?"

"Opium? Hashish? I'm no hophead!"

"Of course you're not, or you'd've realized from the way it works what's in such a mess. You can take it a long time and not be an addict. The case in your favor gets better right along—I mean it, you did a swell job of it while the shooting lasted in Africa. That was something you understood. India fooled you, that's all."

Sincerity touched Kellam. Slade chuckled good humoredly, relaxed his fist, and said, "See that all knives and the like are present and accounted for. Or I'll have to peel her to the buff to make sure nothing's hidden. Or, tie her up so tight it'll be painful. Even then, these dancing girls are so nearly double jointed you can't hold 'em without a blacksmith to make a job of it."

Kellam went to find Yasmini and Halima. When he came back with a dagger and a chopper, which he turned over, along with his service automatic, he said, "This is it, there's nothing more."

"Official statement."

Kellam, despite *post*, drew himself to attention, and saluted. "Official, sir." Slade, forgetting how grotesque he was in vermin infested Pathan rags and sheepskin jacket, snapped to attention to return the salute. "Very good, Captain!" Then, smiling, "Damn good, Steve. And sleep well."

Slade burrowed into Boukharan embroideries, silken carpets from Samarkand, and Tekke carpets of wool more luxurious than any silk. The truck's hood was wired down. He had fastened the tarpaulin, and latched the cab.

"If that beautiful girl lets air out of the tires, I'll make her pump 'em up," he resolved, and yielded to the sleep he had to have, lest he wreck the truck on the dangerous trail.

Somewhere, in the debris littered passages of buried Suastos, Yasmini was awake and hating him. This knowledge kept him from total surrender to fatigue, so that though Slade rested, his consciousness was nearer the surface than it would otherwise have been. And then, he had won Kellam back to returning. In his half sleep, Slade pondered on how to stay behind the scenes, to help Kellam without taking from him the credit of having made restitution of his own accord and effort.

"...losing that jeep'll be tough to explain away...less said about *post*, the better...tried to do girlfriend a favor, and kicked the roof off when he learned the score...so came back...my end's easy...leaving details from a report isn't a false official statement...the guy *has* bucked up his outfit..."

Thus Kellam's redemption, rather than his own danger, kept Slade from entire rest. What awakened him was gasoline fumes.

"Siphoning—"

Just that much; the words pertaining to Yasmini had no time to shape. Flame spewed, red and smoky. Slade scarcely heard the gusty sound, and the crackle of tarpaulin. He was lurching for the front, snatching the extinguisher, and twisting the door handle.

Yasmini, backed well away from the flaming fuel tank, screamed when she saw him. Her eyes were impossibly wide. She was frozen in a dancer's pose. Slade gave her the first jet of the extinguisher. It caught her squarely in the face. Pain made her collapse, choking and clawing her eyes.

After wasting a few strokes on the gas tank, he flung the extinguisher aside, knifed the tarpaulin, and grabbed a woolen rug. This he flung over the tank. Being full, there was no space in it for an explosive mixture to form. He smothered the fire, then whipped out the blazing trails of fuel which had boiled over to the ground.

The extinguisher settled the smoldering tarpaulin.

When he had finished, Yasmini was gone. Kellam came on the run, blinking and confused. Slade said, "She did it. Don't worry, a bit of carbon that won't blind your honey or even mark her, but by the living God, I'll kill her if she makes one more false move. Tell her, make her believe it, or I'll change my mind and finish her right now!"

Kellam believed, and he obeyed.

Slade sleeve-mopped his sooty face. "Lucky that hellion didn't know enough about gas tanks to do it right," he muttered. "Better hold her nose and fill her with *post* till it leaks out her ears..."

He went to the front, and cursed the sun, and the long hours before he could get on his way.

When Slade saw the white-bearded mountaineer coming up over the shoulder of the shelf, he forgot Yasmini, and grabbed his carbine. He would have dropped the man, but for his aversion to shooting without challenge.

At the first move, the newcomer flung himself forward to roll for scanty cover. "Don't shoot!" he yelled.

"Shir Dil—you blockhead—get on your hind legs, or I will blow you loose from your eye teeth! What's the idea barging in like this? Where the devil—who's that following you?"

While Pathans are usually loyal to their salt, Slade had seen too many men slip. He yelled for Kellam, "Grab the gun from my belt and stand by!"

Two bearded Sikhs with carbines loomed up. They were big, brown, stolid, and wearing turbans which made their faces even heavier; unimaginative men, thick-witted men who, once in motion, keep moving. The yelling and Shir Dil's dive for cover had not changed the sway of their broad shoulders. They came on, and two like them followed, guns at the ready. That Kellam had joined Slade, and stood by with a .45 automatic was nothing to them. Each firm step raised puffs of dust. Unless someone commanded, "Halt!" they'd probably march right through the bowels of buried Suastos; if anyone began shooting, they'd answer with marching fire, and keep going until they dropped or else won the decision.

There shouldn't be any Sikhs in the Wali's territory, least of all in khaki uniform. "This is it," Kellam said, in a level voice. "The commissioner sends troops, now that we're both off base and Uncle Sam doesn't count."

Slade blocked Kellam with his elbow. "Hold it! That's my man getting on his pins. That's what smells! Shir Dil, what's this?"

The old Pathan was up, and smiling. "Friends, O Friend of Allah!"

Then Slade saw the veiled woman who rode a cream-colored donkey. Only one eye was visible. Her dusty brown cape made her shapeless as a beehive. Pack animals followed.

Slade groaned. "More women."

Yasmini had recovered from her woes. The splash of carbon tetrachloride hadn't hit squarely. She came out, splendid and shapely, with a figured shawl over her sleek hair. She had dyed her palms red, and stained her toenails; a billow of attar surged ahead, sweetening the air.

Kellam tried to thrust her back into the shallows, but she clung to him. Slade barely noted this, being busy squinting through the glare, and wondering what would come next. When it came, he was not prepared.

The woman on the donkey lowered her veil.

"I knew I'd find you!" she cried.

Slade took a step forward, and choked. "You bungling blockhead! You—"

Her face changed. She had seen Kellam and Yasmini; Kellam's embarrassment had told more than the dancing girl's close-pressed body could have revealed. "Stand fast, you fool," Slade growled, turning his head in time to see Kellam hustling Yasmini back into the tunnel. "Stand fast, you're making it worse."

Yasmini, laughing and breathless, let herself be herded out of sight. The more she insisted she wanted to meet the *memsahib*, the more Kellam felt that he had to conceal her.

Slade then went to meet Diane Crawford, who was followed by two native women, whose leathery faces insured their safety in any company. They helped Diane dismount.

"Get in, you and your army, before someone sees you from miles off, these blasted mountaineers have telescope eyes, X-ray eyes. What the blazes *is* this?"

Diane smiled impishly, as though she had not noticed Kellam trying to untangle himself from a Kashmiri girl whose every pose was enticing art. "You'd never guess, but I made it! Oh, it was so simple, so easy!"

Slade, following her into the ruins, wondered if perhaps he had been drinking *post* in his sleep. But the Sikhs were no illusion, and neither was Shir Dil's bouquet of sheep, tobacco, asafetida, garlic, and horses.

"It was this way, sir," the old Pathan began. "Akbar Khan is a pig-loving son of many fathers! When he came back, he had me beaten till there weren't no more sticks left. He—"

"Skip it! Diane, what's it all about?"

"Oh, a truck!" she exclaimed seating herself on the running-board. "How marvelous!"

"Before I blow my top, *please* tell me what's coming next?"

"Oh. Well, it's awfully simple. I threw a wingding to get you moving, and then I decided to do a few things myself. I met Colonel Sir Pratap Singh Bahadur and told him I could help. I knew you couldn't find Steve, but it'd be easy for me."

"Too easy! He's getting cleaned up. The truck caught afire. All right, marvelous gal, you found us, and with only four guards, and in territory that British armies found too tough to tackle."

She leaned forward to say, confidentially, "That position in Kabul, as head nurse. *That's* what did it. Sir Pratap naturally couldn't come into Swat, but he did arrange with the Wali for me to come over. The Wali's the sweetest old thing!"

"You met the Wali?"

"Well, of course! Or I'd not last ten minutes. He's so modern. Remember, you told me about his hospital. Anyway, he wouldn't be outdone by Afghans and their Women's Hospital in Kabul, and he decided he'd go them one better. Since he couldn't build another hospital, and it'd be indecent, having women in the one he built for men, he commissioned me to be the traveling female doctor, tending to the hill women all over."

Slade nodded. "They'd rather die than be examined by a male M. D. Uh-huh, it is simple. So you heard about a man in a jeep, and—"

"What do you think? The news of you spread. Poor Shir Dil would've been flogged to death, Akbar Khan's so awfully sensitive. So I doctored his women, and talked Akbar out of his rage. You're supposed to be dead, of course."

"Chances are still good," he observed sourly. "So Shir Dil brought you here?"

"Naturally." She smiled up at him like a little girl. "So here I am, to help smuggle the loot back. Nobody'd dare stop me, I'm under the Wali's protection."

Slade groaned. "Oh, God! Coming to Peshawar was bad, but this is the kiss of death."

"Why, Dave? Don't look at me as if I were a leper! I've sacrificed and risked—"

"That's the very trouble!" he shouted. "You're crabbing the act! Get out before I throw you out! Go doctor Akbar's wives and lady friends, and leave me alone!"

"Dave—" She sat up straight, and her voice was cold. "I suspected you of itching to drag Steve back a prisoner, to make yourself a name, and now I know it! Well—well—*to hell with you!* I'm sticking here to see you do nothing of the sort. You may be an officer, but you're no—"

"Nobody in my department," he interrupted wearily, "can be a gentleman. The services we perform are too special. They call us officers purely as a formality. We're all sneaking connivers. Believe it or not, I've connived *for* him, not against him."

She looked as if she half believed. "Then why must I leave?"

"Did you, or did you not, see that hunk of shapely female meat wrap herself all around him? She knew somehow before anyone else that you weren't a native woman, but someone important to him."

Diane laughed. "Oh, good Lord, you're pre-war! Now if she were a woman of our own kind, then I should be worried silly. She's lovely, that Yasmini."

"Oh. Yasmini. You know all about her?"

"How long does anything stay secret in mysterious Peshawar? My *amah* at the hotel told all, and loved it. So I simply had to come here and—well—"

"Go down that tunnel and try to pry them apart!" Slade growled. "Try it, and good luck! He never will come back, now!"

CHAPTER X

The women were not screaming or taking each other to pieces; but after some thinking on it, Slade concluded that this was all for the worst. Echoes warped the voices he did hear, and the rumble of the tunnels tricked his ears. None of which made any difference, since nothing which Diane and Kellam said would affect the issue. But at last came something which reached into the space where the truck was parked.

Kellam screamed, "Quit rubbing it in, or I'll set out afoot! He likes you, he's crazy about you, he wants you, he can have you, now shut up!"

She came to Slade, and sobbed without restraint. "Do something!" she cried, "you fool, do something! Let's leave! Now!"

"Can't. Not until dark."

"But he'll go away on foot. He's out of his head!"

"So were you, when you butted in."

Diane cried wordlessly, and turned on him. Slade caught her arms; he held her fast, shook her. "Pull yourself together. We're both ready to blow our tops. We've got to keep our feet on the ground."

He released her, and went into a vault lighted by slanting rays which reached through rifts in masonry and earth. Kellam got up, still clutching a bowl.

Wild-eyed and gulping, he stared. Then, as if belatedly recognizing Slade, Kellam snarled, "Try and take me back! Pull a gun on me! Your damn bungling, bringing her into this!"

Slade spat from tasting the fumes in the air. *"Panj,"* he said quietly, "and here's where you get all five! I'll make a Christian of you if I have to knock you apart."

Kellam reached for the waist-band of his pants and brought out an automatic; a small bore weapon, not a service .45. It spurted flame. Slade felt the bit of powder flecks on his cheek. Blinded, he closed in, because the shock had not stopped the motion which had started before the shot. He connected, and with his left, he knocked aside the pistol.

Red flashes and green streaks danced before his eyes as he grappled with the crazed man. Yasmini's pistol and hashish promised to make good Kellam's threats.

Slade stumbled. He went down, clawing for a fresh hold before Kellam could boot him apart. A heavy weight flattened him, knocked him breathless. Shir Dil was saying, "Cold caulked him, maybe not too much."

The Pathan still held a chunk of rock in his fist.

"How's the sun?"

"Low."

Slade sighed. "Give me a hand. He'll have to go back, tied and gagged. Where's that Kashmiri?"

"I find her."

"She's not in sight? Ok, give a hand, she's not going with us. Her 'relatives' will take care of her."

They carried Kellam to the truck, and bundled him in.

The four Sikhs stood by, unmoved, and without curiosity. Their job was to guard Diane. Nothing else interested them.

"Get in," Slade ordered.

"Where's that woman?" Diane asked.

"Who cares? She was smart, hiding out. She could have shot me with that gun, but that'd turned him against her, so she tried accidentally roasting me alive."

"That's how the truck got scorched? But the loot?"

"Fire'd hurt nothing but rugs and the pearls."

Four plugs from the jeep's engine, and two spares from the tool kit, put the truck in service. As he backed toward the angle and into the tunnel leading to the shelf, Slade was content with Yasmini's absence.

"Could use her as a witness, or Exhibit A, though she'd do more harm than good—*hell on the sea-beach!*"

Diane, facing the tailgate, called to him, "Stop! Those rocks'll brain us!"

Fragments were peeling from the earth overhead. What made Slade jam the brakes was a chunk of column which smashed to the shelf, blocking the exit. The slope kept it from rolling away. Stains on the fluted marble showed that it had lain lengthwise, somewhere up on the mound. After it came a heavy slab, sliding endwise, and falling in a shower of small boulders.

"Take it easy, it's not an earthquake!" Then, to Shir Dil and the Sikhs, "Get busy, buck the rubbish out of the way."

Shir Dil, who led the rush, jerked back with a yelp. A bundle of burning brush, fiercely ablaze, rained sparks as it fell. The wind drove the sparks into the tunnel. Then Slade saw the riders coming down the opposite slope. A moment later, dust kicked up near the shoulder of the shelf; the muzzle blast of rifles which spattered the entrance with bullets.

There was no clearing the road block as long as snipers covered it with fire. Slade got the truck out of danger.

A few more rocks clattered down. A woman cursed him in English, and challenged him to go out and meet her relatives. Yasmini and Halima, seeing allies from afar, had wasted no time.

"Find the holes before dark," Slade told the men. "So they can't sneak in a surprise party."

As dusk fell, the besiegers crept closer, following channels which rain had carved across the plateau. Shir Dil and the Sikhs blazed away, keeping the enemy under cover. The raiders would not risk a rush for the well-defended tunnel mouth; the besieged could not move, under fires and on flat ground, the marble cylinder which Yasmini and her maid had so levered to roll down the slope of the mound.

Shortly before dark, Yasmini's allies built small fires in the rain channels, so that the glow lighted the tunnel mouth.

"They're going to starve us out," Diane said, as she heated canned rations. "We can't hold long, and there's no water."

"They can't light up the whole shelf," Slade countered, "nor watch all of the draw where I heard water trickling. We'll have enough to drink. We—"

Deep within the ruin, a shot echoed and re-echoed. Slade, pistol in hand, raced toward his best guess at the origin of the report. From one of the danger spots came a Sikh, who pointed, shouting, "Over that way, *sahib!* Not here!"

The exchange had ended when he came to a gap in an inner wall. The Sikh who crouched with a rifle explained, "I am watching there, I hear noise by this place. I come, and they go back, shooting."

"We'll block this. Go get a crowbar and shovel."

Presently, Slade and the guard had loosened sufficient debris from the overhead to plug the narrow approach. "Back to your post, Ram Singh," he told the bearded man. "And look out for more tricks."

When Slade rejoined Diane, he sat in the shelter of debris which was some yards short of the fire light in front.

"Don't worry," he said, "there's a way out. Out, and with the truck. Provided that Akbar Khan doesn't come to investigate."

"They'd not dare touch me, or us!"

"We'd not dare try to keep them from touching that loot. Or what do you think?"

She didn't answer. Finally, after he had touched light to a cigarette, she asked, "What's that you're fingering?"

"Oh. That?" He had scarcely been aware of his nervous fumbling. "It's a hand of Fat'ma. Moslem luck symbol. Brought luck to the chap who used to wear it."

"How was it lucky for him, since you took it?"

"He was lucky I kicked him instead of killing him. This was at Yasmini's house in Peshawar, when three cutthroats broke in to settle her, or—"

He stopped short. Diane, reaching for the blue enameled hand, looked at him, and demanded, impatiently, "Oh, go and say it!"

"Or to loot her house," he concluded. "What'd you think?"

"That you were about to say, *settle her or Steve*. Rather late, trying to spare my feelings, isn't it?"

"You asked for what you got!"

"Why shouldn't I have believed that coming to Peshawar would keep him from going morbid and neglecting his duty? Why shouldn't I?" she pleaded, hoping for a shred of justification. "Why shouldn't I?"

"Because a soldier does what he is supposed to do, whether it's fun or not! And regardless of whether the girlfriend comes to coddle and weep over him! It's you idiot women who started all this G.I. hysteria, I-wanna-go-home stuff, in Manila, in the ETO, all over, writing wailing letters. Wenches in platoon formation, mobbing Eisenhower in Washington, telling him he'd better bring their men back home, or else! Me, I think I'd go for Yasmini, she has guts anyway."

"Why, you—you—" Diane couldn't find a word. "Take your lucky token!"

She got up. She stopped short. They both listened to the sound in the darkness, a choking, gurgling sound, separate from the roar and rumble of Suastos. Diane gasped, "Oh—what's that?"

By then, Slade understood. "Kellam, weeping into his bowl of brandy and hashish. See if you can wile him into snapping out of it, or I will tie him up!"

The watch fires in front had died, for the moon had come up. However, the smack of a rifle answered Slade's first attempt at budging the obstacle.

He was ready. He had been ready. The sniper, seeing a man crawl up with a length of wood, exposed himself recklessly. Slade's pistol blazed. The marksman jerked up like a jack in a box, spun, and doubled, his gun clattering into the channel.

A shot smacked behind Slade. Shir Dil cursed, then said, "Is no Kashmiri, that guy. Is Pathan mountain man, the size, and the turban."

"Yasmini's got all sorts of relatives!"

The following morning, Kellam came to Slade. "Nothing to say for myself. But I'll take any orders you give."

"Stand watch in front, while I make my rounds." He caught Kellam's eye. "Forget what happened last night. I don't remember a thing, Steve. Take your post."

Later Slade wormed his way up into the tangle of earth and roots, of beams and tiles and shattered cornices, trying to find a place through which he could gouge a loophole from whose height he'd command a view of the besiegers. Several such loopholes, with a rifleman firing from each, could scatter the enemy in panic; but for some hours, he succeeded in little more than starting slides, or running afoul of masonry which blocked him. The cracks through which light filtered from the outside proved deceptive, one after another.

And then Diane added to his problem. "We've got to get out," she told him. "I won't stand for any more of this."

"More of what?"

"Your man, Shir Dil, was shot when he went out to get us some water."

"That's no news. Just a crease, he laughed it off. You mean he's crying at long last?"

"No, but I am. I made him let me bandage the wound. I won't drink water bought at such risk."

"Then drink some of Kellam's brandy." This didn't help; she took a new tack. "Your job," Diane declared, "is to bring Steve back. If he drinks himself crazy with any more of that horrible mess, it'll be your fault."

Slade drew a deep breath. "Listen," he answered, with all the patience he could muster, "Steve's doing all right. He's on guard. He's off the stuff. Anyway, it's about gone."

"All the more reason to get him out of here."

"You're being helpful."

"Is that treasure worth the lives it'll cost if those bandits rush us?"

"They're rushing slowly, aren't they?"

She beckoned to the leading one of the four Sikhs, who had come from their ground level lookout posts. Slade turned on the man, demanding, "Ram Singh, what the devil are you doing here? Who relieved you from duty?"

"*Sahib,*" the big fellow answered, respectfully but stubbornly, "our duty is guard the lady. This is danger to her. Taking your order, is not duty. We go with her and the women."

The one following, a gray beard called Hari Singh, took up the argument: "*Sahib,* if she is hurt, we pay. Is this good?"

Slade could neither deny their claim, or call it mutiny. He said to Diane, "You can get out if you convince those devils outside that the rest of us can't hold the fort long enough for you to send help."

"What help could I send?"

"None, and they know it. Toss-up whether they grab the loot from me, or Akbar Khan finally wakes up and comes to grab it. If you must leave, get ready, you, your women, and your guards. Who'll talk to the gang?"

"Zohra, the little one, she's smart."

"Go ahead, then."

Through a crevice near the entrance, Slade watched Diane and her sharp-faced assistant walk out into the open. When they halted, Zohra called. One of the besiegers, cautiously remaining under cover, answered. In a few minutes, Diane was back. She said, "They'll let us leave, provided I'll let Yasmini search me and Zohra and Jauhara."

"And his men'll frisk your four?"

"Yes."

"Go to it, then."

He turned and walked away. When he had gone half a dozen strides, Diane called, "Dave!" and overtook him. Then, "you mean you'd actually stay here, you and Shir Dil, facing all those men; there are over a dozen."

"You forgot Steve. He's staying."

"He could leave."

"He could not. I'd put him under arrest."

Without a word, she turned away. Slade went over to where Shir Dil had watched the entire exchange.

"They're used to your sneaking out to draw water," he said to the old man. "They're used to not hitting you. That gives me an idea. It'd better be good, or they'll nail us, and soon."

"You look worried too quick."

"With the dickering she just finished," Slade went on, "they know we're weakening. They'll soon have guts enough to rush us. They don't mind losing some men, it makes the prize money all the better for those that come up on top. But I can't figure that way. So, it's up to you and me. We'll both play water boy, and one will stay to give them a surprise."

Shir Dil's wicked eyes gleamed as he caught the possibilities of making a sortie against besiegers who expected early surrender. "You tell me plenty more, what?"

But a call from the front made Slade answer, "Wait till I see what's cooking now! You go and have a look at Captain Kellam."

CHAPTER XI

Yasmini was approaching the entrance.

She came to tell Slade, "They say they'll divide the loot, and everyone go his way, not fighting."

"I won't bargain with a woman."

"They expect you to say that. Very well, you go out to talk to them, with a flag of truce."

"Don't be stupid! I'm the trouble maker."

78

"We were afraid you'd mistrust us, Major. But if we send one man, will you let him come back without hurt?"

"Send six," he countered.

She laughed, derisively. "Half of us? Oh, no!"

"Send six," he repeated, "with guns. That will make us even. Neither side can risk any tricks."

Yasmini studied him for a moment. "I don't know whether he'll accept anything of the sort. You're desperate."

Slade laughed. "Desperate enough to gamble on wiping out six men, and then with what's left of us, tackle the others? If they're afraid, I'll go out into the open until one of yours is in the open, gun in hand. Then Shir Dil steps out. If we fire on your one man, the others will have two of us in the open."

She nodded. "I'll go back and tell Marouf."

"Your *cousin*, Marouf?"

Yasmini smiled over her shoulder, and gave him a coquettish wave of the hand, as she went with his proposal.

Slade repeated to the guards and Shir Dil what he had proposed; he concluded, "And no false moves. It'll soon be dusk. This is to keep them amused until I take my turn. Understand?"

Ram Singh answered for the Sikhs: "Understanding, and we do it, sahib."

Yasmini waved her scarf from the rain channel, and called, "Marouf says it is good. He waits for you to come."

Slade would have stepped from the protecting shadows, but Diane, who had heard the bargaining, caught him from one side.

"Don't," she begged. "You're the key man, she knows it."

Slade jerked free. "They're lousy shots!"

Though he had lost little time between summons and response, the interlude had been the cue for another actor. Kellam, stepping from a corner in which, unnoticed, he had been sitting, made for the tunnel mouth. He was empty-handed, though he had a pistol in his hip pocket.

"Hey, you!" Slade called, as Kellam brushed past.

"Let it be!" Shir Dil warned, catching Slade's belt and yanking him back. "Two go out, they think trouble."

"Now the scums think I'm scared, and they'll get cocky!"

Between Kellam and the old Pathan, the damage had been done. Then, out on the shelf, a tall man popped up from the earth, and shouted, "Here I am, send your next!"

"Bad light," Shir Dil explained, "they don't see good, they don't know him, don't know you."

Slade went out. The shelf was already banded with long shadows. "No matter what tricks they pull," he whispered when he reached Kellam's side, "get that man first."

From another rain slash, a second bandit got up, rifle ready, and joined Marouf. Slade then called, "All right, Shir Dil."

The old man pounced out, alert yet bold. Another tall fellow from the opposing side came out of a crevice; but there the only response to Slade's call was Ram Singh's explanation, "Enough to talk now. We stay with the memsahib, by order."

Slade couldn't argue. Instead, he called to the bandits, "Shabash! This is enough. We'll come over to talk to you." Then, in a low voice, to the men at his left, "Nothing else I could do, or they'd make the most of knowing nobody'll back me."

A few yards from the visible bandits, the trio halted. Greetings were ceremonious; compliments were elaborate. During the exchange, Slade was convinced that at least two of the three negotiators were familiar. Karim, who sat next to Marouf, had lost three front teeth. His mouth was still bruised, and he took little part in the talk.

Slade had seen them previously only once, and by moonlight; but that instant before his leap into Yasmini's courtyard had been one during which details were indelibly impressed. When Shir Dil nudged him, there was no doubt left at all; the nudge meant to Slade, "These fellows would rather run than fight."

The haggling was such as might have taken place in any bazaar stall. "We be twelve, not counting our sister, Yasmini," Marouf stated. "You and the captain, that makes fifteen, and your old man, he is sixteen. Then take three parts and leave us thirteen, and go with our blessing."

"You swear on a Koran?" Shir Dil demanded.

"*Aywah!* And by the three divorces," Marouf affirmed. "Name the oaths, and see if we do not take them."

"How divide it? Ask him, Shir Dil!"

The old man asked, and interpreted the answer: "Each thing, one by one, how much is it worth. Then we make sixteen stacks, and God loves the generous."

Kellam turned to Slade. "If we could recover half, we'd make a good showing. But there's something odd about this."

"A good deal's odd! Which queer bit gags you?"

Kellam answered, "The opening deal's too good. They can't expect us to accept the first offer."

"They can rook us in the appraisal, or foul us up one way or another. They're not giving us any breaks." Then, to Shir Dil, "Say this: they *want*, but we *have*. And the taking, it will cost them. So let them pay for the peaceful giving. Take four stacks, and go with our blessing."

Marouf laughed even before the formality of translation. He wagged his beard, and regarded everyone amiably, being pleased at not dealing with a fool or a weakling.

Finally Slade broke into the dicker by exclaiming, "*Shabash!* Enough talking, soon it's dark, and tomorrow is another day." Then, catching Karim's eye, he said, "O Friend! You want presents. Let me offer you the finest." He flipped the Hand of Fat'ma toward the battered man. "Luck and my blessing!"

Karim's face lighted from instant recognition. "Praised be Allah!" He reached into his tunic, drew out a cord from which hung a carnelian amulet, and removed the gem. In its place, he tied the blue-enameled Hand of Fat'ma. He showed his tooth stumps in a happy smile.

Slade bowed, and asked Marouf, "With your permission, we go back. Fire, or do not fire, either is good."

Marouf courteously answered, "Permission, and blessing, O Friend! And what happens, by Allah, it happens."

Each group got up, and backed to its post. Neither could be stupid enough to shoot it out, in the open, and from a cold start.

"Won't be long now," Slade remarked, once they readied shelter. "We've got them baited, and half an hour, it'll be dark, and then—"

But Kellam had not been listening. "That was odd, out there. Marouf recognized the trinket, that blue-enameled hand."

Diane cut in, "Well, of course he did! He lost it at Yasmini's place, the night they tried to murder or rob you."

The words were spoken, despite Slade's nudge and his attempt to carry on with what he had been saying. Raising his voice failed to check Diane, and the attempt only added emphasis to the detail which Slade had tried to gloss over; yet he made a final try: "Just by way of ribbing the fellow, I offered him a lucky charm. Trifles help."

But Kellam, not saying a word, got up and left the group. A long silence followed. Slade broke it by taking a deep breath. Then, "Pretty rugged, but maybe that's what he needed."

"What do you mean?" Diane asked.

"*What do I mean?* You gave him everything but a diagram to prove that Yasmini sold him out."

"Well, good heavens, Dave! As if he didn't know that all the time, and seemed to love it! She's with the enemy—I can't understand—"

"If I ever try to shush you, again, you'd better shush! Listen, darling. You made it clear that Yasmini faked the breaking and entering of her house in Peshawar, to back her stall about being in danger. At the time, I fell for the trick, and I was stone sober—he was owl-eyed drunk, and didn't get as good a look at the three with knives as I did. When I met Sir Pratap Singh, I figured that he had sent *busmashes* to finish Yasmini and search her house, and that failing, he finally appealed to the commissioner. He—Steve—snapped at the bait. Now he can't give himself an alibi. You made it too clear that he wasn't saving the girl-friend by going AWOL. That he was just her custom built front, her made-to-order, benevolent American chump, Uncle Sam in person!"

After a pause, he went on, "Well, he'll spend some time trying to justify her, but this is more than he can swallow. You made a Christian of him this time! You put the kiss of death on that romance, darling!"

"Blame me, always blame someone!" She choked, caught her breath, and went on, "Next you'll say I flashed that lucky hand."

Slade was about to repeat why, after declining Marouf's offer, he had given Karim the holy amulet; but he decided against further words. Instead, he found Shir Dil, who was taking a cat-nap.

"They expect more bargaining. They expect you to sneak out after dark to get more water. They'll be ready to snipe, just for the sport of it. This time, never mind the drink. Shoot back, and keep shooting."

Shir Dil anticipated the finale: "Same time you go with Ram Singh's fellow's to rush them from the back?"

"If I can get those blockheads to follow. Come along, and see what we can do with them."

Darkness had fallen. The fires whose light was to keep the besieged from taking off in the truck once more spread a wavering glow across the shelf, and all the way to the marble column. As an afterthought, Slade said, "Get Captain Kellam, every gun counts." Then he went to the four Sikhs, to explain his plan.

They listened, gravely. Though they admitted the idea was sound, they nevertheless insisted that their job was to guard Diane.

Hearing a discussion center about the memsahib, Diane stepped up to the group. "Now what've I done wrong?" she demanded. "For once, I will be right, I'll make it right!"

Slade told her what Ram Singh and his fellows held to be their first duty. He concluded, "So tell them they can go with me! Sign a waiver, sign a release, pay them off, but whatever you do, do it in a hurry!"

Ram Singh went stubborn. "No, *memsahib*. Begging pardon of your presence, women have no sense, could I go back saying, the woman told me to break my orders? We are your guard, we guard you."

"Dave," she said, helplessly, "what else can I do?"

"Nothing. Steve and I can swing it alone. Move fast, hit hard, panic the bunch, and they'll scatter like quail. Shir Dil, where's Captain Kellam?"

The old man answered in Pushtu, "I beg leave to represent to the Threshold of Benevolence that the captain is pig-drunk."

Though Diane understood not a word, it was easy for her to read Slade's face, and Shir Dil's. "Go on, Dave," she said, "I'll get my four guards to change their minds."

"How?"

She retorted, triumphantly, "Now who's talking out of turn? Please, Dave, go, and if they let me down, well, I tried, and you'll still be under cover, no worse off."

Her voice had changed, and when she caught his hand, he knew that she was confident, vibrant, and that nothing remained of the petulance and weariness which had kept them snapping at each other ever since their meeting in Peshawar.

"Go ahead, don't look back, they'll be on your heels, ready to take off when you're ready to bounce out that side passage. You move the rocks while I'm talking."

CHAPTER XII

Slade went far into the gloom of Suastos, and turned right to pick his way toward the crevice which they had blocked against surprise. After locking the switch of his flashlight, he set to work, carefully removing the pieces of rock he had arranged so that anyone approaching from without would start a noisy slide.

Above the drumming and muttering of the ruins, he caught voices: Diane and the Sikhs, he guessed, as he crept out to skirt the mound until he saw the glow of watch fires. While waiting for Shir Dil's demonstration, he wondered how far he could go in supporting the old Pathan, certainly far enough to disconcert the enemy.

"But they won't be caught from the rear a second time," he told himself. "Unless Diane's blockheads listen to reason, I better stand pat. Shir Dil can duck back without—"

He shook his head; while his reasoning was true, he couldn't swallow it. "With a tommy gun, I could take 'em at a walk...easy meat for one man..."

The man who ran the show had no business pulling rash tricks, needlessly risking the head which did the thinking for all; but this logic made him grimace disgustedly. "Fat lot of thinking you've done—start doing things!" Then a warning voice, from the same source which sent a chill racing all through him: "That's what those wooly outlaws are waiting for, for the head to blow a gasket!"

That chill, that shiver going the length of the spine; the tightness in the throat, and the thumping at the temples—he knew that he was about to buck sense and reason.

He looked over his shoulder. No sign of the Sikhs. Very well, then; they weren't yellow, they were cagey. They'd fight it out, when Diane needed them.

Then, though he could not from his observation spot see the truck exit, he knew that something was happening. The besiegers exclaimed and muttered. Turbans bobbed from cover, ducked back, came up again.

"God, what a chance! One tommy gun, or a sack of grenades!" he muttered, and somehow kept himself from risking it with carbine and pistol. The former was too slow, the latter not sufficiently accurate at such range.

A man lurched into Slade's field of vision. He had a bottle in one hand, and a bowl in the other. Kellam, pig-drunk, zigzagged toward the bandits. Though he shouted, the thick-lipped utterance was hopelessly confused by the wind. The besiegers who were out of direct line of the tunnel mouth laughed and gestured. Yasmini came from her shelter; whether to welcome Kellam, or to warn

83

him back, Slade could not guess. He jerked violently about, startled by the sound of one rock grating clashing against another.

Diane was walking toward Slade.

"Get back!" he said, and gestured.

She ignored him, and came on.

Then hell rattled from the front. Slade spun about, and in time to see both bowl and bottle rise on first bounce, and roll over the shelf. Kellam had drawn a pistol.

He yelled ferociously, he darted toward the men who mocked him. Whatever he had drunk, it had finally keyed him up: Hashish madness, Slade thought, when pistol blast and the end of a long bound coincided; another leap, another shot, timed as a ballet dancer's routine.

One man dropped, drilled clean. Another, though hit, returned the fire. In a matter of seconds, Kellam had no targets; instead, he had become one. Bullets whined and screamed. Kellam advanced, holding his fire so that in the end, he could shoot down into the shallow shelters of the bandits.

Yasmini alone was visible. She screamed, and gestured to Kellam and to her allies.

Slade bounded from cover. This was the chance to catch them from the flank. The surprise, however, was knocked flat by a deep-throated shout behind Slade. Heavy feet thumped out drum-notes as they pounded the thin earth which overlay the buried houses of Suastos. The Sikhs were advancing. Having taken a direction, they would not change.

Above their savage war cry came Diane's voice, very high. "I got them going! They're with you!"

Kellam was down. He bobbed up, leaped, sank into a ditch. It exploded with pistol fire. Yasmini, posed as though she had grabbed at Kellam and missed him, doubled up and rolled out of sight.

Then Slade was in it, and so were the Sikhs, now that the nearest of the besiegers, aware of the surprise, had tried to defend themselves. Shir Dil, instead of opening the show, finished it by picking off one of those who raced in every direction.

"I told you I'd do it!" Diane cried, when the shooting ended. "I ran out, and they had to follow me, they had to!"

She laughed wildly. Slade caught her arm. "Easy, darling. He's out there, I saw him go down. Get back, stay back, til we make sure everything's clear."

Hooves clattered. In the darkness below the shoulder, the survivors of Yasmini's accomplices were cutting tracks. They had suffered far more casualties than any unorganized group could ensure.

Everything was clear. Shir Dil made certain of that by taking each fallen bandit by the beard and slashing him neatly under the chin. He did this while Slade knelt beside Kellam.

Yasmini had collapsed within a yard of the captain. She had one of her late accomplices by the sleeve; she still gripped a dagger. It was red, and the man's coat was ripped. A bullet had drilled her between the shoulders, knocking her against the object of her fury.

Though Kellam reeked of *post*, he was clear headed, despite his half dozen wounds. He tried to wipe off the blood froth trickling down the corners of his mouth. The chill of shock made him gray-faced. He said, with an effort, "Worked better than I thought."

"You damn fool," Slade muttered. "You damn fool."

"Nothing like a drop of *post* for a fast getaway. If you'd only seen the— guys run—" Then, as Shir Dil moved, Kellam saw Yasmini. "Good God—did —I—how—"

"Easy fellow. We'll take care of her—the women will—Yasmini—" He took the dagger from her limp hand. "She went to bat for you, she tried to stop them."

"I thought... I saw...her...in front me...but—"

"She used this on the man you clinched with. When you lost your pistol."

Kellam understood. "Did she? She did! Let me talk to her—why don't you help her?"

"She's done, Steve."

Kellam drew a wheezing breath. He smiled, made a sound which came near being a triumphant laugh. "You never gave her credit—"

Above, Shir Dil was trying to keep Diane from coming near the edge of the channel. Now that she had recovered a little from the tension of her desperate play, she began to understand what Slade had told her, and she cried, "Steve! Steve!"

Slade got to his knees, saying, "It's Diane."

Kellam laid a hand on his arm. "Take good care of her—take—where's Yasmini, I knew all the time—" He let go of Slade's arm. He made a choking, wheezing sound; he coughed blood. A violent tremor ended it.

Diane turned away, and without a sound, Zohra and Jauhara led her back toward the tunnel. Slade got up and said to Shir Dil, "Once more, give me a hand. Yasmini and the captain, we bury them in the dead city." Then, to the Sikhs, "Take bars, and roll the road block away."

Slade turned Diane's pack animals loose to join the horses of the fallen bandits. Later he pulled up at the foot of Akbar Khan's hill to let Zohra and Jauhara go up to the *khelat* to find shelter until they could return to the Wali and tell him he'd have to make other plans for a traveling medical service. And before Akbar Khan's dogs scented strangers, Slade was back at the wheel, booting the truck and its cargo of loot toward the frontier.

Diane sat with him, saying nothing until dawn grayed the summit of Malakand Pass. Her first words were, "I'm glad he knew that Yasmini finally— well—quit selling him out—I'll never forgive myself—for speaking so bluntly —that's why—he got crazy drunk—and—but his wounds sobered him—he knew she'd tried—"

"He wasn't drunk. He'd poured it all over himself, but he didn't drink any. His eyes didn't have the hasheesh stare. When I bent over to hear some of the things he said, there wasn't a trace of it on his breath."

"All the more, then, it was having seen that Hand of Fat'ma, that drove him to suicide."

Slade shook his head. "It was knowing he'd quit his post to help a thief. Knowing he'd pulled us all into danger. He couldn't stay, and he couldn't go back."

After a mile downgrade, Diane spoke. "I heard what he said, right at the last."

"He was confused, wandering."

"No, Dave, he was talking sense. He was happy that Yasmini was finally on the level, and that he didn't have to worry any more about what people would say."

Several hours later, when the sun was blazing down on Peshwar, and Sir Pratap Singh Bahadur had finished checking his treasure, Slade sat in his hotel room, frowning at the report he had not quite finished. "Didn't know it was loot, so he wasn't an accessory for stowing it," he muttered. "Obeyed ordered when inspector told him to get it off the reservation. This after having bucked up his outfit. Was lawfully—um—well—lawfully *ex post facto* anyway—on—leave—died gallantly upholding the honor of the service—that sounds too much like a citation for an award, but the fool deserves a good epitaph—can't give him the court martial he deserves—oh, hell!"

He was reaching for the phone to call Diane; he needed help, and needed it badly. Kellam, if one skipped a few details, had died in the line of duty, but how to put it across? He got no answer, either from Diane, or from himself; then, before he could get back to his task, his own phone rang. Sir Pratap Singh Bahadur begged permission to call.

When Slade went to receive the Rajput dignitary, he met more than he had expected. Diane was with Sir Pratap, and she was smiling.

After ceremonious courtesies, the hard-bitten Rajput offered a small enameled box with a hinged cover. Slade accepted it with both hands, and opened it. An unset ruby, the bluish-red of pigeon blood, gleamed against the white satin. The gem was nearly the size of the nail of his little finger, and cut in the ancient fashion. "Permit me the honor, Major Slade, to offer this, along with my apologies."

"I don't blame you for having suspected me, Sir Pratap."

The Rajput smiled. "I did not suspect you. My apology if for using you to inform me as to the late Captain Kellam's general and special destinations. You were covering his trail, and for but one purpose."

"I had to. But this—being in the service, I can't accept it."

"As Major Slade, perhaps not. But as David Slade?"

"The two become terribly confused." He pointed to the papers. "That report, trying to prove that a deceased comrade died in the line of duty—if I accepted a gift, it'd cast reflections on—no, it's not a false report, but still—"

Sir Pratap gestured and bowed. "I think I understand. When you tell an honorable lie, it must be its own reward. Miss Crawford led me to expect as much."

"I did," Diane said, "but Sir Pratap insisted. He offered me a gift, which I had to decline. Because I'd come so near bundling your effort."

Sir Pratap still smiled, wisely now, and to match the gleam in his deep-set eyes. "Listen, please. Major Slade, I take this from your hand. Now, Miss Crawford, you have it in your hand. Though it is not yours. It belongs to him as much now as before. Just as it once belonged to me, even while far from my house." He closed his hands over the box. "So! Not yours—but since he never accepted it, who but I could say he received a gift?" Before either could answer, he bowed and said, "With your permission, I leave."

When he had gone, Diane and Slade regarded each other for a long time before either could speak. "I can keep it, because it isn't mine, and it's all right as far as you're concerned because you never accepted it!"

"He's a very smart man—listen—you said you'd heard Steve's last words, and you insisted he'd not been wandering at the time—umh—uh—I mean—sit down while I finish that report—damn it, that's something that takes Sir Pratap's wits."

Diane laughed softly, through small tears which jeweled her eyes. "Sir Pratap didn't think of a thing! I told him you could not possibly accept, and figured out a way. Or must I go back to tell the Wali that I insist on doctoring the hill women?"

Slade glanced again at the fool's epitaph. "Tell you what, darling, nothing in the articles of war or the traditions of the service keep me from having a ring made to fit a ruby which isn't mine."

"Oh, marvelous!" She caught his arm. "Let's go right now, we'll go to the goldsmith's bazaar, and watch him make it."

Slade blinked, and shook his head to clear it. "I was wondering, all the way back, how soon it'd be right to ask you." Then he caught her with both arms, and lifted her to her tiptoes. "This is something you're not being asked about, now or ever!"

"I'm not complaining," she answered. "Now, or ever."

HASHEESH WISDOM

Originally appeared in *Spicy Mystery Stories*, **Sept. 1936, under the pseudonym "Hamlin Daly."**

Three sots had just been jailed in Cairo:
"Let us break out!" stormed the drunkard, kicking the bars.
"Better sleep here till they let us out," said the opium eater.
But the hasheesh smoker smiled craftily and said,
"Follow me, Brethren—we will crawl through the keyhole."
　　　　　　　　　　　　　　—Wisdom of Ashraf Ali.

There might have been a fouler dive than Zorayda's Garden, down in the Muski Quarter of Cairo, but thus far Burton had not found it. His pupils were dilated to great black discs, and his face was an aquiline, deeply lined mask, the color of seasoned leather, but his beard was curled and oiled, his turban was clean, and his white robe was spotless.

He drew again at the long-stemmed pipe whose bowl contained a little tobacco and a great deal of hasheesh. The acrid fumes made him cough, but they gave him uncommon wisdom. They made him master of time and space, made him see the point of jests far too subtle for ordinary comprehension.

They left him above fearing the hawk-nosed, white-bearded little man with eyes like black fires who said in a low, grim voice: "The Grand Master sent me from Bagdad to get the five thousand Egyptian pounds you have collected for the revolt against the King of Iraq."

Long silence. Haste is of Satan. Burton had not the least idea what had happened to the money he had collected in behalf of the Ismailian Society.

Finally he spoke.

"The Peace upon you, uncle. I will have it for you after the sunrise prayer."

The sour-faced little man stalked out to the narrow street, frowning and stroking his beard. He seemed to suspect.

Egypt was a hotbed of revolt. Collecting money from radical scholars eager to see the British-owned King of Iraq die of insomnia had been easy, until work began to interfere with hasheesh smoking.

Burton's position was deadly. The Brotherhood of Ismailians, which he had joined in Bagdad, had a long arm that reached across the Moslem world, with dagger and strangler's noose. What was just as bad, old Abbas had but to denounce Burton to the British rulers of Cairo.

Five thousand pounds, Egyptian, or else. Yet Burton had the answer: simple as crawling through a keyhole...

He rose, disdainfully stepped over the snoring sots, and with stately paces stalked down the narrow alley whose gloom even the blistering Egyptian sun could not dispel. When he reached Khan el Khalili, his dignified deliberation clove a path through the confused tangle of tourists and peddlers and donkey boys that thronged the bazaar.

They did not know that that hawk-faced, handsome man with the strangely glittering eyes was an Englishman whose business was overturning a throne.

Who else would have had the cunning to lounge around Zorayda's place, masking his true quality by drinking smoke from sunrise to sunset? A lesser man would have acted the spy, furtive and cautious—but not Burton, the renegade.

A dozen courses were possible, but two seemed brilliant. Sell the house, and the costly trinkets he had bought for Salima, the exquisite Syrian girl whose sultry kisses and smoldering, heavy-lidded eyes had convinced him of the folly of squandering hard-earned money to overthrow a king. Thrones crumble from top heaviness anyway...

Better yet, denounce old Abbas to the secret police, collect a reward for his head, and carry the proceeds directly to the Grand Master as proof of the cunning that had outwitted the invisible network that enveloped Cairo.

That would be crawling through the keyhole!

At the coppersmith's bazaar Burton turned into an alley. He wanted Salima to enjoy the laugh with him.

He wanted to surprise her. He moved with leopard stealth as the door silently closed behind him. She was not in the orange-clustered courtyard, nor was she singing to the somnolent strumming of her eight-stringed *oudh*.

Nevertheless, he heard enough to know that he had indeed surprised Salima...though not as he had intended.

Crouched in the angle of a pilaster, he peered between the bars and into the shadowed room.

Salima was a length of golden bronze loveliness in the shifting shadows. Her legs were amber-tinted modulations that tapered from the smoke-wisp gauze about her hips to the gazelle ankles encircled by ruby-clustered golden bands.

Her anklets were no longer joined by the slender golden chains that permitted her no more than an eight inch pace. Her legs were free, and luxuriously extended against the wine-colored Boukhara rug that covered the lounge.

The slender curve of her waist was not enclosed by the massive girdle whose trailing pendants should be caressing her sleek hips...and her haughty young breasts were poorly confined in their cupped silver guards. Her wanton lips were like pomegranate blossoms.

If Salima had anticipated Burton's return, the gray-haired British major whose saber and spurs were carelessly scattered at the foot of the *mastaba* would not be so deliberate about extricating himself from her serpentine arms.

The insidious smoke distorts all sense of time. Burton did not know whether he had watched for seconds or months...nor even whom he saw...

Years ago, he recollected, he himself had worn a khaki uniform and a saber. That was before regimental funds, and a woman he did not know was a colonel's wife had combined permanently to relieve him of military honors.

But that man with Salima could not be Burton. His hair was too gray.

No, Burton was not at the moment standing apart from his body and regarding it as another person would. Though that was very easy to do when you faithfully smoke hasheesh...

He drew a long, curved knife. But first, listen for a moment.

"Don't be silly, darling," Salima was murmuring. "He won't be back for hours..."

The British officer, however, snapped his saber to his belt, and spoke of returning later that night.

He did not know that a robed man was following him toward the Ezbekiyah quarter. The sun had set, and gloom was invading the narrower alleys.

Burton ducked down a cross passage, looped around. Presently he was waiting in an archway near the gate through which the officer must pass.

The *muezzin* was calling true believers to prayer. The street was deserted. Moslems were in the mosque, or in their houses, kneeling as they bowed to holy Mecca. No one would see.

It was cunningly done, as prescribed by the Ismailian Brotherhood of Assassins. There was no outcry. Just a silvery flash that ended in a ruddy, red throat; a gurgling smothered by Burton's free hand, a sodden *chunk* and a tinkle of scabbard and saber chains as the officer toppled into the dusky lurking place.

Presently he ceased shuddering. The red froth bubbling from his mouth subsided. Burton deliberately probed his tunic. It was easy, when you timed it right. It made no difference, but he wanted to know the major's name.

He learned that, and more. He found a list of trouble-makers the secret police of Cairo were watching. Burton's own was on the document.

As he thrust wallet and papers into his belt, he smiled at Salima's futile treachery. He was entirely above wrath. The red testimony of his superiority lay at his feet.

Burton circled back toward his own quarter. There was scarcely any blood on his hands. He washed them at a shadowed fountain.

At the nearest mosque he paused to pray. It was the polite thing to do. Maybe it would help. Cairo was now doubly perilous. It would be dangerous to try to betray old Abbas. Better just take Salima's jewels and steal from the city.

The major would not be missing until morning. Neither would Abbas strike before then. He did not want to kill the old fellow.

Somehow, Salima's sweetness outweighed her treachery. He would slay no more. There were better uses for his last hours in Cairo.

Salima's loveliness aroused a consuming hunger. He had left her that morning to go to Zorayda's den, but it was now as if he had spent years in the lonely desert.

Salima had done him no wrong. She really could not. Burton was omniscient. The major's body proved that.

When Salima ran across the court to meet Burton, she moved with mincing steps and sensuously swaying hips. Her ankles were again locked together with short golden chains, and her breasts in their small silver hemispheres were like the halves of oranges.

She was dizzyingly fragrant, and her body against him was like a silken serpent. Her lips were a consuming fire, and the entire supple length of her was a multitude of questing tongues of flame. When her breath sighed tremulously in his ear, all the mighty wisdom and subtle hasheesh knowledge that burned in Burton's brain shifted, centering in a single desire.

Peril made her kisses sweeter, and hasheesh infinitely prolonged each exquisite moment into hours...that was one of the marvels of that potent herb which can be smoked, or eaten in confection, or infused into wine.

The last night in Cairo. Sorrow finally invaded the ecstasy of the moon-dappled room that faced the courtyard. Old Abbas would be disagreeable. And someone else from the rear major's office would carry on.

But a caravan would clear the eastern gate of Cairo at dawn. It would go down the Red Sea coast. There would be pilgrims bound for Mecca, and traders for the Soudan. That was the next step: the great desert, or holy Mecca. The last would be especially appealing. Making the pilgrimage as his namesake had done, three quarters of a century ago...

Leaving Salima was intolerable. Tears dimmed Burton's eyes as he drank in the exquisite beauty of that silk-veiled Syrian girl. Her dark eyes widened in wonder, not contempt. To express grief is not unmanly in Moslem lands.

"You are distracted, beloved," she murmured. "What is wrong?"

"I am looking into the future," said Burton. "I see everything. I know everything. Even that you and I part at dawn. That there will be no more love beneath the orange tree by moon, no more kisses when the moonbeams seek the fountain mist. That is over, and I go out on the roads of Allah."

She was silent. Her eyes shifted. She stared at his sandals.

An inner voice warned Burton. A thin whisper spoke to his mind's ear: "She sees the blood stains. She knows you have slain someone."

When her eyes rose, they alarmed him.

"Let me go with you," she finally said.

Burton knew that she was dissimulating. She was too cunning to accuse him. She was waiting for him to fall asleep from drinking wine mingled with hasheesh. Then she expected to tell the major.

He laughed immoderately.

"By Allah, we two will go!" he said.

91

"That is good." Salima's eyes were bright again. "I saw an old man in the bazaar. Twice these past two days. An evil-faced old man with a long beard and cruel eyes. He looked at me. I am afraid."

"Perhaps I should slay the old man first," pondered Burton.

He peeled an orange, then cast it aside. Its acid juice would cut the hasheesh fumes. It would rob him of the wisdom he needed.

Salima was wearing only a few of her jewels. None of them were the costly gifts he had brought her with money won by betraying his trust. For a moment his blood was a bitterness. For years now he had been betraying trusts for the sake of some woman...

Regimental funds...corporation funds...and now the money of a society of Ismailian assassins who planned to overthrow a king. For the first time, the wisdom of hasheesh let Burton see how evil his life had been.

"But it was unintentional," he said to the shrilly fluting voice that piped in his ear. He sharply looked up, but saw that Salima's expression had not changed. She could not have heard.

Yet she might listen to the debate that Burton was now carrying on as his lips planned with her for the flight in the morning. This was a new gift, being able to converse with two persons at once. He decided that it would be safer if he answered the unseen speaker in...well, Tamil—a language Salima could not understand.

"She is hiding those pearls," said the presence that he could now feel beside him. Soon he would also be able to see. "Better get them...you can trick her... she will not know..."

So Burton listened as he planned with Salima, who still believed he would take her with him to holy Mecca.

She poured more wine, but sipped very daintily. The great wisdom told him she was waiting for him to become dead drunk. But she underestimated him. He could drain the Nile if it flowed with wine, and still keep his head.

"Sing for me, Salima," he commanded.

Her chattering was becoming intolerable. It was blocking out the voice of wisdom, but music would not.

She set aside the wine flagon, picked up her eight-stringed *oudh*, and plucked it with a turkey-quill plectrum.

Zabiyat il unsi ilaya
Badri qabl al fawat
Wunsheri tibun zakiyn
Mun 'ashah fi el hayat...

Her song was an ecstasy that stabbed him like many knifes: *"Come to me, O Gazelle, before I die..."* ."

Burton steeled himself against that heart-searing beauty, fumbled in his girdle, and found a large packet of bank notes. He had forgotten them, that afternoon. The faithful in Cairo had given him a heavy payment. Then the great wisdom spoke, and he slumped back against the cushions, mouth agape and snoring…

Presently Salima ceased singing. That made it easier. Burton was not unconscious. Hasheesh was making him unnaturally wakeful.

Through barely parted lashes he saw her eye the money, stealthily pluck it from the folds of his robe, glance warily over her shoulder, then bar the door.

That done, she tiptoed across the room and drew aside an embroidered hanging. Her fingers caressed the masonry. They lingered on a spot that had been polished by many finger tips. A panel of the wall yielded. She thrust the bank notes into the secret cavity, then closed the niche.

Burton now knew where she stored the jewels he had bought her while drunk with her loveliness and treacherous love.

Salima resumed her song, then ceased singing, and for a long time sat staring past him and into the moon-drenched patio.

"See, she is waiting for him," whispered the hasheesh voice from the fourth dimension. "But do not laugh aloud…she does not suspect you have slain him… Burton, she is insulting you by that lack of suspicion. She does not think you are shrewd enough to sense treason. Now do as I say…"

He listened, until at last another voice cut in. This was one that rang sonorously from far above the housetops: the *muezzin* calling true believers to the midnight prayer.

"A-a-a-a-alahuakbar! Al-l-l-l-abu-u-u-a-a-a-akbar!" The cadence rose and fell like a mighty organ note. "God is most great! Come to prayer! Prayer is better than sleep…"

That was the signal. Burton bestirred himself, yawned, and said to Salima, "I go to pray. Then to rout out Saoud, the caravan master."

She kissed him, and for a moment Burton relented. She was luxurious and supple and she clung like a caressing flame. Her eyes were great black opals, splendid with passion, shadowed with concern at his peril.

Peril that she had created, something reminded Burton as he broke away from that shapely form that pressed against him and shuddered with ecstasy.

Then in the cool of the Cairene night the hasheesh presence whispered anew: "Do not weaken, Burton. Treachery always wears a lovely mask. You are a man among men, but a fool among women…verily, this is your night of power when you shall plumb the depths and reach the heights of your destiny, its lord and master…yea, do this thing and redeem yourself from the folly that oppressed you these many years since that first woman with gilded hair persuaded you to borrow what you could not repay…"

So he presently found Saoud the red-bearded Afghan, squatting beside a charcoal fire in a *serai* near the mosque of el Hakim.

"Hakim" means wise and learned. It seemed appropriate, now. Wisdom is bitter, but Burton was smiling as he bargained for a position as camel driver in the caravan. He was too subtle to speak of the money he would have.

Beyond the Gate of Victory-by-the-Aid-of-God he saw the domes and tombs in the moonlight. He shuddered slightly as he thought of what would follow. But they were gracious and inviting, those ancient forgotten tombs. Still, God might give him victory.

A surge of devotion for a moment choked him, and he silently gave thanks for wisdom.

"Yet we may not march in the morning," muttered Saoud the Afghan, spitting and stroking his red beard. "There was murder tonight. A dog of an infidel officer was neatly knifed. By God, who did that killing is my brother. It was well done, but the British will make the King's police find the slayer, else they will bombard the city."

He grinned hopefully for a moment, then added, "Wallah! Maybe there will be rioting and excellent looting!"

"It is with Allah," said Burton, betraying not a sign of the alarm that burned into his hasheesh wisdom. "I go to attend to certain business. But I will be ready at dawn."

"Allah give you strength," wished the Afghan.

Burton needed it. He fingered the haft of his knife as he walked through what had become a whispering darkness. The shadows gossiped of a red-faced major lying in a pool of red. God curse the dog, why could his carcass not have lain concealed a few more hours?

As a special agent of the Ismailians he had thus far handled only cash, not knives. The novelty oppressed him. Then he smiled contentedly at the recollection of his skillful first slaying.

Soon he was again at his house. The hasheesh voice warned him to be stealthy.

"Maybe Salima is asleep...it will be easier..."

But she was neither asleep nor alone. She was talking to a man with an unpleasant voice: old Abbas, and a glimpse through the window confirmed it.

"He will be here soon," she said. "It will be easy..."

Abbas, the crafty dog, had guessed! He had prepared a trap!

Burton consulted with the hasheesh presence. It answered: "You can not slay them both without raising an alarm. But there is a way..."

He withdrew from the court, creeping toward a narrow alley to await the impatience of Abbas. The traitors could not anticipate his cunning. Abbas would finally leave. But he would not go far.

"Unless the red flames of Jahannum are distant," amended Burton, feeling the edge of his blade.

Before he reached cover, the darkness was alive with uniformed Egyptian police. He was surrounded by tall men whose harsh voices called his name, accused him of murder, leveled pistols and demanded surrender.

A knife was a vain thing, and they did not fire as he drew the weapon. They wanted him alive, to try him, convict him, avert the martial law that the British overlords would proclaim if vengeance were not exacted.

Yet Burton's wits were more subtle than any policeman's.

He reeled, chanting a bawdy song as the flashlights blazed into his face. The wildness of his voice shocked them for an instant. Their pistols wavered, and they muttered.

Burton leaped straight up, moving with incredible agility. Only hasheesh gave him the power. He seized the ledge of a low *mashrabtyah* window, and like an ape swung himself to its ornate, out-thrust molding.

The police gaped as he crouched on his perch, one backward reaching hand lacing fingers into the lattice work.

"Come down, Haroun," they said, calling him by his assumed name, "else we fire."

"Haste is of Satan," he amiably agreed. "Beware—I drop—"

But he did not drop. His muscles, exquisitely timed in their surge of power, shot him out and to the fringe of the squad. His feet landed on brawny shoulders. Two policemen were bowled over. Pistols crackled. They belabored each other with feet and truncheons as they tried to seize the elusive creature that had attacked them like a leopard.

There was a roaring and a shouting, then a futile blasting of fire and lead as Burton broke clear and dashed down alleys that no detail of special police could ever thread.

The pursuit was deflected, abruptly, unaccountably. Then Burton laughed as he understood. Abbas, alarmed by the raid, had burst out into the street, and they were pursuing him!

Just a glimpse of white robes and white beard, just one yell of terror that was swallowed by thundering pistols. Then a flash of Abbas pitching headlong, probing flashlights in an instant finding him.

Before the police could realize that they had killed Abbas by mistake, Burton was lost in an impenetrable tangle of passageways. He paused to take counsel of the companion who had not deserted him.

"This is wisdom," said the voice. "They know you dare not return to your house. They are hunting you in the old city, at Zorayda's place, at Selim's. Therefore, get the jewels from the niche, and the rest will be easy. Do not go to holy Mecca. Go to Bagdad, and be the new king of Iraq. This night's cunning proves you a king without a crown."

That was wisdom. He boldly circled, doubled back, threading those narrow ways which no police from the Ezbekiyah could fathom. And in an hour or so he was back to his house, entering this time by a secret door opening from the rear.

Salima was alone.

"For a change," a soft, bitter voice whispered. "She smiles in her sleep, knowing you can not escape the net. Maybe she does not even know that Abbas was killed. But that would make no difference. She has no heart."

He deftly caressed the panel behind the drapery. The niche opened. There was no jewelry. He froze. Then he saw there were many packets of bank notes.

She had sold his gifts.

His smile warped. All the better. He swept the packets and heavy envelopes into a bundle which he tied up with the drape. Before he left, he paused to look at the loveliness curled up on the *mastaba*.

Salima's beauty was like a knife-thrust between his ribs. This was the last of the women who had led him to folly. He did not hate her, even though she had betrayed him to the police.

He might have known she had seen that blood-splash on his sandal. He carefully wiped it off. Then he knelt beside her. The half smile faded, and she stirred uneasily. Her conscience?

He bent to kiss her. The undulant, sweet curves that gleamed through the silken gauze were a memory to take to Iraq. That sense-stirring beauty made treachery a trifle.

But as she sensed his presence, stirred sleepily, blinked unfocused eyes, the hasheesh companion was whispering in soft venom:

"Oh fool and descended of fools, you forgive this? Until the end of your days, some woman will trick you of your senses, and you will be king of beggars, not a king in Iraq. The Ismailian master will mock you. And you will mock yourself, for the sake of all these who have kissed you to your doom... prove yourself, do not weaken—"

But Salima's awakening brought recognition to her eyes. Her arms arose, closed about him.

"Oh—I thought—I feared—"

"Clever," said the prodding voice from the side, as her lips fused to his. "Very clever. She feared. Feared you would escape—"

One arm drew Salima very close, until her young breasts rebelled against the pressure. Burton's other hand found his knife. It was easy...but her shudder was not of passion... The blood that frothed to her lips was hot and salty on Burton's tongue as that last kiss choked her outcry...

He finally let her slip from his arms. He wiped the blood from her mouth. He sheathed the dagger. Then he bowed very low, picked up his parcel of plunder, and stalked boldly into the night.

He was free. He knew that never again would any woman trick him. He had redeemed himself for all those follies.

The false dawn was graying. He knew better than to try to slip out through the Gate of Victory. He made a long loop into the citadel Saladin had built. He climbed the steep ascent, picked his way through the deserted gloom, then perilously climbed down, crevices in the ruined masonry giving him a hold. Soon he was at the foot of the Mokattam Hills, and on the way to the tomb-dotted wastes beyond.

He headed northward to intercept the caravan. If Saoud really was right, then he could lurk in the cemetery until the blockade was lifted.

But presently he heard the tinkle of bells, the grunt of camels, the cursing of the drivers. All was clear. He sat down in the doorway of a tomb and in the first light of the true dawn he scrutinized his plunder.

Money, of course. Thousands of reclaimed pounds. But more than that. Papers—not English, but Arabic. The script was large, formal. Straining his eyes, he read as he waited.

But he knew before he read. That was the great seal of the Ismailian grand master, on a letter addressing Salima, his "beloved sister."

"This Haroun, the English renegade, is a persuasive talker, but an ass. Perhaps you can keep him from other women. Make him spend his collections on you, lest others dupe him…"

"*Do* not trust Haroun to blackmail that British major in the intelligence service. You and Abbas will handle that. That red-faced pig can not endure scandal—let Abbas trap him with you, and—"

He read no more, nor looked at any other papers. He knew now that Salima did not betray him. He remembered her words, "He will soon be back…"

She had meant the major, not Burton.

The camel bells were closer. Burton, known as Haroun the *hasheesheen*, sat erect in the door of the tomb. A red-bearded man mounted on a Barbary horse was reeling drunkenly in the saddle as he headed the caravan: Saoud, the Afghan.

The path was close to the tomb. His voice was thick but loud.

"By God," he chuckled, "and again, by God! I have the price of Haroun's head, yet Haroun escaped, may Allah prosper him! Blood on his shoes, wits in his head, he escaped. By Allah, there is no God but Allah!"

"Yea, brother," hiccupped the Arab riding boot to boot with the Afghan, "He is wise. He is generous! Praised be his name!"

That was mockery and bitterness and frost; but what came from the voice beside Burton was infinitely worse: "Hear, and know that Fate freed you better than you could free yourself. This was the last of the women who beguiled you. You know now that you can not face the Grand Master, whose sister you slew in error. But those many thousand Egyptian pounds, and your cunning—"

Saoud the Afghan had other things to say; but they were not spoken. A squared rock that had fallen from the tomb fitted Burton's hand and purpose. He hurled it, and it soared into the dawn.

Bone crunched. The Afghan toppled from his horse. There was an outcry, a stampeding, and a screech that rippled down the lines as the leaders of the caravan saw a tall form ducking out of a tomb and losing itself among other tombs.

If a lurking demon wants to brain a drunken Afghan, it is not sensible to interfere. The Holy Prophet doubtless sent the devil to punish the blasphemer. They praised Allah, and rode on.

Burton walked to Cairo.

"Fool," whispered that vibrant voice, "go the other way. Catch up with the caravan. They will think you are a madman—one whose wits are with Allah. That you punished a blasphemer. They will think you a saint. It is better to be a saint than a king."

But Burton, thinking of the girl whose blood had stained his lips, mocked the voice of wisdom, and stalked toward the Gate of Victory-by-the-Aid-of-God. His face was no longer drawn. His eyes were no longer uncanny. He seemed much younger in the morning glow, and there was contentment for the first time in years.

He bore a straight course. He passed his house without a glance to the side. He entered the Ezbekiyah, where the British had their headquarters.

Presently he answered the challenge of sentries. The strange gleam in his eyes gave him entrance to a house where no native could enter at that or any other hour.

"Sir," he reported, "Captain Harvey Burton, of His Majesty's Own Seventh Bengal Fusileers reports after twelve years, five months, eleven days absence without leave to face charges of desertion, embezzlement, and—Sir, you might as well add murder to that. Major Harris, and there's a girl—"

The colonel gaped, choked, blinked, and called the guard.

"The blighter's balmy! Blast it, if this happens again—who—"

He eyed Burton for a long moment. He began to remember and understand. Then he said, "It's better this way, captain. You couldn't have escaped, you know."

But Burton's smile mocked hasheesh wisdom, not the colonel's ignorance.

HELL IN DARIEN

Originally appeared in *Spicy-Adventure Stories*, **Nov. 1937.**

The girl who lay in the *hennequen* hammock was a king's daughter, and her lover was the self-appointed governor of Antigua del Darien—Vasco Nunez de Balboa, who had just discovered the South Sea.

A scarlet skirt clung close to generous hips, and outlined her shapely legs, and her full breasts were bound with calico that was an adornment rather than concealment. She was exquisitely formed, yet there was enough of her to fill the arms of a man as large as Balboa, who called her Tula, since her Indian name was entirely too much for any Spanish tongue.

A ruddy mustache fringed his broad, reckless mouth; and that the man was as bold as his face was proved by the red plumed helmet, which hung near his steel corselet. Both were dented by Carib war clubs, and nicked with arrows. But for the moment, pearls filled his hands instead of a Toledo blade.

They gleamed splendidly against Tula's olive skin when he looped the strands about her throat. But pearls were nothing to an Indian girl. She liked them because he did, and as he bent over her, she drew him close, fervently pressing her mouth against his.

"But you were saving them for your king, *querido*," she murmured.

"King Ferdinand got his share," said Balboa.

"Anyway, I'd rather have some more of this red cloth."

"Then keep them till I get some more calico!"

Though Tula did not know it, he was letting her wear the gems because they would age and finally perish unless they drew fresh life from a woman's soft, warm skin.

"And you'll always love me?" she murmured, arms again about his neck as she drew back from the edge of the broad hammock. "Even if my people won't tell me the road to Peru, where every rain washes gold from the earth?"

"We'll go to Peru," promised Balboa. "You and I."

"Don't squeeze me so tight," she panted. "Those pearls—"

Her dark eyes misted; she shuddered ecstatically, and no longer noticed that the pearls were biting into her skin...

* * * *

The blast of a cannon shook the house. Though Balboa's persuasive tongue had made allies of the neighboring Indians, his vigilance never wavered. He was on his feet, reaching for his helmet, when a second shot echoed, this one from the bay. The shouts of his men, pouring into the plaza, explained; those shots were salutes to a ship.

"Garabito's back from Cuba!" he told the wide-eyed girl. "With enough men to guard Antigua, while we are looking for Peru."

There was a pounding at the door. A swarthy man, all soldier, entered the room. Hernan Arguello, after getting a fleeting view of Tula's legs as she slid from the hammock, announced, "Four ships, Don Vasco. Pedro Arias de Avila, flying the king's standard."

"A thousand armed men," cut in a newcomer. He spat, and added, "Indoor soldiers! We can slice them to pieces before they land. *Por dios*, we want no new governor!"

"The king's standard, did you say?" demanded Balboa.

"Si, señor alcalde," answered Arguello.

Balboa commanded, "Parade the guard! As long as Don Pedro is flying the kings standard, we will welcome him. *Muños! Valderrabano!*" He addressed those who had come running up. "Round up some turkeys! Break out what wine we have left. *Por Dios*, we are poor, but give them our best."

He turned to Tula: *"Querida mia,* you'd better go to your father's village for a few days. I'm going to be busy, giving Don Pedro an accounting of lands and treasure."

Her eyes clouded; she sighed, then brightened and said, "That is right. And I'll leave these pearls. If the string broke—"

He kissed her, thrust the jewels into a chest, then strode out to muster his men. Bugles were braying. Arms clanked. And from the bay came the chanteys of sailors dropping anchor. But Balboa's heart was heavy. Pedro Arias de Avila —Pedrarias, as he was often called—wanted all he saw, and seeing everything. There would be hell in Darien, but he came in the King's name.

* * * *

That evening, resinous torches cast wavering light over a long, crude table in Balboa's house. His frayed doublet and hose, and patched cape were mocked by the rich apparel of those King Ferdinand had sent from Spain to rule Antigua del Darien; but two among those glittering newcomers regarded him with increasing admiration.

One was Pedrarias' wife, a splendid woman at the prime of her beauty. And then there was Doña Isabel's lovely daughter, Maria. Her gray-green eyes smiled with her generous mouth. She had copper colored hair, like her mother; shapely as the older woman, and though not as richly curved, her slim figure was a magnificent promise that even now was almost fulfilled by the exquisite curves that rounded her bodice.

Balboa's eyes caressed her, and she answered. But for venturing into the new world, he might have had such a woman beside him, the mistress of his own house.

100

Her father caught their exchange of glances. His closely spaced black eyes gleamed maliciously, and he sneered at the crude colonial fare set out in his honor.

"The land of gold," he mocked, making a wry face as he tasted wine that the tropics had half spoiled. "Raising corn and turkeys, like peasants! *Por dios*, King Ferdinand did me no favor in sending me to govern this place, *señor*!"

Balboa laughed and answered, "Wait! I will show our Excellency."

He beckoned to an Indian servant. In a moment, the savage returned, handing the master a small parcel. Balboa opened it, and displayed the triple strand of pearls. The ladies near the head of the table gasped; Bishop Quevedo exclaimed; and Pedrarias' eyes gleamed avariciously.

"These are nothing," said Balboa. "The best ones went to King Ferdinand, just before Your Excellency arrived." Then, to Doha Isabel, "*Señora*, with your lord's permission, I offer you these trinkets as a token of the esteem we have for your family."

"Oh—but I can't—Don Vasco, they're priceless," Doha Isabel protested; and her daughter's eyes were very bright when she saw that though the words were addressed to her mother, the thought was for her.

"There are more in the South Sea," said Balboa. "Your unexpected arrival gave me no time to find a worthier gift, nor better hospitality. Wait till I raid Peru."

"You are liberal, carrying provinces in your pocket, Don Vasco!" said Pedrarias, unable to conceal the envy in his thanks.

The tropical heat wrought havoc with the unseasoned newcomers, in the days that followed. Doña Isabel and her daughter retired to the hills behind Antigua; but Pedrarias braved the sweltering settlement while he tried to prove Balboa guilty of keeping more than his share of the loot of Panama. Quarrels broke out between Balboa's soldiers and the silk clad grandees from Spain; and hot headed Arguello urged his chief to fight it out and send the whole rapacious crew back to Cuba.

"They come from King Ferdinand," reproved Balboa, swallowing his own wrath. "Now have an Indian take some fresh fruit and game to Doña Isabel and her daughter."

* * * *

By that night, he had finally cleared himself. Later, his troubled sleep was broken by a familiar voice. Before he could fairly arouse himself, he knew that though he had heard Tula, it was not she who had entered the room. He must have been dreaming. One woman, an Indian, remained at the door. The other approached.

Her bare arms were like ivory serpents, and her hair was ruddy gold in the moonlight that came in through the unglazed window. It was Doña Maria. But as she knelt by his side, she drew back in amazement.

"Oh—Don Vasco!" she faltered. "Where's my father? They told me he'd been wounded in a brawl—mother's ill—so I came with my maid—forgive me —"

"Don Pedro—" Balboa swallowed his heart. She was wearing his pearls. They shimmered against her bosom as she breathed. "Is quite safe in his quarters."

Maria caught his glance, and said, "Mother let me wear them. They're wonderful."

"I wanted to give them to you, but I couldn't," he said. "Not after these years—not after what I've become—"

"You're the greatest captain in the New World," she breathed. "Even if my father does hate you."

They regarded each other, and he forgot that she was the daughter of the King's favorite. The sweetness she exhaled dizzied him like old wine. She swayed toward him, and the lips that touched her hands paused only an instant before caressing her bare shoulder and throat.

Then she was in his arms, and neither felt the great pearls crushed between them. Finally, as she caught her breath, Maria panted, "But I must go, *querido*. Someone lied to me. Some Indian girl—told me—father was in here."

Yet not even that hint could chill Balboa's surging blood, or remind him of the Indian girl whose love kept peace between him and her warlike father.

"*Sanctisima madre!*" he hoarsely breathed. "This mistake is too precious! I will find Peru—I will have a hundred Indians make you a gown all of pearls—I will demand your hand—"

"Vasco," she sighed, looking up with misted eyes, "I know you can. And with new fame, he couldn't refuse—"

"Pearls from your throat to your toes," he promised. "Then I will pluck them from you, one by one, let them scatter as they drop—until only the pearl of yourself is in my arms—"

Her little cry of dismay startled him, and he heard the dry rattle as the snapped strand of her mother's necklace spilled the jewels to the floor and over his couch.

"I'll find them—a light—"

"No! Not a light!" she begged. "Someone tricked me."

And before he could stop her, she had fled. But Maria had scarcely cleared the doorway when torches flared, steel rang, and Pedrarias' wrathful voice boomed into the room, "Where's my wife?"

"Don Pedro, you flatter me as much as you wrong Doña Isabel," answered Balboa; "Here, at this hour?"

Pedrarias suspiciously eyed the barren room. Then he caught the gleam of scattered pearls, and saw the lace scarf on the couch. His sword leaped out. Though he was sixty or past, he was wiry and lean and cunning.

Balboa, swift despite his stature, sidestepped, and in one move seized his cloak and whipped the sword from the scabbard beside his bed.

The blades clashed, red ribbons of steel in the torches of the gentlemen who had accompanied Pedrarias. But despite the skill of that bitter old man, Balboa's quickness kept him at bay, parrying the deadly thrusts that danced in and out like heat lightning.

"Don Pedro," panted Balboa, "cease before I strike the king's envoy. By God, sir, if you force me—"

Pedrarias' point leaped forward to slip through a momentary gap in Balboa's guard. But the sword that had carved a path to the Pacific Ocean was in a master's hand. Its dry, crisp beat, *forte* to *faible*, knocked Pedrarias' light weapon circling in a silver arc.

"Assassin!" howled two of the governor's attendants, closing in.

Balboa, cornered, could have called for the guard, but pride forbade. Crouched like a tiger, he faced them, point wavering in small circles, eyes blazing with the wrath that had scattered hordes of savages.

"Santiago!" His voice shook the room. And one of the governor's knights stood gaping as the other, run through, sank groaning in his own blood.

He whirled to engage the remaining opponent as Pedrarias, dagger drawn, slipped up on his flank. But a scream warned Balboa. He flung himself aside, avoiding the treacherous attack. And before any could again engage, Maria de Avila was among them.

"My mother was not here," she declared. "It was I, wearing her pearls. An Indian woman told me that you were here, wounded. So I came. And my maid was with me."

Pedrarias smiled bitterly. That a high born lady would risk compromising herself to clear a common soldier was an affront to Spanish honor, nor could the ensuing exchange of apologies and compliments alter that fact.

* * * *

Balboa's night was sleepless. He now realized that Tula, seeing Doña Maria wearing the pearls, had acted in a flare of jealousy. Nor could he discard the Indian girl. Her father and his horde of savages would again harass the settlement. Though they could be beaten off, many men would die; his men who were his first concern.

The following night, a broad-shouldered man in armor followed Hernan Arguello into Balboa's house. This was Andres Garabito, who had come from Cuba. Warned by the sight of Pedrarias' four caravels anchored in the harbor, he had secretly landed.

"Amigo," Balboa's old friend went on, "it is well that we came silently. Leave this hound to misrule Antigua. We will march across Panama, build ships on the other coast, and sail for Peru."

The bitterness in Balboa's heart burst out, "We will do that! Even though King Ferdinand must by now have gotten the gold I sent, he can not recall Pedrarias. It is too late. So we will find a new empire—richer loot—wider lands —"

They filled flagons with the powerful Estramadura wine that Garabito had brought from Cuba. They drank lustily, and for a while, Balboa forgot his grievances.

Outside, others were drinking, and wrangling. But he did not pause to wonder where his soldiers had obtained wine. Certainly not from Pedrarias' supply, which he had brought from Spain. Maybe it was maize beer, made by the Indians.

"And on our way, we'll find the Golden Goddess of Dobaybe!" swore Garabito, twisting his wine-dripping mustache.

"I lost ninety men, the last time we tried!" grumbled Balboa, somewhat thickly.

And thus, none of them were ready for what sunrise brought.

When they heard the muted clang of steel, they thought that the watch was marching to the guard house. It was not until Arguello roared, "Who invited you in here?" that Balboa started, unsteady on his feet.

Pedrarias, accompanied by a company of his own soldiers and officers was at the door. He commanded, "Arrest the traitors!"

Swords were out. Flagons crashed from overturned tables. Half a dozen blades crossed in an instant. Arguello laid about him, and Balboa's sword was red, but he was being outpointed because of his wine.

"Surrender!" cried Pedrarias, "or we cut you down to the last man! The place is surrounded. And your soldiers are too drunk to rescue you. I saw to that!"

Balboa lowered his blade. His companions had only their swords; their assailants wore casques and corselets of steel. He demanded, "Don Pedro, who calls me a traitor? After I claimed the South Sea in King Ferdinand's name?"

"We have been watching you, Don Vasco. And we heard you plan with Garabito to conquer new lands and hold them against our King!"

That last was false; but outnumbered and only half armed, Balboa could only surrender. He and Garabito and Arguello were marched to the guardhouse.

"I have enough witnesses to your treason," mocked Pedrarias, as the massive wooden gates slammed shut, "to give the headsman's axe its long, delayed dues."

* * * *

Later, kindly Bishop Quevedo, who had become Balboa's staunchest advocate, came to the prison in which the captives sweltered.

"My son," he said, "make your peace with God. I have pleaded with him, but he will take your head and his spies will back him, and King Ferdinand will believe them."

"Sanctisima madre!" growled Garabito. "That *cabron!*"

He was still cursing when the bishop left. But Balboa was fingering a scrap of paper that the holy man had slipped into his hand. He said, "Cheer up! Even if my soldiers have been disarmed, we've still got a friend."

Maria had written, *"Maybe I can help, or persuade him. But if I can't, I'll die loving you. Go with God."*

* * * *

That night, the watch about town was doubled, so that Balboa's soldiers, though disarmed, would not risk a riot with stones and clubs. Finally they were herded into barracks, sullen and muttering. And the captives, though they could see but a little from the barred window of their stout jail, felt the increasing tension.

"Pedrarias feels it," said Balboa, "so we'll meet the axe before the boys set the town on fire and risk it empty-handed."

"They might get Careta on the warpath," hinted Garabito. "But he won't help us. Not with his daughter sore at you. Damn these Indian wenches!"

All the while, Balboa was testing the walls and bars. But the prison he himself had helped build was too strong for empty-handed captives. He tried to engage the sentry in a conversation. If he could only steal a dagger from the fellow's belt!

"Back, traitor!" growled the soldier. "None of your slick tongue."

The night wore on. Moonrise silvered the plaza. Garabito and Arguello snored. Balboa vainly applied his broad shoulders to the bars, but he could not bend them enough for a man to slip through.

The sentry's arms rattled as he whirled, growling a challenge. A woman answered. Balboa recognized Tula's voice.

"What are you doing out this hour?" the sentry demanded.

But before he could call the guard to report the violation of police regulations, Tula was at his side, pleading. "Do not arrest me, *señor!* I'm Doña Isabel's maid. She's very ill. I came down from the villa to get her a jar of wine."

She stood there, body swaying, jar poised on her sleek head. Her legs were gilded by the moonlight, and so was her torso, bare except for the red cloth that bound her breasts.

"Wine, eh?" he demanded, catching her arm. "Give me a swig."

"I can't," she protested, "It's for the governor's wife."

"How'd you like to be flogged for being on the street at this hour?" he demanded, very sternly. "How do I know who you are?"

"Señor—" And then the jar tipped from her head, crashing to the ground. "Oh, it's broken! Now I will be beaten."

"Shut up!" he grumbled. He was attracted by her gilded curves, and worried because of the spilled wine. She might be Doha Isabel's maid! "Wait till I'm off duty, and I'll get you some more from the officer's mess."

"Oh—will you?" With a glad cry, she came close to him.

His breastplate robbed him of the best portions of Tula's curves, but his sleeves were not steel, and he wore no gloves. Then and there, he knew that he had a woman with ripe hips, a supple waist, and legs beautifully rounded above the knees. He set his halberd against the door jamb. Tula protested at his embrace, but he said, "Get in the doorway or someone'll see you—no, you idiot, of course I can't take off this armor. Not on duty!"

But Tula was grateful for the promised wine. Every moment the soldier became more and more bothered.

Balboa cursed under his breath. If Tula, who was unknown to Pedrarias' people, had actually worked her way into his household, she might in her wrath poison Maria. He stepped toward the door, resolved to expose her and warn his enemy's family.

"Oh...that awful armor," she was panting. "It's such a nuisance..."

And then, approaching the jamb, Bal-boa saw Tula and the soldier. She was ardently kissing him, but one of her hands was probing her heavy hair. It was not a comb she was fingering, but a dagger hilt. Once she got a chance to slip it through the joint between gorget and breastplate, his throat would be cut before he could cry out.

Tula had come to help Balboa, and had shattered the jar to arouse him to his chance. But before she had kissed the soldier to utter recklessness, Balboa reached between the bars. He caught the staff of the halberd, drew it stealthily between the bars. Tula's hand dropped from her hair as she caught the move.

"Oh—don't—please," she moaned, suddenly trying to repulse him. "Suppose the captain—" She wriggled clear, tripped, landed in a heap in the doorway, arms and bare legs thrust up as she tried to regain her balance. The soldier was after her now, in dead earnest, kneeling beside her, reaching...

And then the halberd, descending between the bars, smacked him a sledgehammer blow across the back of the head. Despite his helmet, the impact knocked him senseless. Tula had scarcely wormed herself clear of the amorous soldier when Balboa used the heavy weapon to pry the lock apart. And in a moment, the prisoners were in the archway.

"I'm sorry," cried Tula. "I was jealous—I couldn't help it—"

She clung to him, sobbing. He said over her shoulder, "Andres! Hernan! If I go, my men come with me. He'll lead them to the chopping block, figuring they helped me out."

"Can't do it," growled Garabito. "We'll be lucky to get to my boat before we're missed."

"Boat?" Balboa growled. "They'd kill us in Cuba. Peru, nowhere else."

"He'll hunt us down!" protested Arguello.

"What a chance! Those milksops, tracking *us* through the jungle? Listen— let's jerk. Pedrarias out of bed, and take him as a hostage. That way, he'll have to release my men."

So they stole through the silent streets of Darien. Garabito protested, "A boat just came from Spain. He's up late, with a lot of officials."

But Balboa pressed on. Tula, clinging to his hand, was choked by her joy. She said, "Now we'll go to Peru. Or to Dobaybe, the land of the Golden Goddess. Won't we?"

* * * *

Once at Pedrarias' house, Balboa made his companions wait until he reconnoitered. He wore the sentry's sword, leaving Garabito and Arguello with the fellow's armor, halberd, and dagger. He scaled the palisade, crept across the garden, and toward the light that gleamed from a window.

Pedrarias sat scowling at his desk. It was heaped with documents which the two messengers had given him. Gentlemen of such quality could not have come to Antigua with less than letters from King Ferdinand himself.

"Señores caballeros," said Pedrarias, looking up, "you are weary from your long voyage. Let me take you to your quarters, whose poverty embarrasses me. Golden Darien!"

"It will be luxury, after our trip. And forgive us for our brusqueness. But there is a dispatch for Don Vasco Nuñes de Balboa. Coming from His Majesty's own hand, we are not permitted any choice but to—"

"Muy señores caballeros," was the frigid interruption, "is not *my* receipt sufficient? I myself will hand His Most Catholic Majesty's communication to Don Vasco, who like myself, is the faithful servant who kisses your hands. I regret that he is stricken by this accursed fever, and is scarcely to be disturbed."

The two hidalgos stroked their pointed beards. Pedrarias was King Ferdinand's friend. The spokesman conceded, "The King's message is in good hands."

Pedrarias clapped his hands. Two officers emerged from an ante room. They were followed by four soldiers. He said, "Modena, be good enough to show these gentlemen to their quarters, and let Bernal and Sotomayor attend them as orderlies." Then, as the messengers were ushered from the room, Pedrarias said to the remaining officer, "Don Ignacio, dismiss the guard and be seated. There is much to consider, late as it is."

He broke the seals on a document picked from the pile. There was no chance for Balboa to enter by the barred window. He let himself to the ground, spent endless moments, crouching in the shadow of a plantain cluster as the two envoys were escorted out of the compound gate. And as the drowsy porter wrestled with the bars, Balboa slipped from cover and ascended the stairs.

Voices, half muffled, greeted him as he went down the hall.

"You shouldn't have opened it," protested Don Ignacio. *"Por dios,* now it is too late. You have read the king's command."

"Nevertheless, I will have his head, that rebellious dog!"

From the doorway, Balboa saw Pedrarias holding a crumpled sheet to the candle flame. He bounded forward, sword drawn.

"Stop, in the King's name!" he shouted.

Before he had half crossed the spacious room, Pedrarias and Don Ignacio were on their feet; and the two soldiers came clanking out. Behind him, he heard the porter's padding feet. But Balboa was reckless with wrath. His blade licked out, biting into Ignacio's shoulder. His parry blocked Pedrarias' cut to the head.

107

"The king's letter! It is mine, sentence or no sentence of yours!"

"Seize him!" yelled Pedrarias. "The guard!"

Balboa ducked a halberd stroke, slashed a soldier's arm instead of wasting a thrust on a steel corselet. A glancing blow numbed his shoulder. Garabito and Arguello were hammering at the gate, smashing it in. But Ignacio, shifted his blade to his uninjured left. A servant hurled an earthen jar, catching Balboa between the shoulders.

And then a majestic voice rang over the confusion. White haired Bishop Quevedo commanded, "Put up your swords! Give him his letter, Don Pedro!"

At the bishop's heels was Doña Maria. Her feet were bare, and she had only a robe over her frail gown whose lace paneling gave glimpses of white breasts and slim waist, and the ivory sleekness of her legs, all splendid in the candle glow. She was breathing heavily; Balboa knew that she had overheard, and run barefooted to get the bishop.

Pedrarias cursed. These were witnesses he dared not harm. Soldiers and servants drew back. Balboa seized the document, and said to the bishop, "Be pleased to read it, Your Grace."

He read the sonorous Latin, then said in Spanish, "Don Vasco, His Most Catholic Majesty has received your treasure shipment. He appoints you Adalanto of the South Seas, and Governor of Coyba and Panama, second only to Don Pedro Arias de Avila."

Pedrarias' eyes blazed with insane jealousy. Though he was in name the supreme ruler of Darien, Balboa had been assigned the richest provinces. Then he forced a smile and said, "Don Vasco, perhaps I have been hasty. And since my daughter has gone to such lengths in your favor, I will ask the bishop to solemnize your betrothal at once."

Crafty Pedrarias, making the greatest captain of the New World his son-in-law, would have a strangle hold on all Balboa's rich loot. Since he could not ruin his enemy, he would imprison him in silken bonds.

"Let Garabito and Arguello be my witnesses," said Balboa.

But Tula was gone. She must have heard enough to know that she could not be a queen in Peru.

There were no outward evidences of love exchanged by Maria and Balboa, but their eyes spoke to each other, and just before they signed the formal papers —the betrothal was almost as solemn as the marriage that would follow—he whispered, "Tomorrow I march for Peru. To win you a gown of pearls."

Her lashes dropped, and he saw the flush that spread to her breasts. The momentary pressure of her hand was a promise that could not be fulfilled until they were married. A lady of high birth is too closely guarded...

* * * *

The next day Balboa and his company of old soldiers set out across the Isthmus. Behind them trailed hundreds of porters, sweating and bent double by the weight of fittings and cannon they carried toward the South Sea, where ships were to be built.

But Balboa's high heart froze, that night, at the first camp. Grim old Careta came stalking into his camp; and with him was his daughter, Tula, splendid in the firelight that made her luxurious body a golden amber. Her dark eyes blazed, but she said nothing.

Garabito, listening to the parley, was likewise silent; but his eyes caressed Tula's half bare flesh, and in his mind, he stripped from her hips the frail scarlet scarf.

"Don Vasco," said the old chieftain, "Tula is yours. You cannot desert her, since no man of her own rank would now want her."

Balboa remembered the glamorous times with Tula, who had brought him her father's friendship. But while Doña Maria could forgive him an affair with an Indian girl, for him openly to keep Tula would be a mortal affront to Pedrarias' family pride.

Careta went on, "Take my daughter, Don Vasco, or while you are on the way to Peru, I will blot out Antigua. You I could never beat in battle or ambush, but these men who smell like women, they cannot defend the town, nor the life of Doña Maria. And to see that my daughter is well treated, I am leaving some picked men, to serve you and protect her from insults."

He turned and stalked into the jungle. Not a weapon was raised. The night was alive with armed Indians, and Balboa's caravan was not in shape for immediate defense.

Then Tula followed him to his tent. She knelt beside him in the half glow of embers, and the warmth of her luxurious body revived ancient memories.

"Maybe," she murmured, as his kiss drew her life to her lips, "we'll lose ourselves in the lands of the Golden Goddess, after all?"

He drew her toward him, caressing her so that she sighed, and shuddered in his arms...

* * * *

They hewed timber, fashioned a ship, and set sail for Isla Rica, some miles off the Isthmus. And while the other three caravels were being built, Balboa, a few picked men, and some Indian divers probed the water for pearls.

The hearty, affable captain became sombre. He went back and forth between the island and the main land to inspect his shipyard and camp. Day and night he drove his men. His only escape was to Peru, to win an empire. Otherwise he would lose Maria, for the loot he was sending back to Antigua was already a prodigious prize for avaricious Pedrarias. The betrothal could be annulled.

He sat by the fire, having decided against returning to the island that night. To Arguello, in charge of the ship building, he said, "Hernan, I feel the hand of destiny. See that star? It is marching to the position foretold by the Venetian astrologer who predicted that one day I would waver between death and an empire."

"Empire, Vasco! Buck up, man!" chided Arguello. "You're tired."

"Dog tired, *amigo*." Weariness was making him morbid, suspicious. "Suppose those Indians on the island took a notion to butcher Garabito, and sneak away while I'm gone. He trusts them too far. A disaster could discredit me, and give Pedrarias a pretext."

Balboa aroused his sleeping Indians; they were two of Careta's men. He said, "Push off, you fellows! I feel trouble."

They arrived worn out and breathless. Wind howled, lashing the waves to foam. Spray pelted them as they staggered to the camp.

Balboa's heart choked him as he entered his thatched hut. Tula was stretched out beside the hearth. Andres Garabito was bending over her, letting her draw him to her upturned mouth.

"My father," she sighed, "may give me to that faithless hound, but he can't give my love—"

"*Cabron!*" Shouted Balboa, drawing his sword. "You, Andres, doing this behind my back! Tula, you accursed *puta!*"

She rippled to her feet, unbound hair trailing so that it half hid her proud breasts. "Andres," she mocked, "is not marrying the governor's daughter. Though she's probably doing the same, for all you know—"

Balboa flung aside his sword, snatched a whip, slashed it across Garabito and the woman whom his arms could not protect. Before Garabito knew what was happening, he was blinded with blood, and Tula's back seamed with livid welts. Balboa cursed them, flayed them. Then he flung his whip aside, and as Garabito blindly snatched the sword that its owner scorned to use, Balboa hurled himself, empty-handed, knocked him end for end, crashing headlong against a pillar of the house.

That quenched Balboa's fury; soldiers and Indians came bursting in. Among them was the chief of those that Careta had sent with his daughter. Balboa said, "Take her back to her father."

The Indians, knowing what Balboa had found on his unexpected return, had no answer. Tula had violated the code of her own people. He turned to the soldiers and added, "And take Garabito back' to Antigua!"

* * * *

The next day, Balboa watched a pirogue take his faithless friend and Tula to the mainland. Arguello would arrange for an escort, and on his return would bring added supplies for the cruise to Peru. And only then did Balboa realize that since Tula's own father would repudiate her, Antigua del Darien was in no further peril. He began to regret his treatment of his friend. Garabito might have been tempted beyond endurance. At all events, there was no longer any woman between him and Maria...

Days passed. Balboa buried his premonitions. He reasoned that the crisis had passed; for had he not exposed Tula and the infatuated Garabito, they might have slain him so that he would not uncover their secret love.

At last Arguello returned, meeting his chief at the camp on the mainland. He had a letter from Pedrarias, and one from Don Maria.

"Father has listened to my pleas," she wrote. *"Return and marry me before you go to Peru. So that I can go with you when you discover new lands."*

Pedrarias' letter confirmed Maria's: *"My dear son, we parted without full understanding. Come back and receive my full blessing. But go by way of Acla, where there are certain matters in which your experience could benefit me."*

Balboa said to Arguello, "I knew there was some catch in his friendliness. Indians muttering in Acla, eh? Oh, well—for once, trouble is welcome."

"I don't like this," Arguello somberly muttered. "Pedrarias never forgave a man in his life. I beg of you, *amigo*—set sail for Peru."

"Doha Maria couldn't be wrong," declared Balboa, face agleam. "Her intuition would warn her. And I'm Adelanto of the South Sea."

The end of it was that he followed Balboa and a few picked men into the jungle, and across the Isthmus to Acla.

* * * *

The guard was paraded in his honor when, at last, they dragged weary legs past the gates of Acla. Pedrarias was there, with his staff of officers. Trumpets brayed, drums rolled. A squad of musketeers fired a salute; but the martial din had scarcely reached its height when a bedraggled woman came screaming into the plaza. It was Tula, hair streaming, her scarlet skirt a tattered, blood-caked scrap. Her body was a crisscross of red welts, and she shrieked, "Vasco—beware—you are doomed—they tricked me—into signing—"

"I told you!" roared Arguello. "Back to the gate!"

A soldier struck the screaming girl against the palisade. Balboa was stunned by the sudden blossoming of treachery. His sword was out, and he shouted, "Santiago!" as he parried an axe. Yet he could scarcely believe his ears when he heard Pedrarias croak above the hoarse tumult, "Seize the traitor!"

Valderrabano was down, stunned by a halberd stroke. Arguello yielded his gains to come back to his chief's side. Munos and Botello, back to back, drew sparks from the clash of their steel, and Balboa laid about him, hewing and crushing the men who closed in with pikes and cutlasses.

But the city gates were closed. Horsemen with couched lances forced the foot soldiers to their doom at the swords of Balboa's handful. But a rock hurled from a housetop struck him to the ground, unconscious.

* * * *

It was not until he regained his senses that Balboa learned that his four friends had survived the overwhelming attack. He knew now why there had been a rendezvous at Acla; had this treachery come in Antigua, the town would have revolted.

Later, a guard and officers accompanied Pedrarias to the door of the cell. There were notaries and lawyers with him.

"I have finally learned," said Pedrarias, "how you and that Indian wench mocked my daughter, how you planned to desert to Peru, so that you could make her your queen."

"Who says that?" demanded Balboa, rising from attending his wounded comrades.

"I, Andres Garabito!" His former friend stepped forward, gestured toward the sealed documents that Pedrarias had in his hand. "I overheard you and her, planning against King Ferdinand's territories in the New World, so I tricked her into returning and confessing."

No one, not even Pedrarias, could believe that story, but Garabito had sworn to it. It would sound plausible in the court records. And how could King Ferdinand know otherwise, back in Spain?

"It's a lie!" groaned Arguello, sitting up. "Wounded as I am, I will meet any three of you—on horse or on foot, and prove that you lie!"

"You cannot testify," sneered Pedrarias. "Being yourself under charges of treason, along with Munos and Botello and Valderrabano. A priest will be in to see you. Either before you are tried, or after. It will make no difference."

* * * *

And during the trial of Balboa and his companions, Tula and Garabito were in a second floor room overlooking the plaza, where a scaffold had been built. Their presence was not necessary. Their depositions had been taken, and Pedrarias would run on risk of having them change their testimony when they faced the prisoners.

Garabito's hand trembled as he reached for a flagon of wine. Tula was rubbing from her body the healing herbs she had applied to her bruises. Her skin gleamed a golden brown, and in that shadowy room, the welts; left by the flogging and the preliminary torture that had won her false confession were scarcely visible.

"Andres," she suddenly began, "Save him. Good God, I never knew it would come to this! I just thought he'd be in disfavor—"

"And go back to you again?" growled Garabito.

"No," she cried, sinking beside him. "I don't love him. Not that way. But he was good to me and my people. I'll go to court—I'll tell the judges—"

He jerked back to the couch. "They'll kill you. Pedrarias has the court in his pocket."

She clung to him, sobbing, but the luxurious form that had turned him against his friend did not for the moment move Garabito. He snarled, "He struck me with a whip—I could have forgiven him if he had killed me with a sword."

Then, looking out the window, he saw the black scaffold, and his head sank between his hands. Tula's heavy eyes brightened. She stroked his hair, whispered in his ear of the old friendship and perils he had shared with Balboa. And as he wavered, her voice became throaty and caressing as her soft hands.

The sun was dropping toward the jungle that fringed the town. Tula plied him with kisses, with all the allure that not even bruises had robbed of its splendor. She turned her remorse into compelling passion as she pleaded, "Andres, for the sake of my love, save him. Tonight, we can overpower the jailor. I don't care for him as I do you. I can't. But he is a born captain, and he had to marry her to win more fame. So I forgive him. Good God, Andres. So can you. You're not afraid—"

He fiercely embraced her, stroked back the streaming hair that half veiled her thinly clad body, read the glow in her dark eyes. He was sure at last that Tula had sought him for his own sake.

"Love me, Andres," she pleaded. "Never stop loving me. I'm an outcast. My father has disowned me. Your people will spit at you for betraying Balboa. Save him—tonight—or he dies at sunrise. Your honor dies with him—and I die —being guilty with you. But my father loves Balboa, and for his sake, he would receive us. You and me, Andres—my people are your only hope. Balboa's friends will find you, surely slay you. Save him, or you die. And I perish alone in the jungle—cursed by my father—"

"*Dios!*" he groaned, fingers sinking into her arms till she winced. He crushed her to him, and remorse more than desire fused them together for a while. "Holy saints! You have tricked me out of my vengeance. Tonight I'll get him loose!"

"We two, Andres!" She made a sound neither a laugh nor a sob. Then she clung to him, and their wrenched emotions blended in tears and inarticulate cries. And with fear and vengeance driven from that shadowy room, Tula and Garabito found each other anew; their kisses mocked the scaffold. For the first time, there, was no shadow between them as they found each other's arms...

But as the sun dipped toward the jungle's crest, the blare of trumpets and the solemn roll of drums shook the room. A priest was chanting in sonorous Latin, cadenced to the metallic tread of marching soldiers.

Five men, bare headed and manacled, ascended the scaffold. Balboa, chin high and nose jutting like a crag, stalked boldly ahead, and his four friends in file behind him; solemn but unafraid, since they had often faced death when he was not saluted by the rumble of drums and the heart wrenching cry of trumpets.

A masked man tried the edge of his axe. Halberds gleamed from the ground; musketeers stood by with matches smoking. Pedrarias was in the center of a picked company; even in Acla, he feared revolt.

"*Sanctisima madre!*" groaned Garabito. He was unarmed, except for his dagger—caught off guard by Pedrarias' haste to behead his victims. Tula's sigh seemed to deflate her frozen breasts and draw her color until her lips were leaden.

She sagged, and he did not catch her. She lay there, sprawled in her hair and the little scarlet skirt from which her lovely legs grotesquely reached.

The headsman was kneeling, begging the personal pardon of his victims. Balboa's deep voice did not tremble as he absolved the masked man. Long red shafts lanced through the jungle, and shadows marched across the square.

"Let me go first, Don Vasco," said stout Arguello.

"Your captain leads," retorted the man who had claimed the South Sea for Spain. *"Vayan con dios, compañeros!"*

The roll of drums drowned the prayer that the descending axe cut short. A frozen silence in thickening light. Another trumpet blast, and that awful rumble...another—

Then Garabito saw what lay at his feet. For this sprawled flesh he had sold his friend. Yet he was sick, and she was all that he had. He knelt beside her, mumbling what prayers he remembered.

And he died with a prayer on his lips. Tula, rousing herself, snatched his dagger and thrust it home.

She laughed shrilly, and as the axe for the fifth time fell, men in the square wondered whose mirth could profane that moment when the captains licked their lips and groped for the next command.

Then feet tramped, trumpets blared, and no one heard the cries of the king's daughter whose bare body gleamed as a last sun ray kissed it. With red laughter and red dagger, she was running to the jungle that hates all lonely creatures, and destroys them.

* * * *

But before the sun rose, Tula knew that it was only her sensuous beauty, and the safety of Antigua del Darien that kept her in his tent.

They reached the South Sea whose waters kissed the coasts of the Indies.

UNFIT FOR COMMAND

Originally appeared in *Short Stories*, September 25th 1941.

CHAPTER 1

For a long time now, the commanding officer of the Philippine Scout post at Bacolod had been wondering whether to decorate Dan Riley, or to try him for conduct unbecoming to an officer and a gentleman. And what Sergeant Piomonte brought from Headquarters was not a Congressional Medal.

Riley said wearily, "Come in, Sergeant!" But Piomonte remained at the threshold, straight and trim in his well starched chino blouse. He wore side arms, so he kept his hat on, and he tried to avoid Lieutenant Riley's eye. Like every scout on the post, he knew what had happened, and he was sorry; but his wrinkled brown face showed none of this as he began, "Sir. The commanding officer sends compliments to—"

Riley raised a hairy paw, and grinned sourly. "To hell with the compliments. Sit down; it'll take me from now on to read the charges."

But Piomonte would not sit in the lieutenant's presence; not on this solemn occasion. No one was certain whether the C.O. was trying Riley under the 96th Article of War, or under the 95th, which last made dismissal mandatory.

Riley was only a few inches taller than the sergeant, but he carried fifty pounds more weight, most of it in his square shoulders and strong arms; and none of it, according to Major Crann, in his head. The cavalry trumpet hanging on the wall of the dark paneled room, just over the iron bed with its mosquito netting, Major Crann said, explained that distribution. Trumpeters, he insisted, blow their brains out, not with a service .45 as they should, but by mere performance of their duty; and Dan Riley had served an enlistment as a trumpeter in the old Seventh Cavalry.

Riley opened the official envelope and took out the original and carbon of the charges. "Long as a Chinese dream," he grumbled, and for a moment poked around among the ash trays, dobe cigarettes, unanswered letters, and canned gadgets of carabao horn and marine ivory which littered his table. Then he found a pen, made a tentative splash on the floor, and put his John-Henry on the dotted line. "Here you are, Sergeant. And have a cigar!"

He reached for the box of Excellentes. Piomonte approved of a gallant fellow who cared so little about orders that he wouldn't bother to read the one which probably meant his dismissal from the service, but the sergeant was also practical. "Sir. If I breeng back thees paper with signature, the Commanding Officer knows you 'ave not the time to make proper reading."

"Oh, all right, light up and wait." Riley began to read, *"Charge 1: Violation of the 95th Article of War."*

His long jaw tightened just a little, his mouth hardened, his sandy brows bristled for a second. Major Crann was out for a hide. The only way to stay in the service was to beat the charges, and these could not be beaten. He read on:

"Specification 1: In that First Lieutenant Dan P. Riley, Philippine Scouts, did, at Bacolod, Mindanao, P. L, in the tienda of Ah Chin, on or about January 11, 1914, engage in a brawl with one Balabac Charlie, a civilian. And in that the said First Lieutenant Dan P. Riley did throw a coal oil lamp at the said Balabac Charlie, the lamp exploding and burning to the ground the tienda of said Ah Chin and two other houses of nipa construction in the said village of Bacolod."

Riley shook his head. Captain J. C. M. Wilson had witnessed most of the show. So had Spud Marley, a copra trader who hated soldiers on general principles. And then there were enough natives to testify.

"That the said First Lieutenant Dan P. Riley, Philippine Scouts, did then, at grave risk to his own life, rescue the said Balabac Charlie who was then unconscious from a blow from the fist of said First Lieutenant Dan P. Riley."

This last was not included because Major Crann intended to give the crack-brained officer a chance to plead heroism; as the C.O. saw it, Riley was just lucky not to be facing manslaughter charges, and the court was being so reminded.

During his hasty signing without reading, Riley had noted the closing paragraphs of the impressive document. They did suggest a very slim chance; that next to the last specification, plus one Datu Andug, a hill Moro who knew too many gun runners. Major Crann's saddle-colored face turned a deep purple whenever Andug was mentioned; he knew the *datu* was accumulating guns, but war department orders kept him from taking the initiative in cleaning out that nest of trouble makers. This was in the tradition: never lock the barn until it's too late.

Riley began to brighten. He rose, thrust his feet into his straw *chinelas*, and walked over to the cavalry trumpet. It reminded him of court-martials he had dodged as an enlisted man. Resourcefulness had gotten him out of more than one tangle, though this time, it would take some getting. He turned back to the table, and still thinking of the last paragraph, he said to Piomonte, "Sergeant, I want you to watch for Crazy Tom. The minute he comes out of the Lanao country, let me know, day or night. Do you understand?"

"Si, mi teniente."

Riley resumed his reading: *"Specification 2: In that First Lieutenant Dan P. Riley, Philippine Scouts, did then bring said Balabac Charley, a civilian, and another civilian known as Crazy Tom, to the military reservation of Parang,* and did, while standing on the trail in rear of bachelor quarters of said military reservation, at or about three o'clock, A.M., blow a cavalry trumpet, the same being equipment not authorized for issue to officers, a tune commonly known as ZAMBOANGA, after having encouraged the said Balabac Charley and the said Crazy Tom, both civilians, to accompany him vocally, the words of said song being indecent, improper, and unbecoming an officer and gentleman: This all to the scandal of the military service."

"Specification 3: In that First Lieutenant Dan P. Riley, Philippine Scouts, was drunk and disorderly in the presence of enlisted men."

This last savored a bit of anticlimax, Riley thought. It had all started when he learned that Balabac Charley, just returned from Borneo, had once soldiered in the 31st Infantry, a regiment which, somewhere or other, Riley couldn't remember, had been quartered near the 7th Cavalry. So they began drinking; and presently they began to feel sorry for Crazy Tom, with whom no one would drink. They asked Crazy Tom to join them, and the list of charges neatly summed up the results.

Just incidentally, Crazy Tom had, years previous, soldiered in a cavalry outfit. Now he was a sunshiner, definitely whacky from nipa gin. Whites despised him, natives feared him. He had four wives; one in Bacolod Village, and three in the Moro country, this trio being kept in shacks a day's march apart. The hostile tribesmen feared to harm him, since madmen, whose wits had been checked with Allah, were under divine protection. All this gave Riley a glimmer of hope.

That glimmer became a blaze as brisk as Ah Chin's *tienda*. An inner voice began to sound like a cavalry trumpet. Riley paced up and down in his slip-slapping *chinelas*. Then he noticed the sergeant, who still stood there, face no longer blank; he looked confused, uncertain. Riley asked, "What's the matter, Piomonte?"

The sergeant gulped, stood up straighter than was natural even for a Scout at attention. "Sir. Regulation say, enlisted man cannot say de officer right or wrong. Cannot make de *reclama*."

Riley tried hard not to chuckle at Piomonte's scruples in the presence of one who had always considered regulations something to be evaded.

"Go ahead, go ahead, what is it?"

"The men—of thees company—the other company too—express the regret. They will sign the petition, begging the *commandante* to—"

"He'd throw you all in the mill, do you hear? What good'd that do me? Now get out, and watch for Crazy Tom."

"*Si, mi teniente.*"

Riley's big idea was too good to keep. He wanted to see the commanding officer at once, but being under arrest in quarters, he could not call on Major Crann. However, an hour later, he was crossing the parade.

He wore his white uniform, but without belt or saber. Wiry little scouts, lounging on the veranda of barracks, snapped to attention, the senior member

117

of each group saluting. Riley's hand rose a little, then dropped, and he said, "Cut it out! I'm under arrest, don't you understand?"

"*Si, señor*. We know that."

Being a damn fool did have its rough moments. Riley gulped and blinked, thinking of how tough it would be, no longer commanding a platoon of these little brown apes.

It was mid-afternoon, but he stopped at the mess, just for a minute. When he came out, he tried to pat his blouse into shape, though not with any success. One pocket bulged. Then, instead of going directly to quarters, he detoured to Major Crann's office. The orderly who paced back and forth on the veranda, at each end making a precise about face, started to do a rifle salute, and then remembered not to.

Riley knocked smartly at the screened door. A professionally brusque voice answered, "Come in!" Then, "Lieutenant, what in hell's hinges and Tophet are you doing here? Who gave you permission to leave your quarters? Do you or do you not understand the meaning of arrest?"

"Sir, after reading those charges, I had a splendid idea."

The major's long sharp face became two shades darker. He pushed his chair back, and stood there, straight and scowling. Then he sighed gustily and the double row of campaign ribbons on the breast of his white blouse settled back a little. "Riley, I do not wish to add charges of breaking arrest, though after all, I do not see that would make much difference."

"That's just about correct, sir," Riley brightly agreed. "Now, my idea is—"

"I am not interested in your damned ideas! You've had too many of them, and fraternizing with sunshiners, with that polygamous madman whose very existence is an affront to white prestige in Mindanao, that is the limit. Let me explain again, Riley. I am patient because, with your long record as a bugler—"

"Begging the major's pardon, but I was a cavalry *trumpeter*, sir. Buglers are —"

Crann's teeth grated audibly. "I know, Riley. Bugler is not the designation used in the mounted service. But you've blown your brains out through your mouth just the same. Now, the meaning of arrest in quarters is—damnation, am I to believe that you don't know you are permitted to leave only for sick call or meals?"

Riley dug into the pocket of his blouse. "That's what I was about to explain, sir." He displayed a sandwich two inches thick, made of issue salmon. "I went to get a meal."

Crann sat down. He said, with a mixture of regret and anticipation, "You won't be disgracing the service much longer. In many ways, you have the makings of a first-class officer, but damn it, sir, your breaches of discipline make you utterly unfit to command men in battle. Unfit to command men, you understand?" He raised a hand. "I know, you have good showmanship, the men follow you. But in the end, you'll sacrifice a company. Now, what is that idea?"

"I've found a way to learn where Datu Andug gets those guns and cartridges, sir."

"What?" Crann's face changed. He leaned across his desk. "Don't try to trade with me, you'll win no leniency. But I'd like to know how."

"Crazy Tom goes all through the hills. He's loco, and Andug's men won't touch him. Now, he wears a mask to hide a big scar, the poor devil thinks his wives won't love him if they see that *kampilan* slash. I'm his size, suppose you throw him in the hoosegow, while I go into the hills. The Moros will take me for him. The mask, sir, don't you see?"

Crann smiled bitterly. "Impersonating a madman. Appropriate, in a way. Now get out of here, and stay in your quarters. The idea is too wild for words. Even though I am preferring charges, I don't want you staked out on an ant hill. That is all, Lieutenant!"

CHAPTER II

It was around five-fifteen when Sergeant Piomonte, fairly crackling in the chino khaki freshly starched and ironed for retreat, came to Riley's quarters. He burst in without knocking, and began to gesture: "Look, *mi teniente!* She is coming from the mountain."

"She? Who?"

"Crazy Tom, *el loco*, the accursed one, *señor!* I watch for heem."

Riley followed the little sergeant to the veranda. The sun was sinking toward the Celebes Sea; the red and magenta and the green splashes were mirrored in the water, and seemed to reach all the way to Borneo, but Riley had no eye for the beauties of nature.

Crazy Tom, stumbling down the mountain trail toward Bacolod Village, looked finer than any sunset.

Riley's shoulders swayed just a bit, in unconscious imitation of the madman's slouching gait. "By God, I can walk like that, it's easy!"

And he could also have carried the little deer that scarcely hampered the sunshiner. Glance fixed only a short distance in front of him, his face hidden by the red bandanna he wore, in the manner of a western road agent, Crazy Tom seemed always on the verge of falling or tripping, but he never did.

In one big hand, he gripped a single-barreled shotgun. This weapon, loaded with buckshot, kept the market hunter in money for gin, and for gewgaws that fascinated his four wives. The ladies made quite a fuss over him; all, that is, except his first wife, Catalina, who bitterly resented the three younger ones.

So Tom had to beat her thoroughly, whenever he was in town.

But in his rough way, Crazy Tom was kind to Catalina. He gave her as much red calico, and as many bits of tinned jewelry as he gave to Conception, Carmen, and Conchita. These last ones were Moro girls with outlandish Malay names, and from some queer quirk, he had given them Spanish names all starting with "C."

119

While Riley had always been sorry for that caricature of a white man, he now found Tom's psychology intensely interesting. Sergeant Piomonte, though a Christion Visayan, was ill at ease from seeing his *teniente* stare so earnestly at the accursed one. He and his fellows feared Tom almost as much as the Moslem mountaineers did; but aside from their squeamishness in the presence of the uncanny, the little scouts feared nothing on earth, least of all the Moros and their long *kampilans*, and leaf shaped *barongs*, and the deadly *sundangs*. These were fighting men, and led by a fighting captain, they were hundred and thirty pound packets of hell.

"*Señor*, ees not good to watch heem too much."

"Carries a deer like it was a rabbit—hmmm—I can do that." But Riley was troubled by the thought of what would happen if one of the wives thought they saw Tom approaching, up some narrow trail, and ran to meet him. "Oh, well, it's a good gamble."

Women, who had no souls, were exempt from any of the harm an accursed one's proximity could cause a man. Neither did women have brains, hence, nothing would be addled. But a Moro warrior would as soon eat pork as come within arm's reach of Crazy Tom.

"Maybe the old man's right, maybe I'm nuts too," Riley pondered.

However, the Moros had not officially classed Riley as a madman, and not a man of the hill tribes but would love to dissect the solid Irishman, for fun, for glory, and for his pistol and cartridges.

A bugler sounded first call. Piomonte had to leave. Riley bolted into his room, kicked out of his slacks, and put on a civilian suit. Out on the parade, commands rumbled, and there was the smart slap of leather slings against Scout palms; the thump of pieces coming to the order. When any more snap is possible, the Scouts will display it.

The retreat gun boomed; it echoed from the adjoining headland, and from the wooded hills. "Pre-z-e-n-n-n-nt—*ARMS!*" That was when Riley bolted. Aside from himself and the cooks, every man on the reservation was at attention, eyes front, waiting for the colors to be lowered. The bugler sounded, *"To the colors."* Riley's instinct almost made him halt. Then he stretched his legs, having found a precedent: "Hell, I'm under arrest, I am not entitled to salute!"

The sentries were at present arms, facing the direction of the field music. So Riley cleared the limits of the post before the captains commanded, *"Order, arms!"*

But even in his bolting, Riley had noticed one significant thing: Crazy Tom, who had stopped to rest along the trail, had risen, had raised his hand to the brim of his sloppy old hat when the bugle screamed. Way back in that gin cooked brain, there was perhaps ten cents worth of soldier.

"Which makes me and him about neck and neck," Riley said, once he ploughed through the high *cogon* grass and readied the rocky trail to Bacolod. "But Crann, he's nuts, claiming I can't command men in battle."

120

Major Crann, for all his worship of the I.D.R., was a field soldier, and a good one. He did his best to conceal his mistrust of Scout officers, who in the main were ex-enlisted men of various grades, commissioned temporarily in time of emergency. Though he did not question their valor and experience, he simply could not quite accept them as real officers. And Riley, the horrible example of a self-styled "field soldier" who had won a commission, was breaking arrest.

For all Crann's insistence that finding the source of Andug's guns would not and could not get the charges withdrawn, Riley still gambled, and so he followed Crazy Tom, mimicking his gait, trying even to think like a madman, a sunshiner, a market hunter who kept four native wives, and yet was not a Moslem.

Crazy Tom entered the tangle of nipa-thatched shacks that sprawled along the waterfront, alternating with tin-roofed *tiendas* and copra storehouses. Mud splashed under the sunshiner's heavy tread. Dogs yapped; mangy, starved creatures drawn by the smell of blood from the freshly killed game. Flies buzzed about Crazy Tom and the deer, but he ignored them and the dogs as well.

The garbage and offal under each shack had a stench that drowned the reek of the waterfront, and the odor of copra, and of rotting pearl shell in the vintas that were moored along the quay. Their masts and raking yards were black against the red sky, and their brown crews strutted about town. Women and naked children milled about, going from one open front market to the other.

Riley edged away from a tub of *guinamos*. In spite of all the spices and bay leaves, that mess of pickled fish had the foulest odor in the Islands. The natives loved the tang, and once Riley had eaten a portion, rather than offend a local *datu*. No one had ever decorated him for that feat.

Crazy Tom, now surrounded by the women of the "coast" Moros, and the wives of the local sunshiners, was hanging the deer to the bamboo roof support of the open front stall which he shared with Lin Fu, the Chinese butcher, as part-time tenant.

The squaws chattered, pointing. Tom grunted, the big *sundang* rose and fell, and the customers caught the chunks he lopped off. In a few minutes, nothing remained but a gory tangle of guts and other odds and ends, evenly divided between the dirty table and the crowd of growling dogs. It reminded Riley pretty much of the battle of Mount Bagsak, after the jackass batteries had shelled the Moro outlaws, who, refusing to surrender, fought it out to a finish in the extinct crater. And now Datu Andug, patiently collecting guns from smugglers who must come from the Borneo Coast, seemed to be preparing to duplicate Datu Ali's bloody revolt.

When Tom had thrust the last peseta into the side pocket of his ragged pants, Riley stepped from the corner post of the shop and gestured toward Wing Lee's *tienda*.

"Come on, I'm buying a drink."

Tom stared, dull-eyed, and backed away. Years of drunkenness, of jungle solitude, of ostracism by his own kind, had made him wary of white people. He muttered behind his dirty red mask, and pulled it up a little higher, concealing the barely visible end of the ugly purple scar that reached slantwise to the hair just above his ear. Riley had never gotten a fair look at the man's right cheek and jaw, but a glimpse had been enough, people would stare.

"How about a drink, Tom?" he repeated, with all his Irish persuasion.

Tom grunted, nodded. "Aw right, *teniente.*" And now there was half-brightness in his eyes, for he began to remember the only white man who had drunk with him since he had become a sunshiner.

The walk down the main street was ticklish work, and Riley's recklessness was not equal to keeping him from uncomfortable tension.

One provost guard would upset everything. Once, a native policeman in khaki stared for a moment, then hastily turned away and darted down a side street. He must have recognized Riley, but it was none of his business, a white officer breaking arrest. Yet he might make a report to Headquarters, just to forestall a future disturbance.

Wing Lee's place was perhaps thirty feet long, and little over twenty wide; its bamboo framework, sides and roof, were thatched with nipa palm, and the floor was of hard packed earth. One door opened to the street, the other to the beach. For the rest, there was a zinc-topped bar, four or five yards long, and half a dozen small, greasy tables.

Wing clasped his two hands and bowed double. "Velly glad see you, *teniente.* Lo, Tom. Catchee dlink? Velly nice fire, velly nice, burn up Ah Chin's place." He cackled, and pointed to his own lamps. "Too high up, *teniente,* no throw-ee lamp!"

"Make it whiskey, Wing. Old Crow, understand?"

"Ol' Clow, hab got, catchee, chop-chop."

He was proud of his English, and would not dream of using Spanish or Moro. As he trotted to the bar, Riley went to the table in the furthest corner. Like the others, it had a top that was solidly carved with dates, initials, Gibson girls, and Indian chiefs; all the work of soldiers, sunshiners, copra traders, and pearlers; and by the time Wing touched light to the two hanging lamps, the customers began drifting in.

Riley kept his back to them, and they ignored Crazy Tom. After the first round, which was on the house, for Wing insisted on being grateful for a bit of accidental arson, the lieutenant called for a bottle.

As he refilled the glasses, he asked, "You sell any deer up in the hills?"

Tom lifted the lower corner of his mask, and downed the drink with not enough exposure of his mouth to give more than a hint of the scar. "Uh, plenty. To Tsang Wu. Got a good *tienda.*"

Riley knew the place, having marched through with a detachment, months before Andug had seriously considered revolt. Throughout the jungle of the interior, there were Chinese traders; it was important to know which one Tom favored.

"Smoke?" Riley produced a pack of Sweet Caporals.

"Nuh-uh."

"Rather have *dobes*? Or a cigar?"

"Nuh-uh. Don't smoke." He spat out a well worn cud which, kept far back in his cheek, did not interfere with drinking. "Chew," he said, and fumbled for a package of Five Brothers.

That was another thing to remember. Tom stumbled to his feet. "Catalina raises hell when I get in too late." He giggled. "Chased me all the way to the bundoks with a bolo, one time. So I beat hell out of her. Uh-huh. Got to beat squaws. White women too, I guess."

"Come on, come on now, sit down, it's whiskey you're drinking, Tom."

Riley held the bottle as if it were the crown of England; the stuff cost ten times what native gin did. The sunshiner shrugged, slumped back in his chair. "Lieutenant," he stuttered. "Lieutenant—"

"Cut out the frills, hell, didn't I tell you I used to be a buck private in the old Seventh? I'm liable to be something like that again, looks like they're fixing to bob-tail me for starting that fire and socking Balabac Charley. For a plugged peso, I'd go over the hill, and to hell with 'em!"

Tom was goggle-eyed. "Go over the hill," he mumbled, "and show 'em. I did, only they sent a patrol after me."

"How do you manage to get along with the Moros?"

"Aw—anybody can—it's easy—huh—just don't pay any attention to 'em. Leave their women alone—buy one for yourself—for some calico—and canned salmon—hell, I get along, don't I?"

So Riley listened to the details of how to go native and without being sliced in half, or tied to the horns of a fighting buffalo. Tom's answers were perfectly logical, except that they omitted the basic principle: a man first had to be established as thoroughly crazy.

Riley thought. "Poor devil doesn't realize he hasn't got regulation equipment above the ears."

Then Crazy Tom made gurgling sounds, and fell face forward across the table. Riley beckoned to Wing, and said, "Keep him dead drunk, I'll pay." He handed him a thick roll of twenty peso bills. "And there's more when I come back. Tie him up, don't let him get away till I come back."

"Me sawee plenty."

"That's not all. Help me carry him to your shack. I want to swap clothes with him, I want his shotgun, too. Understand? Don't let him get away! Or I'll take you to pieces."

Wing didn't understand anything except money, but he said, "Me sawee plenty, you catchee Clazy Tom's woman?"

"No, I am not interested in his girls! Now get busy, and shut up."

"Me sawee plenty."

An hour later, Riley was heading for the jungle. His life depended on a madman and a Chinaman. As long as there were not two Crazy Toms in the hills at once, there was a chance of spying out the country, learning the location of that one among the hundreds of coves where gun runners could land on the jagged Mindanao coast.

CHAPTER III

The first mile up the trail that wound into the Ambol country was easy enough, and leaving by night was quite in accord with the character Riley had assumed. He had Crazy Tom's jack-light on his hat, ready for deer hunting; he carried the sunshiner's old shotgun across the crook of his arm.

With each uphill step, the air became hotter and more humid. The jungle's silence was pointed by furtive stirrings, chirps and twitters. Monkeys, always wary, shifted their perches, and chattered warnings to sleepier companions. Once, the sharp bladed *cogon* brass rustled, and Riley caught the phosphorescence of a deer's eyes.

The long thorns of *julat anay*—the "wait a bit" creeper—raked his legs. *Bejuco* vines set traps for his feet, and Crazy Tom's rope-soled *alpargatas* were another handicap, though their silence would later be a help. It was a stiff climb, a slow, all-night ascent, unbroken except for Riley's halts to rest. Swarming mosquitoes kept him from napping more than a few minutes in any place. And when the sun finally rose from behind the peaks about Lake Lanao, he had covered only a short distance in an airline.

He heard the animated chatter of the monkeys and knew that they were as glad as he was at having lived through another jungle night. Fresh water was not far ahead; he could make camp, cook some coffee, and rest a while.

Then, as he rounded the turn, he saw a file of Moros: at least forty of them, and strangers to the district. They wore the peculiar, floppy turbans of the tribesmen from beyond Lake Lanao. They were not Datu Andug's men, who had long accepted Crazy Tom as one under Allah's protection.

Their unexpected presence indicated that Andug's deviltry had gone much further than anyone at Headquarters had suspected; the trouble-maker was calling for allies, and the presumption was that only an offer of guns and cartridges would have induced those Lanao men to team up with the forces of a rival chieftain. But Riley's first thought was, "How the hell do I convince these fellows that I'm loco?"

The strangers had come for a prolonged visit. Their women led the way, carrying pots and baskets on their heads. Their black hair and their brown bodies gleamed from palm oil. The reek of this cosmetic blended with the smoky tang exhaled by their close-fitting red *sarongs*: they had only a little while previous been sleeping beside smudge fires, as partial protection against mosquitoes.

The procession was heading for a fork that led northeast, toward Datu Andug's *cotta*. Already, the women were chattering, and the men were running forward, drawing *krisses*. It was not cowardice that made these fellows put their wives in the advance guard; it was plain logic, for, since women have neither souls nor sense, no one kills them, and thus they can give the warriors warning of ambush.

Riley had one move: to convince them he was crazy, and before they sliced him in half. While he could make himself understood in the Lanao dialect, this was not an occasion for logic and argument. So he advanced, very straight instead of slouching. He held the old shotgun as if it were a drum major's baton. And while a comb and some tissue paper would have helped him imitate field music, he did very well behind his dirty red mask. He shouted a command, gave the gun a spin, and went on with his vocal imitation of a military band, with *oomp-pabs* worked into his droning of the melody.

A one man band in the hill country was unique, to say the least; yet every Moro, trying to bushwhack a sentry and steal a rifle, had spied enough near military posts to understand Riley's pantomime.

The men with the drawn *krisses* lowered their weapons. The women began edging back, and into the *tigbau* grass; they spoke to the waiting warriors. Riley could now see the wrinkle of scowling faces, the fire of narrowed eyes, the play of sunlight on oiled skin. Only a few more yards to go.

He made a brave flourish with his baton, and halted, smartly, one-two. Then a command, and a hand salute, which he held as he whistled "To the Colors." For good measure, he made the four *burrrnps* of drums rolled in honor of a visiting general.

Compliments rendered to a visiting dignitary, he made a grandiloquent gesture, said in Lanao, "Welcome to my capital!" Without waiting for any return salute, he marched on, carrying his gun once more as a hunter.

They did not cut him down. The fighting men scrambled to avoid even the touch of his elbow. But getting that file of forty-odd Moros at his back took longer than Riley's first three enlistments in the ranks. When he reached a high spot from which he could watch the visitors swinging into the trail toward Andug's *cotta*, he slumped down under a tree, and sat there for some minutes before he noticed the biting of ants.

He felt sick, and he looked it. He said, unsteadily, "If I'd only had a bugle, I could have made the set look and sound like something."

While he had sold hostile strangers the idea that he was crazy, he could not shake off the fear that these strangers might, with their animal intuition, begin to wonder if they had not been taken in: simply because, unlike Andug's people, they had not learned to take Crazy Tom for granted. He had to get away from the main trail, lest he meet other delegations to Andug's fortified village; a one man band might fail to convince the next party.

Soon he was following a branch which wound through dense jungle. The trees were overgrown with purple cattalyas and white butterfly orchids; the lovely parasites nodded in the humid breeze, like well groomed women confident of their charm. Monkeys made faces at him, and shook their fists at the scolding parrots, far overhead. And then he heard the booming of kettle-shaped Moro gongs. Andug was welcoming his visitors.

Riley halted near a small stream, and with his heavy *sundang* he cut bamboo and *cogon* grass for a lean-to. He would spend the day sleeping, for the all-night climb had thoroughly tired him. Regardless of the importance of his mission, he had first to kill a deer, and carry on with Crazy Tom's routine. To go near the Moro *cotta* without game would be fatally out of character.

Just for luck, he cut a heap of thorny creepers with which to make a barrier about his shelter. Then he opened a can of salmon from his pack, and cooked a pannikin of coffee. Within an hour after making camp, Riley was asleep; fatigue overcame his impatience, and the thumping of Andug's gongs did their part.

Around ten o'clock that night the mountain chill awakened him. He was shivering when he pushed the thorn barrier aside and crept from his shelter.

Stalking deer was simple enough, though as a sport it was more like assassination. With shotgun and jacklight, Riley picked his way back toward a burned-off area which, freed of the tall *cogan* grass, invited deer. They liked the new crop, which was tender and juicy.

He stepped slowly over the black clearing, swinging his jacklight beam from side to side. Presently, two luminous eyes gleamed ahead of him. He advanced, deliberately. Curiosity kept the animal fixed in place, fascinated if not actually blinded and bewildered.

Riley raised his gun and cut loose with the charge of buckshot.

Simple butchery. Simple as the way the Moros cut down a sentry, or a coconut planter, or a Christian native.

So, an hour after leaving camp, Riley was back again. With a flexible strand of *bajuco* he hoisted the little buck to the limb of a tree, out of reach of the ants. Left anywhere near the ground, the carcass would have been cleaned to the bones, and long before dawn.

In the morning, Riley shouldered the sixty-pound deer, and worked his way back to the main trail. At the fork, he followed the course taken by the visiting Moros he had met perhaps twenty-four hours earlier. Hampered by gun and venison, Riley began to appreciate Crazy Tom's industry in keeping four wives.

When he finally came near enough to Andug's *cotta* to smell the rotting offal, and the lines where the fighting stallions were kept, he saw Tsang Wu's *tienda*, which stood in a level clearing. Aside from being *cogon* thatched, it was similar to the one where he had left Crazy Tom, in Bacolod.

Nearby was a lean-to, where the Chino's Moro wife squatted beside the cooking fire. Though Tsang Wu was an infidel, and as much the enemy of Allah as any white man, the Chino's native wife won him tolerance.

For all the ventilation, the place had the high odor of dried fish, *guinamos*, and, worst of all, durian. Riley stood there, staring stupidly, which was easy, since his eyes could not at once accustom themselves to the shade of the *tienda*.

Tsang leaped from his seat behind the littered counter, and snatched up a "working" bolo; though designed for household service, such as cutting bamboo and beheading chickens, it was versatile enough. "Whatchee want?"

Riley grunted. "Sell meat."

The Chino looked puzzled, then lowered his bolo, and grinned broadly. This last was easy, for his face was round, gleaming, and there was lots of it.

"Oh—Tom—you fool me, come back too quick."

In his haste, Riley had not learned all about Crazy Tom's routine. Apparently the sunshiner, after selling Tsang a buck, moved on to the next hunting ground, on the Malabang trail, instead of making a follow-up sale.

The Chino, still chuckling, went on, "Wassa malla, mebbeso flaid see Ca'mencita, likkee Conchita mo' bettah?"

This was dangerous ground. He wasn't even sure where Conchita lived, and what was more, he didn't want to stumble anywhere into the vicinity of the lady's shack, somewhere on the plateau. Each wife had a battle-axe of a *duena*, nominally a companion, but actually, a guardian. Conchita might overlook a bit of mistaken identity but the *duena* would not. Old and ugly, she would be resentful enough of a shapely young trick to watch every move.

Riley answered, "Nuh-uh. Datu Andug—lots of company—need plenty meat, huh? You can sell, huh?"

"My savvee plenty." Tsang laughed until his belly shook his blue shirt, which hung outside his green silk pants. "Velly flighten, you come back too quick."

The Chino meant that he had for a moment feared that some other white hunter, wearing a mask, had come up for a bit of robbery. Yet that made no sense, for with a village of warlike Moros less than half a mile away, Crazy Tom was the only white man who would dare come so near. But then, Tsang's dress and his fat face showed that he was prosperous enough to be wary of the most improbable threat to his hoard.

Ten to one, the hill tribes had been bringing him bits of gold dust, or perhaps some pearls, from the coast.

Riley set his shotgun against a bamboo upright, and dropped the carcass of the deer. The bargaining, however, had no chance to start. A long shadow reached in through the door. Riley turned, and saw a man whose height, unusual for a Moro, identified him. He was close to six feet, and his curved nose proudly advertised Arab blood, which the Malay race especially reveres. His *sarong* and turban were of silk, fine and heavy, colored red and black.

This was Datu Andug, who stood there with one hand on the silver hilt of his *kris*. Riley grinned foolishly behind his mask, and pointed at the butchered buck. The Moro's nostrils flared like a stallion's, and he backed away, to avoid contamination from a madman's nearness. There was more than revulsion in his expression; and since a chief is a degree nearer to Allah than ordinary men, he might go for that *kris*.

With war brewing, Andug would be suspicious even of madmen.

"You like?" Riley asked in the Maguindanao dialect, and pointed.

It was very plain that there was something which Andug violently disliked. And Riley knew that he could never reach his shotgun before the *kris* got into action.

Andug spat within an inch of Riley's toe, and stepped to the counter. He spoke to Tsang in a bastard Chinese patois that the disguised officer could not understand. Tsang handed him a packet of cigarettes, and made a gesture toward Riley. Then he said in English, "You no 'flaid, I tell Andug you velly nice man, you no likee soldier, you no talkee."

Riley mumbled, "That's good. I just hunt for a living."

The *datu*, apparently mollified by Tsang's interposition, tore open the pack of *Hebras*. "Smoke," he invited, in Maguindanao.

Riley readied for the pack, and had almost brushed a corner of his mask aside when he remembered that Crazy Tom did not smoke. His eagerness to make the most out of Andug's amiability had recoiled. Worse than that, he had fumbled for a pack of matches.

When he realized his error, he grunted, fumbled in his other pocket. He put the cigarette in the corner of his mouth, and with both hands digging, he located his jackknife.

Then he split the smoke, and grinned. "I don't smoke, I chew," he said, and thrust the tobacco under his tongue.

Andug eyed him intently, then stalked out, where his parasol bearer and a groom waited with the stallion which the datu rode on ceremonial occasions. Riley hoped that his error might be attributed to the confusion that is bound to muddle any ordinary man when a chieftain personally offers a smoke, but he lost no time in pocketing Tsang's cash, and heading out to hunt again.

CHAPTER IV

Riley had ceased to love his work; all day he admitted that, and before mid-afternoon, he also realized that he was thoroughly frightened. It was not that choked and sick feeling a John-recruit gets the first time some Mausers pop from ambush, and a buddy topples over, right beside you. It was not that instant of paralysis you get the first time—or the tenth time!—the *cogon* grass rustles, and a swarm of Moros rush a column, with *kris* swishing and every man yelling, "O-o-o-ah buguy!"

What had Riley by the throat that long day was uncertainty, a strange and new feeling. Andug might want to gain "face" by killing a madman, and again, he might fear to kill one, lest his followers become uneasy. Andug might be having a conflict of qualms, just from wondering whether Crazy Tom would let slip some fatal trifle, in the market at Bacolod, about having seen Lanao Moros so close to the coast; wondering whether the danger of letting him live was greater than that of finishing him.

When a Moro becomes introspective, he has to do something about it, and the only thing that comes to his mind is to draw a *kris* and start slashing, which is what makes him one of the world's best fighting men.

To keep from thinking too much, Riley built a super-fancy shelter for the coming night. After cutting a supply of bamboo and *cogon* grass, he sliced off a length of wiry *bajuco*, and split off some strips with which to lash the grass thatch, and secure the skeleton. Then he took the feathery branches from the crest of each bamboo stalk, lopped off the leaves, and staked the thorny pieces down in a tight hedge about the lean-to. Raiding Moros couldn't get through such a barrier without awakening him.

This was sheer panic, and he knew it. There was some sense in a company hedging itself in, but if a handful of Andug's men came to get him, they would get him, regardless of his being warned of their approach. Riley would be afraid until they arrived. After that, for a little while, he would be a fighting man again.

He wanted a smoke, but he did not dare risk it, so he chewed sweat soaked "Five Brothers," and waited for darkness. The increasing noise of the Moro *cotta* told him that Andug's men were whooping it up, while the elders and junior *datus* squatted in the big house and chewed betel and spat as they planned.

He shot his deer.

He did very little sleeping. And when he roasted the buck's liver, he knew why it was so hard to swallow. He was too worried.

And when the sun rose, Riley shouldered the carcass and headed for Andug's *cotta*. Being worked over with a *kris* was better than trying to decide what a *datu* and a Chino were thinking.

But Riley's wire-edged nerves did finally help him. He was perhaps halfway to his destination, when he saw the mass of *julat anay* that blocked his path. Thorn brush was just routine on the infrequently used trails. He paused, looking around for footprints, and though he found none, he still did not like that obstacle.

Riley dropped his burden, and cut a length of *cana bojo* about the thickness of his forefinger. That done, he used a strip of rattan to tie his *sundang* to the light piece of cane. Standing well to one side, he slashed at the thorny entanglement. There was a sound like the twang of a bowstring. A hunting spear shot across the trail, waist high; the wrought iron head buried half its length in the tough trunk of a *kemagon* tree.

If he had tried to kick the *julat anay* out of his way, as he had often enough done before, the spear would have impaled him. Was this a general precaution, or did it have a personal touch? It is hard luck, it is hoodoo for a Moro to kill a man whose wits are with Allah, but if a madman just blunders into a spear trap, where will the curse land?

Maybe on the spear. Maybe on the warrior who, obeying the *datu's* order, had had no idea as to why his chief had wanted traps set out. There was no telling just what fine turns Moro logic might take.

Then Riley straightened up, and grinned. "Why, the stupid *bugao!* That's a dead giveaway, he still thinks I'm Crazy Tom, or he'd've sent the boys to *kris* me!"

Riley was a fighting man again. He spent some minutes working the spear head from the tough *kemagon* trunk. If there was a curse on the weapon that had tried for a madman's life, he wanted it, just for fun. He began humming an old ballad that dated back to "Bridge of Spain" days, before his time: and he fitted the *datu's* name into it.

> *"Here's to Audug, the son of a—*
> *May he have lice and fever and the dobie itch—"*

With the sixty-pound buck, and Crazy Tom's shotgun, Riley already had a handful, but it took him only a moment to find a way of taking the spear along. He lashed the animal's legs together in pairs and swung the carcass across his back, so that the legs reached forward, on each side. With his burden so balanced, he worked the spear through the lashings; thus, one hand on the shaft that passed across his chest did double duty, leaving the other free for the shotgun.

He did not pause at Tsang's *tienda.* Now that the build-up was completed, Riley meant business. And when he reached the clearing in which the fortified village stood, he saw that he had rightly interpreted the sounds and signs. Datu Andug had a swarm of visitors, and he had made lordly preparations for their entertainment.

The *cotta* was surrounded by a moat, and a fourfold palisade made of bamboo stalks better than six inches in diameter and lashed together with rattan. Behind this barrier of sharpened stakes was a wall of earth, pierced at intervals by bamboo tubes: these were the ports through which flintlock and matchlock muskets were pointed, as well as the muzzle loading brass *lantakas.* But these were the routine details of a *cotta,* and Riley was more interested in a bowl-shaped depression which was perhaps a hundred yards from the fort.

The ground had been cleared of its natural tangle of vines to make room for pony races, stallion fights, and carabao fights. And all around this natural oval, women and boys and slaves were at work, building shacks and lean-tos. The entire clearing swarmed with visitors.

Dogs yapped at the heels of the horse ridden by a newly arrived dignitary, and naked brats milled about. The harem, as usual, went ahead, and on foot. And in the excitement of greeting a newcomer, no one paid any attention to the man they assumed was Crazy Tom, bending under a load of venison.

The visiting datu reined in his under-sized stallion, and the fifty odd fighting men who followed him halted, not far from the bamboo bridge which spanned the dry moat. Women and children crowded the parapet, leaning over the sharpened bamboo stakes to look at the imposing stranger. The gate was blocked by Andug's men, all wearing their newest turbans and sarongs, and loaded down with krisses and daggers.

Those at work building shelters dropped their tools and gathered about the retinue. Riley had already recognized the flopping turbans; this datu had come from beyond Lanao, forty miles away. The fifty men behind him were only a fraction of his force; these were just his personal guard, his "household troops," so to speak. And already, Riley knew why Sahipa waited at the gate of the *cotta*.

He was too important to go in to greet Andug. He sat his runty stallion, and pretended to ignore the excitement. He kept his wrinkled face blank, and held his head high; his white hair was bound in a knot that peeped through his turban, and his cheeks and throat and arms were corded with old scars, white against his brown skin. Sahipa, the old man of the mountains, was almost a sultan; the big yellow parasol which an attendant carried had a gilt fringe, and the staff was overlaid with gold leaf.

Riley was thinking, "Sahipa's here because Andug has or can get so many guns that there'll be enough for all."

The sensible thing to do was to leave while there was a chance, but while returning and reading the social register of Inner Mindanao, as represented at Andug's *cotta*, would warn Crann, Riley was not certain whether that would dispose of the court-martial.

Then the crowd at the gate parted, and Andug came out, followed by his parasol bearer, servants, and his retinue of *datus*. He would have been imposing had his horse not been too small for him. The shaggy little brute snorted, tossed his head, shook the red tassels of the bridle; the reins tinkled from their silver decorations. For all his runtiness, he kept his tall rider from seeming ridiculous.

Riley was impressed when Andug reined in, at the outer end of the bridge, and raised one hand. *"Tabay, sultan!"* he said. "Greeting, Sultan Sahipa!"

Then Riley's glance shifted to the saddle. It was made like a sawbuck, with very little padding, top or bottom. It was bad for the rider, and worse for the mount. Instead of stirrup leathers, there were lengths of braided *bajuco*, knotted at the lower end. Andug gripped the cord, just above the knot, between his large toe and the next one. Like all Moros, he rode only for short distances, and then only on occasions of ceremony.

Riley, ex-trooper of the Seventh Cavalry, ceased to be impressed with either *datu* or sultan. "Depress your heels, you bastards!" he said to himself, thinking of the instruction he had given many a John-recruit. "Get your legs back!"

And the spear in his hand gave him confidence. These mountaineers were superstitious and they couldn't ride for sour apples. If a trumpeter sounded "Charge," they'd be clawing dirt the first jump. That settled it. He wasn't going back until he knew where the guns were.

Then Andug put on the final touch of ceremony. One of his men had a battered bugle, picked up after some skirmish with white troops or brown, and now he was giving it hell. Whatever he was trying to play, made no difference, but the intent was plain—this was American style field music to salute a sultan who would soon be using American style ammunition to clean up the infidels on the coast.

Both dignitaries were heartily sick of their murderous saddles, and at the bugle tooting, Sahipa dismounted. This last frill touched him, and so he unbent enough to be the first to get on foot.

Andug practically slid his stallion from under him. Two grooms fought the shaggy devil to keep him from bolting, and while everyone was dodging, Riley ploughed through the crowd, straight for the two chieftains. He dumped the deer on the ground, pointed with the spear. "Present for Andug."

There was a snarl, and the whisper of a *kris* slipping out of a wooden scabbard. A man yelled at Sahipa, "No, he's crazy!" Andug eyed the spear in Riley's hand. He eyed the butchered buck. He said, "Thank you, but get away from me." Then the *datu* gestured to Sahipa and toward the bridge. As host, Andug had to go first. The warriors followed. Riley, staring dumbly about him, tagged after, with the women and the dogs.

Now that Sahipa had arrived, the council would get to business, and with luck, Riley would learn about the landing of the ammunition, and where the *cargadores* would pick it up. He needed luck, needed it as he never had before; but he was too close to victory to hesitate.

CHAPTER V

Riley moped around, feigning the dull, shifting attention of the man he impersonated. His interest seemed most centered on the red earthenware pots which steamed over crackling fires of bamboo joints, but as the day wore on, he went to watch the carabao fights. These combats between 1,200 pound buffalos were sluggish affairs, a head to head butting, a pushing back and forth as the heavy, downward drooping horns clashed and locked. Broad beamed, short legged, short necked, these brutes depended on weight; there was a lot of grunting, a ploughing up of dirt as one forced the other back.

And they spent much of their time blowing, glaring at each other, until the shouts and tail twistings and spear proddings of the spectators made them lumber toward each other. As sport, it was dreary enough, but to the Moros, a fight was a fight. And presently, more exciting battles were arranged in the newly cleared arena.

Two rival stallions were brought out, and at the first challenging snort, Moros poured out of the shacks where they had been chatting and spitting. Some wore tight fitting silk pants, red or yellow or green, instead of *sarongs*; all wore their *krisses* or long-bladed *sundangs*, and quite a few came running with their most prized possession: fighting cocks in wicker cages.

But now, the stallions had everyone's attention, and the spectators howled and cheered as the shaggy little fellows, scarcely twelve hands high, reared and squealed, striking and biting. They wheeled, they feinted; sometimes Riley was certain that they blocked and parried. Chunks of hide flew, and the combatants dripped blood from neck and shoulder and sides.

Blood-soaked earth spattered the spectators, and flying foam from the snapping jaws splashed them. Both were blowing, and neither was steady on his feet, but they knew no more about quitting than the Moros did.

Riley turned and shuffled away from the group. He loved horses, he hated to see them baited to death. Each jaw snap and each hoof thump hurt him. But more than that, leaving a good fight proved conclusively that he did not have all of his original equipment. So he sat down in the shade of the wall, and nodded while flies buzzed about him. After all, there would be no plans to overhear as long as the fights and gambling went on.

Yet his loitering about the *cotta* served one purpose: no one was wondering, uneasily, whether he might be heading back to Parang with a muddled bit of gossip. And the dogs were becoming used to him. They liked the scent of deer's blood that had dried on his dirty shirt. Later, a lot might depend on getting around quietly.

Riley avoided the cock fights, for these often ended in free for all battles so brisk that no one had time to decide who was and who was not a madman. So, after begging for a chunk of meat out of one of the big red pots, he found himself a spot inside the *cotta*, not far from the *lantaka* that guarded the right of the gate.

There he waited for night, and the end of the fiesta, and the council that should follow, when the *datus* met in Andug's big house. It was larger than the others; it had a veranda, and a reception room, and the rattan walls had patterns worked into their basket weave.

Under each house, a smudge fire smoked. The fumes rose between the bamboo floor slats, and to a degree protected the natives from the malaria mosquitoes. Riley could do nothing but slap and squirm. However, the smudges finally did help him. That was when, satisfied that the village was asleep, he began to work his way toward Andug's house; the low hanging fumes kept him from being conspicuous to any of the restless visitors who slept outside the gate.

There was just enough sky glow to make the smoke a vague, blurred gray. Each shack seemed a solid black mass, with the stilts looming up in front of him, abruptly.

Once, a Moro came clumsily down the notched trunk that led to the ground. The fellow was half asleep, and presumably going to get a drink, but this reasonable guess did not make Riley any more at ease. For moments, he crouched among the refuse that rotted under the house whose smudge concealed and choked him.

Crazy Tom, stumbling about by day was natural enough, and so was Crazy Tom, hunting by night in the jungle, but stealth in the village was something else. That Moros will not hurt a madman is a general rule, not an infallible law of nature.

But he did at last reach the *datu's* house. A stallion tethered there snorted. There was a jingle of accoutrements, a dull gleam of metal. For a moment, Riley thought that the presence of the horse was Sultan Sahipa's final touch of formality. Then he distinguished the man who crouched to one side of the ladder to the entrance. The wavering light that came through the door made several details clear enough.

The man had his *sarong* pulled up over his head, for added protection against mosquitoes. Across his knees, he had a drawn *kris*, and near him was a bugle. This was Andug's personal attendant, waiting to escort some important caller from the conference.

Above, men were speaking, and of course, spitting. The bamboo floor creaked. Probably a slave was passing around more betel nut. The preliminary harangues were over; there were none of the usual exhortations to whip the minor *datus* to the desperation needed for a raid on a coast town protected by a Scout battalion. Riley edged slowly under the floor. Betel-charged saliva plopping down between the slats guided him, and the torches in the room above made thin bands on the ground.

This was a ticklish spot.

"Do not worry about the rifles, Sultan Sahipa," a man was saying. "With your pearls and my gold dust, we can pay for them. The three *prahus* from Borneo will land at Tanjong Merah. The Chino has arranged all that."

The Chino? That must be Tsang Wu.. It was now clear to Riley why the storekeeper had been so startled at seeing a masked white man so soon after Crazy Tom's departure for Bacolod; and just about as clear why Andug had made a personal call at the *tienda*, instead of sending a messenger.

Delivering guns to Moros was like trying to hand steaks to a tiger. Tsang Wu and his friends from Borneo would have to be careful lest the weapons be seized before the payment was received. All this would take care, move and counter-move against trickery. Riley pondered on this as the voices blurred, submerged by a general muttering and spitting and stirring about. Then one bit came in clear: "I should have cut him down, madman or not." That would be Sahipa, who had half drawn his *kris*, that morning.

Another *datu* protested, "Too many of our men would be worried. It was better that you did not."

There were plans for the surprise attack on Bacolod; men rushing from the hills behind the garrison; others, hidden in Parang Barrio, coming from cover; and all this timed to accord with the landing of those who would arrive in fishing *prahus* and pearling boats. Altogether, it was a sound plan. With only *kris* and *kampilan*, such a concerted attack would be beaten off after heavy casualties among the Christian villagers of Bacolod and Parang; but with rifles, the swarm of Moros would have a fair chance of swamping the battalion of Scouts.

That would be bad, but the moral effect of such a victory would be worse. Riley needed no further details. He did not know exactly where Tanjong Merah was, and perhaps the charts did not designate the "red cape" by its native name, but there was a chance of breaking up the formation. If he got back to Bacolod before the guns were landed and distributed.

Slipping out of the *cotta* was slow work. Riley's rope-soled *alpargatas* were worn thin, and while they made for silence, they did not stand up like service shoes. For a fast march to the coast, he had to have the extra pair he had left in camp, along with his reserve rations.

The council broke up before he reached the corner of the adjoining house. Sultan Sahipa and the visiting *datus* came to the veranda; attendants lighted their way with torches. When the man with the bugle rose from beside the steps, Riley crouched in the shadows, and for a while he forgot the mosquitoes.

The sultan had not brought his horse, so Andug and the minor *datus* walked with him to the house reserved for him and his women. The chatter of the dignitaries half aroused the neighbors; there were stirrings and sleepy mutterings, and awakened dogs growled and yapped a little.

Dawn was not far off when the *cotta* was again asleep. Riley's face itched and burned from countless bites, and he shivered from more than the mountain chill. But finally he cleared the gate, and worked his way past the encampment outside the palisade.

At Tsang Wu's *tienda*, he swung into the jungle, and his progress was all the slower for remembering the trap he had escaped on his approach to the *cotta*. Spear thrust ahead of him, he felt his way along the trail, for with all the dawn sounds, and the chilly mists that preceded sunrise, it was still dark in the jungle.

Soon he heard monkeys stir about in the branches, and felt the breeze. Bit by bit, a murky light picked out tree trunks, and presently a red ray reached across the trail. The sun had come up over the distant peaks, beyond Lake Lanao.

Then, as he neared his shelter, he caught the smoky odor of men who had lain over a smudge all night. Some *cogon* grass stirred, and he saw a splash of red, a blot of yellow. He was within sight of his shelter when the Moros popped up, on both sides, and in front, blocking the approach to the clearing.

Riley thrust his spear head into the ground. No use explaining that possession of that weapon proved how Allah guarded him; if they did not get the point, the jig was up. They closed in, slowly, silently except for the crackle of leaves and the rustic of grass. Those coming from the clearing exchanged glances. Riley wondered if someone had been picked by lot to risk the curse.

One of the Moros said, "Go back. You stay at the *cotta*."

The horseshoe of drawn *krisses* contracted, and came nearer. They were not striking, but if he did not retreat, a point would sink home.

"Want to see Conchita," he mumbled. "My woman."

"You see Tsang Wu first," the spokesman said. "Later, you see woman."

He grinned, showing betel-blackened teeth, but that effort was forced. None of the others spoke. They did not like dealing with a madman, yet they had their orders. Riley was to be detained until the guns were landed, and the raid

135

was under way. Once that was done, he was harmless, and in the meanwhile, Allah would not send a custom-built curse.

These men were shaky, nervous; a false move would crack their last restraining qualms. Tsang Wu, Riley began to suspect, had not been entirely convinced by that first meeting, and had in his Chino patois advised Andug to wait and see, to play it softly.

CHAPTER VI

The continued games and amusements in the cotta did not interest Riley. His captors neither bound nor guarded him; they gave him full liberty, except that there was no chance of slipping into the jungle. Freedom was what made the day a torment, for he did not know what to expect next. Anticipating a clash with Tsang Wu's Mongolian wit had been bad enough, but it was worse, waiting for the Chino to appear and to settle it, one way or another.

Andug and Sahipa circulated about the *cotta* and the camp outside. Both had their saddled stallions; sometimes they rode, but most of the time grooms led the mounts, half a dozen paces behind their respective masters. And the *datu's* bugler trailed along with the others who made up the retinues of the two dignitaries.

Tsang Wu, Riley decided, was even now arranging for the munitions to land. He might have left the day before. What worried Riley the most was the words of the Moro who had led the party which had snared him: "You see Tsang Wu first." They must all have known that the Chino was gone. Apparently, their idea was to let hours of increasing tension crack their captive. Crazy Tom's gin-blurred mind grasped only a few primitive notions. Nothing worried him, and he had not the slightest concept of danger, whereas an impostor, however rugged his nerves, could endure just so much anticipation. This became plain as Riley found it increasingly difficult to regard his surroundings with feigned stupidity.

Wherever he went, he was under the increasingly pointed scrutiny of Datu Andug, of Sultan Sahipa, or the minor *datus* who followed the leaders from carabao fight to fencing matches, from stallion fights to feasting. No one spoke, no one made threatening gestures; but those hard, bright eyes became sharper, sharper, boring into the dirty red mask. Riley could now feel their thoughts as plainly as if they had said, "You're not Crazy Tom."

To jerk the handkerchief from his face would really prove nothing. Tom, sensitive about his ugly scar, would hardly have explained why he kept his features so well covered. And back there at Bacolod, he had told Riley how simple it was to mingle with the Moros. Not realizing he was crazy, it never occurred to him that there was any special reason for his immunity. And now Andug had devised a third degree.

It all had a Chinese flavor; Moro cunning takes less subtle twists. That was why dread of Tsang Wu's ultimate return became overpowering. At times Riley became light headed. He had to fight the urge to dash for the jungle. He began to tell himself, "Hell, why wouldn't a fellow that's loco just forget he's under arrest and then check out?"

This was dangerous logic. He knew all too well that once he started, he would display ambition and eagerness that Crazy Tom never did. And stumbling along, casually, would not work. Whenever he tried this, early in the day, men blocked his way with drawn *krisses*; silent, uneasy little men who would themselves go wild if pressed too far.

And somehow, Andug and Sahipa's wandering from point to point showed a pattern and a purpose. Riley could never get from their sight for more than a moment.

His head was beginning to hurt him. Not an ache as from a clouting or too much whiskey; rather, the pain was as if an inner pressure had scrambled his brains and now threatened to pop his skull. His pulse was hammering, hammering, hammering at a crazy rate, and the distended veins at his temples now caused a pain of their own.

The smoke, the dust of the clearing, and all those red and yellow and black turbans began to blend and quiver and whirl. The voices dimmed to a silky whisper, expanded to a rumble, rose to a horrible shrieking and screeching. He was fearfully tired, he was hungry, but most of all, he had waited too many hours for an uncertain threat.

They had taken his shotgun, and though he still had a *sundang*, he knew that he could not check the revolt by making a rush for Andug and Sahipa. He'd never live to scratch either.

Long shadows were marching across the clearing. The day was ending, and so was Riley's endurance. The women were busy at their fires again, and the men who had been watching fights, gathered in groups to squat and chew betel. Concentration on the suspected captive was bound to lag; not much, but enough for a man who took off at a sprint to win a few yards. The idea of winning a race through the approaching darkness was, after all, no wilder than the beginning of Riley's venture. And once the Moros had eaten, they would be handicapped. So he rose from beside the rock where he had squatted, and ambled toward a tree, near the edge of the clearing.

He could feel the eyes that watched him, even when he halted, scratched his head, and finally remembered the pack of "Five Brothers." That, however, was one chew which did not get behind the red mask.

The man who was lumbering into the clearing toward Riley was ragged, dirty, and tired. He had neither shotgun nor jacklight, and instead of a *sundang* thrust into his belt, he had a weapon equally serviceable: a *barong* with a satinwood grip, and a leaf-shaped, eighteen-inch blade. The dull eyes that peered over the top of the new, blue mask were dull, but they lighted a little when he saw Riley.

Something had slipped. Crazy Tom had come to the hills.

The Moros were all talking at once as they closed in on Riley. This was the payoff, and he knew now that he would not run, simply because it would be useless. As he turned and half faced them, he saw the man who ran after Crazy Tom, yelling and waving his arms. It was Tsang Wu, who had seen the sunshiner, and was on his way to spread the news.

Riley was now so calm that he was able to think, "He was here all the time. That proves it was a Chino trick, keeping me here, waiting."

Andug, Sahipa, and their retinues surrounded Tsang Wu, Riley, and Crazy Tom. The tall *datu* snatched the mask from Riley's face. The newly arrived madman made a warding motion to protect his own mask, then said, "Hullo, Lieutenant. Been drunk three-four days. My squaw come and turned me loose. I beat hell out of her."

Tsang Wu's gestures had silenced the Moros. The sunshiner went on, "I knew you went over the hill. I come up to help you get along. Whole damn battalion coming up to get you, you got to move on." That was the longest speech Crazy Tom had made in years. Gratitude for whiskey and friendly words had brought him into the hills to keep a deserter from being arrested. Riley said, "You're sure a real buddy, Tom."

Tsang Wu translated the speech into Maguindanao dialect.

Andug demanded, "You believe this officer is a deserter? An outlaw among his own people? I think he's a spy."

They all respected the Chino's wisdom as to the ways of the white man; and his gun-running had made him important.

The answer was sound: "If a battalion is on the way, as this madman says, it makes no difference what this officer is. Without guns, you will have a hard time facing so many Scouts."

Sahipa said, "Datu Andug, the true madman has helped you. They come into the hills, while we go to the sea for the guns. Meanwhile—" He drew his *kris.* "No, he's your man, you kill him."

Now that they knew who was crazy and who was not, so many Moros seized Riley that he could not have struggled had he tried to. He said to Andug, "No use quarreling. Why don't you draw straws for the honor?"

The Moros cheered. They liked a prisoner who could take it. Andug smiled appreciatively. "In the old days, when all the soldiers were Americanos instead of Visayan monkeys led by a few white men, we would cut you down and start running into the hills. But now, we have time."

"For what, Datu Andug?" Riley knew, and wished that he did not know.

"To stake you to an ant-hill. The last act of our fiesta."

Crazy Tom was not paying any attention. He was busy stuffing another chew into his mouth, for he could carry only one idea at a time. He had delivered his warning, and having found his one military friend in good hands and unharmed, he dismissed the matter.

There was some discussion as to the nearest ant-hill. The common tribesmen kept a respectful distance, waiting for their chieftains to decide the details.

Tsang Wu stood there, beaming, and said to Riley, "Plenty clazy, think I make mistakes. So I tell Andug how make sure. Catchee plenty guns, catchee plenty gold, go back to China."

Riley shrugged as best he could, with the strong hands that held him, and spat some "Five Brothers" smack between the Chino's eyes. Everyone laughed, and two men lunged for Tsang Wu when he drew a knife. Andug said, "*Teniente*, spit on me too if it is not too far. No one will cut you down."

Riley answered, "Tsang is a pig. But you are a soldier. I am a soldier. So you will do me one favor before we go to the ant-hill."

"You wish me to tell Major Crann you died like a man?"

"He'll know that. Now this is what I want. Your man there has a fine bugle. It is our custom to blow certain music when a man dies."

"I will have him make the music," Andug promised. "Ever since I cut down the soldier who owned that bugle, I have been proud of it. It belonged to the man who followed an officer all over the battlefield. A brave man, who made music when everyone else used bayonets against us."

Riley shook his head. "I heard your musician, he does not do well. Let me blow my own music, and then let us go. And make a circle. Do not crowd me. Take my *sundang* if you are afraid."

This was a real show. There had been nothing like this within the memory of the oldest *datu*. The attendant handed Riley the bugle, and the circle widened. In their interest, they forgot Crazy Tom, who had shouldered a place for himself.

Riley wondered if his lips could produce a sound, and he wondered what Crazy Tom would do; but whatever happened, they would speak of this at campfires as long as a mosquito buzzed in Mindanao. He raised the bugle, closed his eyes, saw himself, ten years previous, mounting guard; himself and others, smartly stepping down the company street, playing marches between first call and assembly.

He sounded these, with only a pause between.

Riley opened his eyes, and played "Retreat." He saw Crazy Tom's dull eyes brighten in the setting sun. Then, "To the Color." The sunshiner raised his hand as he had done that evening on the trail to Bacolod.

The *datus* and dignitaries stood there, impressed. They liked the music, and the man's gallant gesture appealed to their sense of the dramatic. No one was impatient. Not even when Riley played, "To Horse!"

Crazy Tom cocked his head. "What's that call, Lieutenant? Which hosses?"

Then it came: "Charge!"

The madman got it. He yelled hoarsely, and bounded across the circle. He whipped out his *barong* as he leaped, and the blade hissed. The horse holder dropped, head and left shoulder hanging by a shred. Crazy Tom was in the saddle, and the stallion snorted.

Riley, playing for this break, had a split second advantage over the Moros. He slugged Sahipa's groom, drew the fellow's *kris*, and mounted up as half a dozen blades slashed at Crazy Tom.

Wild cuts raked the fierce little stallions, though that was hardly necessary to make them bolt. In the scramble, none of the men on foot had a fair chance. An explosion could hardly have given them less time to draw or cut or parry, much less move together instead of into each other's way.

A second, two seconds of bobbing turbans, hissing *krisses*, howling men, upturned faces—and Riley was through, with Crazy Tom at his side. Then a flintlock roared; a muzzle-loader charged with rivets, nuts, bits of scrap iron. Slugs spatted through the foliage, smacked the bamboo. Pieces cut Riley, and he saw Crazy Tom lurch forward in that outlandish saddle. The sunshiner bawled, "I got that Chino—*teniente!*"

"Shut up and ride!"

Riley pulled into the lead, and he did not notice the thorns and slashing blades of *cogon* and bamboo. He was not sure just where or in how many places he bled, but there was no time to look.

Ordinarily, Moros dislike night problems. This would be an exception.

Finally, however, the sounds of pursuit could no longer be heard, though the drums were thumping, high up in the hills. The air became thicker, more steamy; the vegetation more dense, and progress slower. And when he pulled up to give his mount a breathing spell, Riley said, "How'd you make it, Tom?"

The sunshiner muttered something. He toppled when Riley caught him.

Kris and *barong* had raked Crazy Tom but that charge of scrap iron was what had done the damage. Riley staunched the wounds, tore up a shirt for bandages, and tied the sunshiner to the sultan's horse, which by now had been whipped down to a bit less fire and cussedness. Then he turned his own mount loose, and led Sahipa's stallion. He was too weary, too weak to manage one horse and lead another on that difficult trail. Riding was harder than walking.

Riley had lost all track of time when he heard a sentry challenge, "Halt! Who's there?"

He couldn't be near Bacolod, not even with a downhill pull; but that was a Scout's challenge, and he answered, "Armed party!"

This was not what the sentry had expected. He yelled for the sergeant of the guard, and then Riley recognized Vicente Piomonte.

Someone said, *"Es el Teniente!"* As he got the order to advance, he heard Major Crann cursing.

Riley shouted, "Turn out the guard! Deceased comrade!"

That, he felt, precisely described Crazy Tom, one time trooper in the regular cavalry. He explained this to the major, before he told of the guns that were to land at Tanjong Merah.

Major Crann finally said, "You damned fool, of course I'd turn out in force when I got enough *barrio* gossip to know that you'd gone into the hills. But now I'll have to draw up some new charges, Lieutenant."

"New ones, sir?"

Crann grunted. "New ones. Plain A.W.O.L. 61st Article of War. Probably cost you five files and half a month's pay. If you give yourself half a chance, you may amount to something yet. Anybody who could make Crazy Tom have a lucid interval is fit to command men in battle."

Riley said, after a moment, "It's my fault he died, but maybe I did him a favor. Look here, sir—could we give him a military funeral?"

"Huh! I guess you'll want to blow taps, eh, Lieutenant? Well, I'll see if we can arrange it, but it'll be the first one on record with four widows involved."

CAIRO TANK TROUBLE

Originally appeared in *Thrilling Adventures*, May 1943.

CHAPTER I
A Fight in an Alley

Mike Rayne, civilian specialist, was beginning to wonder if it wouldn't be a real break to get out in the desert after Rommel. He was tired of sweating here under the floodlights. He was weary of trying to invent ways of mating up parts from three different models of tanks. The result had to be one mongrel tank that could roll, and dish it out, and take it for a while.

Here the greasy concrete floor quivered from the impact hammers which straightened plates, ripped and warped by those roaring 88s. Hissing torches welded cuts, and built up tractor treads. Here, just as much as the desert gap between the Qattara Depression and el Alamein, was the front.

And Rayne, who had left the factory in Detroit to go to Egypt to supervise tank repair, had been doing it the hard way. His crew had to recondition damaged parts, while Rayne robbed what he could from hopeless wrecks. There was nothing else to do. For the *Iron King,* loaded with spare replacements, had been torpedoed in the Red Sea.

A stooped, thin man with silver eagles on his shirt stalked through the shop. He halted, cocked his head.

"Rayne! You working yet?" he bellowed. "When the simmering blazes do you sleep? How many hours do you think a man can stand in this furnace?"

Rayne's swarthy face twisted. He gestured at the line-up.

"All right, Colonel. Take over for me, will you?"

Colonel Mitchell made a gesture, palms up.

"Enough's enough. Don't you work your crews overtime?"

"Won't do. If they get groggy things might happen."

The Colonel snorted with disgust.

"I know why. They can't use a micrometer, they can't pour a bearing, they can't balance a crankshaft. Especially the ones which ought to go to the scrapheap instead of back into service. That's so, isn't it?"

"Sure. Simple enough."

"All right," the colonel went on, "and if you don't ease up, you'll drop dead. Get out of this place, right now."

Mike Rayne was tired, more tired than he had ever been in his life before. Lines of weariness had cut into his young face, injected his eyes with blood and furrowed his brow. But he wouldn't quit. His square jaw set itself. He felt inclined to argue.

"Aw, nuts!" he said. "Don't you realize Rommel's advancing?"

Even as he spoke the shop had a tendency to spin. He put his hand to his wet brow and managed to control the dizziness. Colonel Mitchell caught the gesture. His manner grew triumphant.

"Ah, ha, you see that?" cried the Colonel. "What did I say? You need time off. I'll wager you haven't even seen your grandmother; I'm putting you out."

To emphasize his remarks, Mitchell caught Rayne by the shoulder, whirled him about and hustled him toward the far-off entrance. Mitchell's hand was far more powerful than it looked. Effortlessly he managed the weary man.

"You follow instructions," he told Rayne. "Get yourself a bit of shut-eye, see your grandmother, or go out and get drunk. Do something." At the door he halted the young mechanic. "Trust your crew," he said. "You trained 'em. Now give 'em their heads. They depend too much on you. If it weren't for that you could go to the front. But you're too valuable to lose. So you must take care of yourself, boy. Understand?"

Rayne sighed. The old chap with the silver eagles was right, no doubt about it.

"You win, Colonel. I'm going."

Not until he left the shower, did Rayne realize the colonel's order. He put on his clean whites, which accentuated the swarthiness of his face, the keenness of his deep-set eyes and the darkness of his brows. He still did not feel any too steady on his feet. His head was giddy from long sustained tension.

Maybe he ought to see his grandmother, out in the Salahiya Quarter, as the colonel had suggested; The old lady was past eighty. However, going to bat for Cairo had been a mania with Rayne since he had come back to Egypt. Though born in Denver, he had spent his boyhood in Cairo, with his grandmother.

On the Detroit payrolls, he was listed as Mike Rayne, and not Mikhail Matar. An American, he once told his parents, ought to have an all-American name, so he had translated it. Though "Rain" he figured, had a bit more class if you spelled it "Rayne."

The paving billowed a little under his feet. He knew that he could drink arrak by the bottle and not feel the blistering stuff. He understood now why the survivors of a torpedoed transport, after several weeks in an open boat, had that blank look, why they could not say much.

Rayne was exhausted. Exhaustion parts the thin veil which separates a man's everyday knowledge from the hidden knowledge which comes to him in hunches. To Rayne, the lights and the voices, the café laughter and the whine of "rebeks" and the crying of flutes carried a shocking message. Most of the town felt Rommel did not want to bomb Cairo.

Rayne knew Rommel wanted to blast the British and American armored forces. Rommel wanted to shoot the R.A.F. and the U. S. Air Force from the sky. But he wanted to keep Cairo intact for the Nazis. Rommel could plan this way because at least half of Egypt hated the British, and believed that Hitler would bring a bright new day to the Nile.

Rayne could have gone to the Continental Roof, where Hekmet did the Egyptian version of a strip tease. Also there were the cafés on the Ezbekiyah, crowded with officers. Instead, Rayne, drifted toward the Muski Quarter, the town he knew from boyhood days;

He had lived in the States too long not to notice the smells. But for all his crinkled nostrils, it was like meeting an old friend, a friend who was making a deadly mistake. A woman's voice, and the plucked strings of an *oudh* tugged at his heart. Such things brushed back some fifteen years. Mike Rayne became Mikhail Matar again, an American thinking in Arabic.

Robed figures flitted about shadowy alleys like the unburied dead. "Effendis" strutted in European clothes, and tarbooshes rakishly cocked. At times, he heard English and American voices. These began to sound foreign. He stepped into a *loqanda* where much arrak and only a little coffee was sold. No one gave him a second look; he belonged. But when two men in civilian clothes entered, Kassim's customers eyed them. Kassim, sharp-eyed and greasy, went into his tourist bait routine.

"Nix, we want a drink," growled the two men.

They were seamen. Rayne knew that. They needed the anise flavored brandy to turn the Red Sea jitters out of their rugged frames. U-boats did slip past Aden. Submarines still plied On Mozambique and Madagascar.

"Talk about horseshoes," the red-Haired sailor said, after a snort to welcome the "arrak" home. "That *Iron King*. Torpedoed, she's abandoned. Gosh knows what happened to her crew, but she settles on a reef and hanged if he's not towed in."

"Says who?"

"I talked to a guy at Suez, that's who. Cargo all okay."

Rayne almost choked on his "arrak." The *Iron King*, leaving New York some six weeks ahead of him, had been loaded with spare parts. And these men had sighted her, limping homeward after emergency repairs at the southern end of the Suez Canal. Then why had not her cargo reached the shops?

The seamen's speech, already thick, was becoming more so. Rayne left his bench in the corner and sat down with them.

"What ship you on?"

Where they had been dishing out news for all to hear, they now froze up, "Who wants to know?"

The other put in his bit. "Beat it, mug," he said. "Shove off before we wrap a table around your head."

That a customer, so much at home in Kassim's, spoke English with an American accent, aroused their suspicions. This was no place for Rayne to explain himself. Particularly be did not wish to debate matters with a couple of drunks who belatedly remembered their orders against mentioning ships by name. He shrugged, and went back to his own table, where he called for more liquor.

"That buzzard likes the stuff," the redheaded seaman muttered, his voice carrying much further than he had intended.

This remark solidified Rayne's suspicions. Fellow Americans were mistaking him for an "effendi."

Kassim, meanwhile, directed a sharper scrutiny at Rayne. Apparently, the encounter had made him wonder. Rayne, realizing he was getting nowhere, headed for the street.

Decidedly he had a hunch. Heavy cargo could not be dumped into the Canal. Nor could it be buried in the desert. But it might be sidetracked and hidden in Cairo's many warehouses. That would be simple enough. If hidden, with the records altered, the spare parts could remain out of service for several months. That would be sufficient to cripple the defending army. Replacements might take weeks to arrive.

A good hunch. But Rayne needed more details. No matter who he told, the *pasha* responsible would block investigation. The official clique, barring a few honorable exceptions, had for the last century been Egypt's worst enemies. No wonder the *fellahin* were not worried about Rommel. Nazis would be a treat in a land looted by native officials.

Rayne stepped into the darkness of an archway across the street. His wits were sharpening now. He was having one of those brief stretches of alertness which alternated with periods of intolerable sleepiness.

His legs were tired. His feet burned. He squatted in the archway, easily and readily as any native. Then, hearing a mumbling and gurgling, he realized that he was not alone in the gloom. The varnish odor and the incoherent words told him that someone was polishing off what remained of a bottle of Greek "mastika."

"Have one, brother," the drunk sputtered, and passed him the flask of resin-flavored brandy.

Rayne thanked him and pretended to take a pull. Meanwhile, the sailors, after making unsteady silhouettes in the doorway of Kassim's place, reeled down the murky street.

"That's hot music," one said, thickly.

In some other dive, a girl was singing. *"Zabbiyat il unsi ilaya..."*

"Koochie dance."

Probably he was right. The song ceased. The little kettle drums began to mutter. A sistra jangled metallically. Voices raised raucous shouts of *"Ya sitti! Kamaan!"*

The seamen were in no shape to barge into a native cafe which featured dancing girls. Just the wrong quip, and they would get their throats sliced, or they would be slugged.

Rayne also wanted to know what ship had brought them in. That thin hunch needed building up. So, still holding the mastika bottle by the neck, he set out after them.

Though the Muski is not such a bad place if you knew the answers, it is not for two drunks in civilian clothes. Nor can it even be called healthy for a handful of hard-boiled men in uniform.

Ahead flickered a yellow light. Rayne knew it marked the dive where the drums pounded, where Christians and renegade Moslems swilled arrak and cheered as a dancer shook her torso.

Then Rayne saw business was picking up. From a cross alley, dark figures suddenly blended with the silhouettes of the seamen. A wrathful growl sounded, followed by the pop of a hard fist, and the sinister gleam of steel.

CHAPTER II
Into Moslem Byways

Although outnumbered by assailants, the seamen defended themselves stoutly. So far as Rayne could tell, the attack had been launched utterly without justification. Regardless of that, he would have intervened, anyway. What now drove him on was the conviction some other reason than robbery, vengeance for breach of custom, had instigated the attack. As Rayne dashed forward he felt this fight embodied all of the hidden fires that he had sensed in his walk through modern Cairo.

The town was ignoring the war. It had ignored it to a degree which had shocked Rayne. Though the eight-sided Ezbekiyah had not been festooned with neons, it might as well have been. Pompous-looking *pashas,* rolling by in long, sleek cars only conceded to Rommel's air force the flattery of blue headlights. In side streets, marriage processions still wound heedlessly along, torches flaring. Until this evening Rayne had not suspected the true state of affairs.

Too many merchants of Cairo had figurative welcome signs for Rommel on their doorstep. That made things bad for sailors on shore leave.

Rayne, with a bottle clutched by the neck, fairly swooped toward the battle. Excitement brought out his last reserve of energy as he swung the bottle.

"Ruh, ya kilab," Rayne yelled, and cracked down on a felt skullcap.

A police whistle shrilled.

For a time there was no sound in the darkness other than heavy blows and the other noises of furious combat. The sailors continued to swing their fists recklessly, letting go at every head they saw.

After his first shout and efficient use of the liquor receptacle, Rayne had intervened no more in the battle. He had an excellent reason for this. A chance wallop from one of the seamen had laid him down in the Egyptian mud, stunned and breathless.

The men from the ship continued to use their fists with effect. Soon their assailants began to dodge away. One of the seamen now had opportunity to speak to his companion who, likewise, had backed up against a wall.

"That feller who helped us out with the bottle," growled the sailor. "He ain't no pansy. What d'ye say, friend? Shall we check out of here like he did? The cops is on the way."

"Aye, aye, shipmate," responded his companion. "Let's shove off quick."

And they merged into the shadows just as the police rushed into the street from another direction.

Rayne, still groggy from the punch, was unable to get away either. In addition to the blow a kick from a hard shoe had nearly knocked him unconscious. The police approached, flashing lights upon the scene.

The scattering thugs distracted them. By the time they collared one prisoner, and given the others up as a bad job, Rayne had crawled painfully into the angle of a wall. A flashlight played on the arena.

One of the khaki-clad policemen seemed surprised.

"*Wallah*, this was the grandfather of battles," he said. "One of these dogs has a crushed skull. Doubtless he sings in Paradise at this very moment."

"Infidels did this thing," a groggy ruffian mumbled through shattered teeth to a policeman. "Allah knows we were innocent."

"Silence, thou father of thieves," snapped the policeman.

One of the officers flashed a light into the alley. He saw Rayne. So did the man with the thickened mouth.

"There's one of those sons of pigs," he cried. "They wore *Feringhi* clothes."

One man lay dead, one badly gouged, one in need of some dental work. And there in the angle rested Rayne, just recovering from his bruises. Thus he seemed to be an ideal candidate for a scapegoat. Spectators came flocking out of houses, although thus far no one had emerged from Kassim's place.

Assembled policemen held a conference in Arabic.

"*Wallah*, this fellow wears *Feringhi* clothes, still he doesn't look like one of them," they said.

"He's an unbelieving dog," muttered the man with the broken teeth. "He stole my purse."

"But he's not one of the men who were beaten up by the infidel," muttered a policeman. "Who can he be?"

They hoisted Rayne to his feet.

"The peace upon you, but ruffians knocked me down," he gasped, with difficulty. "They kicked me in the stomach. Allah, first I am booted asunder, and with the father of all boots, and now they accuse me."

"By the prophet, a true believer," the cops exclaimed. "Which way did the infidels run?"

Things looked better for Rayne.

"Allah knows all things, but it seemed that way," he answered, pointing in a wrong direction.

Then Kassim waddled out.

"O Men, what is this thing?" he puffed. "Who makes these riots?"

"Wisdom is with God."

Kassim squinted at Rayne. "This fellow lies like Iblis, the condemned. He is a friend of the *Feringhi*. He sat at their table."

"Let us take them all to jail," decided the policemen.

Well, things could be worse. Though Grandma would shudder, bailing her grandson out of jail, Rayne figured he could live it down. But a real wallop knocked the relief out of him.

From the doorway opposite Kassim's lurched a man who reeked with *mastika*. "There's the eater-of-filth who stole my bottle," he bawled, as he stumbled and wove through mud and offal. "O True Believers, make him return my bottle."

That fatal bottle! It had killed a man and Rayne's fingerprints, whether sharp or blurred, were nevertheless on the glass neck. This looked like it would be something from which Grandmother could not extricate him. The old lady's influence did not carry weight enough with the *pashas*.

Rayne made a lunge. He tripped one policeman and cold caulked another. The uniformed men had barely hit the dirt when he was darting into the darkest of the Muski, and he thanked Allah that he knew where to go.

The effects of the kick and the punch had worn off and he moved easily, lightly upon his feet. After him followed the police and various idlers, like a pack of hunting dogs, raising their voices in wild yells. But this did not bother Rayne. He thanked his stars for the training of his youth and a thorough knowledge of the furtive alleys of the city.

He went through murky passageways, around the corners of wooden shops, past shadowy buildings, twisting and turning, but holding to a general direction. Pedestrians whom he met were careful to draw back and give him room. For this was the East where a man's business is his own, and they knew not what crime he had committed or what weapons he carried.

Rayne headed for the more lawless sections of Cairo, knowing that in such a section on general principles, all men aid a fugitive from the law.

In a few minutes by skill and quick wit the sounds of pursuit had died out and he had lost the howling pack. Then he swung around another corner and halted, leaning against the side of a building in the dark. He was breathless but calm. For a few minutes he waited, regaining his wind.

Then he sauntered off as if nothing had happened. And as he strolled along, he was thinking hard.

Rayne was not old, but he had not become a master mechanic by having folks pat him on the head.

Battered and half asleep, he began to reckon the score. Kassim and his *loqanda* were off color. That the ambush had occurred so near the place proved nothing. But it was odd, during the riot, no one had come out of Kassim's to get a look until the police had arrived. And then that effort to connect Rayne with the seamen, when Kassim knew well that he, Rayne, had been rebuffed as a prying foreigner.

His last waking thought was, "When I can think straight, when I'm not so dopey, I'll get to the bottom of this."

Again weariness seeped through him and he longed for rest. His course now took a definite direction. He turned his steps toward a ruined mosque with which he was acquainted and soon stopped before the wide steps of the deserted building. Further along was a coppersmith's bazaar but not a light showed either there or here.

Rayne slipped down along the structure out of sight. Halting before a door he cast a quick glance up and down the narrow lane. No one was near. In a minute or two he was inside the mosque. It was pitch dark inside but he managed to find a clean corner which would do for a bed. In a minute or two he was settled down and composed for sleep. He had a last waking thought.

"Tomorrow, when I'm not so tired and dopey, I'll find out what became of those missing tank parts," he said to himself.

Rayne passed the night undisturbed in the mosque. At dawn, awakened by the *muezzin's* call to prayer from another mosque nearby, he crawled further into the crumbling masonry and caught up with some more sleep. After the bedlam of the tank shop, the sounds of the market failed to disturb him.

Not until mid-afternoon came had he rested enough to notice the discomfort of his rocky bunk. This told him how correct had been Colonel Mitchell's diagnosis, and how near Rayne had skirted utter collapse.

He plunged his head into a nearby fountain. His hat was gone, and in Egypt, running around bare-headed is a worse breach of etiquette than roaming about without pants. So Rayne lost no time in buying a tarboosh. Then he got out of that quarter of Cairo.

Near Khan el Khallili, where caravans from the Soudan used to unload gum and leather and ostrich plumes, he found a *loqanda*. Here he ordered sour milk, cucumbers, and a flat cake of bread. Borrowing an Arabic newspaper from the proprietor, he read an account of the previous night's fray as he sipped his coffee.

The two sailors, Walt Kearney and Robert Irwin, were in jail. They had been held in connection with the death of Zahir-ud-Din Mohammed, a resident of the Kordofan Bazaar. In addition to this, one Abu Najeeb, who had been severely cut by broken glass, was in the Ismailia Emergency Hospital. Kassim, restaurant proprietor, stated that the two sailors had come in with a bottle of *mastika*, and had left in a quarrelsome mood. Therefore, the street fight had not surprised him, Kassim informed the police.

Since every paper in Egypt is government controlled, this was official. It bothered Rayne. According to that version, the actual owner of the bottle, despite his loud protests to the police, did not and never had existed. Neither could the seizure of the bottle by Rayne matter much to the police since Rayne, likewise, had no official existence. All of which seemed odd to say the least.

"Kassim, is a liar," Rayne told himself. "Kearney and Irwin didn't have a bottle, and he knows they didn't." The only reason Kassim could have for building up a case against two seamen would be that he had some good motive for covering up the fact that a gang had jumped the sailors at the first alley beyond his place. But why cover that up?

Rayne had two guesses: first, the Garden was a deadfall; or, the men had during their brief visit said or done something which made their disappearance necessary to Kassim. What made Rayne want to follow through was the fact the two seamen might know more about the *Iron King* and her cargo than they had let on.

Still puzzled, Rayne left the restaurant. His chief needs were suitable garments in which to carry on his investigations.

Wandering from shop to shop, he bought sandals here, baggy trousers there, and elsewhere, a jacket. In a ruined house he made a quick change. Then he resumed his tour of the bazaars. When it was done, Rayne had become a lemonade and cigarette peddler, raucously offering his wares to the shoppers who crowded the narrow street.

The customers he really wanted were in jail. The official smoke screen and the distortion of facts told Rayne anyone trying to get in touch with Kearney and Irwin would be blocked by miles of red tape.

Whoever, consul or otherwise, tried to investigate would surely run into a yarn about the prisoners having just been shifted to such and such station. So Rayne asked no questions. He settled down to patient guessing.

At each station, he gave the man at the desk free lemonade and a pack of cigarettes; there was similar baksheesh for the jailer. This detail settled, he was allowed to peddle his wares to the prisoners.

CHAPTER III
The Toils of the Law

It was near sunset when he found the two sailors in the tank with half a dozen natives.

Rayne pretended a lofty scorn of the seamen. "Have these two infidel pigs any money?" he asked the natives, in Arabic.

"*Ya* Allah, they have," was the answer. "We tried to rob them, and they kicked us breathless."

Kearney and Irwin indeed looked as though they had been battling for their rights. So did their cellmates.

"Then stand back, little brothers, and the blessing of Allah upon you," said Rayne. "I speak their language a little, they will think I am a friend. Watch me loot them."

"God give you strength," came the pious wish, and the natives edged as far away as, they could.

Rayne addressed the sailors in dragoman-English.

"Lemonade, Mister," he inquired. "Cool and freshing. Fine Egypt made cigarettes, cheap."

150

"Go jump in the lake, you greasy swab."

The other, seaman nudged his companion.

"Bob, don't you remember this guy? Only he was wearing white man's clothes then."

For a few moments Rayne continued his patter. He displayed his jug, his greasy little cups, the packages in his basket.

Then, in Americanese, "Dish out a bit of small change and keep on cussing me out. I told the others I was out to give you a rooking."

Red-haired Kearney offered a *piastre*. Rayne babbled for more.

"Who are you, anyway?" asked Kearney.

"Army Intelligence. You fellows are buried so deep no consul will ever find you, but maybe I can give you a break. You're wanted for murder."

Both sailors started; their faces changed. "Cut it out, brother."

"Gospel truth," Rayne insisted. "It's not in any English or French paper in town, just in the Arabic papers. The whole yarn is phony. Dig up some more dough, and take some cigarettes. Keep up the game, and growl at me a little." They wrangled and bartered. Rayne winked at the interested native prisoners, elaborated his gestures.

"Wait until this unbelieving fool gives me a one-pound note and wants his change," he smirked.

Meanwhile Kearney and Irwin carried on. "How come we went to that dump, Kassim's? A dragon-man or something met us on the train and said he'd show us around reasonable. In Suez, a black fellow gave us cards, be sure and go to Kassim's and was it a washout when we got there. That's what we were sore about, no girls, nothing but that arrak."

"Do you remember the dragoman's license number?"

They did not. Tourists should, but never do, take their guide's number. Rayne went on, as he palmed a pound note and slipped it to Kearney.

"When I start walking out, wave this folding money, call me back, and buy something. I'll take the money and run out on you, and you yell and raise the roof, like I'd robbed you. Get it?"

They did. "All right," Rayne continued. "Now what were you fellows talking about before I came into Kassim's?"

"About the cargo of the *Iron King*, how lucky it was they salvaged all those spare parts for tanks. We were in port when she was being loaded, back home. We knew what she had."

"I'll do my best to get you fellows out," Rayne promised. "Do you know any more about the cargo?"

"No, how would we? Except it landed at Suez."

"Okay. Go into your dance."

The act was good. The prisoners got several packs of cigarettes, and Rayne made off with a pound Egyptian, worth close to five American dollars. The cursing was an inspiration. And the native prisoners howled with glee.

Mike Rayne grinned at the sergeant, tossed him a piece of silver, and went on. The sergeant caught the backsheesh on the fly, and thought it was a grand joke.

* * * *

That night, Rayne sat in a restaurant, eating an eggplant and mutton stew. He mopped the gravy with a flap of leathery bread, and wished that he had time to take the interurban train to Grandma's house. But for the time, he was too busy piecing together the information Irwin and Kearney had given him. Though it did not seem important, actually it was dynamite.

First, runners in Suez handed out cards to merchant marine sailors with shore leave to Cairo. Second, a dragoman met them in Cairo to guide them to the spot, and apparently, managed to get them moderately drunk on the way. Third, two men who discussed the cargo of the *Iron King* had narrowly missed being murdered. And fourth, after escaping from ambush, they had been jailed on false testimony largely concocted by Kassim.

Rayne did not know whether to tell Colonel Mitchell, or carry on alone. The colonel, in his official capacity, would have to confer with whatever officer handled much matters. Then that man would confer with the British, who in turn would have to take it up with some of Egypt's swarm of *pashas*. These tricky scoundrels would decide it was consular business, and the merry-go-round would keep whirling.

Meanwhile, Rommel was kicking up sand in the wrong direction.

"A short circuit," Rayne told himself, "may blow some fuses, but it is also the shortest distance between two points."

To save time and avoid lengthy explanations, he had been forced to tell the sailors he was Army Intelligence, and they had accepted it. Rayne hated the deception but there had been no other way. Now he figured it might be wise to make that harmless lie a temporary truth.

Rayne hurried away from the jail and turned his steps back in the direction of the place where he had left his clothes. He nearly dropped his lemonade peddling kit when he approached the place where he had made the change.

A crowd had gathered and the police were bringing out of hiding the shoes and suit which Rayne had concealed.

Now it turned out in his haste, he had not performed the task as well as he should have done.

The hat, lost in the alley brawl, must have started the search. Rayne raised his voice, adding to the chatter, but got no customers. Then he edged into the crowd. Whether the police had found the wallet he had buried under a loose slab, was not certain. But if they had, Rayne's identity would soon be disclosed by cards and papers.

As nearly as he could gather, however, an American cigarette, in the side pocket of his coat, along with the stamped corner of an envelope mailed from the States, told them what brand of infidel was on the loose.

"Now he's trying to disguise himself as a true believer," a policeman told one of the spectators.

Rayne sold some lemonade. The policemen helped themselves, sans payment. Rayne, though still shaky, left the corner with increased confidence. However, he realized that from now on, the police would be going from one shop to the next to pick up the trail of a man who had shed a white suit in favor of native dress.

Once more, he was tempted to phone or see Colonel Mitchell, but he ended by resisting the temptation, simply because an officer could not take part in any free and easy snooping fest. Whether he liked it or not, Rayne had to play the hand out himself.

Then the game began to have a thrill. As he ate, that night, he chatted with fellow diners and got their ideas on the mad infidel. They were betting a hundred to one the fellow would be nailed before dawn. His way of eating or drinking would betray him, even if his speech did not.

While they admitted that infidels might learn Arabic at school, none could speak it convincingly. Rayne, after belching in the fashion prescribed by the Egyptian Emily Post, wagged his head and agreed. "By Allah, brother, that is verily the essence of truth," he said.

He rented a cubicle in the old caravanserai, and spread out the palm leaf mat he had picked up near the restaurant. From now on, this was his address in the Muski. Having a visible means of support, his chances were not the worst in the world.

In spite of having gone native, Rayne dared not risk entering Kassim's place. But he prowled about, waiting for dragomans to bring customers from the merchant marine. With the ever increasing flow of ships from the States, there would be more and more American seamen.

These seamen did not have to be indiscreet. Just a casual remark, harmless in itself, was enough. But it could be dangerous when fitted into other equally trifling bits contributed by sailors from a different ship. A man can hardly help but let his hair down after making a safe landing. While Rayne had always known the peril of unguarded remarks concerning a ship about to sail from the States, he now realized, from the past night's mishaps, the enemy could make good use of facts pertaining to a safe arrival in port.

CHAPTER IV
Into Enemy Clutches

From his lurking place across the narrow street, Rayne saw and heard three Americans who trailed after their dragoman. The guide's leathery face was plain for a moment as he stood under the light in Kassim's doorway. He turned to bow and gesture, and to go into his patter, "This way, gents," he told the Americans. "Famous rendezvous. The real Cairo. Boss spiks good Inglees, like me." The man's number also showed for an instant. Rayne would not forget either. The Americans filed in. But they came out before long and the dragoman followed them, wailing.

"You wait, I show some other place," he promised. "Kassim uncle just die. No more business tonight."

"How about us going to the funeral?"

"Do they have grub and fireworks?" another quipped.

"You're thinking of the Chinese," said a third. Then, to the dragoman, "Shake it up, Abdul!"

"Name is Selim," the guide corrected. "Poverty struck son of one time pasha."

"Aw, nuts, it's Abdul, do you get it?" The three went on, everyone offering an idea as to the next place. "Kassim's looked like a funeral anyway. Hey, take us to a juke joint, we want to dance." Rayne did not follow them. Just why Kassim was turning down customers was worth finding out.

He headed Nile-ward for perhaps a hundred yards, then swung into a yard-wide alley. It opened into a dark and odorous court which opened into another passageway. This was Cairene town planning, at its craziest.

Above him, he heard the voices of people lounging on the flat roofs. The scent of Ajami tobacco drifted down to blend with rubbish reek. He met no pedestrians, and presently, he had doubled back, reaching the rear of Kassim's place.

In the dark, he found the wicket, which was latched, not locked. Patiently silently, he worked the door open, then closed it after him. Once in the gloom of the court, he made a slow circuit of the wall. It was lined with storage sheds and packing crates were heaped in corners. Liquor cases, saved up for fuel, he surmised, to stretch the charcoal supply.

Above him, *mashrabiyehs* bellied out, projecting from the second floor and overhanging the court. In these screened bay windows one could get the river breeze almost as readily as on the roof. But at the moment, lack of either light or voices told him the occupants of the building were elsewhere.

Rayne could barely distinguish muffled speech from somewhere in front. In view of Kassim's having turned customers away, that conversation was worth hearing.

The door ahead was apparently bolted from the inside. Rayne headed for the corner of the court, stacked up some empty cases, and from that footing, pulled himself up. He doubted the carved latticework of the nearest *mashrabiyeh* would offer a toe-hold strong enough to support his weight. Then there was the matter of noise. So he tried another approach.

An upward leap, risky because of his narrow footing, gave him a precarious grasp of the parapet which guarded the flat roof.

For a moment, he doubted that he could make it. Worse yet, there was the chance that he would lose his hold and drop down into the court, making enough noise to alarm Kassim. But he made it. Skylined, he was at the mercy of any neighbors who might be looking.

When he had cleared the parapet, he crept across the roof to the head of the stairs which led to the lower floor. Echoes distorted the words, otherwise, he could have halted midway to listen. Not until he had reached the edge of the patch of light which wavered on the lower stair treads, was he able to understand what was being said. From that distance, also he got a partial view of the back room.

Kassim was conferring with two men. One, wearing European clothes and a tarboosh, had an oversized diamond in his necktie. Heavily-jeweled rings flashed on his lean brown hand. The other, in native dress, was familiar, which puzzled Rayne for an instant. Then he realized that this was the jailer, now in civilian clothes. Kassim was protesting to the bejeweled dignitary.

"Your Excellency, I couldn't leave my post to call on you," Kassim said. "I had to send a messenger." He made a helpless gesture. "Really, Daoud Pasha, this was no time for etiquette."

"Etiquette!" The *pasha* snorted. "You fool, you son of several pigs, I'm not thinking of ceremony. But if Army Intelligence is watching you, it is not helpful to have me come here to be included in their suspicion."

Kassim gulped, turned to the jailer for moral support, and got only a blank look.

"Excellency, we have only Musa's word for it the accursed lemonade peddler is connected with the British or American Army," Kassim assured the official.

Musa, the jailer flared up.

"So you think I can't understand Inglesi? I speak better than you. No, I was not so near, but I can't be mistaken. That's what he said to the sailors." Daoud Pasha went wild.

"Satan blacken you, Musa. And you waited till now to tell us."

"I didn't know it was important. Not till I began thinking a while, after I was off duty. Anyway, what if the officers or the sailors do find them and get them released?"

From this it grew clear Musa did not know the score any better than Rayne did. Under ordinary circumstances, neither Kassim nor the *pasha* would have enlightened him. As it was, the *pasha*, believing himself in a tight corner, wanted to impress Kassim's friend with the importance of being vigilant in the future.

"Listen, Musa," he said. "Foreigners are swallowing Egypt, piecemeal. First the British, and now the Americans. For what they call defending the country, they'll take an even stronger hold. Kassim and I are patriots, you understand? Egypt for the Egyptians. Despite all that it takes you hours to decide you ought to tell Kassim about an Intelligence officer finding those sailors in jail!"

Musa, seeing how worried Daoud Pasha was, forgot his deference to the man's rank.

"What happens to your excellency is none of my business!" he snapped, insolently. "I had Kassim in mind. Allah! What have you ever done for me?

None of this makes sense anyway. The British are bad, but no worse than the Germans. They pretend to be friends but only a fool would believe that."

As Rayne now saw it, Musa, knowing the sailors had gotten into a serious riot outside of Kassim's place, had been worried only by the thought that his friend might run into trouble with Army Intelligence. However, Daoud Pasha's hasty drive in response to a restaurant keeper's summons convinced Rayne that his original hunch had been right. The anti-British *pasha* must have been conspiring with Kassim to obstruct the defense of Egypt.

Daoud probably was, according to his lights, a patriot, and neither a Quisling nor a traitor. But Rayne's job at the moment was to trail the missing spare parts, regardless of the *pasha's* being or not being a Nazi agent.

"Only a fool would believe those Germans," Musa repeated, enjoying the spectacle of a badly-worried *pasha*.

But Daoud was frightened and jittery. He had been pushed too far by an insolent jailer. He cursed, drew an automatic pistol from his pocket, and fired.

Kassim, however, bounded toward him. This deflected the *pasha's* aim. Musa, panic-stricken, did not wait for the outcome. Though there was a door leading to the front and another to the rear, both were barred. With a yell, he leaped over a bench, and darted toward the stairway.

Meanwhile, the *pasha* dropped the pistol as Kassim, wrenched his wrist. "Excellency, Musa means no harm," he shouted. Then, shouldering the hotheaded official aside, Kassim darted after his friend, calling, "Wait, Musa! Wait!"

Rayne, cramped from squatting on the stairs, could not move rapidly enough to race Musa to the roof. The way was narrow, and even as he hoped that the jailer would be blinded by panic, Kassim's shouts took effect.

The frightened man, thinking he had two enemies now, leaped to his left, colliding with Rayne.

Just then Kassim charged into the tangle. The stairs were steep and narrow. Rayne's efforts to disengage himself failed. He was still kicking and struggling when the three thumped down a dozen treads and crashed against the low table in the center of the floor.

Rayne doubled Musa with a boot to the stomach. He disentangled himself from Kassim and tried for the pistol which the *pasha* had dropped, but Daoud, apart from the three-cornered melee, had kept his wits. He snatched the weapon.

"Hold it, you fools!" he cried. "We've got a spy here!"

Rayne, failing to get the *pasha's* pistol, seized the table, which was knee high, and a little over a yard in diameter. The silver and ivory inlay deflected Daoud Pasha's hasty shot.

Then, as the weapon jammed, Rayne straight-armed the table, knocking the Egyptian off balance.

One more move, and he would break for the roof. He had plenty to tell Colonel Mitchel. Moreover, stealth had no further use, now that Daoud knew a spy had tuned in. He whirled, and from the corner of his eye, caught a glimpse of Kassim, who had regained his feet.

Rayne's ankle turned. A splash of coffee dregs made him slip, and for an instant, he floundered. Kassim, for all his fat, was agile enough to use the brass tray he had picked from the floor. It rang like a temple bell as it smashed down on Rayne's head, knocking him face forward to the floor, too nearly out for either flight or fight.

CHAPTER V
Torture By Fire

The disturbance had not alarmed the quarter. The stone walls muffled the sharp crack of the small bore pistol. Kassim's waiters had apparently gone home when the proprietor closed the *loqanda*, since no one had come from the front. Once Rayne's wrists were lashed together with a length of cord, Kassim and the pasha yanked him to his feet.

Musa had by now regained his breath sufficiently to gasp, "By Allah—that —is—the Intelligence—officer."

Daoud, despite his bleeding and battered face, was amiable enough.

"You did very well, stopping him," he said to Musa, who presumably was supposed to forget the attempt to shoot him down. "I'll speak to the chief of police in your favor."

That, Daoud assumed, would fix it up. Pashas had not changed much since the days when arbitrary floggings and capital punishment were a routine privilege they exercised freely.

"Your excellency," Kassim said, "we must get this fellow out of here before his superiors search the place."

It was not clear to Rayne why they had not already cut his throat. As his captors marched him, blindfolded, down through a maze of alleys, he reasoned that it is usually easier and safer to let a man go to the execution scene under his own power.

If there were any spectators on the nearby roofs, or in the over-hanging *mashrabiyeh* windows, they would see nothing significant in the group which filed through the darkness below.

Rayne was sure that even if he had been one of a group of Intelligence officers, it would have been impossible to trail him. At least twice during the march, the party entered and passed through a building, and emerged in the labyrinth at its rear.

Odors finally helped Rayne to orient himself. When he caught the tang of the spice bazaar, and the reek of the saddle-makers quarter, he knew where he was. These landmarks were scarcely out of nose range when his captors prodded him over a threshold and removed the blindfold.

By the light of an oil lamp, Rayne saw that he was in the reception room of a long unoccupied house. Dust coated the floor, and the worn upholstery of a low platform which ran along one wall.

"There is a well in the courtyard," said Daoud Pasha. "It is about your size."

"Nobody is stopping you," retorted Rayne, hoping that his voice did not betray his dismay. "Or are you waiting on my account?"

"There is a way out, if you are reasonable," cut in Kassim. Musa stood to one side. His eyes were narrow and glittering. He seemed to be wavering between hatred of Daoud Pasha, and loyalty to his friend Kassim.

"What was the purpose of your spying?" the *pasha* asked Rayne. "Do you realize you are wanted for murder? Not even your superior can protect you from that."

A good deal more could be found in that idea than the pasha himself realized. While Rayne may have intervened to help two fellow Americans fight off a treacherous attack, he would nevertheless have to face the local laws. Certainly he had no legal defense for his invasion of Kassim's quarters. But what heartened him was that Daoud Pasha was temporizing instead of using that ready gun.

Rayne's mind raced as Daoud Pasha's intent eyes bored into him.

"This buzzard must believe I have something on him, he's trying to blackmail me by using what he's got on me," he thought to himself.

"You aren't too sure what my superior can or can't do, are you?" Rayne retorted to the *pasha*. "Otherwise you'd give me what you tried to give Musa."

"You've not told me why you were spying," Daoud Pasha persisted.

"Those sailors were led by an unlicensed dragoman to Kassim's place," Rayne retorted. "They were ambushed on the way out because they knew too much about something you are interested in. Naturally, I reported that. But if you're sure they won't be released from jail until you've covered your tracks, you have not a thing in the world to worry about."

With an oily smile, the Egyptian official stared at Rayne.

"Army Intelligence won't find you so easily," the *pasha* countered.

"Maybe not." Rayne shrugged. He tried to force himself to believe, rather than hope he could find a loophole in the *pasha's* defenses. Then he staked it all on a bluff: "They don't have to find me. What is one man, more or less, in this whole show? As long as they find the tractor parts you sidetracked, you'll get what will run your friend Rommel the full width of Africa and push him into the ocean."

The Egyptian official was not poker-faced. The thought of Army Intelligence on his trail cracked his resistance. His snort of derision did not sound sincere. So Rayne hammered away. Though his hands were tied, he had, for a moment at least, won the initiative.

"Official Egypt may be pretty rotten, but there are some sound spots. Maybe you've got your reasons to be anti-British but a lot of your people don't agree that the Nazis are a blessing. There's a well waiting for me out in back, but do you know what's waiting for you?"

Daoud Pasha's laugh was forced.

"You are almost threatening me. Very well, if your superiors know where the spare parts are, why haven't they seized them? I never heard of that American game called poker. So—I am calling your hand."

The *pasha's* confidence had returned. He stalked grandly out of the room, and into the court, where he called, "Ali! Marouf!"

Two men answered.

"Aywah, effendi!"

A low-voiced consultation followed. Rayne was not able to get a word of what passed between Daoud and the two he had called. That they were at hand, awaiting summons, seemed significant. They must have been there all evening, for Daoud Pasha had not taken time, since Rayne's capture, to order henchmen to appear at a rendezvous. A thrill of realization buoyed him up and out of the depression which the ominous conference in the court had induced.

The *pasha* remained in a huddle with Marouf and Ali. They were planning the first step toward murder and its concealment. Their having been on hand indicated that the warehouse which contained the sidetracked tank parts must be near.

This was a quarter devoted largely to the *wakkalas* which in the old days had received goods hauled by camel caravans out of the Soudan. So, despite the growing menace, Rayne felt that he had gained a point.

He realized that this might be wishful thinking on his part, yet he could not deny the logic. Daoud Pasha, worried and caught off guard, would inevitably take a prisoner to a place associated in his mind with concealment.

When Daoud returned, two lean and wiry Arabs followed him. One had a copper brazier and goatskin bellows. The other had iron tongs. These household implements implied that Marouf and Ali cooked their meals somewhere in the rear; that they kept day and night watch, taking turns.

Instead of going to their homes or to *loqandas* to eat, and thus laying themselves open to native curiosity, the two watchmen never stirred from the supposedly abandoned *wakkala* and the house which abutted it.

But their faces told Rayne that they were not preparing to cook coffee or grill mutton.

"If you had given your superiors any real information, they would have raided Kassim's place, and then this place," said Daoud Pasha. "I am giving you just one chance to keep from being buried in a dry well."

"Thanks," Rayne retorted, ironically. "Allah will reward you."

"You must convince your superiors that you have so far discovered nothing, but that you have a clue. Which perhaps you have."

"Turn me loose and I'll tell them just that," said Rayne.

Daoud Pasha scowled.

"You will not be so witty when Ali and Marouf set to work." He turned to his men. "Get busy, now!"

CHAPTER VI

159

A Desperate Chance

The Arabs squatted by the brazier. One slopped a bit of kerosene from the lamp bowl, and struck a match. The other pumped the bellows, first gently, so as not to extinguish the yellow flame which rose from the charcoal. Then, as the black chunks began to glow, he increased the force of the air blast.

Sparks showered. The glare presently overwhelmed the murky light of the lamp. Tongues of blue flame rose from the incandescent heap in whose center the tongs were thrust.

"You'll write your message," Daoud Pasha said to Mike Rayne, raising his voice above the evil hissing and creaking of the bellows. "Either now, or after we've cooled some iron on your hide. You will say you have gone to Alexandria to watch a suspect."

Once he had written a message to throw his imaginary superiors off the trail, Rayne knew he would be murdered.

His hands were tied behind him. Furthermore the odds were five to one, and then there was the *pasha's* ready pistol. The machine shop beyond the Nile seemed a long way off, now. So also did his grandmother's house in the Zeitoon Quarter.

Rayne regretted a tactical error on his part.

He had gone too far in convincing Daoud Pasha that he, Rayne, had been playing a lone hand. Though the *pasha* could hardly suspect Rayne of being certain the missing tank parts were only a few yards away, the earlier bluff, teaming up with circumstance, had shaped itself into a trap. The *pasha* believed Rayne could disappear without any danger of being traced.

"Let me think this over for a minute," Daoud Pasha said, and moved back toward the bench.

Ali gleamed with sweat as he pumped the bellows. Marouf took the tongs from the heap of glowing coals. The metal shot out white sparks. Waves of heat billowed toward Rayne. The small room had become stifling. Daoud Pasha and Kassim stood there, eyeing him. Musa, somewhat apart, was blank faced, perhaps in his mind already enjoying the promotion and pay which the hot tempered official had, after relenting, promised him.

Marouf approached, slowly, bringing the iron nearer.

"*Effendi*, we ought to tie him first," he suggested.

"*Wallah!*" the pasha exclaimed, as though he had forgotten such trifles. "Of course."

Part of the buildup—the preliminary terror to crack the victim's will. Rayne knew this, and also he had no chance against such odds. Yet he resisted when they seized him.

He writhed and kicked and twisted until booting and sheer weight won out for the Egyptians. Four men did the job, while Daoud Pasha stood by, polishing his rings on his coat sleeve. Not until the men had lashed him to a bench, did

Rayne appear to wilt. To Daoud Pasha the beating and mauling had been enough to crack any man's spirit, even without threats of the red hot iron.

"Wait, *effendi*!" Rayne howled, as though in abject terror. "Don't let him touch me. I'll write it. Untie me. Let me sit up and give me a drink."

Rayne made his act good. His life depended on it and, besides, he did not need to pretend fear. So he babbled with terror. The *pasha* nodded. Ali and Marouf removed the bonds, and yanked Rayne upright. The act ticked like clockwork. The *pasha* looked pleased. Then Rayne went on with the desperate plan he had conceived.

"My hands and wrists are numb. How can I write?"

"Try and see." Daoud Pasha took a pen and notebook from his pocket. "And no trickery, no codes either."

"Who is going to deliver the message."

"A detail I shall handle," the *pasha* reassured him.

Rayne took the pen and paper. Then, for a moment, he wondered if his hysteria had been convincing for the official had drawn his pistol and stepped back a little.

Closing his eyes as if dazed, Rayne fumbled, opened them and gazed blankly about. He rose, mopped his forehead with his sleeve. Then like some half animated dummy, laid the pen and paper on the bench. The Egyptians regarded him with contempt. Apparently terror had cracked him more completely than they had expected.

Rayne took off his jacket, and muttered about the heat. Then, after dropping it on the floor, he decided to pick it up out of the dirt.

Now that their task of intimidation had ended, the Arabs had moved away from the blistering heat of the brazier. Daoud Pasha lowered his pistol. In another instant he might even have pocketed it, but Rayne was not gambling on that possibility. He preferred that weapon to be within sight and reach.

Clutching the jacket Rayne went into action. Leaping forward he seized the glowing brazier before a man of the group sensed what he meant to do.

The coat muffled his hands. There was the stench of burning wool. Then, despite the penetrating heat, Rayne spun in an arc, showering red coals and ashes as he whirled.

A fiery cascade showered the barefooted Arabs. It sifted down into their loose garments. Glowing fragments peppered Daoud Pasha's face and hands.

He was not a good shot, and the startling counter-attack made him jerk the trigger. The bullet went wild.

Rayne let go the hot brazier. It hurtled straight for Kassim, who yelled and bounded to one side. This maneuver knocked the *pasha* off balance.

The floor became carpeted with red hot flame. Rayne, making the most of the confusion, snatched the tongs. He ignored the howling Arabs, whose every step brought their bare feet down on chunks of glowing coal. They danced about like fleas on a stove lid. Rayne darted for Daoud Pasha who, trying to scramble to his feet, tried at the same time to shoot.

161

He made a bad job of both. Rayne smashed down on his wrist with the hot tongs, knocking the pistol from his grasp. Next Rayne jumped back to face Kassim, who was drawing a knife.

The restaurant keeper did not like the still glowing jaws of the tongs. He hesitated, bounded for the door.

In the courtyard, the Arabs screeched and shed their smoldering garments. Rayne charged for Kassim, combining escape with vengeance. Out of the side of his eye, he saw Musa, the jailer, lunge for the *pasha's* pistol. Already the room was roaring with fire. The lamp, kicked over, had spilled its oil on the floor.

It was Musa's move for the pistol which saved Kassim. As the fat man raced down the alley, Rayne halted and spun about to heave his tongs at the man with the gun.

Too late!

"O son of many pigs," shouted Musa. "This is my day." Then the weapon commenced to explode.

But Musa did not fire at Rayne. He was pouring lead into the official who, perhaps an hour previous, had tried to cut him down. Daoud Pasha dropped.

"Stop it, you fool!" Rayne yelled.

Musa straightened up, eyes blazing. "There are too many *pashas* like him. I was afraid until now. Then I saw you, and by Allah, I am your protector."

"Give me that gun," Rayne demanded, walking back. Without waiting for obedience, he twisted the weapon from the man's hand. "Now turn in a fire alarm."

The blaze did not yet bar him from the court. So Rayne, pistol in hand, raced through the room to the rear. By the light which reached into the paved space, he saw Ali and Marouf clambering over the wall. And beyond the further archway, Rayne learned his suspicions had been well grounded.

He was looking into a barn-like warehouse loaded with crates and cases. The stenciling on the nearest told the story: they had been consigned to the S. S. *Iron King.*

So long as the *wakkala* did not go up in smoke, the shipload of spare parts would after all help roll Rommel back into the desert.

Rayne retraced his steps. His first act was to examine Daoud Pasha's wounds. They were not serious. Next, Rayne dragged the man out of the blazing room. That done, he raced to a telephone. It was about time to speak to Colonel Mitchell.

A fire company was on the job before Rayne got in touch with the colonel. "There are two American sailors in the Saiyida Zaynab jail," Rayne told the officer. "They were framed. While I was trying to help them, I located the missing spare parts."

"What?"

"Yes, sir. Near the Soudan Bazaar. You can't miss the place. There's a fire, half the town's turned out, and Daoud Pasha was shot up by some native who had a grudge against him."

"I'll be blasted," the colonel exclaimed. Then asked and received the remaining details. "I thought you were going to see your grandmother?"

"That's where I'm going now, Colonel," Rayne replied. "If you think that you will be able to spare me for another day."

NAVIGATION SIMPLIFIED

Originally appeared in *Short Stories*, May 25th 1943.

Tarrant was solid, deeply tanned, and clear eyed. For a beachcomber, Jim Tarrant was certainly presentable, and the hard-drinking Netherlanders of Pulau Besar seemed to have hit upon the answer: "That home-made *arrak* would gag anyone, he takes just enough of it to get him to the point of feeling damn good and sorry for himself. What he needs is something to do and to worry about."

And now the entire settlement had plenty to worry about; so much so that they ignored Tarrant, who had warned them. He began to wish he had left with his friends, the Malay fishermen, during the night. Being ignored made him sorry for himself, as usual.

Jan Dekker, the *posthouder*, said to the twenty-odd men who sat on the counters and on packing cases, "When the stock of trade goods is gone, we either have to leave or else be sure we can defend ourselves for the duration."

Adolph Maartens brushed back his shock of sandy hair and laughed sourly as he faced the lean and leathery *posthouder*. He gestured at the shelves, and included the storerooms, and the bales of rattan which the kinky-haired head hunters had brought from the interior.

"If my stock is all there is between us and hell, I think we had better start swimming."

A hatchet-faced Australian asked his comrade, "What's he saying? It doesn't sound good." His companion, who had a better command of Netherlands, interpreted, adding, "He's bloody well right. When Malays start slipping out, it's time to follow suit."

Maartens turned and picked Tarrant from the farther side of the group. "If this draft dodger or fugitive or whatever he is had let us know—" Tarrant reddened, and took two steps forward.

"I didn't know they were leaving so suddenly."

The storekeeper snorted. "Probably not, or you'd gone with them. Or wouldn't they have you?"

"Ali asked me," the American snorted. "I had my chance."

Jan Dekker, representing what law and government remained in that isolated reach of the Indies, raised a lean hand. "Never mind blame or argument! We could not—let me say, we *would not* have seized their boats." His fierce eyes gleamed beneath white brows; his shifting glance nailed the key men of the little settlement. "Those days are gone. Even if *Mynheer* Tarrant had been sober enough to notify us, we would not have seized any Malay boats. Now let us have something constructive."

"Guvnor, why in hell don't you suggest something? You're the *posthouder*," Sims, the red-headed Australian demanded.

Dekker smiled enough to relieve the hardness of his uncompromising mouth. "First I listen to you, to all of you, before I tell you what is to be done."

He heard patiently the blend of panic, ill-timed defiance, impracticable schemes of defense against the beetle-browed Papuan head hunters of the interior. And Jim Tarrant knew that his draft dodger's paradise had become a mirage.

Pulau Besar, midway between the Jap-infested Moluccas and Jap-occupied Timor, had for several years sheltered him, and even after Pearl Harbor, the island was a cozy haven. Tarrant had a grudge against the government, his own government, which, as he saw things, had sold him down the river. So, in this outlying bit of the Indies, which Jap cruisers and bombers considered unworthy of their attention, Tarrant had coddled his grudge and his self pity.

Until the Japs swooped down on Java and Timor and Sumatra, a K.P.M. steamer called once every eight weeks to pick up tortoise shell, *agag-agar*, rattan and *trepang*. It brought mail, and supplies and trade goods—calico, knives, fish hooks, stick tobacco for barter with the wild Papuans of the interior. And now, with shelves almost depleted, the trading post proprietor could not bargain with the savages when they came to town.

"Don't barter with the bloody beggars!" the Australian prospectors decided; an idea whose English expression most of the Netherlander understood, or had already phrased in their own language. "Just close the place."

All eyes centered on the *posthouder*. Dekker said, "The steamer has missed two calls! Since the Malays could not help us, they left so as not to see our end. The only hope is that the Papuan brain—" He made a cutting gesture with right index finger against left thumb. "About this size, or a little smaller—will take a while to grasp the point."

A guffaw greeted this first cheering bit. Even Tarrant chuckled, and the missionary moved over toward him, to make him feel somewhat more like a white man. But Dekker, like so many of his nation, was a realist and not a wish thinker. He added, "Do not forget, gentlemen, that what a Papuan lacks in brains, he makes up in animal instinct."

Tarrant cleared his throat, and took an uncertain step forward. The missionary's implied friendliness smoothed some of the awkwardness of the start: "We can build a boat and make for Australia."

Someone made a derisive sound. Dekker however interposed, "We are less concerned with a man's past than we are with his future. Mr. Tarrant, can you navigate?"

"I came from the Philippines in a Buginese *prahu*. Between us, we can piece together enough navigation to get us to Port Darwin."

Albeit risky, that sounded reasonable enough, until the *posthouder* learned that not another man of the group had even Tarrant's skimpy knowledge. "Don't worry too much, men, and don't get your families excited. Before we can face the perils of the sea, we'll first have to survive what comes from the land."

A battered *prahu*, abandoned by the Malays, served as a model; the jungle offered trees large enough, and there were sufficient hand tools. Dekker, at once admitting the wisdom of making a large dug-out according to the proportions of the model, told the men of the settlement, "We could risk ribs and planks and perhaps get something which would be seaworthy. And again, we might not. Unless Yut Li and Ah Wong have blueprints for a junk, we follow Malay design."

Since the two Chinese merchants had no suggestions, a tree was felled and manhandled to the beach.

Anthropologists claim that certain primitive races cannot count higher than five, others no more than ten, with twenty as the upper limit; but the shock headed Papuans, regardless of theories, had a clear concept of fifty-six, for on the day when the steamer should have anchored out in the bay, the knotty muscled savages arrived from the interior to trade.

Dekker, not being an anthropologist, was prepared. Tarpaulins and empty cases concealed the partly shaped hull on the beach, and on the face of things, Pulau Besar was normal. Everyone, however, had blistered palms, and whoever owned a pistol carried it in his pocket.

Though the aborigines were odorous enough, Tarrant could also smell trouble. There was a new gleam in those cunning little Papuan eyes. The thick lips had an insolent twist, and the flaring nostrils twitched as though they had half-scented a change in the white settlement. Someone muttered, "Naturally, they miss the Malays. That's a dead giveaway."

Dekker was in his official bungalow. Yut Li and Ah Wong were in their little shops. Luden, the missionary, waited as usual in the dispensary behind the church. But the half-dozen women and children were in the old blockhouse.

With not a radio in operation for some months, the white settlement had lost all touch with the world. When the K.P.M. steamer for the third time missed her scheduled stop, it was clear that something had gone wrong all the way from Sumatra to Timor, and that the fall of Singapore had been only the beginning of calamity. Where the absence of bombers and cruisers had made the war an unreality to Tarrant, the long continued absence of the interisland steamer began to bring the conflict closer. And now, watching the clucking savages crowd into the trading post, he realized for the first time that law had left the Indies.

True, their stone axes and their carved clubs were at the fringe of the jungle, along with the spears tipped with cassowary bone; they still obeyed the law which, in terms of their logic, was a taboo proclaimed centuries ago by Jan Dekker's predecessors, and terribly enforced by soldiers and gun-bearing ships.

Though they suspected that the power backing the taboo had faded, they still lacked the courage to test their suspicion. They wanted hatchets, they wanted knives, they wanted canned goods. Maartens, bluff and hearty, told them that the steamer, arriving ahead off time and leaving early, had left only calico and tobacco, and very little of either. "And how about some mirrors?"

But the story was falling flat, and Tarrant began to get a taste of the war he had evaded in advance. His own government had sold him down the river, several years previous, when "good neighbor" legislation, favoring vegetable oils from Brazil, had killed the copra and cocoa nut oil business of the Philippines. And rather than accept the hospitality of natives who had once looked up to him as the owner of a prosperous plantation, Tarrant had sailed away with a Buginese skipper, finally landing in Pulau Besar. There, with homemade *arrak* to help dramatize his troubles, he had enjoyed the role of draft evader.

Looking from the veranda of the trading post, Tarrant saw that suspicion would quickly become certainty. Three Papuans, fully armed, were rounding the headland and creeping toward the tarpaulin and the heap of cases which camouflaged the partly completed dugout. To give an alarm would take too long, moreover, every white man in the settlement would dash to the water front and leave the settlement exposed to whatever other armed savages might be lurking on the landward side.

Casually, loitering along, he headed down the path; and in spite of the revolver in his hip pocket, he did not particularly like his task. Each step away from his fellows made him more uneasy, more and more conscious of the unpleasant aspects of the isolation he had so long sought.

Once below the level of the town, he broke into a run. The three Papuans, hearing the thud of his feet in the sand, whirled from their objective.

"Get away!" he shouted, gesturing.

They stood there, grinning insolently. White prestige had taken a long drop in the past six months. One hefted a stone axe. Another, spear in hand, continued on his way toward the camouflaged hull. Already, they must have seen, from that short distance, that this was not a straggling heap of freshly loaded merchandise.

"Get away!" he repeated, hesitating to use his revolver against Papuans who had only primitive weapons.

The man nearest the cache made a quick gesture. Tarrant had heard of Papuan slingers, and he had seen them, but never in action. Almost as quickly as one could draw and fire a pistol, the knotty legged giant had whisked a stone the size of a baseball.

Tarrant flung himself flat; and with little time to spare. The sound of the heavy missile's passing told him how narrowly he had missed a fatal wound. Barely flat on the sand, he drew his revolver, firing from rest.

He drilled his man squarely. The other two fled, howling.

There was no shooting in the settlement. With pistols, shotguns, and two rifles confronting them, the aborigines had no choice but to withdraw. By the time Tarrant reached the level of the store, the place was clear of Papuans; but he liked neither the looks nor the mutterings of the men he faced.

"If you're so anxious to fight, you could have picked a better time and place than this," they reminded him.

"If you'd been keeping your eyes open," he retorted, "you could have headed them off before they got close enough to see that we're building a boat."

Jan Dekker remained neutral. "Two got away, do you say? Then you may depend upon it, they all know by now. So let us stop this everlastingly-damned argument before it starts. There is a boat to be built."

He did not add that, in view of the weeks which had passed without the arrival of any supplies, the settlement would have to live off the country; and that the country was now alive with Papuans who, sensing the end of law and order, would collect whatever heads they could, and renew their acquaintance with long pig. All this was too plain for discussion.

And as he sweated with adze and chisel, Tarrant did not know whether he had or had not used his head, down there on the beach. He was sure of nothing other than that his hands were horribly blistered, that he ached in more muscles than he ever had suspected himself of having, and that the Japs might as we'll have bombed and shelled Pulau Besar.

Though he was not really conscious of the fact, Tarrant had quite forgotten to curse the skillet-heads who had ruined the copra business. However, he might have got around to that routine, later in the evening, had Jan Dekker not furnished an antidote: "A guard must be posted at the hull as well as at the blockhouse. Line up and draw lots."

Everyone but the two Chinese had suggestions, brilliant ones, on guard duty. But the *posthouder*, after listening patiently, simplified matters a good deal. "Just stay awake and on your posts. No drinking, sociable or otherwise—Tarrant, I mean you, too! Since this is not an army, I cannot tell you that sleeping sentries will be shot. Still I can assure you that sleeping sentries will be eaten. Good night, gentlemen."

* * * *

There was no attack that night, and none during the shaping of the hull, or the stepping of the mast. She had a square sail, like a Moro *vinta*.

No champagne for the launching. She was long and slim, without any keel; outriggers kept her from capsizing. For a chronometer, there was the *posthouder's* watch. For charts, his atlas, and a 1904 edition of a British Admiralty pilot book, dug out of a corner of the trading post. One of the Australian prospectors had a prismatic marching compass.

Tarrant, meanwhile, had been solving problems of his own. Buginese navigation was based on principles contained in manuals written in that obscure language. Where he had expected elementary sea knowledge among at least a few others of the settlement, he found that every man, from the *posthouder*

168

down, had cheerfully dumped the responsibility on him. What had started as a suggestion for public consideration had ended as a personal responsibility. So, during the completion of the war canoe, Tarrant had been at work.

He was tempted to confess to Luden, the missionary, but thought better of it. Instead, he said boldly, "There's probably not a sextant between here and Timor, and probably not even a surveyor's theodolite."

Mynheer Luden nodded. "That is true. But the old mariners steered by the stars, and we have a compass. After all, we do not expect frills, *Mynheer* Tarrant, the Buginese method you know is good enough for us."

Tarrant was thinking, "Yeah, swell, until we wander around in circles, and run out of rations and water, and then who'll they be lynching?" He said, "Maybe you have some drafting instruments, a protractor?"

"But of course. Right here."

So he set to work with an aluminum dishpan, wire, and a piece of gas pipe. What he finally carried aboard was something he hoped would pass for an astrolabe.

The women, crowding amidships with the half dozen children who had not been sent back to the Netherlands to go to school, cried out against the impossibility of living in such a cramped space. Jan Dekker said, grimly, "As we run out of rations, there will be more room to stretch your legs, ladies."

Dekker was in command, by virtue of age and rank. Tarrant's job was merely to set the course. "And," Dekker whispered to him, once they were under way, "to be thrown overboard if something goes wrong. And I will be next."

Tarrant glanced back at the settlement, which Dekker had ordered set afire, so that nothing could by any chance serve the enemy. "Better than being eaten," he retorted.

She knifed the water. Once well from the lee of the headland, she raced along, spray drenching the closely packed passengers. Tacking was a simple business, for with both ends alike, either could be bow, or stern. Luckily, no heads were cracked when the boom came about. But she had scarcely made three cable lengths beyond the bar when Sims, the carrot-topped Australian yelled, "Look there! A whole bloody navy!"

Two Papuan war canoes were converging from port and starboard. Apparently they had been waiting to catch the refugees all packed in a vibrating hull, too cramped for defense of concealment. Or perhaps, with their walnut-sized brains, they had reasoned that once the whites left the taboo-protected settlement, their magic would fail.

Their oiled black bodies gleamed in the beating sun. Leaf shaped paddles flashed, and wooden drums set the cadence. From the deck of a destroyer, the spectacle would have been beautiful to see.

For a while, it seemed that sail and the Malay pirate hull would win. With a Buginese crew, and all the canvas she could carry, it would not even have been an interesting bet. But here, amateurs were competing with experts. And the black men, beyond any doubt, felt that they had to cut off the fugitives so that there could not be any future vengeance.

Bone tipped arrows began to rake the bulwarks as the Papuans narrowed the gap. Black slingers cut loose with rocks polished round in torrent beds.

"Heads down!" Dekker shouted, rather needlessly. Then, "Who can shoot?"

"I ain't bad, Guvnor," Sims answered, and Pitt, the other Australian, admitted no greater incompetence. "But the way she pitches don't help."

One pointed port, one to starboard; the ripping whack of the two rifles made a long drawn sound. Dekker, spotting with his binoculars, shouted, "Good! Both good!" But a realistic Chinese trader observed, "Still come too damn fast."

And the gap in the rank of rowers was filled up. Tarrant said, "They've got more men than we have ammunition."

No doubt that Sims and Pitt were handy. Neither arrows nor sling stones shook their aim. Not even the scream of a woman nailed by a bone-headed shaft made them flinch. Dekker, however, said, "We are short of cartridges."

"Hell, Guvnor! We won't have any more if we wait till they overhaul us." Someone shouted to the women, "Quit that screaming!"

Dekker nudged Tarrant. "Bad case of nerves. Wish we had another dozen Australians."

A sling stone bounced off the taut sail. Another, dish-shaped instead of spherical, cut a hole. The canvas began to tear. With the least freshening of the wind, there would be a ripping, and the race would end.

Dekker's lips were knife-thin. "If you know any other Buginese customs, my lad, let us hear them within the next couple seconds."

Tarrant was breaking out hatchets and knives. Pistols and shotguns were served to their owners. Each tack gave the Papuans a definite advantage. Then Tarrant said, "Dekker, one chance. Make for the nearest boat, to hell with running, close in on one!"

As he spoke, he dug for the tin of homemade alcohol which was to feed the little stove amidships, and slashed its top.

Dekker shouted to the man at the sweep, "I'm not crazy, do as I say!"

Sims and Pitt grinned. The redhead said, "If we get across their bow, maybe we can string four of them with one bullet!"

The Netherlanders had tightened up, stubborn and silent, no longer shaken by the moan of the woman nailed by an arrow. The two Chinese were blank faced as they crouched with their hatchets. Nobody paid much attention to Tarrant. The helmsman groaned, dropped. Luden took the helm to put her hard a-port. If the missionary was praying, he did not look it.

The tack was good. One outrigger in the air, one deep in the water, and the sail catching hell; but not ripping. Not yet.

"Now!"

Rifles whacked. Shotguns bellowed. Pistols smacked and roared, and for a moment, the flight of arrows and stones had to cease. The war canoe lost way as paddlers dropped. Then, when it seemed that the outrigger would foul the enemy's prow, Tarrant flicked a cigarette lighter and heaved the slashed can of alcohol.

The fire ball landed among the enemy, scattering flaming fuel. Dekker followed up with three beer bottles amidship. The archers and the slingers and the paddlers neglected their work; for the blazing alcohol floated on the water the fast running canoe had shipped. And her crew was too tightly jammed for good dodging.

Sims shouted, "See how *you* like roast meat!"

The Malay *prahu* came about, and now the other Papuan canoe was pulling nearer. "Get the drummer!" Tarrant shouted. "Pick him off!"

Pitt frowned. "You don't like their bloody music?"

"Pick him off, damn it!" Tarrant howled. "Break their beat!"

The Australian's second shot did it. And whether the cessation of the war drum, or the fire flinging which had demoralized the near canoe, the fact remained that the Papuans began to lag further and further astern.

Luden relinquished the helm. "That poor woman with a barbed arrow in her arm," he muttered, and dug into the supplies.

The anesthetic was four ounces of brandy. Taken in a few gulps, the patient was practically paralyzed. The missionary forced the shaft home until it appeared on the other side, its barbs tearing all the way. Tarrant leaned over the side, and when he looked back, wiping his chin, Luden had cut the arrow head: and could thus withdraw the shaft.

"I guess that hurt me more than it did her," he muttered, and went astern.

There he found Dekker white faced and coughing blood. He turned to shout to Luden, but the *posthouder* caught his arm. "No use. This is one he can't shove through. Call Maartens and Doom."

These were the *posthouder's* two cronies, and next to him, the oldest residents of Pulau Besar. When they saw him, and the result of the farewell volley from the second canoe, they tried to tell him of cases where men had recovered. But Dekker snorted. "Shut up, you two fools. Listen to me, you are witnesses." He coughed, a gush of blood choked him. "This Tarrant—no one thinks much of him—maybe they are right—but he's the only man—who can —navigate—I leave him—in command—of—"

"But—see here, Jan—" Maartens protested.

Dekker persisted, "One eyed man—is king—among the blind—damn it— you can't—navigate—at all. Shut up. Do—as I say."

And though he lived for some minutes, Dekker could not say any more. When the missionary learned what had happened, he said, "You should have told me. The other wounded could wait."

Tarrant shook his head. "Reverend, the only consolation he wanted was knowing you were taking care of those you could save."

On paper, the Banda Sea is small, and crowded with islands; and the Timor Sea looked just as easy, but before many days had passed, Tarrant began to worry. Islands were totally lacking, and both water and food were running low.

A *prahu* manned by Buginese sailors apparently made three times as much way as a similar craft handled by landlubbers. Tarrant's own misgivings had made him ration water almost from the start, and thus he had handicapped himself with thirsty and doubting people.

"Where's those bloody islands you said you'd have a hard time dodging?" Sims demanded.

The Netherlanders, though they kept a stoical silence, had the same question in their bloodshot eyes and drawn faces. The *prahu* was no longer crowded. Nearly every arrow wound had led to a fatal infection, in spite of the missionary's first aid kit. "Poison," he told Tarrant, one night. "But I didn't have the heart to tell them. Probably they knew, and tried to believe they'd be exceptions."

Tarrant's astrolabe was a wonderful thing to see. The azimuth circle had been scribed on the bottom of an aluminum dishpan. The column was a piece of gas pipe.

The telescope, a bit of copper tubing, was wired to the straight-edge of a draftsman's protractor, to which was attached a plumb bob.

He shot the sun. He shot stars. He consulted the Buginese manual. Unhappily, for all his thumbing of the Admiralty Pilot, 1904 edition, there was no landfall.

Pitt, taking up Sims' refrain, demanded, "Where's those bloody islands you told us about, with lots of tucker and water?"

Tarrant carefully set the astrolabe down. "I cannot call this mutiny. Any sea lawyer could prove that my being put in command was irregular. But the first island we reach, I'll beat the living hell out of both of you!"

"Chum, take off that gun, and have at it."

Tarrant shook his head. "A *prahu* is too crowded. If I thought you could navigate any better—want to try it?"

They eyed each other and the weird astrolabe. "We can't read Buginese tables."

A squall carried away mast and half the sail. Bamboo and rattan, stolen from the outrigger struts, furnished what an optimist might have called a jury rig. "It is better than paddling," Tarrant contended, "particularly since we don't have paddles."

When they did sight an island, it proved to be rich in guano, devoid of vegetation, and without any water. Flying fish and a shark stretched the scanty rations. Tarrant, regarding the gaunt and hollow eyed passengers, could see that they eased their misery by telling each other that this was his idea; that his bluff and brag had induced them to leave a blockhouse which they might have defended, and in whose immediate vicinity they might have foraged. They at least would have had water aplenty.

He sustained himself by thinking, "They've got to blame someone. They're sorry for themselves."

Now that supplies were dismayingly low, he knew that there had to be a guard against pilfering from the stores. The passengers would be short sighted enough to express their resentment by stealing. More and more often, he had to say, "I am sorry, but a child does not get any more thirsty than a grown person. A ration is a ration."

Luden said, one day, "You can't keep it up, with just cat-naps. Let me watch. You need sleep."

"No, Reverend. They'll wheedle you out of water for the kids."

Luden had no answer. Tarrant napped at times, but never for long. He would awaken, shocked from a sleep in which passengers crept upon him to steal; and then, awake, he would see that none had moved from their places. Sometimes he thought that Jan Dekker was saying to him, "Don't be afraid of them, they know the supplies have to be rationed."

Dekker's presence became very real. He knew now that he was in command only because of Jan Dekker's final words. But he also knew that beyond a certain point, a dead man's will and courage could not sustain people who suffered far more from fear and doubt than from actual hardship.

When a squall pelted rain into the bellied remnant of the sail, and doubled the water supply, there should have been an easing of tension, but there was nothing of the kind. Maartens and Doom and the two Australians came to him and said, "We're not getting anywhere. We're going in circle. No matter what way we went, a straight course would certainly have brought us to land long before now."

Tarrant said, wearily, "You've all steered, and you've all held the course, and even if the compass is off, we could not go in circles."

"But where the bloody hell *are* we? What's your log say? You're shooting the sun, you're getting some sort of latitude or longitude or whatever it is you're supposed to get, where are we?"

Tarrant turned to the fly-leaves of the atlas, on which he had kept his log. "See for yourself."

"If we knew anything about right ascension and declination and the rest, we'd be navigating."

Luden cut in, "What can you expect of home-made instruments and a Buginese manual? This is still better than staying at Pulau Besar."

"We want to know where we are."

"Twelve degrees south, one twenty-nine east." Tarrant jabbed his pencil to the map. "Right here."

"Right there, eh? But how many days, how many bloody miles?"

They were hard and angular and desperate, but they were also querulous, underneath it all like children begging for reassurance. Their maddening reiteration, their unspoken promises of violence, of wrath which would have to destroy someone when it burst out—they at last stopped oppressing Tarrant, for these people, though hating him, blaming him, nevertheless looked to him for reassurance. He began to think of himself, sulking on the beach, finding comfort in self-justification and in the repeated recital of how his own government had ruined his plantation.

Everyone wanted comfort. Even a bungling navigator, a navigator in whom no one had any trust, was still tolerated instead of being thrown overboard: provided that he could offer encouragement, and plausibly.

"I hate to tell you this," he announced, "but we have at least five more days."

He sounded as though he believed every word, though he might as well have said seven or twelve or fifteen. But he had seen the effect of assurance, and he saw it work again. All but Luden went away, and Tarrant said to him, "Take over, while I sleep."

"Good! That will give them more courage than anything else could have done."

For the first time, Tarrant did not hear Jan Dekker, nor did the red sun dance behind his eyelids: and his cracked lips and dry mouth failed to disturb his sleep. It made no difference now what happened when, five days from now, there was no landfall. Let them do what they pleased.

At first he thought that the concussion which had awakened him was thunder, and that a rainstorm was drenching him. But the *prahu* was not breaking up on a reef.

Two rifles whacked. Sims and Pitt were blazing away at a plane which was beyond their range. Another stick of bombs hit the water, and geysers gushed high. Then he saw the fighters swooping down. Smoke poured from the bomber, masking the red rayed sun on its wing tips.

It began to spin. All ablaze, it nosed into the sea. Some of the victors had concentric red and blue and white circles on their wing tips. Others had a red circle in the center of a white star, in its turn on a blue circle. The people of the *prahu* waved ragged shirts, and shouted, gestured until they dropped. But the planes, having done their work, streaked home, and without seeing the *prahu*. Or if they saw, they may have assumed that the waving was applause for a good job.

"They'll send help," Tarrant declared, confidently. "We're nearer than I figured. Line up for an extra ration."

The following afternoon, Pitt sighted land, and green jungle. There was an inlet whose waters were alive with grumbling and bellowing crocodiles. Parrots chattered, and flights of birds whirred from cover.

The difficult landing was made. Some distance inland, poles with crossarms readied black against the sky. Tarrant did not need an astrolabe to tell him that he had made Australia. Cutting a telegraph wire would bring a maintenance crew, and in a hurry.

He laid his pistol on a rock, and beckoned to Sims and Pitt. "Come and get it. Lots of room now."

They chuckled, and shook their heads. "Digger, we have nothing to fight about," Pitt said. "You can't be more than a hundred miles from Cape York or

Port Darwin, which is close enough for us. And we're two years behind time, getting home."

"Two years behind time?"

Sims nodded. "Same as yourself. Hated to leave a soft spot like Pulau Besar."

"Practical minded," Pitt cut in. "Never the ones to go looking for trouble." Then, to Sims, "Let's cut the bloody wire, while the skipper picks a spot to camp."

They plunged into the jungle. Luden said to Tarrant, "I think they—I think we've all met the war. And how is *your* grudge?"

Tarrant laughed. "Oh, that! I've got a brand new one. It's been growing ever since things blew up on Pulau Besar. Say, they must have some American troops in Australia, judging from those planes, yesterday."

"You wouldn't think of joining the navy," Maartens asked, as he joined the two. "See here, Tarrant, where did you learn to read a Buginese pilot manual?"

"I can't read it. And it's not Buginese, it's a Koran I picked up in Mindanao. It was just as clear to me as the working of an astrolabe."

"I thought as much," Luden said. "But how—" His gesture, including all that part of Australia, completed his question. "Nothing to it," Tarrant answered. "With a compass, I figured it'd be simple heading south. Australia was too big to miss entirely. Now, when we head the other way, it'll be just as simple. With Japs in practically every damned island, we can find some wherever we land."

SCORCHED EARTH

Originally appeared in *Speed Adventure Stories*, July 1944.

When Mu Lan fingered a curl which was already faultless, and paused for a moment to admire the hair-do which she had invented, a blend of Chinese and Manchu styling, plus a touch of her own. All her life, Mu Lan had been revising rules to suit herself, but this was the first time that the freedom of a sing-song girl promised to have real meaning.

Her *amah* stood behind her, watching with pride and apprehension; Yu Tang was glad when her mistress smiled and said that all was perfect. Then Mu Lan twisted a jade pendant of her ornate head gear. The jewel separated into hollowed halves, into whose cavity she put several small pellets. This was not her first invitation to appear at General Yasuda's quarters, but it might be her last.

General Yasuda was Japanese, and a gentleman, and so, particularly disliking his guest of honor, he had outdone himself in arranging the dinner to welcome Gunther Dreckhauffen, who had come to observe the workings of Co-Prosperity in the Rice Bowl. The bullet-headed Nazi, on the other hand, true to the training of his kind, was not content with being as boorish as nature had made him: he pointed out how German efficiency would have improved every course from bird's nest soup and steamed sweet doughnuts to the flattish and sticky champagne.

"General Yasuda—" Dreckhauffen consistently ignored both field and company officers, his gesture including them with the litter on the table. "It is already plain that instead of occupying China, and then breaking the Russian truce, you are becoming as Chinese as your cuisine."

Yasuda smiled. He was a delicate-looking little man, as frail and unsubstantial-seeming as the evasion which he offered, instead of a retort: "After all, the Chinese are better cooks than we are."

The Nazi was so shocked that his monocle dropped from his eye. *Um gottes willen*, what kind of a man is it who can see good in another nation? Not a bit more character than the *Dagos!* With such allies, no wonder that *der Fuehrer* had to save the world single handed.

Yasuda had a fair idea of what passed behind the envoy's fat face, but his amiability did not waver. "Mr. Dreckhauffen," he went on, using the English which served as a common tongue for the two, "when you see the final Chinese touch, I think that you do not blame me for—for—making concessions to art."

"Eh? More food?"

He mopped his dripping face, and ran a thick finger inside his collar, over which his neck made a red bulge.

"Oh, not at all. Now that we have titillated our palates, we have a feast of wit and reason. Chen Mu Lan, the Shanghai sing-song girl, consents to entertain us."

"*Consents? Herr Gott!* Could she refuse?"

"Of course not. But one can hardly be entertaining, witty, and charming by command."

Dreckhauffen snorted. "In Germany, one can, and one does."

And then the Number One announced Chen Mu Lan. Yasuda nodded, beamed at his guest; the general, having the soul of an artist, took pride in being the patron of China's loveliest sing-song girl, and ignored the possibility of her having had unusual motives in leaving Shanghai.

She moved with a mincing pace, artificial as it was graceful. Jade ear pendants, and the jade pendants handing from her satin hood made a thin, sweet tinkling, fragile as the conventional twitter of her voice when she kowtowed, greeting host and guest of honor.

Dreckhauffen eyed her from tiny embroidered slippers to the arch of close-packed curls which framed her forehead. Mu Lan was neither tall nor as slender as she seemed, for the knee length tunic combined with her silk trousers and prim, high collar to exaggerate her slimness, while the Manchu styled headgear increased the illusion of height.

The Nazi grunted, and with not quite his usual disparagement. "Nimble enough, for her crippled feet."

Yasuda hissed, somewhat out of politeness, and somewhat to conceal his amazement at ignorance. "Please, begging pardon, those are naturally small. Sing-song girls never binding feet." Mu Lan's training had taken more time, and covered more ground than an American debutante and an American Doctor of Philosophy could claim between them; she knew how a wine glass should be touched, and how even the incorrect inflection of her smallest finger could detract from the perfection of the gesture: and so with her repartee. But none of the company knew enough Chinese to be worthy of her talent, so she sang in that studied falsetto, and pantomimed with all the finish developed in forty odd centuries of training sing-song girls.

The *sam yin* wailed. The drums muttered; drums, and the shivering, hissing brazen gongs. Dreckhauffen shuddered, and growled, "*Herr Gott!* This is worse than those stupid *geishas!*"

Between songs, Mu Lan drank tiny cups of *mui kwai lu*, which tastes like sewing machine oil flavored with attar of roses. Though she wheedled Dreckhauffen into emptying cup after cup of orange-red *ng ka pay*, her glance slid always to Yasuda, a glance which, as to angle and the droop of eyelids, had been prescribed a thousand years before the ancestors of both Gunther Dreckhauffen and the Son of Heaven had quit raw meat and smoky caves.

The general smiled his appreciation. Of the girl, the Nazi thought; he didn't know that the Jap relished the triple-edged mockery of Mu Lan's song about the foreign devil with the eyes of a pig and the manners of a buffalo, sweating and grunting and fingering his tight collar.

Mu Lan knew now that she had not wasted those weeks of establishing herself in Cheng Teh, to make her presence the touch without which a dinner would merely have been a meal.

To impress the Nazi observer, Yasuda had inevitably to make an important move to convince him that the failure to complete the seizure of this sector of the Rice Bowl had been according to plan. Sooner or later, such a gesture would have had to come, if only to maintain Yasuda's "face" in Japan. Dreckhauffen's presence had merely hastened the climax.

The next move would be toward Ching Pao, Mu Lan's native village; so she was going to her own people. The same instinct which once made Chinese section hands arrange to have their bones shipped from California to the ancestral burial ground, now drove Mu Lan to Ching Pao, "Precious Gold," as the dumpy little village called itself, to sound more impressive than its neighboring rival, Yin Pao, Precious Silver.

She seated herself, smiled dazzling at Dreckhauffen, and proposed a game of *chai mui.*

"Like this," Mu Lan explained, thrusting out three fingers. "I call *three!* You answer, seven, and put out enough fingers to make ten. A mistake, and you lose."

"What do we bet?"

"You have to drink a cup of General Yasuda's brandy. And if I lose—"

Dreckhauffen brightened some more. "You drink one, eh? Very good."

But it wasn't what he expected. Voice and fingers tricked him, and when it came his turn, he could not catch Mu Lan off guard. Though the general lost, he took it good-naturedly, while the Nazi considered that honor was being affronted.

The more bets he lost, the more *ng ka pay* he drank, and the more he fumbled. Yasuda began to enjoy the thus far unpleasant dinner, and so did his officers, until they fell on their faces to snore into the banquet remnants. Food rather than brandy had overcome them, since years of short rations had made them unaccustomed to hearty eating.

The amiable little general blinked owlishly through his misted glasses when Dreckhauffen crumpled in a heap, knocking down bottles and jugs and glasses.

"The foreign devil cannot even pass out like a gentleman," Mu Lan said, laughing. "Now with your permission, worthy general?"

Though Yasuda handed the sing-song girl's maid an envelope containing more than the customary fee for making an appearance, his enjoyment of his triumph made him reluctant to dismiss her; and Mu Lan, after pleading another engagement, let herself be talked into staying.

She did not stay long. A song and three drinks settled Yasuda, and without the assistance of the opiate in the hair pendant.

Yu Tang gathered up Mu Lan's cape and fan and discarded bracelets. The musicians had long since left. Then, as the *amah* watched at the door, Mu Lan searched first the general's pockets, and next the living quarters. She returned with a sheaf of orders, all in Japanese, which she could not speak; but since the monkey men had cribbed their hieroglyphics from the Chinese, lacking any writing of their own, the significance of many of the characters was clear to anyone who could read.

Rumor had been right. There was an order to make a demonstration because of the Nazi's presence.

Once outside the house, Yu Tang awakened the coolies who snored in a corner. Mu Lan got into the sedan chair; her *amah* followed, then drew the curtains. The coolies shouldered their burden, and set out at a trot.

The pass which Yasuda had given Mu Lan to smooth her late return from his quarters was more than enough for the sentries posted at intervals beyond the outskirts of Cheng Teh. All night long the knotty-legged coolies trudged down the yard wide trail which wound and snaked among the rice patches.

During the hours of darkness, little more than instinct kept them from stumbling over slabs placed lengthwise to bridge ditches which led water from higher to lower terraces. There was no shoulder, nor any allowance for swerving; once off the paving, a pedestrian dropped into the knee-deep mud of the fields on either side.

When the moon rose, Mu Lan looked between the drawn curtains, and out across the headed rice which swayed in the hot breeze. Some of the terraced plots were no more than a few yards square; other reached a *li* in every direction.

Irrigation had for the time ended. Only here and there was the moonlight reflected from a dyked field. When once the waters sank, invaders and harvest time would come to the unoccupied stretches of the rice bowl.

Mu Lan had no reason to hope that her warning could put into the field enough guerillas to block Yasuda's troops. The best she expected to do in Ching Pao was to persuade the villagers to destroy their crops rather than to harvest for the enemy. Now she wondered how any argument of hers could succeed when all others had thus far failed; for, seeing again, after those years of absence, how much backbreaking work went into building dykes, and ploughing knee deep in mud, planting rice shoots by hand, and ladling fertilizer to each cluster, she understood why the peasants stubbornly held out against scorched earth.

And the loneliness added its bit. She was in another world, a rural world cut off from news, from cities, from the rest of China. Her parents, if they still lived, bending in the mud of rice fields, could not see beyond local feuds, and the rival village, Yin Pao. To them, an enemy in Cheng Teh was an enemy in the moon.

Unless she could convince them, they wouldn't learn until it was too late.

At times shelters loomed up, dark and massive: brick columns, supporting a tiled roof, flanked brick benches. Here the coolies rested, smoked a few pipes of finely shredded tobacco, and trotted on.

Mu Lan was not afraid. There could not be any pursuit until Yasuda emerged from his stupor, and had occasion to refer to an order whose contents already formed an unpleasant part of his memories. And though suspecting Mu Lan, he would hardly issue an order for her arrest, for to do so would make him lose face with whatever subordinates he detailed to execute his commands. Having been outwitted by a sing-song girl was not a subject he would care to mention, all the more so since the inevitable rumors which no vigilance ever prevented would certainly have warned the villagers. Every Japanese plan was so sure to become public property before being put into effect that Yasuda as a matter of routine included precautions to offset leaks.

Yet she craned her neck, and begrudged the coolies their short rest, some time after sunrise, at a grimy little inn, a hovel of brick and timber, where pigs and chickens shared quarters with the proprietor and his family.

The day's heat was made worse by steam exhaled by the drying rice fields. In some villages, farmers were already cutting the clusters, and beating the grain out of the heads. The continuous drumming and thumping was like the far off rumble of thunder.

Toward evening, the coolies waded ankle deep. Premature rain, falling in the far off hills, had flooded an area before the harvesters could gather the crop, No need here for scorched earth. Famine was already on the way, and men and boys plunged into the mud and syrup-thick water, salvaging what they could. Sunrise to sunset, from year's beginning to year's end, there was rarely a day not given to outwitting hunger.

Mu Lao's shoulders sagged, and more from the weight of her task than from weariness. Seeing these men fight to save the shreds of a crop made her mission in Ching Pao seem impossible.

* * * *

Near sunset of the third day, the coolies stumbled toward the wall which enclosed the rammed earth houses of the families who owned the surrounding acres. This was home, and the sight and smell of it made her for a moment regret Cheng Teh. Then, as the tea shop loafers set down their cups to gape and point, marveling at the gilded sedan chair and the splendid person it sheltered, Mu Lan smiled a little, and held her head high.

She had left this grimy village afoot, and to avoid marrying the village idiot. Far from postponing flight until her wedding day, she had shaken the dirt and dung of "Precious Gold" from her unbound feet the day after the betrothal feast, making her parents lose what little face they might have had. Nothing but instinct brought her back; instinct, and the urge to show her one-time people how to outwit the vicious barbarians from Japan.

180

Mu Lan's parents, driven by famine and revolt, had not been able to encumber themselves with a daughter agonized and helpless from bandaged feet and when the times finally permitted the family to return to Ching Pao, the girl's feet had grown beyond binding. They could have sold her as a slave girl, rather than lose face by keeping their big-footed disgrace, but they had managed to avoid that solution, for, luckily enough, there was a neighboring family which would accept a bride who did not have "golden lilies."

Since the son was a half-wit, and the parents were as poor as Mu Lan's, they had snapped at the chance.

Thinking of these things, she smiled a little more and said to her *amah*, "Yu Tang, ask that yokel where the house of Chen Ah Tien is."

The *amah* had some difficulty in making herself understood. A crowd gathered, gaping, chattering, and spitting. They shook their heads, and marveled, saying, "*Hai!* What is this? Chen Ah Tien pretends to be poor, and see the concubine he's buying!"

The local money-lender brightened. At this rate, it wouldn't be long before he'd get possession of Chen Ah Tien's acre, for when the number one wife is dead, it doesn't take a young successor very long to settle an estate. He followed the village elders, when they called to give Chen Ah Tien indirect advice. Like them, he was shocked to hear that Mu Lan was not a concubine, but the village disgrace coming home to roost.

There was even a greater shock when, upsetting the final shred of rice belt propriety, she boldly addressed her father's callers. "The monkey men are coming, but there is still time to burn the rice and wreck the granaries and drive away the buffalo."

She had fully expected an outcry of incredulity, then of horror, and was prepared to explain herself: but this was needless. A hard-eyed young man with a bandaged arm and ugly scar which twisted one side of his face addressed Chen Ah Tien: "Honorable First Born, this lady brings from Cheng Teh the advice I bring from commander of the night-marching army. Burn what is dry, flood what is wet, break down what stands, drive away what can walk, and carry what you can. The barbarians come for food, and having not enough guns, we must starve those we can't ambush. They come for rice, and without rice, they can't march."

Like face and eyes, his voice was iron. Mu Lan, though used to monopolizing the spotlight, was grateful for an unexpected ally, particularly a man, and above all, a fighting man. But she had overlooked rural wit. An old man with stringy mustaches got up, bowed ceremoniously, and said, "Young Brother, we also will starve. And this young lady does not look hungry, she ate enough rice among the monkey men. Far better that we compromise."

Mu Lan's jewels and silks and sleekness had betrayed her, and worse yet, she saw the cool amusement in the glance of Zeng Hai Wong, who as much as assured her, with a look, that despite her bungling, he was not whipped.

Nor was he. Zeng's wounds and scars and voice commanded respect, and so did his uncouth rural accent. A one-time farmer, he now harvested Japanese heads. Yet these were stubborn people, who could see no further than the neighboring village.

"Gung ho!" he concluded. "Work together!"

"Starve together," they retorted, not mockingly, but rather, regretting the necessity of their logic. "When we leave with fire behind us, and what rice we can carry, will we be welcomed at the next village?"

"The Generalissimo will feed you."

Zeng said this in good faith and certain truth, yet the retort was not slow: "But if the next village, and every other village destroys its crops, where does the Generalissimo get rice then?"

He could not make them believe in the extent of China. He described, but they could not conceive of a land so broad that by dint of advancing into newly made desert, the invaders would finally have to halt or go beyond their own lines of supply; yet it was not amazing that farmers could scarcely picture the needs of an army, nor believe that anything so powerful was also vulnerable.

"Fight them with scythes, that is good, and if we die, we die," they agreed. "But that is not famine."

Simple enough, to be faced stoically, but they could not gulp the nonsense of a sing-song girl and of a guerilla agent who had more valor than sense. However much he told of what he and his kinsmen had endured in occupied areas, they still held that famine was the ultimate enemy, and particularly, self-made famine.

The money-lender, having a stake in many a plot of rice, led the outcry, and then the old feud came into everyone's mind, for Zeng had slipped sadly in mentioning the adjoining village.

"We destroy what we have, and in Yin Pao, they do not destroy. And they eat what the little monkey men allow them, while we eat the nothing we have made ourselves. That is not wise."

Their bitter logic dismayed Mu Lan. No rapier play of wit could serve where the grim sincerity of Zeng Hai Wong failed. Then she rushed from the smoky room, and came back with all the money she had hoarded. She flung it to the rammed earth floor, and added her jewels to the heap. "This will buy your fields and your crops. Gold and may it choke you!"

Her father jerked to his feet, regained his poise, and said, "My disgrace has become an idiot, do not listen."

She was Chen Ah Tien's daughter, and her hoard belonged to him, and to whatever kinsmen might hear of it and come to town to share the family fortune. This was so well established, though long independence had made her forget it, that not a man of them considered her offer.

But Zeng Hai Wong addressed Chen. "Consider, Prior Born, how much face you will gain, buying all the village lands and offering them as a sacrifice to the ancestors. And how much face the misers of Yin Pao will lose if they don't make an equal sacrifice."

There was a growing mutter, first of wonder, then of approval as they saw the possibilities. The village would win either renown or cooperation.

Mu Lan was thinking, triumphantly, "My jewels, his wit." For the first time in her life, she had met a man whose thought kept ahead of her own.

But she had not reckoned on Confucius. The eldest of the elders announced, "The Master Kung said, think before you act, and act before you speak. I would not willingly associate with a man who would empty-handed fight a tiger, or cross a river without a boat, or die without regret."

Mu Lan flared up, "And the Master Kung also said, First Born, a man must have humiliated himself before he is humiliated by others: A nation must have defeated itself before it is defeated by others. And how can you better defeat yourself than by feeding your enemy? The ancestors of any of you would have committed honorable suicide to call to heaven's attention the oppression of an unjust mandarin. Why not a village destroy itself to bring heaven down on the monkey men?"

"Heaven has no favorites," the village wise man retorted. "And if we join the monkey men, perhaps we can each of us cover our floors with gold."

The ironic quirk of his voice brought laughter. She lost face, and so did Zeng Hai Wong for having supported her argument. Ridicule drove Mu Lane from the room, and according to tradition, it should have silenced Zeng Hai Wong, but he stood firm, and he said, "I will prove this for heaven to witness. My honorable suicide, going to the enemy's camp to kill their general. Then perhaps you can kill a field."

The silence which followed his leaving told Mu Lan that he had won, and that through him, she also had won. Then her victory became a coldness and an emptiness: for they had believed him because they had not been able to doubt that he had devoted himself to death.

There was no smoke to redden the sun on that day, or the day which followed; whatever Zeng Hai Wong's fellow-agents had said and done, they had not succeeded in scorching any earth belonging to the villages between Ching Pao and Cheng Teh. And the Japs were on the march. Swift-racing rumor, and the flights of bombers and fighters coming out of the southwest to harass the enemy made that clear enough.

Zeng lounged in the tea shop and played *mahjong*. The failure of his fellows to the east had apparently pulled the teeth of his resolution. When he went to keep his word, it would be too late. There was nothing he could do: for if he went to meet the invaders, already delayed by guerillas, he would find his fate too far from Ching Pao to convince the skeptical farmers.

And he might escape alive, in which case, heaven would not be the least interested. The sensible thing to do about radical proposals was to let the other fellow try them.

But Mu Lan had her thoughts. In the first place, a wounded man could not possibly get through the enemy lines. He'd be suspected of guerilla activity. They'd not even bother to question him. A sing-song girl, however, had a chance to do her work, and escape. Since a woman amounted to nothing at all, her survival would not affect the issue any more than would her death. Heaven simply wouldn't notice.

But the villagers might; and if she settled the commanding officer, there would be no occasion for Zeng Hai Wong to make a sacrifice which she now felt would be useless. Had the enemy approached only a few days sooner, Zeng's resolution would have had weight, but now time had dulled the edge of his words.

Zeng was useful. He should not waste himself.

She went to the market, and made a great show of buying red bands. It was noised about that Chen Ah Tien's disgrace was going to make the gesture of binding her feet. While she could hardly cripple them at her age, they were exceptionally small, and only a little cramping would satisfy convention.

The coolies, homesick for Cheng Teh, trotted eastward with the empty sedan chair. It gleamed bravely, all gilt and red and tasseled, exhaling the perfume of its one-time occupant. The villagers said, "So she didn't own it, after all." Others laughed and said, "She sacrifices a chair, we sacrifice our fields."

But Mu Lan was not there to hear their irony. She was one of two ragged women who trudged eastward along the flagstone trail. Both were bent double under bundles. Her father would not miss her for some hours. Then let them all guess.

The coolies lagged. That night, Mu Lan and her *amah* overtook them at the first inn, a good many *li* to the east.

In the morning, Mu Lan wore her silks and her jewels; her hair-do was perfect. She was exactly as she had been on her arrival at her old home, except for one detail—her feet were bound, mercilessly, torturingly, a sample of the three years of torment she had escaped in childhood.

Well, she'd avoided marrying the village idiot, and now it was nice to think of Zeng Hai Wong. She'd often think of him. She might even see him, some day, though a guerilla's grave was always open.

The coolies were not worrying. The worst that could happen to them would be some forced labor, and there was always the chance of escape, and flight to Cheng Teh, where their advance pay waited at their *hong*. Their only complaint was the jam of refugees on the flagstone trail. There was no shooting. The guerillas worked from the flanks, chewing off unwary detachments, luring them into blind ravines, or knee deep mud.

Finally Mu Lan had a chance to try the pass which General Yasuda had given her that night in Cheng Teh. A non-com, recognizing the official seal, did not bother to read the details. As for the interior guard, her presence spoke for itself.

She demanded to see the general. The splendor of her dress and polished haughtiness of her manner protected her.

Yasuda, despite his rank, was well to the front. Since he had to make a showing, it behooved him to leave little or nothing to subordinates, and thus Mu Lan faced the ultimate test sooner than she expected.

While waiting at his headquarters tent, she lost, as she expected, both coolies and the gilded sedan chair. Then, in the private tent, a slave girl searched Mu Lan, and finding no weapons, took the long pins from her head gear. When she went to greet the general, she had not even her maid with her.

Yasuda had to deny to himself that Mu Lan had once outwitted him, even though the information she had gained had been useless. She wondered where the Nazi observer was, and what he would have done in Yasuda's place. And then she said, "I have canceled many engagements to sing for your excellency."

"So now you have golden lilies?"

"I am retiring. This is my farewell performance. For you."

"Thank you. But this time, if you insist on playing *chai mui*, the forfeit is hot *saki* and not rice brandy."

She laughed, and spoke of the pig-faced man and the murderous headache he must have had: and Yasuda was happy, remembering how the Nazi had been the first to collapse.

An orderly gestured to the attendants, and then drew the tent flap. Outside, an army; inside, a gentleman of Nippon, who wondered whether he had become as Chinese as his favorite dishes.

She sang, and without musicians. Her pantomime made him follow the slender hands, each of which seemed to have a life of its own. It took an artist to appreciate art.

He found an interpretation for the dainty gesture toward a jade pendant, and ignored the possibility of a second meaning. The hands rippled on, weaving their part of a story told by face and voice and step.

His glance followed her as she shifted. Though he did not know it, Mu Lan had designed for him to turn, and upset the porcelain *saki*-jar. And she was ready, catching it by the neck before it broke or even spilled more than a gulp.

"And now," she wheeled, "see if you can beat me at *chai mui*."

He could not. He had never taken that strenuous course of charm, which included the finesse of beating wealthy aristocrats at that popular after dinner game; sober on *saki*, he was no more skillful than when drunk on *ng ka pay*. If for no other reason, eye and hand and voice were always a little out of step for he was distracted by the concealment and primness of that high-collared silken tunic, far more devastating than any décolleté.

And the opiate she had not needed in Cheng Teh now served its purpose. He had lost five games to her one, and he could not stand five times the drug.

Mu Lan continued her mirth and her gestures, mimicking the male falsetto and giggle of the unconscious Jap. The lights were low, and there would be no

185

betraying shadows against the canvas. So under cover of the noisy game, she had one hand free to unbind her tortured feet.

Still calling numbers, she twisted the bands to make a cord, and she did her work to a double take of laughter. Strangling does not take great strength or much time.

Then she glanced about. The final thought which came to her at the end should have come from the beginning, yet she was still glad that she had used foot bindings. Her search was short. Habit and tradition favored her. A Japanese gentleman's sword can never be far from him. She found it, drew it, cut once, and put out the light.

Now that it was done, her feet claimed their due. Better even have married an idiot than be a lady!

Finding her *amah* was beyond trying, so, since Yu Tang, who might have carried the unexpected head back to China Pao, was not there, Mu Lan had to hobble with it as best she could.

She took off her conspicuous head gear and jewels. Muffled in a long quilted jacket, she set out, pass in one hand, and a compact bundle in the other. As verification, she had even taken Yasuda's insignia.

Her luck held until the interior guard was well behind her, but as she approached the outposts, there was a shot, followed by a challenge, and the groan of a man mortally wounded. Sentries at adjoining posts quite needlessly passed on the alarm. A non-com answered, and brought a detachment of the guard. A large disturbance about nothing at all: not a raid but a solitary prowler, who no longer made any sound.

Either he was dead, or had taken cover.

An officer wanted to know all about it. While listening to explanations, he sensed rather than saw the vague movement when Mu Lan made the mistake of trying to slip past under cover of the distraction. Zeng Hai Wong would have waited.

A yell—a challenge—the blaze of a flashlight, and the thin, spiteful snap of a six millimeter pistol. A second and a third shot. She felt the bite of the puny slugs. Her stride broke, but she recovered, and prayed for the life to return to her aching feet.

The blundering pursuit was brought up sharply by the officer, who said, "Just another camp follower. Woman. Get back to your posts."

By now Mu Lan knew where she had been hit. She coughed, and the taste of blood was plain in her mouth. What worried her most was that leg. Given time, she might get to Ching Pao, but she had no time, for they would miss the general's head in the morning.

"Mu Lan," someone said in an iron whisper. "Mu Lan!"

Zeng Hai Wong came out of the darkness and found her; groping, he found the bundle and guessed from its shape. "You—you did it—"

"You came to do it? Did they hit you?"

186

"No, I groaned to fool them, I wasn't where the sound seemed to come from, I thought they were shooting at my false voice. What's this—you're bleeding—?"

"No, it's his head."

"It's not. This is warm."

"Just a scratch."

But her cough betrayed her, though she choked it to a gasp which carried no more than a yard. "How'd you know me?"

"I knew you'd left. And then that flashlight, though the perfume made me sure." So he remembered her perfume, what little of it he could have picked from the reek and smoke of her father's house. That was the happiest of all her extravagances.

"It's my feet," she explained as she stumbled. "I bound them."

Zeng Hai Wong half-dragged, half-carried Mu Lan and her proof of victory. When she lagged hopelessly, he set her on his shoulder, and jogged along like a porter. He knew what a race he was running with the enemy, but he was too intent to realize what a race Mu Lan was losing.

At the dawn rest, she toppled, and would not mount his shoulder. "You can't go fast enough. Unless you go alone. Hurry, Hai Wong, take the proof or we both lose face—" The feigned rattle in her throat tricked him. Without a backward glance, he swung into a trot. When he was almost beyond her sight, she struggled to her feet, and tottered on. She knew that she could never reach Ching Pao, yet she had to walk as long as she could.

The small bullets lengthened her torment, yet in the end, she blessed them. Had they been larger, she would have dropped many *li* further from her goal. There was no chance of being buried among her own people; that was clear, and she was resigned to reality when she knew that she could not again pick herself up.

Finally she raised her face a little from the flagstones. The height of the embankment above the fields gave her a small advantage, and the rise of a crest furthered it.

Though she could not see Ching Pao, she saw smoke, and ever spreading flame. Mu Lan twisted a little. The men of Yin Pao were not being shamed by their rivals. She saw the smoking fields of the neighboring settlement, and she had even a moment to be glad for that, and for Zeng Hai Wong's fast march.

ALLAH MADE THEM AS THEY ARE

Originally appeared in *Short Stories*, December 1944.

CHAPTER I

Ahmat had plenty of time to get the people of his village organized to welcome the Japs when they came to take over the most important town in Northern Sumatra; and when the invaders landed in Kota Raja, he said, somewhat for the benefit of all of his waiting people, but mainly for his lovely young wife, "Praise be to Allah! This is my day of days!"

Zeynab answered, dutifully enough, "May Allah make it happy for you!"

The yellow scarf which all but hid her sleek black hair was caught about throat and shoulders, and with an instinctively achieved elegance. Gilt embroidery adorned her blue blouse, but then, everyone had that; Zeynab's real triumph was high-heeled red shoes. They murdered her feet, but they were worth the pain.

"Don't forget," Ahmat said to the betel-chewing group of elders who crowded about him, "to yell *banzai* when you wave the flags."

White-haired Saoud, who wore an ink and pen case at his belt, left off polishing the silver-rimmed spectacles which served no purpose other than to make it clear that he was a schoolteacher and a scholar. "By Allah, that *banzai* is nonsense! Ten thousand years for what?"

"For the Emperor," Ahmat snapped; he'd explained everything the previous evening.

"No man lives that long. The Japs are doubtless an absurd people, the one who used to come to take our pictures was."

"Yell it anyway! They like it."

Ahmat scowled fiercely, but seeing that the teacher did not flinch, he turned his bitter gaze on the others.

Ahmat was a brown and wrinkled man in blue silk jodhpurs, gold embroidered jacket, and European shoes which tormented his feet. His eyes slanted slightly, his nostrils flared like those of a stallion scenting a rival; the beetling of his brows made dark depths from which his eyes gleamed as challengingly as the topaz eyes of the red-and-yellow plumed fighting cock he carried in a wicker cage; Merah, the local champion, stood next to Zeynab in Ahmat's affection.

Smoke from the ruined airport, the docks, and the railroad yards reddened the setting sun, so that by contrast it exaggerated the green rice fields which

188

terraced the Acheen hills; but Ahmat's village a few miles away from the river, was untouched.

The soldiers disembarking from the barges wore dirty and sweat-stained uniforms. Though no air attack menaced, each had leaf and grass camouflage on his helmet.

Ahmat waved the small white flag on which Zeynab had stitched a rising sun. *"Banzai! Banzai!"*

The villagers followed the mayor's example; all, that is, except Saoud, and Zeynab, outstanding examples which did not improve Ahmat's disposition. Certainly the country had gone to the devil under Dutch rule!

The invaders tramped past, a dirty ragged, reeking column of tired but triumphant soldiers from Singapore. Some grinned at the cheering Malays; most, however, walked in their sleep, since they had time only for advancing from one victory to the next. There was nothing clean about them except their rifles, which were as well kept as the straight-hiked swords the grimy officers carried.

"These be fighting men," Ahmat said to Saoud when the villagers broke to trail after the column for a way.

"So are the Dutch."

And now that Zeynab was out of earshot, Ahmat released what he had kept to himself, lest his wife overhear it, when the elders met at his house, the previous evening.

"These men are not ruled by a woman! We are free of the Dutch Sultana, and once more a man is chief."

Though Saoud's smile kept the day from being what it should have been, Ahmat carried on, "It is unmanly to be ruled by a woman, it is against *adat*, it is not fitting, it is not proper!"

They followed the troops to the plaza of Kota Raja, where Dutch officials formally surrendered the town. Loud-speakers blared warnings in Malay and Japanese, repeating the text of the notices which, posted on all the buildings, set forth the rules of the new regime.

The townsmen chattered, gaped, craned their necks. All but the Chinese had turned out; they kept under cover. Ahmat's villagers, well in the background, had to tiptoe for a look. Then, despite the cordon of soldiers who kept the crowd from the plaza, those in front surged forward, driven by the curious and the impatient in the rear.

An officer yelled a warning. The thin line of soldiers plied rifle butts. Thus far, it was no more than the khaki-clad Malay police were doing in their effort to maintain order; but native curiosity was not to be controlled, and those in the rear could not hear for the crackle and snarl of loud speakers.

There was another general surge.

Ahmat frowned. He smelled trouble as well as Japs. His early disappointment became acute uneasiness.

"We have seen and heard enough," he said to Zeynab and the nearest elders, "let us go home."

"Oh, but it's just becoming interesting," Zeynab insisted, smiling impishly. "I want to see the Dutch *lurah* make a speech." Then, whispering in his ear, "It'll look bad, leaving now, you told us to cheer."

"Very well," he had to concede, though grudgingly, for she was uncomfortably right in her logic.

Ahmat got up on the hub of a *kerbau* cart wheel. Dignity or no, he had to watch this. He did not like the Japanese faces; it was not that they were offensive, as such, but that they showed all too plainly weariness and tension. They weren't men to be crowded or startled. "Sleeping dogs," was the thought that came to him, an odd comparison for their welcoming committee, yet he could think of nothing else. They'd bite without thinking.

No one seemed to share the uneasy foresight that had become almost a premonition. No one seemed aware that the officer nearest Ahmat's side of the square was worried, and fearful lest he neglect his duty. A soldier was knocked sprawling by the billowing of the crowd. The captain saw this, shouted, waved his sword.

The machine guns at the entrance of the city hall snarled, a short burst, needling the crowd, stabbing here and there; the gunners cared little whether they hit or missed their widely separated fellows who tried to maintain the cordon.

The fire was high. Not more than half a dozen spectators dropped. The soldiers plied bayonet and butt, and without doubt in what they called moderation.

The sightseers broke in panic. Ahmat, diving for the ground at the first burst, led the retreat.

The firing ceased as quickly as it had begun. It had not been intended as a massacre; it was merely a warning to hotheads who might have considered rushing the handful of soldiers.

"You see what I mean?" Ahmat demanded, after he had explained the psychology of it all to old Saoud. "Tired men, and only a few of them, the advance guard, and our people were thousands."

"And if we'd had *krisses*, we might have done them harm?"

The teacher spoke so smoothly that Ahmat agreed before he was aware of the trap into which he'd blundered.

"But there weren't any *krisses* in sight," Saoud went on. "Did you see any from where you stood?"

Ahmat spat out the cud of tobacco and lime and betel, and told Zeynab to roll him another chew. "No *krisses*," the mayor growled, "because the Dutch Sultana made us quit wearing them, and we became women!"

Saoud smiled gently. "No one was angry with us. Just half a dozen shot down as a reminder. No evil in their hearts. They are as women, flaring up when there is no cause."

The smile became thin and bitter, and then the voice deepened, surprisingly for such a frail old fellow. "Yea, but when they have cause for anger, it will not be as the clawing of women! O Man, may Allah be gentle in His enlightening of you!"

CHAPTER II

Life, however, was not so bad, back in Kampong Baharu, where Ahmat and his people were all too content to remain, after having had a glimpse of Greater East Asia's mild discipline. The surly water buffaloes, submerged until only their noses and crescent-shaped horns were visible, enjoyed their mid-day siesta in the pools just off the hard-packed square; wiry, long-legged chickens cackled, and scratched for rice which had leaked from the thatched granaries or had been lost during the winnowing.

Of a morning, the women went to the market, carrying on their sleek heads the wide rattan baskets of bananas and mangos, fresh fish, plantains, and yams. Meanwhile, the elders, and the men not busy tilling the terraced rice fields, lounged in the shade and arranged cockfights. There was nothing to worry about, least of all about finances, a matter which the women handled, as Allah and custom had ordained.

All this was good. And it was good to be sitting in the shade, chewing and spitting. Long silence, then grave rebuttal of some previous speaker's impressive words about nothing of any importance. Being a Malay gentleman was, after all, the ultimate of human existence, now that the Dutch Sultana no longer ruled Sumatra. And collaboration—as Ahmat saw it, a few *banzais* and a bit of flag waving—was a splendid idea.

Ahmat's first doubts came a week or so later, when Japanese trucks, guarded by soldiers, and preceded by an officer riding a motorcycle side car, came to Kampong Baharu. Captain Tashi stepped briskly from the sputter-bike. He found the mayor, and he lost no time at all in announcing the number of *gantangs* of rice he had come to requisition.

Ahmat protested, "There is not any such amount, we have had a poor crop, there is barely enough until next harvest!"

Captain Tashi smiled indulgently, opened his briefcase, and got his records. "Honorable Mayor," he said in excellent Malay, "the Imperial Government has records indicating figure I name. Be kind enough to load same into waiting conveyance."

The soldiers lined up by the trucks too businesslike for argument; and Ahmat now preferred the smile of the Jap officer to the bitter looks of the village elders.

Captain Tashi went on, "Payment is in cash."

Ahmat brightened. This was not so bad. More than that, he was able to protest enough to get Captain Tashi to whittle down the requisition by a considerable amount.

When the rice was loaded, Tashi dug into his case and said, "Here is payment, now give me a receipt."

"Allah! Is that all? That is not what we get—"

"That is the controlled price. Government curbs profiteers."

"But we'll have to buy rice later! It'll cost us more—"

Tashi was patient. "To meet a temporary emergency, you will patriotically contribute to the army liberating you from oppression. Later, everything will be cheaper."

The trucks had scarcely left the granary when the villagers crowded about Ahmat to get their share of the cash just received, since the rice had been community property.

"What kind of money is this?" they demanded. "It is different."

Ahmat made a virtue of necessity. "It is liberation money, naturally it is not like Dutch money. But it is good, go spend it as you need it."

And then he settled down to strengthen his position. His voice rang, his air was commanding, his gestures were emphatic. "As the captain said," Ahmat went on, "thousands of soldiers who liberated us need rice. Can they stop to plant and harvest? Of course not! Perhaps we will run short, though Allah is the best provider. Certainly we'll have none to sell. But liberation is worth paying for. *Banzai!*"

There were answering cheers; not quite the volume or enthusiasm he had hoped, but still, a very good response.

Despite the gutted granary, Ahmat did not feel too disillusioned by collaboration; but Zeynab's first trip to the bazaar in Kota Raja, a few days later, gave him a shock.

She came back with an empty basket, and a handful of liberation currency, which last she flung to the floor. She screamed, "Those sons of lewd mothers! Those eaters of filth!"

Ahmat's jaw sagged, and a red trickle of betel juice leaked from the corners of his mouth. "What's this? Allah, what's this?"

"I said, it's no good!"

"You mean the merchants refuse it?"

"No, but—" She contemptuously gouged her toe into a five guilder note. "That dirty paper, it's no good at the bank."

"You went to the bank to ask?" he asked sarcastically.

"I did not! But Ah Ling knows, his uncle works in the bank."

"But they've got to take it, it is the law."

"Oh, they take it! They take it," the outraged girl screamed, "but you're lucky to get one guilder's worth for each five in paper! Now, the Dutch paper —"

"Silence, women!" The mayor got up. "There are temporarily few things for sale, that Chinaman is trying to get rich on what stock he has. By Allah, I'll—"

She caught his arm. "You'll do nothing of the kind, you stay here, you'll talk yourself into trouble with your Japanese friends!"

Her unfeigned alarm and dismay made Ahmat cool down in a hurry. "How is that?" he asked, and sat down.

192

"They beat Ah Ling's neighbor for not wanting to take the money. And then some people tried to steal rice, they got their hands chopped off."

"Both hands?"

"Oh, no, just one hand apiece."

Neither Ahmat nor Zeynab really understood what was wrong with printing press money. While inflation was a meaningless term, they did realize that the mere difficulty of replenishing stocks had already made prices zoom, and that "real" currency went further than the Japanese kind.

"But there isn't any Dutch money in town," Zeynab went on, "those fathers of little pigs took it away from the shop keepers and gave them this kind. That proves it's not good, if our old kind weren't better, they'd not be taking it."

Ahmat held his hand over his eyes. His head was spinning from the intricacies of high finance and foreign exchange. "I betake me to Allah for refuge from Satan!" he groaned. "Don't ask me to figure it out."

"God does what He will do," Zeynab said, resignedly.

And Ahmat was grateful that she had passed up the chance to remind him that he had had it all figured out in advance.

Voices from neighboring houses gave a hint as to what other husbands were hearing. Those gentlemen, however, could always blame it on the mayor; and toward sunset, when the usual visitors failed to show up at Ahmat's place, he knew that he had been made the scapegoat.

This was Bad, but worse was on the way. It arrived a month later, when Major Okama, a political officer, came to Kampong Baharu. He was grim, tight mouthed, sharp eyed, and it was plain that nothing he saw pleased him.

Major Okama's companion was a white clad civilian, a bland, smiling little man who wore rimless glasses; and his face was all too familiar to Ahmat. Mr. Hagawa, who had gone from village to village, long before the invasion, giving the natives bargain rates on the pictures he took of them, had returned.

The political officer began, "You are Ahmate, the mayor, yes?"

Then, to verify the answer, he dug into a file of pictures, selected one, squinted at it and at Ahmat. "Just as represented. You are the one who offered patriotic greetings. So I call on you first. Before any others, you benefit by Great East Asia prosperity and right thought. This is Mr. Hagawa, he is to open the Japanese language school for this village."

The gathered elders rearranged their wrinkles, trying to conceal their skepticism. Ahmat said, "We appreciate the high honor, but it is difficult for our boys to attend two schools, we are very busy, everyone works in the field, no matter how young, there is still part time work for him."

"That is proper," the Political Officer agreed. "So, I send Mr. Hagawa, then your Malay teacher can devote time to farming. Learning Malay writing is of no use, the future speech is Japanese. And Mr. Hagawa is to instruct in Right Thought, he will organize the Junior East Asia League, with parades on Moslem holidays."

This last was a redeeming feature. "All holidays?"

"All. Your Emperor, the Son of Heaven, he loves Mohammed and Allah. You will name him—" Major Okama pointed to the primitive mosque, "in all public prayers."

He made a curt bow, a brusque dismissal rather than a courtesy, and went back to the waiting car, leaving Mr. Hagawa standing there with two rattan suitcases and a box of books.

The pleasant little man smiled to show all his teeth. He sucked in his breath, very politely. "Unexpected pleasure, coming back for duty in your pleasant village, Honorable Mayor. Inspiring scenery, salubrious climate, this is my favorite of all villages viewed as itinerant photographer."

"You have no bicycle," Ahmat remarked, after returning the flowery courtesies. "Difficult traveling from village to city."

Mr. Hagawa hissed again. "Having pleasure of all-time residence in honorable town. As soon as you have built me a humble home."

With rattan, bamboo, and nipa palm thatch, a house can be built very quickly, so Ahmat at once set some villagers to work. Then, as Mr. Hagawa watched them clearing the site of his future home, Ahmat said to Zeynab, "There is no power save in Allah! He took pictures of us all, and now he comes to spy, to see and to hear."

Zeynab proved herself the perfect wife by answering, "There is no evil except Allah has willed it."

CHAPTER III

While it was hard to see old Saoud deposed and forced to the manual labor for which his dignity, his age, and his years of scholarly inactivity had unfitted him, it was worse for Ahmat to hear the metallic jangle of the Japanese language which the boys were learning; but worst of all was to see the Malay boys aping the tricks of Mr. Hagawa. They bowed as he did, they made that absurd intake of breath, they addressed their elders in stilted Japanese honorifics.

The weeks went by, and not knowing the face and the shape of the next evil, Ahmat sat up at night, long after the village was asleep. He sat in the darkness, and fingered the wavy bladed *kris* which he had carefully buried under the house, rather than surrender the weapon when, years previous, the Dutch had forbidden a gentleman to carry arms.

In the gloom, he could just catch the dimmed glint of the damascened blade. It was cool to his fingers, and smooth with the smoothness of steel oiled to protect it against rust.

The flame-shaped blade was little short of razor sharpness, but he wanted it perfect, for in the end, he would have to redeem his honor, and make his face "white" again.

For some time as he fingered the steel and felt his hands tingle from the touch, he wondered if slashing Mr. Hagawa would be sufficient.

A soft stirring in the gloom made him start. Zeynab was beside him. She had moved without making a single creak of the bamboo floor slats.

"If you go *amok*," she said, "I'll be left with nothing but a dead man's honor. Stay with me, for better days."

"The elders are getting ready to put me out of office," he whispered, fiercely. "I can feel, I can smell their thoughts. Satan made me a fool, and now I am as a bird without any feathers."

"The Japs have done the same things to people who did not go with flags to welcome them," Zeynab retorted.

"Being a woman, you have no honor! When a man's words have become as the chattering of apes, when it is clear that there was no sense in him, what else is there to do?"

"O Man, live for your people! Can a dead man's honor help them?"

She went silently back to her mat in the back room.

For several nights thereafter, he sat, and without getting the *kris*. His brooding was not disturbed. But the next time he got the weapon, Zeynab appeared.

"Woman, what devils, what spirits talk to you?"

"I just woke up and felt danger. Must it be explained?"

"Go back, I am thinking!"

She obeyed without a word. The spell of the ancient steel had been broken, and she knew this, and she was content.

On another night, she said, "If you *kris* Mr. Hagawa, you get only the death of the rest of us, is that right for a headman?"

He didn't ask how she knew he had been thinking seriously of Mr. Hagawa's future; he merely retorted, "That pig-lover wears his shoes to the mosque, yet he takes them off, properly, when he goes into his home. He honors his own place, and shows contempt to the house where man talks to Allah."

"Is God unable to defend Himself?"

She did not wait for an answer, and Ahmat laid aside the *kris*.

Better let the elders depose him, then he could leave, and being no more a part of the village, he could make his face white again, and without hurting his people.

This required pondering, and without the intoxicating touch of a blade that had been handed from generation to generation, with the score of its blood drinking, so he settled down one evening to think as Saoud might, with coolness and level head.

The snarling of a dog startled Ahmat.

The sudden cessation of the alarm was even more disturbing. A wary and cunning man was approaching. Then Ahmat heard the soft, muted whimper of the dog whose first snarl had been quieted. Ears sharpened, eyes sharpened, he could just distinguished that someone moved along the edge of the hard packed square.

The stealthy figure became plainer, and a man said, *"Ana dakhilak!"*

This was Arabic, the language of the Holy Koran, and the speaker repeated the appeal in Malay: "I am thy protected." Ahmat's pride came back, for after all these black-faced months, there was finally someone who begged his protection. He said, "The Guest of Allah is welcome! Blessing and the peace be upon you."

"Allah will reward you."

Hearing the man's speech close at hand, suspicion set Ahmat on edge. He struck a match, and then he groaned. "I betake me to Allah for refuge from Satan!"

His guest, his protected, was a Dutchman.

The man wore a skull cap, a tattered jacket, a ragged sarong. Instead of being big and ruddy and heavy faced like most Dutchmen, he was short and swarthy; yet clearly he was one of the Sultana's people, and not any Malay.

"I bring you a gift," the man answered, and it was very hard to tell that it was not a Malay who spoke. "And you have given me your protection."

This was dangerous, this was deadly; one whisper to Hagawa! Desperation made Ahmat think with a sharpness he had never known before; a gentleman had no use for wits, except in battle or gaming, but this was certainly battle. The village and its people hung on what Ahmat next said and did.

"You are my protected," he said blandly. "But no noise, a Jap spy lives in the *kampong*. I was surprised to see a Dutchman, I thought you were all in prison, or living in guarded houses. And you, when did you become a Moslem?"

"I testify that there is One God, and that Muhammad is his apostle, and on him be the peace, and on his family, and on his pious companions!"

Protection given in error to an infidel could be withdrawn by dishonorably stretching a point, and Ahmat was desperate. "You made the testimony, but how do I know you speak it sincerely?"

"It is written, *Hell is for him who calls a true believer infidel.*"

Ahmat was beaten. "Allah does what he will! So hide before there is talk, and I'll bring you food."

For three nights, Ahmat smuggled food to the hidden Dutchman, whose name was Jan van Stappen, and for each minute of the seventy-two hours, he wondered when Zeynab would begin to wonder. He had quit fingering the buried *kris,* lest that diabolical instinct awakened her out of a sound sleep and so made it impossible for him to feed van Stappen.

And feed him he had to. Whenever Ahmat felt rebellion arising within him, pride reminded him that no Moslem could deny hospitality to another True Believer; and that to be sought out as a protector had kept his soul from utterly perishing.

Mr. Hagawa, bland and smiling as ever, called at the house.

"I am also Deputy Thought Police, Honorable Mayor. What do you think of Greater East Asia?"

"Only Allah is Great!"

196

Mr. Hagawa let that pass.

"How is rice shortage being received by your people?"

"Allah gives as He wills!"

This certainly was not a seditious utterance, Co-Prosperity was not being blamed for the ration pinch, yet Mr. Hagawa did not like the tone.

"Restless juveniles speak of man walking by night from village. Honorable Mayor has comment?"

"If I knew what child dreamed and spoke of his dream, I could answer. Please tell me whose child?"

Mr. Hagawa made a gesture of futility. "Diverse children spoke among themselves. Who could say which one? So I ask the Honorable Mayor."

"I apologize for my stupidity."

Mr. Hagawa got up, still smiling. "It is vital that the Honorable Mayor knows what all villagers think. About strangers in the jungle. Un-cooperative evaders of labor."

He made his jerky little bow, and set his bow-legs for the plaza.

Zeynab came to the front. "Is it true that people are hiding in the jungle because they do not want to work on the roads?"

"Does anyone like forced labor?"

She smiled, and sweetly. "You can trust me. And if you have fed a fugitive, Allah will reward you."

"It is dangerous even to think about such a thing."

But that night, Zeynab gave him a bowl of rice and chicken for the fugitive.

Ahmat used all his stealth and cunning to avoid the water tenders who watched the irrigation. Whoever had chattered could not have realized what was going on, else there would have been nothing for Hagawa to overhear; had there been a disgruntled adult, or a schoolboy won over by the wily Jap, the information would have been more definite. The Jap had only been fishing.

He left the path, and picked his way among volcanic rocks which made a jumble in a ravine. Finally he came to the grotto in which van Stappen lurked both day and night.

"Bismillahi!" the Dutchman said, and dipped into the bowl. And when he was through, he exclaimed, *"El hamdulilahi!"*

In speech and gesture, he was correct in fine points of observance which most of Ahmat's people ignored. But there was one point on which Ahmat still depended.

"Friend, the three days of guest-right are over, and there are others who would be blessed by your presence, we have no further right to detain you."

"I have been thinking of that. But I cannot leave." Van Stappen paused. "For your sake, I would like to, but it is not permitted."

"Who forbids?"

"The government, and my duty."

"The Dutch Sultana?" Ahmat queried bitterly.

"Yes." Van Stappen spoke softly, evenly, yet there was no mistaking his resolution. "Doubtless this seems wrong to you, since you serve an emperor who is the son of a female god."

Ahmat spat. The idea that any man could be of divine descent was the ultimate abomination to a Moslem; and even indirectly admitting the existence of Amaterasu, the Sun Goddess, a "female God," was a blasphemy.

"It is not that!" Ahmat retorted.

"I didn't think so. But a Moslem may pretend to infidel belief, as strategy, if he keeps his thought clean. And I am a danger to your people."

"Thou hast spoken. So leave, and even if they catch you, they'll no more than put you in a cage, or put you to work."

"No brother, they'll shoot me."

Ahmat had to believe the man. "But they'll shoot some of us if you're caught here, under my protection."

"Then tell the school teacher where I am. What I have to do must be done, and there is no help for it."

"As one Moslem to another, I beg you, go!"

"As one Moslem to another, I would. But my duty is to more than a man."

"For the Dutch Sultana! An infidel woman!"

"Is a piece of paper holy?" van Stappen asked quietly.

"Allah forbid!"

"Is there holiness in ink?"

"Filth upon such a thought!"

"But you wash your hands before you touch paper on which in ink is written *That Which Is To Be Read.* The Holy and Excellent Koran is paper and ink."

"Not so! It is a revelation Allah sent to Muhammad, on whom be the peace!"

"And so is loyalty sent from Allah. And it is not a woman I serve, any more than it is ink and paper you keep wrapped in a clean scarf!"

This glib, undersized, swarthy Dutchman knew more than el Islam than Ahmat himself did; he might even outpoint Saoud. Ahmat could not get rid of the man, nor could he turn him over to the Japs. So he sat there, and the sweat slowly trickled down his cheeks, as he said to himself, shaping his resolution:

"I'll tell the elders to throw me out of office, then the new mayor can blame me when van Stappen is finally arrested, and my people won't be held guilty. Maybe Zeynab can think of something."

At last he got up and took the bowl. "O Man, stay for another day, and our blood be upon your head, you are taking our lives."

"You can save yourself," the Dutchman calmly retorted, "by turning me in. And the peace upon you!"

Zeynab was waiting when he returned, and she listened until he had finished telling her what had come upon them.

"He is a small man, and not red faced?"

"That is right, and he is sun browned, and his eyes are not blue."

198

"Then it's easy! Let him come out into the open, a half-caste kinsman from town. And let him work. We need men at work, not squatting in grottos!"

"Mashallah!" he gasped. "But that Hagawa has pictured us, named us, described us, how long would this last? It could have been done at first, but now it is too late, that father of little doglings will ask why a kinsman was hidden for three days?"

Zeynab was silent for some moments, and then she said, "Knowledge is with Allah, and wisdom comes with the sunrise."

"Inshallah!" he muttered, though without the least conviction that Allah would grant any benefits by dawn.

CHAPTER IV

In the morning, the women went to market, Zeynab with them; and all that forenoon, Ahmat heard the maddening jangle of Japanese from the schoolhouse. With a madman lurking in the ravine, and resentment of his people concentrating on the house, he thought again of the *kris*, the way of honor.

Mr. Hagawa marched his pupils from the schoolhouse and countermarched them about the square. They sang the new anthem, *Greater East Asia*. They carried little flags; and the sight infuriated him.

The teacher halted the column and came to Ahmat's door. "Honorable Mayor, be pleased to cooperate. We drill for a parade in Kota Raja. I am impersonate reviewing officer, while you march past, commanding the salute to officer and colors."

The whole world went somewhat redder than the rising sun on the little flags, but Ahmat somehow did not run *amok*. "I have no military training," he said stiffly, "therefore not able to command a parade."

Mr. Hagawa smiled. "In which case, be pleased to impersonate high officer and return salute of parade and colors as they pass."

Having no out, he had to endure. Round and round they went, grinning and bandy legged Hagawa heading a column of honest Malay brats who had become little Japs. Ahmat was sure their expressions had changed. They seemed to have borrowed that blend of supercilious blandness, that tinge of apishness; he wondered if they'd all end by needing glasses, and by developing buck teeth and bow-legs. Anything, anything at all was possible to Allah, and Allah seemed no longer to care what happened!

Then one of the older boys took charge of the procession, and Mr. Hagawa joined Ahmat. "Very nice, brisk, smart," the Jap observed. "Performance above standard." He shouted a command. The column halted, and faced him. At the dismissal, the boys bowed, hissed, and recited "respects and thanks to honorable instructor."

There were no compliments to the mayor. Not that Ahmat wanted any, but being left out was hard to take.

Hagawa said, "This evening, when all workmen come from fields, there is more ceremony."

"What for?"

"Distribution of Koran, printed in Nippon, by the Son of Heaven's permission, who desires to show how he loves Mohammed and Allah."

"We have a Koran already. It is three hundred years old."

"These are one for everybody. Modern, not old-fashioned hand writing with error. Please assemble subjects before dusk."

As he watched the Jap head for the living quarters near the schoolhouse, Ahmat exclaimed, "I take refuge from Satan!"

If this kept up, he'd be joining the people out in the *padi* fields. There remained neither respect nor dignity. And from work on the terraces, the next move would be disappearance. If he could only take Hagawa with him!

Then Ahmat saw two strangers coming. They were haggard, their *sarongs* were ragged and dirty, their faces sullen and perplexed; they were sure of nothing, and there seemed no hope of their finding certainty.

The foremost saluted Ahmat, and he returned the peace.

"We are kinsmen of Nuh and Majid. We come to work in the fields. We are porters in Kota Raja."

Neither Majid nor Nuh had any such kinfolk. Nevertheless Ahmat said, "Come, I will show you where they are."

He led the strangers from terrace to terrace, and when he found Nuh and Majid he said, in a low voice, "These men are liars, but let them work, accept them as kinsmen."

Majid, whose glance had strayed, pointed down into the village. "*Wallah*, there are others coming."

Something was happening, and not accidentally.

Ahmat, drinking back, began to see Zeynab's fine touch. He hurried down, and got to the level shortly after the dogs had come out, sniffing and snarling. He hailed the strangers, called them by names he hoped they would like, and inquired after the health of Uncle Abbas and Uncle Amru.

Mr. Hagawa came out.

Ahmat explained, "Distant relatives, they leave a village short of rice, and come to work with us, their families will be here later."

This bit of foolery offered Ahmat a chance to settle the Jan van Stappen menace.

After leading the second pair of newcomers to the terraces, Ahmat went boldly along the ridge, and toward the head of the ravine, and when he came near van Stappen's grotto, called, "O Man! A dozen friends and kinsmen have come to the village, there are now many strange faces. Come down, this is your chance, before that son of many pigs can make his count. And there is no help for this thing, either come out and eat, or stay and starve!"

The invisible Dutchman chuckled. "Very well. Doubtless you have some half-caste relatives. And maybe what I have to do can be better done this way."

Without further parley, Ahmat picked his way down the tricky jumble. If the Jap had suspected, and presently investigated, he'd either find nothing, or else he'd find van Stappen. One way or another, something would happen. The suspense had been drawn from the future to present. The relief of cutting it short was intoxicating.

"It must be," he told himself, "like going *amok*. The event is immediate, and in the hands of Allah, and whatever happens, it is good!"

Presently, the women came from the market, Zeynab among them.

He said to his wife, "Those kinsmen you sent, there will be one more than you counted on, the hidden man is coming out, and who will think him more strange than the others?"

"That is what I intended, but I was afraid to tell you before they came."

"That was well done, *sitti!* Yea, it is as if I had done it myself, and it is on my head. And now, I will deal with this madman! I'll make him work till he is glad to leave us!"

Then Mr. Hagawa came to distribute the new Korans. The beating of a gong, and the running of schoolboys from door to door, summoned the villagers to the plaza. Four carried a rattan hamper which they set where Mr. Hagawa stood.

The Jap dished out the little books as casually as though peeling dirty bills from a fat roll. The schoolboys said, *"Arigata,"* and added the appropriate foreign honorifics, but the grown men and the elders were sullen and hard eyed. To receive from the unclean hands of an infidel *"That Which Is to Be Recited"* was cause for rioting, and murder.

Ahmat felt the bitter gaze of the men who gave him precedence. That he could not do anything about it did not absolve him; that this would have happened, even though he had not gone to welcome the invaders, in no wise helped him. He took the black book, and begged pardon of Allah. Those who followed him did the same. And then he saw that van Stappen had placed himself at the head of the newcomers. When he got his copy, he stood there, instead of passing on, and he said, after opening the book, "This is not fitting! This is printed in Japanese, and it is not lawful to write the word of Allah in anything but the language of Allah!"

Hagawa's face froze. "What name?"

"Abdul Mumineen, the Servant of the Faithful! And the cousin of the mayor."

He dropped the book, kicked it aside, and folded his arms. The Jap was without words for a moment. So was Ahmat. Zeynab's eyes were wide with terror. There was no sound except the cackle and cluck of a busy hen, and in the silence, it was loud as gunfire.

"What is this?" the Jap finally sputtered. "Not Malay! What is this?"

"My grandfather was Dutch, but I am Malay, I am the cousin of the mayor. And Allah punishes those who put his word into a language he does not care to speak!"

The Jap was so shocked that he demanded, "Allah does not understand Nippongo?"

"He knows all things, even your cackling, but he speaks only Arabic."

"Dismissed!" Hagawa croaked. "Go, go away!" He turned on Ahmat. "I hold you responsible, this is sedition! This is treason, this is mutiny!"

"You are protected," Ahmat said. "You came unarmed. Go tell the Political Police and say that I did this, and that my people did not do it. Pick out any mayor you want, I am leaving and I go on the highways of Allah, and whatever happens to me, it happens. And God curse the Emperor, God curse the father and the grandfather of whoever does not curse the Emperor!"

He darted under the house, and came out with the gleaming *kris*. "*O* Men! This man is your protected, his life is on your heads. As for me, who knows where I go, or why I go?"

He thrust the sheathed *kris* into his sash, and without looking back, he headed straight for the path which led to the hills, and the winding game trails and the jungle. But he had scarcely put the first thicket between him and his people when he heard a sound behind him, and he saw that the Dutchman, "the Slave of True Believers," had followed him, and was carrying a bundle tied up in an old scarf.

Ahmat whipped out his *kris*.

Van Stappen halted, smiling. "You are not angry. You thank Allah for the return of your honor. I did what I had to do, seeing that you did not do as you should have done."

The gleaming point dropped, and then Ahmat slid it slowly into its wooden sheath. "Thou hast spoken, brother. But *you*, why do you do this? He might have shot you as you stood! For all you knew of it, he could have been armed! You were a stranger among strangers, and now—"

Van Stappen rubbed his palms together, and nodded contentedly. "I needed a comrade to work with me, doing what is to be done, and here you are, an outlaw now like myself."

CHAPTER V

As he followed van Stappen along the narrow trail, a thorn armed darkness which finally led toward the sea, Ahmat told himself that Hagawa would surely wait until sunrise to report to the political police in Kota Raja, for as long as the school teacher remained in the *karri pong*, he was protected; once he ventured beyond the village limits, he faced the risk of being *krissed* by some hothead. Ahmat hoped that the Jap would have sense enough to stay put until the villagers relapsed into their habitual calm and indolent resignation, for as long as no harm came to him, they would be safe enough from reprisal.

But already, it was a lonely business, following a Dutchman to an unknown destination. True, he had many times gone even as far as the island three miles off the coast. He had gone upstream a number of miles beyond Kota Raja, to visit kinsmen; yet his world centered about his own village, and the thought of exile horrified and appalled him.

Over the centuries, Malays had spread from Palembang, the cradle of their race, into Java, and to Singapore, to the very edge of Burma, and others had crossed the seas to Macassar and to the Philippines, and to the coastal fringe of Borneo: but by clans and groups of clans. Only the outlaw, the damned, and the renegade, ever went alone or left his people, or wanted ever to leave them, for leaving one's people was like being torn from one's proper earth, since the Malay is like the rice which gives him life.

The cutting of the stalk of rice must be done politely and ceremoniously; and thus with leaving home.

The smell and the sound of the sea were both strong when van Stappen halted.

"From here, it will be dangerous. So I go alone."

"I am not afraid." Then, with childlike candor, "Except of being by myself at night in the jungle. What do you do?"

"We go to the island, Pulu Weh, to Sabang Town."

"Why?"

"There are some men to kill, only a few. Me, I'll be too busy carrying things. So I need someone to help me."

"With carrying things?"

"Oh, no, I can carry things easily myself."

Ahmat smiled for the first time. "I think Allah will make this pleasing to me," he said, and did not even ask what size or color the several men would be.

Ahmat was too busy learning things, such as, that there was a very small outrigger prahu hidden in the brush, well up from the beach; also, a box of things, presumably those which van Stappen was going to carry.

"I hid them," he said, "before we were driven from Kota Raja."

"You lived there?"

"In a way, yes. I was a soldier there."

"Ordinary, or a *tuan-besar* soldier?"

"The last. A captain of militia. I was wounded. I got away, very far from any Jap. Then I came back."

"Alone?"

"Alone. I jumped from a plane."

"God, by the One God, by the One True God! Is that possible?"

"The Japs did it at Palembang, it is easy when you know how and your parachute opens in time."

They set to work getting the little *prahu* to the water, and then while Ahmat fixed the outriggers in place, van Stappen went back to get the box of things he considered so important. It took him an unusually long time; so long that Ahmat was done, and beginning to worry, for evil spirits walked by night. To offset them, he recited, "I fly for refuge unto the Lord of the Daybreak and from the evils of those things which He hath created, and from the evils of the night

203

when it darkeneth, and from the spells of wizards when they mumble, and from the envy of the envier when he envieth."

He was actually glad when his companion returned, carrying a small wooden box, and as though it were delicate and precious.

Van Stappen wore a wrist watch with a luminous dial.

"How long to get to Pulu Well?"

"It depends on the tide. Four cigarettes, possibly."

Van Stappen translated that into time. "Good, no hurry."

He opened the box. It contained fuse and primers and dynamite.

"You have been in Pulu Weh?"

"No, only near it, with fishermen."

"You know the petrol tanks, the big ones?"

"*Ay wah!* They looked like silver. Some were round like balls."

"Mmmm—and guarded by soldiers. No moon tonight—"

"What good will this thing do?"

"Who knows? Possibly none at all. But we are outlaws."

"You made me one."

"I had to. And I came to you because you waved the flags when the Japs landed."

"You saw?"

"No, but I heard, and I know of your village."

"And came to me, the friends of the enemy?"

"I knew you would be the first to hate them. Your face would be black for welcoming them. Your people would blame you, even though it was not your fault."

"You knew these things would happen?"

Van Stappen looked at the watch. "In the long run, yes. I didn't know of the Korans at all. They just helped. I did know that the moon would be dark, and that I had to do something, and your kinfolk coming made it easier for me, and so did the Jap."

Ahmat pondered for a moment. "You, a Dutchman and a True Believer. Have you really some Malay blood?"

Van Stappen sighed. "I don't know. For three hundred years, my family has lived in Djawa and Sumatra. Many Dutch-men have some Malay blood. Many of us are your kinsmen."

"Hard hearted ones!"

Van Stappen did not evade the issue. "In the years past, hard and unjust. But so were the old sultans of Djawa. But what was the belief of your ancestors before Islam became the faith of your people?"

"We were pagans, children of the fire! We lived in error."

"Just as the Dutch in the old days. The Malay abandoned his error, so are we trying to abandon ours."

"I had never thought of it in that way. What you say sounds true. But it was not Dutch rule that made me welcome the Japs. It is because we do not think it

204

proper and manly to be ruled by a woman."

"Tonight we do more than serve the Dutch Sultana."

"El Islam?"

It was so dark that the two men could not see each other, except as shadowy blots, yet it was as if they were looking each other in the eye. Finally van Stappen said, "We are going to a place from which we may not come back. So there must not be any lie between us. I am not a Moslem." Silence, almost like a blow.

Ahmat said, gropingly, "But you spoke the testimony, and you know more of our faith than anyone but old Saoud."

"I said, there is no God but God. That is true, and I believe it. The Jap says the Emperor is a god, and that is false. I said that Mohammad is the apostle of Allah. That is true, since he taught good things, and made his people a better people than before. And the *fatha* which Moslems recite has the same meaning as the prayer which Christians recite. So I told no lie, I merely honored a truth in another form."

The bewildered Malay gaped in the gloom, and then stuttered, "But then you are a Moslem!"

"I give no alms, I do not pray, I do things forbidden to True Believers."

"You are a very poor Moslem, a sinful one, doubtless, but still, no infidel! Let us do what is to be done."

CHAPTER VI

Pulu Weh was blacked out. Neither buoys nor lights marked the approaches to the harbor. The Japs, though having every reason for feeling secure, kept good guard. If the tiny *prahu* had made a phosphorescent wake, it had not been observed by any sentry. Once ashore, Ahmat and van Stappen crept along the waterfront, and toward the harbor where by starlight they could just distinguish the lean, low shapes of Japanese destroyers, and the dark wallowing bulk of tankers.

The air was reeking with the exhalation of gasoline and of fuel oil. Though the Dutch had destroyed a hundred million dollars worth of petroleum and equipment at Palembang, this island off the very tip of Sumatra's thousand mile length had become a supply base for the China Sea patrols, the Indian Ocean patrols which controlled the waters all the way to the Andamans, and Aykab in Burma.

Petroleum which had escaped destruction in the Indies; Burmese oil; aviation gas seized in Singapore and Penang and Malacca—fat booty, and safe from any raid from Ceylon.

The tanks, aluminum painted, loomed up in the skyglow. Mesh fences were just perceptible. Iron gates jangled softly as the wind shifted. Water lapped, the surf mumbled; phosphorescence crested the combers as they broke, and then

205

distinct from all, Ahmat caught the vague sound of mooring hawsers, going taut, then slacking off.

He became acutely conscious of these things as he crept after his guide, and for the time, carried the case of explosive, for van Stappen had to pick and feel his way.

The Dutchman stopped crawling, and twisted enough to reach back and catch Ahmat's wrist. No need for signal or speech. Already, the footsteps ahead were clear, measured, military; who but a soldier or European would wear hard shoes?

Huddled, face averted, Ahmat was motionless, and with nothing resembling cover. It took all his faith and all his courage to remain motionless, not trying to improve his posture. Obeying van Stappen's instructions was the hardest thing he had ever done, for Ahmat was a farmer, and not a hunter in the jungle, nor had his people for two generations stalked human enemies. Dutch peace, come to think of it.

But Ahmat lived up to his faith in van Stappen, who had thought enough of the Moslem faith to study it as few Malays did. Even in that danger, Ahmat did not lose his sense of wonder and of discovery. Despising the Dutch had been an abstract business, like hating infidels—he'd rarely seen any, and then not long enough for any but second-hand opinions.

Clump—clump—clump—he wanted desperately now to look up, so that he could dodge if the soldier tired, or lunged with his bayonet. He could smell the eater of unclean food.

"Maybe the son of a lewd mother can scent me," Ahmat told himself, and went cold, and had the urge to whip out his *kris* and settle everything.

But the breeze, though gentle, was cool against his hot face; it blew the Jap odor toward him.

Clump—dump—

The sentry was past.

Then van Stappen made a wailing, whimpering cry, not quite like an abandoned infant, not quite like a woman all worn out from weeping. The sound was very near, yet hard to place. Gravel crunched as the Jap turned. A step, and he halted. At first startled, he was now curious, and not alarmed.

It was working as van Stappen had predicted. Ahmat became tense again, and the pounding of his heart made his throat fill, and then of a sudden he became calm. The Dutchman must have devils serving him. Ahmat knew where van Stappen was, yet the sound came from some other spot a few yards distant.

This puzzled the Jap. Uncertain, he caught his rifle at the balance, no longer holding it at the ready. He stooped as though he was within reach of that which made the whimpering, and Ahmat could hardly believe that nothing was at that spot.

His eyes were long since accustomed to the gloom.

He eased the *kris* from its muffled scabbard, now that the enemy's back was turned, and his bare feet made no sound. He held his breath and stretched his legs, and he struck.

There was a gasp; his own, and the Jap's. Van Stappen, already on the move, caught the rifle before it dropped. Another slash, and a stirring, a wheeze and a bubbling.

Then only the breathing of the two raiders.

"Like a commando! Like a commando!" van Stappen whispered.

They went on for a few yards, and then the Dutchman set to work with heavy wire cutters. He snipped a hole in the mesh. There was a gunny sack in the box. This Ahmat filled with loose earth and gravel. Then, though ignorant of firearms, he squatted outside the barrier while van Stappen laid the dynamite against the big tank of gasoline, and weighted it with the bag of earth.

It was not plain to Ahmat how van Stappen got a light; there was no flame, merely a flick of sparks, and then a dull glow. Then came a momentary spit of fire, and van Stappen wormed through the hole, tearing his shirt.

He took the rifle, and led the way. Ahmat, *kris* drawn, followed him. The Dutchman had explained how the time had been figured out and the fuse cut in accord; yet the impending explosion kept him from being as deliberate in retreat as in approach. His brief, intensive training had not been sufficient to curb impatience an instant longer than necessary. Ahmat never did fully realize the self-discipline which had controlled van Stappen in this first attempt.

Simultaneously, the two stopped and froze in place.

A sentry whose beat was at right angles to that of the one who had been finished was approaching from the left. He now had the advantage of the wind. He may have been accustomed to hailing the man on the other beat. There was no explaining why he halted, wary, alert; veteran's intuition was as good an explanation as any.

Maybe the bayonet gleam of the captured rifle which van Stappen had not had time to cover with his body as he flattened.

"Why doesn't he mew like a baby?"

Only van Stappen had the answer to that.

The sentry said something in Japanese.

"That rifle!" Ahmat told himself, and worked his *kris* free.

Van Stappen made a choking sound, something like the sentry who had eaten half a yard of steel. The Jap repeated his query, presented his bayonet, advanced slowly; no rookie, barging into something strange. Not this man.

A stirring and gurgling. Gravel rattled.

The Dutchman was playing up the disabled comrade act. Ahmat knew that this would be bad. Even with a surprise lunge with the *kris*, when the Jap had his attention fixed on the man lying with the rifle, would ten to one result in a shot. Even one report would be fatal. It was still quite a distance to the boat.

Then the air compressed and the earth shook; Ahmat felt both as he heard the rumble, behind him, and saw in the water before him the reflection of the flash. Fragments whistled.

The premature blast was helping, he told himself as he yelled fiercely, and leaped up, blade hissing.

The rifle blazed. Its flame fairly blinded Ahmat, and the muzzle blast shook him savagely, but he felt his *kris* bite in. Van Stappen was up, and then he dropped. So did the sentry. And all this was plain, since fire leaped up the side of the tank, and ignited gasoline surged out and over the path and into the surf. Thirty, forty, fifty thousand gallons of it, rushing out as fast as the ripped plates allowed.

CHAPTER VII

Sirens screeched. Sentries fired alarm shots. Men yelled the alarm. Bells jangled. Searchlights lanced the harbor; the ships were on the alert, since the docks were in danger. Barges were already surrounded by floating fire.

"I'm all right," van Stappen panted, "get going, get going!"

He flung away the rifle, and clutched his side. Ahmat, covetous, snatched the weapon and overtook the wounded man.

He felt naked in the ruddy glare. The light was now like that of a red sunset. Fire engines raced about. There were rumbling explosions. Ships cut their mooring and put out into the roads.

Ahmat could not believe it when he and the Dutchman reached darkness and the *prahu*, and without having been spotted. It was good to look back at the hell they had made. And then, as Ahmat made ready to shove off, van Stappen lurched headlong into the boat and lay there.

When Ahmat began to ply his paddle, the Dutchman sat up, seized the other, and dug in. "If you'd not yelled, he'd've got me square, I was trying to stop him without a shot, and—"

He coughed, and though clutching the leaf-bladed paddle, he nearly fell overboard. Ahmat pulled him back.

Then, "There is no God but God! Behold the sun rises in the *west*, verily the dawn and its redness!"

Van Stappen sat up, and made motions with the paddle.

"Dawn! Dawn! Allah could, but—but—He wouldn't want to! Against the rules, you know. His own rules." Then, as the sheet of fire spread, far off, far off, the Dutchman croaked hoarsely, "The fleet, lots of it, all of it—the planes too—" There was a sound from the west, and now Ahmat could catch it, for the uproar of Sabang was well behind him.

"Not planes," he corrected. "Thunder now, earthquake sound."

What Ahmat heard was the grumble and roar of shells, eight-inch and ten-inch, and larger, racing on ahead of the muzzle blast of the guns which had reddened the western horizon.

And then the flames of Sabang geysered up in a tall pillar. The shells had landed, dead center. The simultaneous explosions made a wave of sound which nearly knocked him over.

"Dead center!" the Dutchman yelled. "They were sneaking up, I expected them some time tonight; and they saw our fire—" Bit by bit, Ahmat began to get it: the lone spy, the one man commando, planning his destruction so as to make it perfect for the ships in case they did come to Sabang according to plan. Fire alarms, sirens, confusion; the Jap spotters wouldn't hear the carrier-borne planes until too late.

Ahmat heard them, and saw them swoop down, and heard the concussion of the bombs they planted from mast-height, taking the ships silhouetted, mercilessly exposed by the blaze of Sabang. Intent on the danger of floating flame, the town had been caught off guard by the greater peril.

Bombers made pass after pass. Fighters hosed and raked the air-field runways, tracers made curves of red and green.

Then, looking toward the mainland, Ahmat saw flame, upstream.

"They're getting—Kota Raja—too—go home—your people—need you—"

"Don't paddle, I'll do it," Ahmat yelled.

He dug in. This was no sightseeing trip. The blasts terrified him. The screech of shell fragments and bomb fragments and the pieces of structural steel torn apart and scattered like straw were too much for any Malay farmer. Verily, Allah was using fire, his especial weapon, and he might be angry with men who blasphemously toyed, in their small way, with fire.

"I betake me to the Lord of the Sunrise—" He began, and then the grandfather of all explosions knocked him overboard.

When he came up, he saw that the *prahu* was swamped. He did not see van Stappen. He circled, yelled, squinted as he tried to get into position so that the far off flames of Sabang would silhouette van Stappen; but he saw only water. Another flare made him duck. He was afraid of flying fragments. A flaming plane made a seaward comet, and though it vanished a mile or so away from Ahmat, he finished the invocation he had started, moments ago: "—for refuge from the evils which he hath created—"

No van Stappen.

"Behold," Ahmat said, "what it did to me and I was not wounded. Am I God that I can find this man in Satan's own sea?"

So, not trying to right the capsized *prahu*, he made for shore; and it was not far to go.

He had lost everything but his *kris*, and the clothes he wore. And now the dangers of his home town seemed petty, and its inconveniences trifling; and while his people would learn what had happened to Sabang, he had to tell them about van Stappen's hand in the destruction. He'd forgot all about Hagawa.

It was close to dawn when he came to the village. Mists rose from the rice terraces. But there was no smell of cooking from the houses. People milled and chattered. And then he saw Zeynab, and Saoud, and the eiders.

They stared, and then remembered to salute him; and he returned the peace. "Where is Mr. Hagawa?"

Everyone looked confused. There was a crossing of glances. Zeynab stepped forward and showed him a chopper. "That son of dogs," she said, "sneaked out late at night, to tell what there was to be told, and even though you ordered us to protect him—you big fool, why not protect your people?"

And then her voice cracked and she began to cry, and begged his forgiveness, and added, "But I didn't chop him till he was well out of the village, he left the place of protection!"

Ahmat straightened up. "Well done, *sitti*." He whipped out the *kris*. Despite sea water, the runnels of the blade were caked with blood, for the scabbard had protected it. "We also struck, I and the Dutch Moslem."

"Where is he?"

"The sea belongs to Allah, and the sea took him. Now in the old days, when pestilence struck a village, it was burned, and its people moved elsewhere. Are we less than our ancestors? So set all this afire—after we've packed up our rice —we go into the hills until the Dutch Sultana's men come back again and again —*Wallah*, that one who served her was a man among men—wait till you hear —"

Saoud came up, as Ahmat watched Zeynab hasten to pack up. "Women, my friend," the old man said, "have always run things somewhat, but never entirely, and Allah made them as they are, and doubtless it is good. Now tell me of the slayings you and the servant of the Sultana made last night."

Ahmat sniffed the breeze and smelled the smoke of Kota Raja, a few miles away. "No one has time to think of Mr. Hagawa. We have time, some time, not too much, but still enough. *Bismillahi*, it was in this wise that the Dutchman and I trapped the first soldier—" And others came to listen. Zeynab, balancing a bundle of household goods on her head, wedged herself next to Ahmat. With a bit of managing, he'd become a good mayor and a good husband and better yet, everyone was proud of him.

PASSAGE TO MEKKA

Originally appeared in *Short Stories*, May 10 1945.

Rahim came running from the rice terraces which overlooked the Sumatran village of Kota Alim. "The Inspector," the boy gasped, "he broke from the stockade last night, the Japs didn't miss him till late this afternoon, the soldiers are looking in every kampong, they'll shoot anyone who hides them, and they pay a hundred *guilders* to anyone who catches them."

"Them?" asked Yakub, sharply eyeing his son.

"*Aywah!* Inspector Hydrick and another Dutchman."

The news began spreading even before Rahim had told the end of it. Already, the volcanic peaks cast their long shadows across the bay, and after a few minutes of dusk, blackness masked the village. Except for the cordon of troops watching the trails into the mountains which commanded Lampong Bay, the Japanese search had ended for the day, but in Kota Alim, the natives' hunt was just beginning, As for Yakub, he took no part. He sat in his house, thinking about it, and of Inspector Hydrick's chances, and the odds in favor of the Dutchman blundering into Kota Alim, whose people he had so rigidly ruled. This might be the hand of Allah.

Presently, Rahim came in to tell his father, "Someone hides in the straw stack, a dog sniffs at it."

Yakub quit chewing his cud of *betel*. He listened to the ransacking of sheds and the beating of bamboo clumps. "If he escaped last night," Yakub said, more to himself than to the wide-eyed boy, "he may have been hiding here all day. Who else knows?"

"I was alone when I saw."

Alimah had come to the front. Yakub studied his wife's face for a moment, but could not read her thought. "What say you, *sitti?*"

"The long-nosed Dutchman is not our friend, but he is the enemy of our enemies."

"He is a danger to our people."

"Oh. So you'd sell him for a hundred *guilders?*"

"I take refuge with Allah! But it's easier for Hydrick to go back to live in a cage than for some of us not to live at all. Rahim, go tell the elders, let them look."

"That was wise," Alimah said, when Rahim had left, "but does your wisdom make you happy? We should help him. Allah loves the generous." Alimah

211

seated herself on the floor beside him. "And you are going on a pilgrimage to Mekka. Those dog-loving Japs promised to let the pilgrims go in a steamer and now you'll have to sneak out in a tiny *prahu*, you may never get across the water! Now, Hydrick, he was a hard man, but he never lied to us. Did he?"

Yakub chewed both grudge and *betel* nut.

Alimah persisted, "I know our villagers shouldn't blame you because Suzuki teaches the boys heathen manners and makes little Japs of them, only they do blame you, and the power is with Allah! But don't take your grudge out on Hydrick. Look, Yakub, when you come back from the pilgrimage, you won't be mayor, but you'll be a *haji*, you'll be the only pilgrim for miles around—give Hydrick a chance."

Yakub spat. "Dutch or Jap, what difference?"

But when he had come to hope that it was all a false alarm, and that he would not have to choose between helping the Inspector, or turning him over to the Japs, there was the sound of men moving with needless caution. Then a shapeless dark cluster of villagers crowded into the dim light of the peanut oil lamp, and Yakub saw among them two tall strangers in ragged and mud-caked dungarees. One was Hydrick, gaunt and sallow, half starved for months, and freshly clawed by thorns.

This was the enemy, the infidel who saw no difference between manslaughter and the violation of a law as trivial as the one prohibiting cockfighting except on holidays. Hydrick held his head high, and at its usual truculent angle, just as he had when, after meeting the invaders, he had returned under guard, to face the derision of Yakub and the villagers he had once arrested. His mouth, broad and tight, was stubborn as ever; it still matched the set of his long jaw.

He said, "You found us, so I'm sure they would have when they came to look."

The other, shorter than Hydrick, and dark, and thin-faced, said to Yakub, "We can go to the hills instead of being caught here. That will keep you out of trouble."

The villagers said, "You are still mayor, Yakub, do with these men as you please, that is *adat*, that is fitting."

Hydrick understood, and smiled. "That is *adat*. So tie our hands and turn us over, and take the reward, and everything is even."

In the faces of his people Yakub could see that once more, Allah loved him. He drew a deep breath. "Inspector, I sail for Mekka in a *prahu*, and Dawad, you remember, you jailed him for fighting? He goes with me. If he still knows how to navigate by the stars, and if the sea does not hate us, it will be well. And if you are not afraid, then go with us."

"The Japs, or else the Indian Ocean in an open boat?"

"*Aywah!* Let God and the sea judge between us."

The Dutchman said to his companion, "It won't be fun, Van, but I'm for it." The other nodded, and Hydrick went on, "Where's the boat?"

Yakub grinned wickedly. "Until the soldiers have searched everything and passed on, we can't get to the bay. So tonight I must hide you, and perhaps uncomfortably."

In the morning, Mr. Suzuki, the school teacher, arrived with the search party. "I am sure Honorable Mayor will volunteer to take responsibility of cooperation," the bland little man murmured.

All of which told Yakub that Suzuki had not forgiven him for his outburst against having the local schoolboys bow to a statue in honor of Japanese soldiers fallen in the "liberation" of Sumatra.

"Try the roofs," Yakub suggested, and then prayed that the wily Japs would not look in the opposite direction.

The soldiers swarmed up bamboo ladders, to bayonet the heavy thatch, while others went indoors; and as he watched the search, moving from house to house, Yakub felt Suzuki's eyes, alert for any sign of worry.

And Yakub had cause for concern, since the captain of the search party, taking half the detachment, was covering another quarter of the rambling village. There wasn't a chance in a thousand that they'd stumble across the Dutchmen, yet time and again, a yell, a harsh command in the language he could not understand, all but caught Yakub off guard; for one apprehensive glance could betray him.

They forked and fairly winnowed a straw heap. They set villagers to emptying a granary. As long as all were busy, it was not so bad; the danger would come when all but a few points had been covered, giving idle soldiers a chance to blunder into what they had not been able to find.

"Watch the dogs, Suzuki-*san*," Yakub advised.

He spent uneasy minutes wondering if there had been any mockery in the smiling answer, "Too many stranger, dog-sniffing meaningless."

One of the buffaloes lying in the shade opened his eyes, and grumbled. The surly beast objected to the noise, and to the presence of strangers. He shook his head and got up. The increasing heat reminded him of the comforts of the wallows. Already, several of his fellows were submerged.

The search had taken far longer than Yakub had expected. The brute's uneasiness was becoming dangerous. Everything depended on his choice of pools. Suzuki was asking, after the manner of the Thought Police, "Yakub-*san*, what are you thinking of? What sentiments on Greater East Asia?"

The buffalo took a few more paces, and toward the fatal pool. To drive him away would arouse suspicion. To let him go—but there was nothing Yakub could do but pray for himself, his people, and Hydrick. Tension made his senses so acute that, behind him, he plainly heard Alimah whisper to their son.

And then Rahim, laughing and yelling, ran forward to his playmates loitering in the street. "Let's have a parade, like in Palembang! I'll ride, and you be soldiers." He mounted the buffalo, prodded him with a stick. The brute grumbled, but obeyed, and the game was on. "The Junior Order of Enlightenment,"

Yakub said to Suzuki, "maybe it is better than I thought." He knew that the Jap had not understood what had happened.

* * * *

That night, the fugitives came from hiding. They had been lying in the muddy water of a wallow, submerged except for their faces, which had been camouflaged by buffalo skulls over which hide had been stretched to mask the bones.

Half an hour later, Yakub and Dawad made sail. They had scarcely said, *"Bismillahi!"* when Yakub learned that the chances of survival were better than he had hoped; Hydrick, opening a waterproof tobacco pouch, showed him maps torn from a school atlas, a small compass, and a watch. "These will make navigation easier," the inspector said. "But that buffalo wallow took the place of the danger you thought we'd face at sea. That game I'd not counted on when we came to your *kampong.*"

"*Mashallah!* You came on purpose, not lost in the dark?"

"Best of all places. Because you and I had met so often, we'd understand each other better. You'd never prayed for me, but I knew you'd help the enemy of your enemy."

"By Allah! That is what Sitti Alimah said!"

"I'd not be surprised. You see, she helped us hide in that straw stack, the night we escaped. Smart lady you have, Yakub."

FEUD'S END

Originally appeared in *Spicy Western Stories*, July 1937.

"Simon! You, Simon! Whut the tarnation hell yo' think this is, a gol danged hotel?" Uncle Carter, bawling like a four year old bull, shattered the early morning silence.

Simon Bolivar Grimes had heard the first raucous bellow some minutes earlier, but untangling himself from the ranch cook's lovely daughter took time and determination. The girl had developed the art of clinging to the utmost possible degree.

Susie Wrinkled-Meat, slim, shapely, and brown, had inherited an inappropriate name and piquantly prominent cheek bones from her late father, a Comanche chief; and her Spanish mother's contribution was a pair of devil-haunted black eyes and an insatiable urge for just one more kiss.

She wore a gown heavily paneled with hand-made Mexican lace. It concealed this and revealed that—particularly *that*, of which Susie had plenty: such as sweetly rounded hips, and firm little breasts, coyly hinted at by the transparent yoke of her gown. She was sultry enough to need ventilated garments...

"Simon, darling," she sighed. "I hate to think of you're going with the pool herd to Abilene. I'll miss you awfully."

She kissed the gangling, tow-headed boy from Georgia until he tingled all the way to his cowhide boots. He had been telling Susie good-bye since eight o'clock the night before.

"Honey, I jest got to be rep of the Box G," he panted. "But—"

"Simon, you blasted girl-crazy horn toad, wheah are you?" howled Uncle Carter from outside the cook's *'dobe* shack.

Grimes pried the armful of torrid lace from his shirt front and stumbled toward the ranch house. His coffin-shaped face was longer than usual. Maybe if he stalled long enough, he could devise some way of taking Susie with him.

"Uncle Ca'tah," he began, planting himself at the kitchen table, "I got a whale of a headache. Anyway, they ain't going to be through putting the trail brand on all them critters till tonight."

Grimes' uncle, however, was almost psychic: "Bub, they ain't no use thinking of takin' Susie along. Them cowpokes would be so danged busy murderin' each other fo' one of her kisses, they'd plumb fo'get ridin' herd."

"I warn't thinkin' of that!" flared Grimes. "I jest been tryin' to figger out why Melinda Patton ain't putting any of her H-P critters in the pool. They's suthin' funny theah."

"You might ask Melinda," was the malicious retort.

Grimes, white with wrath, leaped to his feet. He and Melinda had been very much in love until he shot her father, the crooked banker, who as front for a cattle rustling syndicate, had nearly put Uncle Carter out of business.

The impending civil war was blocked when a sweet voice purred from the threshold, "*Señor* Grimes, I 'ave jest notice there ees no flour and the bacon she ees damn' near finish."

It was Susie's mother, Catalina. Her comely face had a well-kissed look; and every quiver of her firm, generous breasts made Grimes wonder if his uncle wasn't mighty lucky in his arrangements to take care of John Wrinkled-Meat's daughter and widow.

"Simon," grunted Uncle Carter, "mebbe you an' Susie bettah take the buck-board and load it up with vittles. She kin drive it back."

It was so arranged; and presently they were on their way.

* * * *

While not quite half way to Skeleton Creek, Grimes noted a large herd near the bank of the creek that gave the town its name. The critters were branded BB. He had never heard of such an outfit. Frowning, he handed Susie the reins.

"You wait heah. I'm goin' ovah to the camp," he said, mounting the saddled *palomino* tethered to the tail gate of the wagon.

Grimes was moved by more than mere curiosity; it was part of his business to keep posted on who was who.

He skirted Skeleton Creek; but he had ridden scarcely fifty yards when he pulled up. The woman at the edge of a dawn-kissed pool, just visible through a thicket, was built to make Venus at the fountain look like a Piute squaw. Her hair, gilded by the early light and streaming to her hips, was a passable substi-tute for the last flimsy garment that was settling about her ankles.

He got just a flash of a bosom that quivered like delicate pink tinted jelly. Then, before he could get a look at her face, she turned to the creek, tentatively tested its temperature with an outthrust foot. Though that move cheated Grimes of a fuller view, it gave him a chance to remember that no gentleman would spy on a lady's morning bath. He headed for the camp.

Two men squatted at the fire. Half a dozen others, likewise black dots against the horizontal rays that made Grimes blink and squint, were hustling about with their work.

As he approached, the two at the fire started to their feet, hands darting to their belts. The move, however, was checked when Grimes hailed the camp; but while that gesture had been natural enough, they did seem just a shade jumpy. One, short and squat, ducked out of sight; the other, tall and rangy, rose and approached Grimes.

As the gap closed, Grimes for the first time was able to see that the boss of that outfit had a black beard, a hatchet face and bushy brows; a salty, hard bitten hombre if there ever was one.

"Light and set, stranger," he invited. Then, gesturing at the pot on the fire, "they's still time fer some cawfee."

"Thank you, suh. I done et. I'm Simon Bolivar Grimes, suh, an' seein' yo' critters, I thought at fust you was some local outfit headin' fo' the pool herd."

"Yo're jest half right, bub," grinned the bearded man. "I'm Bart Bailey from Del Rio, which ain't exactly local. But last night I heard about a pool startin' from here and with so many cattle thieves on the prowl, I reckoned it'd be sensible tuh join up."

They chatted for a moment, then Grimes wheeled his horse and rode back to the buckboard. Susie was at the creek ford, waiting. The blonde woman was no longer in sight. But Grimes was not thinking of the beauties of nature.

"Mistah Bart Bailey," he pondered, "sho' drove his herd slow-like, fo' a gent what's afeerd of owl-hooters. Them critters is too fat fo' a fast run from Del Rio."

* * * *

Half an hour later, as they approached the mouth of an *arroyo*, he heard the whinny of a horse. It came from the right; and the greeting to his beasts was cut off before it was fairly out. Someone had blundered. The abrupt choking of the sound was a dead giveaway. There was an ambush ahead.

Grimes, pig stubborn, refused to retreat. In the *arroyo*, the light was still tricky for long range fire. As they were for a moment sheltered by a thicket, he said to Susie, "Grab my hoss and git out while I attend to that gent."

"I'm not scared," she countered; but she wisely dropped to the bed of the buckboard.

Grimes' drawn pistol, a single action .45 the length of a siege gun, lay on his knee. He was ready—

"Whack!" But the rifle blast came from the side of the *arroyo* opposite from the one where the concealed horse had whinnied.

A slug gouged a ragged welt along Grimes' ribs, thudding into the seat beside him. He yelled, pitched to the floor boards. The fuzztails bolted. The clattering drowned everything but the triumphant hoot from the left, and the answering shout from the right.

A man popped up from cover, high above the bottom of the *arroyo*. He was certain that he had plugged his victim; but a correction was on the way. The galloping mustangs had closed the gap; and then the long barreled .45 bellowed like artillery firing in battery. The lurker pitched headlong down the slope.

The mustangs wheeled sharply, wedging the wagon wheels on a boulder. The impact spilled Grimes from the seat, and piled Susie on top of him. The resulting a pinwheel of bare legs, cowhide boots, and red calico settled to the rocky bottom just in time to miss the hail of pistol slugs that poured from the opposite bank. The choked whinny from the right had been guile, not stupidity; but for poor marksmanship, Grimes would have been plugged from the left before he caught the trick.

Sheltered by the half upset wagon, he hosed the slope with lead. His second gun, however, had dropped far beyond his reach; and as he frantically jacked the empties from his smoking weapon, a howl and a clatter of departing hoofs mocked him.

No chance to pursue. The saddle mount had broken from the tail gate and bolted. Susie was screeching to the high heavens, "Simon, they killed me!"

For a mortally wounded person, she was tolerably noisy. Helping her to her feet, he saw that a slug had creased her hip. So while Susie nonchalantly tore a strip from her skirt, Grimes pacified the mustangs, who were industriously kicking the dashboard to pieces, maneuvered them to extricate the wedged wagon wheel, and then caught his saddle mount. That done, he approached the pie-faced man who lay gaping stupidly at the sunrise.

He was a stranger, and the contents of his pockets were not enlightening. His accomplice, escaping with both horses, had removed the most serviceable clue; but Grimes, after bundling the stiff into the buckboard, circled around the scene of the ambush.

One of the hidden mounts had a broken shoe, he learned from the hoof-prints; and he found a lead-riddled hat near the spot where the lurker had watched the horses. It was a Stetson with a silver ornamental band. On the brim was an old bloodstain, almost obliterated. Though the law would not accept such a flimsy identification, it was good enough for Grimes.

That hat belonged to Lem Potts, the shyster lawyer who had been the sole survivor of the gun fight in which Grimes had blotted out Melinda Patton's father. There was no mistaking that blood stain.

The implications, however, reached much further. The signs indicated that it had been an impromptu ambush. There were no cigarette butts, no blur of foot-prints to indicate a long vigil. Potts and the rifle man must have hastened from Bart Bailey's camp to intercept him.

Then he caught the play: Bailey and his companion had not realized that Grimes, dazzled by the horizontal rays, had not been able to recognize the man ducking from the camp fire. Thus the ambush was to keep Grimes from drawing any conclusions as to why Potts, survivor of the rustler syndicate, had had important business with Bailey.

Grimes, though unable to prove his suspicions, drove on toward town with his convictions.

* * * *

The law against carrying belt weapons in Skeleton Creek had just been repealed, mainly because everyone homicidally inclined concealed guns in bootlegs, hip pockets, and shoulder holsters instead of wearing them openly. This repeal, mainly due to Grimes' blasting the gizzards out of a pair of ruffians who had underestimated him, got him a sour glare from old Hob Terrill, the town marshal, who sat near the jail.

"Mawnin', Hob," beamed Grimes, jerking his thumb toward the corpse in the wagon. "I got some new business fo' you, an' the sheriff."

"I guess yuh got another alibi?" He helped Grimes unload the dead.

"Suttinly I has. Ef I'd fired fust, this gent wouldn't never lived to pour a .45-70 along my ribs an' through the wagon seat. An' I got a witness."

The gritting sound Grimes heard as he clucked to the nags was the marshal's teeth. He turned back and added, "An' fo' six bits extry, you kin look an' see wheah that wild shot scraped Susie."

"Six bits, nothing!" mocked Susie, patting her hip. "It'll cost you both your eyes, *Señor* Terrill!"

The marshal, regarding the shapely bare legs Susie had cocked up on the dashboard, looked as though that would be cheap enough. Then he said, "I'll git yuh yet, yuh gol blamed trantler."

Grimes pulled up at Link Simpson's general store. Then, leaving Susie to stock up the wagon, Grimes headed toward the Corkscrew Inn, which was headquarters for the cattlemen who were pooling their herds for the long drive to Kansas.

Half way to his destination, he halted, confused and embarrassed. A girl wearing stitched boots and a trim riding skirt that flattered the most fascinating hips on that side of the Pecos was approaching him. Her sweet, serious face was framed by pale golden hair. The upper fullness of a vee-necked silk blouse rippled deliciously with each stride. She had everything!

This was Melinda Patton. Dreading this first meeting since he'd shot her father, he turned to duck into the Last Chance Saloon; but the swinging door slammed outward, blocking him.

Grimes, lips dry and heart hammering, caught the glance of her blue eyes. She recoiled; a gleam of tears contrasted strangely with the sudden hardening of her face.

"Melinda—honey—" he blurted.

She swept past him. He suddenly was glad he was riding with the trail herd. That meeting had undone every effort to forget the way she had once smiled at him in the moonlight stealing through her window. She had to hate him now, just as it had been his duty to avenge the unexpectedly revealed duplicity of her father.

Worst of all, the blow off had come just as they'd decided, after an evening's conference, that they'd be married the following day.

He stumbled back and into the Corkscrew Inn, where he gargled two shots of whiskey. Then he glanced about and saw the reps of the other outfits who were to pool their cattle. Sitting in their midst was Bart Bailey. White-haired Gil Stewart of the Lazy M was saying, "Shore, I'm trail boss. But we kain't let in any outsiders onless the reps from each ranch agrees, unanimously."

"Hell," said Bailey, "you gents has jest as good as admitted they ain't no objections tuh me."

"Makes no difference," contended Stewart. "We ain't heard from the Box G outfit yet, and until—" Then, seeing Grimes, he hailed him: "Hi, thar, Simon! Come here an' meet Bart Bailey—"

"I done had that pleasure, Gil," the boy cut in. He grinned guilelessly at Bailey.

The bearded man, if he really were surprised to see Grimes, betrayed no amazement. He nodded, then said, "I'll jest leave whilst yuh do this votin', Stewart. An' as soon as yo're done, I'll get started trail-brandin' my critters."

Stewart led the local cattlemen to the proprietor's private room.

"That was jest a formality, fellers," he said. "Ain't no objections, is they, lettin' Bart Bailey team up with us."

"I'm objectin', suh," Grimes interposed. "Fo' the Box G, what's got mo' critters in this herd 'an any other outfit."

For a moment there was a clamor of amazement at his vote. Bailey, apparently, had won the good graces of the four reps during the time he had gained by riding instead of deliberately driving to Skeleton Creek.

"What fur, Simon—? What's wrong with him—? What yuh got agin him —?"

"That's none of yo' dang business!" he retorted to the babbling trio. "Yo' asked, is I got objections an' I done said I has."

"Listen, young whelp!" Jeb Terry, broad as a chuck wagon and belligerent as an old bull, advanced a pace. "I asked—"

Pop! Grimes' fist snapped him back on his heels; but the blow just enraged Terry. With a wrathful bellow; he recovered, tugging leather.

That was a mistake. Before his gun half cleared the holster, a blast shook the room. Jeb yelled. Blood spurted from the hammer thumb that had been cut by fragments of the bullet that knocked the gun from his hand.

"I'll knock the two of yuh loose from yore eye teeth," growled salty old Gil Stewart, interposing. "Simon, what yuh got agin' Bailey?"

Grimes scratched his tow head and frowned. "Gil, I jest don't exactly know. Yo' might call it a permonition. Kain't prove it, so I ain't sayin'."

To explain would only warn Lem Potts, if he actually were in cahoots with Bailey in some devious piece of skullduggery. Grimes had a deep-seated grudge against that slick customer; but for Potts' twisted legal advice, Melinda's pappy might have stayed straight, and young love would not have gone up in gunsmoke.

"Yo're right, not sayin' what yuh kain't prove," Stewart grudgingly conceded. "But yo're a damn ornery brat an' ef I was yore uncle, I'd lambaste yuh till yore hind end looked like a Scotch plaid."

"My uncle has been doin' that fo' months, an' ain't another man living what'd have guts to try it," Grimes frigidly retorted, stalking from the room, and the others followed.

Before Stewart could break the news, Bailey chuckled sourly, shrugged, and said, "I done heard most of it. Grimes, I dunno whut yuh got agin' me, but supposin' you come up tuh my room at the White Hoss Hotel? It's only fair tuh tell me in private."

Grimes had to concede the justice of his contentions.

"I'll sho' admire to give yo'all satisfaction, Mistah Bailey," said Grimes. "In two hours, ef it's agreeable to you. I got to see how many of my critters is branded."

"It's Room Four," added Bailey, as Grimes turned toward the street.

The drover's affability in the face of that direct affront convinced Grimes that Bailey was too diplomatic for an honest man; but that was all the more reason to accept his proposition. Bailey could hardly have guessed that Grimes had connected him with Lem Potts; and, in his efforts to placate the stubborn boy, he might unconsciously drop a revealing hint.

Grimes headed for the branding pen at the further side of town; but he at once looped back, and down a side street to find Potts before Bailey met him.

* * * *

Lem Potts, he presently learned, was not in his hotel or office. Neither was he at the bank, the jail, nor in any of the other saloons. It took Grimes only a few minutes to make the rounds. Then he played his last hunch.

Melinda Patton's sorrel mare was no longer at the hitching rack. She must have left town during the conference at the Corkscrew Inn. Grimes reasoned that Potts, who could not be proved guilty of the attempted dry-gulching, would scarcely shake his hocks; instead, he'd merely hide out until the trail herd left Skeleton Creek. And Melinda's ranch house was the one place where he'd expect to stay clear of Grimes, a gun slinger no one in Skeleton Creek cared to face.

Half an hour later, he was approaching the ranch house of the late Hank Patton. Though neat, it already showed signs of dwindling fortunes. The cracking of the rustlers' syndicate had cut heavily into the fortune Melinda's father took in and spent each year. Then he noted hoof prints: rider and a led horse had not long ago galloped toward the house.

One of the beasts had been bleeding. *And the led horse had one cracked shoe*; the sign Grimes had noted at the ambush. Melinda had sent Potts to bushwhack him.

A feud was a feud, and he couldn't blame the gal. But if Potts were carrying on her vengeance—

"Gawd a-mighty!" he groaned, catching all the implications. "She wouldn't *hire* anyone to plug me. She ain't that low. But ef someone was making love to her, she'd have a right to *ask* him to settle me."

He dismounted, stealthily approached the house. He knew all too well in what wing the living room was. As he came nearer, he heard a murmur of voices. The garden afforded him adequate cover from observation by any employees who might be about the bunk house or stables.

He was tall enough to get a peep between the curtains that screened the barred windows; and what Grimes saw was more than enough.

The woman must be Melinda. A man was bending over her, drawing her toward him. Her face was thus not visible, but there was no mistaking that riding skirt, well over her knees, nor the dazzling curve of her white legs.

"Oh... Lem...you mustn't...not now... I do appreciate what you've a done—what you're doing for me—but I can't—please—"

Grimes drew his .45; but those slim arms, and her incoherent gasps unnerved him. His entire body trembled, and a red haze blurred his eyes. He turned from the window.

Killing Potts in Melinda's house would damn Grimes, who had no right there. If he were jailed, he'd be foiling Uncle Carter, whose old wounds kept him from going with the herd.

"...Lem, darling—please don't—but tomorrow night—come back at eight—"

Grimes stumbled back to his horse, spurred his beast to a gallop. He'd made a fool of himself, suspecting Bailey. The only thing to do was to apologize for a piece of Georgia orneriness and square himself with Gil Stewart and Uncle Carter's other neighbors.

* * * *

His two hours were almost up when he came larruping into Skeleton Creek. As he dismounted in front of the Corkscrew Inn, he saw Gil Stewart, and said, "Jest fergit what I said about Bailey. I done made a hell of a mistake."

"All right, bub," answered the trail boss. "I'll tell him—"

"I'd ruther tell him myself, Gil. But ef yo' want to tell Jeb Terry and the others, I'd sho' thank you. I feel so't of foolish about this mess."

He stalked toward the White Horse Hotel. Bailey was not at the bar; Grimes therefore ascended the rickety stairs to the second floor. He tapped at the door of Number Four. A woman bade him enter.

He halted a pace across the threshold, and devoted the next moment to gaping and stuttering. Her blue robe trailed half open, and what little she wore beneath it, accentuated the high spots between waist and collarbone. There were the sleek legs he'd viewed by sunrise; and now he caught more fully the dazzling beauty which distance had that morning withheld. Her smile was a crimson challenge.

"Uh—ur—beg yo' pahdon, m'am—I'm lookin' fa' Mistah Bailey's room—I'm Simon Bolivar Grimes, m'am—"

"Oh...Mr. Grimes? If you don't mind—" She paused, basking in his hungry glance, yet seeming to grope for a tactful way of reminding him that she could dress just as well without an audience.

The comb slipped from her fingers. Grimes sank to his knees to retrieve it, and did his best to keep his eyes on the floor and his fingers steady. When he straightened, she was so close that he felt her warmth and roundness against him.

But that was nothing to the next shock! Hungry lips pressed a moist, clinging kiss on his mouth, choking his gasp of amazement. Her arms twined about him, and she arched herself closer, breathing an inarticulate sigh of contentment.

"Lawd, m'am!" He was thrilled and horrified. "You kain't do that—not heah —with that door—"

His mouth went dry and ice raced through his veins when heavy footsteps came clumping down the hall. Then the robe slipped from her shoulders. Sheer horror paralyzed him.

In desperation, he reached for her wrists. She cried out, and while one hand broke away, her feet laced treacherously with his boots, tripping him. He was hopelessly tangled with a writhing armful when the door burst open.

Bailey was at the threshold. At his heel was the marshal, Hob Terrill.

"I'll kill the skunk!" roared Bailey, gun drawn before Grimes could kick clear and protest that it was a frame-up.

"Drop it!" snarled Terrill, knocking the weapon aside just as Grimes got to his own gun. "Yuh fool, yuh'll jest embarrass yore wife ef yuh kill him and have tuh explain why. She ain't been hurt none, not exactly—"

He cocked a critical eye at the hysterical Mrs. Bailey, who was laughing, sobbing, and pouring out an incoherent account of how Grimes had gone wild seeing her state of array when she turned from the dresser. Terrill didn't blame Grimes for having notions; he was getting a few himself; but he sternly went on, "Yo're under arrest fur assault and battery, improper and unfittin' conduck, an' attempted—"

He choked, groping for just the word to use before a lady. But Bailey cut in, "Hell, marshal, ef yuh arrests him, *yuh'll* be advertising my wife's humiliation. Supposin' him and me go outside the city limits and settle this."

"Kain't do it." Terrill was adamant. "I kain't countenance dueling. If a couple gents gets riled an' on the spur of the moment shoots each other, that's jest a act of God. But planning it, with malice aforethought, it's down right iniquitous an' it don't go. Not in Skeleton Crick."

Bailey's wrath subsided. "Maria, I done tol' yuh that that dang open front nightgown—"

"Bart, it's a negligee—"

"That open front nightgown was downright indecent," he persisted. "So mebbe I shouldn't git too hostile, specially as he ain't done no—no—uh—damage."

Grimes was sweating, embarrassed, and wrathful. Bailey was a skunk; but having told Gil Stewart that he'd withdrawn his objections, Grimes couldn't back down. And then Bailey said, "Since this here ain't got beyond the four of us, I'll fergit it, ef yun let me in on the Skeleton Crick pool."

"You damn' ornery polecat!" fumed Grimes.

"Yuh agrees," Terrill cut in, "er by God, I take yuh to the hoosegow."

"I ain't agreein' because Terrill's caught me with my galluses hangin' halfway to my ankles," raged Grimes. "I jest done told Stewart I was mistaken about you, and that I wouldn't vote agin you. So I kain't back down. But once this trail herd gits to Kansas, I'm scatterin' yo' guts all ovah a quarter section! Now ef yo' wants to join, yo' ah plumb welcome, suh."

Bailey chuckled. Grimes stamped into the hall. And to forget the morning's humiliation, he spent the remainder of the day at the branding pen.

The following morning, the trail herd surged northward, chuck wagon and remuda at the rear.

Grimes, watching Bailey's critters joining the pool, saw something he had not noticed the previous morning. It became plain enough, once a trick of the early light made him for a second time scrutinize the "BB" on the flank of one of the beasts that supposedly had come all the way from Del Rio.

It was slick and skillful branding; but his resentment and his initial suspicions had sharpened his eyes. The "BB" had not long ago been "HP"—Melinda Patton's brand! Instead of having come from Del Rio, Bailey had by a circuitous route taken Melinda's disguised cattle from her spread and then back again to Skeleton Creek.

Neither could it be wholesale theft; particularly not when Potts, Melinda's lover, had been conferring with Bailey the morning previous. It was becoming intricate beyond reckoning; each possible answer was contradicted by some other fact.

Gil Stewart, though he had heard nothing of the clash between Bailey and Grimes, kept them far apart, just on the chance that the boy's initial opposition might, in the tension of the long march, cause an outbreak of hostilities. The most even tempers would crack after the first week of long marches, nights broken by guard duty, by alarms real and false, by rumors of rustlers, by threats of stampedes.

* * * *

For the first night's camp, Grimes was assigned to the third watch. Instead of spreading his tarpaulin near his fellows, he made his bed somewhat apart, and near the river. All day long, whenever a BB could be picked out of the herd, he received fresh confirmation; positively no doubt that they had all been HP. He was still simmering with wrath and humiliation and jealousy; he had to get to the heart of the riddle.

Something crooked was in the wind. He now had two on his list of men to blot out, once Uncle Carter's cattle had been delivered and the money banked: Bart Bailey, and Potts, Melinda's new lover.

Yet despite his brain wracking, he finally must have dozed. Something was creeping toward him; a silent shape whose advance he had felt rather than heard.

The hair on the back of his neck bristled from the shock of realizing that an enemy had almost crept up on him. Then, silent as the stalker, Grimes drew his pistol, thumb ready to flick the hammer back when the enemy was too close to retreat.

"Simon, I thought it'd never be dark," whispered a soft voice. "Last night I sneaked to the chuck wagon—"

"What? You hid in it?"

"In that bull's hide stretched under the wagon bed. I shoved out some of the brushwood they put in fer fuel."

She was in his arms, eyes agleam in the dim light, hungry lips seeking his mouth, stopping his protest, "Yo' kain't follow us. Uncle Ca'tah was right. Though I did so't of 'low it'd be nice ef yo' could—"

"Just tonight and tomorrow night, honey," she explained, wriggling closer, a supple length of quivering loveliness. "Then I'll take a hoss and go back. Won't be nothing—I can make it in a day, riding. I hid some grub—"

But by that time, Grimes wasn't interested in details concerning the bull's a hide "hammock" in which Susie had stowed away. He drew her closer, thrilled as her breath sighed in quick gasps in his ear…

The trail day is long, and the night woefully short, yet there were a number of hours before Grimes was due to stand watch. And though kisses made them drowsy, he watched the slow circling of the dipper overhead.

An owl hooted…then another…just a night sound; and but for the girl in his arms, Grimes would have ignored it as did the herd guards and the nighthawk of the remuda. But it would be a mess, having the second watch slip up on him and catch Susie.

He relaxed. Then, peering toward the men stretched out near the chuck wagon, he saw a dark shape emerging from a blacker patch. The moon's upper edge was just peeping from the horizon, though trees still shadowed most of the camp.

The figure moved silently, infinitely cautious. There was a gleam of steel.

Murder! Grimes, thrusting Susie aside, snapped his .45 into line. The blast shook the silence; but even as the gun jumped in his hand, he knew that he had been an instant too late. The blade sank home. The slayer leaped, whirling toward the report.

Grimes bounded forward. Tongues of flame laced the gloom. Susie cried out, stumbled; but that shot stretched into a prolonged drumming. The gunner, bolting toward the remuda, pitched headlong.

"Cut down, hip high!" yelled Grimes. "Susie—fer Gawd's sake—"

She was on her feet, but the hand that caught his wrist was wet with blood. And then the camp became a howling madness.

"I got him!" Grimes roared. "Quit yo' shooting—see who he knifed—You, Jeb!" Matches flared. Gil Stewart plucked at the knife haft in his chest, coughed, and slumped back, dead. The assassin Grimes had shot down was Bart Bailey.

The reason for his treachery became apparent an instant later. Rifle fire crackled from the flank of the bedded herd. Horsemen charged out of the darkness. That explained the owl hoots!

Grimes made a dive for the wagon, passing out rifles. The cowpunchers aroused in time to beat the ambush, raked the raiders with a withering fire. Saddles emptied, horses pitched end for end. Instead of a camp gutted by a stealthy assassin, they charged into a hornet's nest.

They broke; and as the drovers piled into their saddles, Grimes got the answer: Melinda, Potts, and Bailey had conspired to plunder, then peddle the stolen cattle to traders in wet beef.

But as the enemy fled, a new peril threatened the camp. The cattle were stampeding. A long, rumbling line thundered along the flank. The raiders, defeated, had precipitated a panic to block pursuit. The drovers again were on the defensive; and against a deadlier peril.

Grimes jerked Susie from her feet and into the saddle in front of him. No time to get a second horse. Not a chance to fan out the roaring herd. They had gotten too good a start. Moonrise revealed a surging sea of long, deadly horns; and the main body, blindly following, was adding to the irresistible flood of beasts.

"The river—Simon—the river—" gasped Susie.

"Not a chanct, honey! They's cut us off, both sides—"

She tried to worm from his arms, but he checked her.

"Simon—you're silly—I can't last long—I'm just tiring your hoss—a wild shot—plugged me—"

Good God! Then he remembered how she'd let out scarcely a yeep. The morning before she'd yelled bloody murder, just at a scratch. She must be badly injured.

"Shut up, you little fool," he snapped, turning in the saddle. "We'll make it."

His .45 crackled. A longhorn pitched in a heap another, and a third. The mountain of beef was too high for those behind to hurdle. Horns locked, they could not swerve. Bones crushed as tons of frenzied beasts piled up, held like a timber jam by one key log.

"We're gainin', honey—hang on—"

He swung to the left, trying to outrace the further tip of the crescent. He emptied his other gun, gained a few more precious yards.

Then the overloaded mustang's stride broke. He had lamed himself in a gopher hole.

Terror drove him on, but he couldn't last long. Escape every instant became more hopeless.

"Simon—you fool—"

Susie's frenzy caught Grimes off guard. She slipped free, thudded to the earth. One bit of devotion in a solid front of treachery. He wheeled, reloaded his guns, bounded to her side. It was insane; perhaps Grimes knew he hadn't a chance, even though he did ride on.

"That buffler wallow—scrunch into it! I'll shoot the hoss!" he yelled. "And pile up some cows tother side of it—"

And then, far ahead, he saw a rider skylined in the moonlight; a rider suddenly blossoming white, and wildly waving something white. A pistol blazed. The point of the onrushing crescent swung, fanned out. Hundreds of frenzied beasts with a single, insane mass mind responded to the new terror. Those further to the rear wheeled, snorting, bawling, hoofs rumbling, horns clashing. Grimes whirled, picked up his limp burden, swung to the saddle.

He flogged his lamed mustang with his pistol barrel, booted and spurred the beast till it forgot its tortured leg.

And when the horse finally pitched in a heap, the stampede had been turned. Other riders, who had outraced the right wing of the herd, came scrambling up the bank to press the advantage. The critters were milling now. Hundreds dead, but the most were saved.

Grimes, struggling to his knees, saw the white rider reel in the saddle. It was Melinda Patton, peeled down to her boots and a few scraps that only an expert in ladies' wear could have described. She slid to her feet, swaying as she clutched the saddle horn.

"Simon," she panted, "I came to warn you—they were going to murder—you and Stewart and as many others—as they could—then loot—"

Grimes, kneeling beside Susie, looked up and snarled, "Yo' came to save yo' own critters!"

"No! It was you. Do you suppose if they planned to stampede the herd they'd try murder by hand, when the herd would do that?"

That clinched it. Grimes felt Susie snuggle closer. She smiled and murmured something, then slumped against his arm.

"I wonder," he finally muttered, voice dry and strained, "if you really are in a class with this gal?"

Melinda knelt beside him. "Let's forget our feud. Dad was in the wrong. I finally saw your position. Then I suspected Potts—"

"Potts?"

"Yes. After dad was exposed, and all the cattlemen got damage judgments against his estate, the bank began wobbling. The only way I could save myself was to disguise my HP cattle as BB, and get Bailey to drive them north. The money I'd raise would go into the bank in a blind account and tide me over, instead of having everything cleaned out by judgments against dad's estate. Just judgments, but ruinous.

"I was wrong, but desperate. Potts had been courting me for some time, and finally I pretended to encourage him. But when he came in yesterday, with a wounded horse, and a confused story, I suspected dirt.

"Then the marshal told me how Bailey and his wife tricked you. That nasty play set me thinking more. And when Potts, early this evening, left me on a flimsy pretext—instead of trying to force himself on me, I became more suspicious, and followed him."

"Mebbe," said Grimes, very slowly, "yo'll are in a class with Susie after all. When I git back from Kansas I got a shooting party with Potts—"

"No, Simon." She leaned closer, till he felt her warmth against him. "There's been too much hate and killing. This is feud's end. I'm grieved—but dad was wrong—you couldn't help it—"

"Honey," he groped, "ef yo' mean that, I'll even kiss Potts when I git back."

TOO MANY CLIENTS

Originally published in *Spicy Western Stories*, May 1939.

Jane Cokey's eyes glowed with pride as she paused at the hitching rack on the main street of Aztec Hill and glanced at the freshly painted sign which read, *"SIMON BOLIVAR GRIMES, ATTORNEY AT LAW."* The harness maker, just across the street, looked up from the eight-strand reins he was braiding and ceased work, then and there.

"I shore wisht I was a lawyer," he said to himself, as the breeze ruffled Jane's copper colored hair, and made her low necked blouse outline some nicely luscious curves. He half rose to his feet, sank slowly back to his bench, and shook his head. "Taint no use trying to holler now. Pore Simon!"

Half an hour previous, the harness maker had seen Kitty Baxter heading for the young attorney's second floor office. Her shapely legs, unhampered by riding boots, had thrown his braiding all out of gear.

Kitty's presence had done almost as much for Grimes. At the moment, he was trying to get her arms untangled from his neck. But the frock coat which he had bought along with the musty law office was a handicap. So was Kitty's seductive fragrance, and the upturned lips that pleaded, "Now, Simon, didn't I help you win your first case?"

"I know you did, honey," he admitted, brushing back his tow colored cowlick. "But it ain't any way fo' a professnul man to cut up, entertainin' ladies during office hours."

"Don't be silly, Simon." She wriggled close enough to make a kiss compulsory. "I just wanted to dust your office a little."

The scarlet gown that set off her cream-colored skin and blue black hair did not seem appropriate to house cleaning. Neither did her tiny satin slippers, nor the frail silk hose whose tops were exposed by the disarray of her skirt.

Kitty's lashes fluttered. "Oh, Simon," she murmured as he ceased trying to pry her arms from his neck and began holding her closer.

Just then, a window pane spattered into dirty fragments. Kitty yeeped and ducked for the corner. Grimes drew a .45 Colt from his hip pocket and bounded toward the sill.

Lem Boggs, the harness maker, was gesturing. Grimes yelled, "What the tarnation hell? What y'all mean?"

Boggs kept on gesturing. Then Grimes saw the blue roan at the hitching rack and recognized the beast: Jane Corey's cayuse!

He whirled. Dainty boots were click-clocking along the hall floor.

That must be Jane. A man's weight would have made the boards creak. He made a lunge and caught Kitty by the shoulders. "Git in that closet, quick!" he whispered. "I'm expectin' a client."

Grimes nearly fell over his own oversized feet, but somehow, he reached the door without a bit of lost motion. He stood there, blinking and brushing back the cowlick that persistently invaded his coffin shaped face. "Uh—um—mawnin', Mis' Jane."

"What's the matter, Simon? You look sort of worried."

Grimes wiped the sweat from his forehead. "I sho' am." She tiptoed, and her arms slipped around his neck. He went on, "I'm jest crackin' my skull, studyin' the Ree-vised Statues."

Before her kiss got serious, he caught her arm and steered her back toward the head of the stairs. "Let's you an' me take a ride out to yo pappy's farm."

"But I wanted to consult you," she persisted, backing to the door and reaching behind her to twist the knob. "We ought to go into the office."

"Uh—um—it's po'ful dirty and dusty."

"Then I'll clean it up for you," she brightly answered.

Grimes was quite helpless. But to his intense relief, Kitty Baxter had closed the closet door. Jane daintily picked her way among the fragments of glass and seated herself in Grimes' swivel chair.

"Dad needs some money," Jane explained. "And now that Hickman is back in town, we'd like to have you arrange the loan."

Grimes shook his head. "Mistah Hickman's bank hates nesters like pizen. He won't loan nothing."

"That's just it. But with the way you won your first case, you've got a lot of prestige. I know you can persuade him." She rose, snuggled up against him and whispered, "You've not forgotten that first night we met? When pa and ma were away from the house?" Grimes had not forgotten. He did not know, for a moment, whether her heart or his was pounding so violently against his vest. But he had to get Jane out of the office. So he said, "Honey, y'all jest run along whilst I draw up the papers. I'll see Hickman this afternoon."

When the door closed behind her, Grimes reached for his blue bandanna. And then Kitty Baxter emerged from the dusty closet.

"You do have lovely clients, Simon," she caustically observed.

Without waiting for an answer, she walked out, head high. Grimes sighed and headed for the bar.

Once at the free lunch counter, Grimes scooped up a handful of jerked beef, a bowl of chili, and a pocket full of salted tortillas. "Doctor" Harrigan ceased fiddling with his diamond studded scarf-pin and reached for whiskey and a glass.

"Have one yo'self, doctor," the young attorney invited.

A tall man came in by the side door. One arm was bandaged; a scarlet shawl supported it against his bear-skin vest. His face seemed to have been hewn from a chunk of knotty oak. He limped perceptibly, and muttered in his throat.

"Top of the mornin, to ye, Mr. Hickman," the doctor greeted.

The banker grunted, gulped his whiskey, and stared at the large silver cup on the back bar. Its gleaming surface was engraved in old English letters *"Won by Hammerhead Hickman, Aztec Hill."* The next line read, *"Glass-Eye Regan, Timber Creek."*

Grimes said, "Mistah Hickman, when y'all git finished takin' a appetizer with me, I'd admire to discuss suthin with yo', on behalf of my client, Mistah Ab Corey."

"Ab Corey? Hrrruhp! He selling out?"

Grimes met Mr. Hickman's blistering blue gaze for a moment. As the banker's glance shifted back to the silver trophy, Grimes answered, "Don't reckon as how he is, suh. Fact is, he's aiming to stay. If y'all renew his note, and lend him another thousand dollars on a second—"

"Second mortgage? Hell's hinges! You think I'm crazy!" He stamped across the hand hewn puncheons, and toward the door; indignation made him for a moment forget his game leg.

Grimes shook his head, and sighed. "He's sho' a onsociable gent. Looks like he had a accident, jedging from his face and arm and laig."

"Sure, and that's what's making him peevish."

The doctor pointed at the calendar at the back bar. Penciled crosses blocked out the dates up until the 22nd; the 25th had a ring around it. "It's this iligant trophy he's worrying about," Harrigan explained. "He won it once, and Timber Creek's champeen won it once. This time, it's fer keeps."

"Looks like it'd hold a quart of likker," Grimes estimated. "What do y'all do to win it?"

"It's a dude sport," the doctor explained. "Shooting a scatter gun. Hickman's the champeen, only his arm's busted."

"What all yo' shoot at?"

"Clay pigeons."

"*Clay* pigeons? Hell, that's plumb silly, busting crockery." Grimes left half his chili uneaten. His face lengthened, and he walked down the dusty street, absent-mindedly munching tortillas. It was not until he heard the full throated boom of a shotgun that he perked up.

Another blast; a shout. "Dang ef he didn't hit that one!"

Grimes headed left, toward the disturbance. Instinctively, he reached for the pistol in his leather lined hip pocket.

Just outside the limits, the young attorney halted. Hickman was pacing up and down near a group of men, one of whom had a shotgun. Not far from the party was a shallow pit. In it a man crouched, behind a barrier of logs that sheltered him on two sides. He was working with some iron contraption the like of which Grimes had never seen. Its purpose, however, was soon apparent.

The man in the pit jerked a string. There was a click, a metal arm snapped out straight, and a saucer shaped black disc skimmed over the barrier. The man with the gun blazed away. Hickman cursed when the flying target vanished, far out in the mesquite.

"Why, Windy, you—you—damn' jughead," he roared. "Even a dude kin hit them things on the fly. By gravey—"

Windy whirled and angrily cut in, "Ef yuh hadn't fell often yore hoss, yuh pot-bellied fossil, mebbe yuh could be firing yoreself."

He made as if to slam the weapon to the ground. Hickman yelled. The man in the pit, startled, jerked the release. Another clay pigeon skimmed over the pit. Grimes hated to see a target go to waste. His .45 roared, and the black disc spattered to bits.

"Shucks," he said to the gaping crowd, "if y'all could jest eat them dang things—"

"What—uh—what in tunket?" demanded Hickman. Then he saw the fuming Colt. "Yuh mean yuh hit that with a six gun?"

"It was a gol dang accident," Windy flared.

But Grimes refuted that by nicking the next clay pigeon. The banker demanded, "Look-ee here, bub! You got to shoot fer Aztec Hill."

Grimes shook his head. "No, suh. It's plumb silly. Besides, I ain't never used a scatter gun, excepting onct, in a saloon fight."

"It's yore civic duty!" Hickman contended. "Tuh keep that air trophy in Aztec Hill."

Grimes countered, "If y'all loan Mistah Corey a thousand dollars, I'd sho' admire to represent yo' in this competition."

There was a lot of wrangling and haggling. But finally Hickman consented. "And yuh use my pus-sonal shot gun. Be dang careful of it. She's hand made, full choke, Damascus barrel, and cost four hundred bucks."

"Gosh," muttered Grimes, "that'd buy purty nigh a dozen Colt!"

"Take these yere cartridges," Hickman added. "They's special loadings. Ain't no use yuh wasting none practicing."

"Gents," said Grimes, "if y'all will jine me, I'm buying liquor."

* * * *

Hickman had somber moments, pondering on the thousand dollars he had risked; but when Grimes bellied up to the bar and had the silver trophy filled brim full of whiskey, the banker began to appreciate the young attorney. "A right pert jasper," he confided to Doc Harrigan, "even ef he does look too dang dumb to come outen the rain."

The news spread, and the saloon filled up. Despite Hickman's broken arm, the honor of Aztec Hill no longer hung in the balance.

Grimes took time out to scrutinize the gold inlaid lock and breech of the costly shotgun. "Gosh," he muttered, "fo' hundred bucks! What in tarnation is them funny little lines all around the barrel?"

"That there's hand made Damascus," the banker explained.

"Damascus? Shucks, this ain't a sword!"

"Bub, mebbe yuh kin shoot, but yo're plumb ignorant. That there barr'l is made outen hoss shoe nails wrapped around a form and welded." He had his details slightly scrambled, but the general idea was right. "It's the strongest barr'l made. Yuh couldn't bust it onless yuh stuffed her with dynamite or plugged her muzzle with mud or suthin."

Then Hickman filled the silver trophy with whiskey and passed it around. Aztec Hill settled down to celebrate the impending victory.

That night, Grimes had the precious shotgun cradled in both arms as he headed through the hotel lobby. Somehow, he got to his room.

There he wrapped the gun in a blanket, heaped the cartridge on the table, and sat down to enjoy his liquor. He had lost track of time, and he did not care...

A gentle tapping at the door startled Grimes. His hand streaked for his .45, and he said, "Come in, but keep yo' arms folded."

Then he saw that no Timber Creek gun slinger had tried to trick him into the hall. Kitty Baxter was at the threshold. She wore her saffron yellow negligee. Though she drew it together at the waist, it gave him alluring glimpses of lace-hedged bosom.

"Simon," she said, softly closing the door behind her and tiptoeing toward him, "I heard all about how wonderful you were this afternoon."

"Them's scrumptious slippers yo' wearing, honey."

Kitty planted herself on his knee. The skirt of her robe trailed away at the knee, delightfully exposing a silk clad leg. She slipped a plump arm about his neck, and cuddled comfortably close. Then she glanced at his bed and wondered, "What on earth have you got wrapped up so carefully?"

"That there is a fo' hundred dollar gun. If I win the competition, Hickman's got to loan my client a thousand bucks."

"Oh, isn't that wonderful!" Kitty's voice registered admiration, but her black eyes were narrow and pointed. "Your client? Which one?"

He made an expansive gesture. "Jest a client, honey."

The lovely brunette wriggled closer and kissed him. For some moments, Grimes' thoughts had no room for Jane...

Kitty sighed. "You're kind of sweet on your client, aren't you?"

The Grimeses of Kennesaw Mountain had their moments of brutal frankness, particularly when drunk.

"She's a mighty lovely little critter." He gently pried her arms from about his neck. "Supposin' y'all trot along. I got to be pondering about a case."

Before she had slid from his knee, Grimes' chin was drooping to his chest. He was muttering to himself, "Jane, honey, don't y'all fret yo'self about nuthing..."

Kitty glanced back from the threshold. "Jane, honey!" she venomously echoed. "Drunk as a skunk, and got that bleached blonde on the brain!"

That burned her to a crisp. She really liked Grimes...

He spent the next day sobering up on a mixture of canned tomatoes, Worcestershire sauce, Tabasco, and raw eggs. By night fall, he was eating a two inch steak the size of a blacksmith's apron. The four hundred dollar shotgun, muzzle carefully protected, stood in the corner. A dozen leading citizens watched the champion eat.

"Hand ain't shakin' a bit," muttered the marshal.

"Ef he kin plug 'em with a six gun sober," said another, "he kin bust 'em open with a scatter gun, blind drunk."

Hickman dug out his poke. "Me, I'm riding to Timber Hill tub make some bets. Leastwise enough to cover that there bum loan I got tuh make outen civic pride."

A dozen citizens crowded around to add their rolls to the pot.

* * * *

The night before the contest, Kitty Baxter tiptoed to Grimes' door. He was carving Jane Corey's initials into the table top, and he needed only one more stroke of his Bowie knife to complete the heart that enclosed the letters.

"Mebbe," he was saying to himself, "if I put a arrow through it, it'd be mo' poetic-like."

When he heard the tap at the panel, he dropped his knife and hurried to the door. Kitty's gown was a crimson haze that scarcely blurred her shapely figure. Nestled in the crook of her arm was a bottle. She said, "Simon, I know you like good liquor. So I brought you a bottle of sixteen year old bonded stuff."

"Mighty sweet of you, honey," he said, brightening perceptibly.

He did not bother to kiss her. He was too busy finding and then using a corkscrew. Kitty's glance shifted toward the table top. Her lips thinned slightly when she saw the fresh initials but she pretended interest in the cartridges that Grimes had arranged in symmetrical groups, just beyond the bleeding heart.

"Ooooh…are you firing all those shells?"

"Ug—ug—glug." He lowered the bottle. "Sho' am, honey. Hundred shots, and ef Glass Eye Regan kin tie a perfect score, then we shoots a second batch." He wiped his lips. "Mighty nice whiskey, but dang if I'd not ruther have corn likker like my grand pappy makes."

"What's wrong with this whiskey? They told me it was awfully good."

Grimes stroked her lustrous black curls, and then got a long arm wrapped about her. He nodded, took another long swig, lowering the level by three inches. "Uh—nothing exactly wrong, honey. Only, it's jest weakish-like."

Then he saw the injured expression that clouded her lovely face. Penitent, he set the bottle aside and caught her in both arms. "Now, don't y'all think I'm ungrateful. I sho' was gittin' thirsty, only the committee won't let me drink a drop tonight. But this here don't count, being mild."

"Simon!" She pouted a moment, then dimpled. "You drink every bit, or I'll never speak to you again."

234

But before he got around to that, she wrapped both arms about his neck, and she kissed him, avidly. "Mmmm… Simon," she sighed, "you were awful mean to me the other night…"

"Ohhh—" She gasped, and her eyes were misty when her fluttering lids finally parted and she regarded him between long lashes. "Kiss me that way again, Simon…"

He did even better than that…

* * * *

The next day, Timber Hill's citizens swooped down in a whirl of alkali. The marshal met them, and the sheriff was with him. The latter announced, "Gents, this here ain't going to be a leather-slapping contest. Therefore, me and the local law is axing yuh visitors to jine our local talent in checking yore hand guns, rifles, Bowie knives, and such like weep-ins, in the interests of fair play and clean sport."

"That air," admitted the mayor of Timber Creek, "is mighty agreeable."

And it was so arranged, then and there.

Grimes did not like the look in his opponent's eye. The ironic twinkle irritated him. And then came a surprise. "Gosh," he muttered, nudging Doc Harrigan, "his glass eye points wrong, but by gravey, it moves!"

"Faith," chuckled the bartender, "it's not really a glass eyes. It jest looks like one. Staring that way, independent and disjinted, so to speak."

"That gent," Grimes muttered, stalking toward the firing point, "hadn't oughta be able to hit his reflection in a back bar looking glass. It jest ain't—gol dang it, where yo'all pinting that there gun!"

The cockeyed Mr. Regan grinned, spat a jet of tobacco. He good humoredly apologized, "Sorry, pardner. I wasn't fixing to pint whar I looked like I was looking."

Grimes felt foolish. Regan's crabwise ambling about was as disconcerting as his unmatched eyes. Facing death at the muzzles of blazing Colts was an old story, but competing with a human scarecrow who could look in three directions at once was getting under Grimes' skin.

As Regan loaded for his first shot, Grimes regarded the tiptoeing crowd. He caught one glimpse of Jane, red-gold curls rippling in the breeze that pulled her thin blouse against her bosom, and urged her skirt to model the curve of her slim legs. She waved once. Then Kitty, closer at hand, suddenly turned her back, ignoring Grimes' gesture of recognition.

"*Boom!*" The recoil of the twelve gauge gun threatened to disorganize Glass Eye Regan's spindly frame, but through the puff of smoke, Grimes saw the pigeon disintegrate in black dust.

"One fer Timber Creek!" droned the score keeper.

Then Grimes cut loose, and the duel was on…

* * * *

235

When he had unraveled his fiftieth shell, Grimes followed his rival's lead and took time out for a drink. Hickman was sweating. "Bub, with neither of yuh jaspers missing one so fur, she's gittin' to be a competition! Don't yuh blow up durin' the last ten rounds. That's how I done lost out last time. That, and that whopper-jointed hombre's disconnected eyes. Is yore shoulder achin'!"

"Shucks, no! I kin burn a hundred shells in a buffler gun!"

"Don't git yore timing outa step. I seen fellers miss two an' three of them pigeons right in a row." Grimes registered dignified condescension. Glass Eye Regan's grin was fixed and irritating. The groups of leading citizens were spitting tobacco juice and rubbing their hands. The second round began—

Then it happened. A black disc zipped from the trap. The four hundred dollar gun boomed. For a split second, a speck of black soared against the blue. Grimes stared, incredulous. Timber Creek roared, and Aztec Hill groaned; loudest of all, Mr. Hickman.

"Gawda mighty! I told yuh! Damn it, whut'd I tell yuh, yuh—"

"Don't you dast talk like that, yo—"

But the marshal intervened. Order was restored, and Glass Eye Regan, grinning from ear to ear, snapped his weapon into line. Grimes wiped sweat from his forehead, rubbed his palm in the dust, and stamped his feet. The firing went on.

They ran neck and neck. Regan missed a pigeon. Hickman hooted, slapped Grimes on the shoulder. Aztec Hill, all tiptoed, watched the boys settle down to the last twenty-five rounds. And then the kid from Georgia missed again. This time, Hickman just glared and gnawed his mustache.

"Gosh amighty," Grimes muttered, teeth gritting.

He could not believe that a man could fail to blast a soaring saucer with a gun that spread shot in a thirty inch circle. Maybe fatigue had broken the smooth rhythm of his pull. But Regan was not missing, despite Grimes' prayers for a slip to even the score.

Damn that gun! It was kicking like a mule. He called for time out to pass a cleaning rod down the bore. Hickman growled, "Fer two cents, I'd kick yore head off. Dang-nation, I might of knowed it was a accident, busting pigeons with a six gun."

"Shut up and quit gettin' him rattled," howled the Aztec Hill crowd.

Grimes shattered the next ten straight. Regan, overconfident, missed two in a row. That cut his lead down to one.

Grimes, tense and tight lipped, was pulling carefully as though using a rifle. The glare of the sky, the blast furnace wind, and the flying dust conspired against him. He saw Jane's white face, down the line. Something was wrong. That last pigeon had just broken, and no more.

A man could not miss. Again the trap whisked a target. Grimes swung his gun. A terrific impact hammered his shoulder; flame and dust blended, and the earth came up to meet him as blackness swallowed him up. He never did hear the agonized groan that finally came to the lips of the Aztec Hill crowd. He did not know that the last three inches of the barrel had blown off; that flying fragments of metal had creased his scalp and cheeks, and that the concussion had knocked him senseless. He did not hear Kitty Baxter's shrill scream, nor Jane's moan as she wavered and crumpled, only a moment after him...

* * * *

When Grimes came out of the haze, he was in his room. The contest, lost by default, was tragic history. Jane knelt beside him, eyes reddened from weeping as she pleaded, "Speak to me, Simon."

But all he did was mutter, over and over again, "I couldn't've got mud into the muzzle..."

Finally, however, the roar and rumble of the explosion ceased echoing in his bandaged head; though dazed, he noticed Jane, and the arms that closed about his neck. He avoided her gaze and mumbled, "I'd've lost even if that dang blasted gun hadn't blowed up. I missed too many..."

"Don't feel bad about it, Simon. We're no worse off than if you'd not tried. Dad's just glad you weren't killed."

He shook his head, gently thrust her from him. "Honey, y'all run along. I feel too dang low to look at anyone."

The more Grimes thought about it all, the more urgent it became for him to leave Aztec Hill, whose citizens had lost their shirts in betting on him. That they did not blame him in no way helped. The town was broke and humiliated.

He put on his gun belt and boots and hickory shirt. He had no further use for his frock coat.

Aztec Hill could auction that off, along with his law office, and use the proceeds to buy Hickman a new shotgun.

Before going to the stable to get his horse, Grimes tapped at Kitty Baxter's door. He'd see Jane on his way south.

"Go away," Kitty sobbed. "I don't want to see anyone. Go away!"

He tapped again, and said, "Kitty, it's jest me. I come to say goodbye."

"Oh—!" She came on the run, jerked the door open, and stood there, anxiously scrutinizing his face and bandaged head. "They told me you were seriously hurt! I'm so glad you're not!"

She clung to him, her tears trickling down his face as she kissed him and went on, "It was my fault! Oh, I never realized—honest, I didn't—think— you'd nearly—get killed—I've been worried—silly—"

"Huh?" He took a stride forward, and closed the door after him. Kitty would not let go. "What's that?"

"That night—when I brought you the whiskey—I cut some of—the cartridges—just below—the wads over the powder—so you'd miss—"

"What?" He thrust her from him, holding her by both shoulders.

She looked up, blinking. Then her eyes hardened and she defiantly continued, "I helped you win your first case. And then you got into that fool contest to help that bleached blonde—"

"Don't you dast talk thataway!" He shook her till her teeth rattled.

"I don't care! I was good and sore, and when One Eye Regan told me how to fix things, I snapped at it. I was afraid you were killed, but now that you aren't I'm glad I did it! Now hit me! I don't care!"

For a moment they eyed each other. Then he scooped her off her feet. Before she could begin to kick or struggle, he had her plopped down on her bed and was rolling her up in a blanket, her arms pinned to her sides.

As he plucked a pair of stockings from the back of a chair and lashed her ankles together, he said, "Don't you dast holler, or I'll snatch you bald headed."

"What are you fixing to do?" she quavered when she found her voice.

"I'm cinching you up!" He improvised a gag. "So you can't raise no ructions until I'm through taking care of Glass Eye Regan. Dad blast it, a ignorant woman wouldn't know that a solid hunk of shell and shot'd likely blow up a full choke barrel, but he'd ought to know that, and if he don't, I'm teaching him!" And for good measure, Grimes dumped his captive into her own clothes closet.

* * * *

When Grimes galloped out of Aztec Hill, he had a shotgun borrowed from the harness maker. In his pocket was a handful of cartridges which had not been tampered with. No wonder he had missed; and no wonder that the taper bored barrel had burst under the strain!

Timber Creek was celebrating its victory. Every saloon was jammed with men spending the day's winnings. Grimes dismounted and set out in search of Glass Eye Regan. He ignored the risk; though this was reduced by artificial light, and the bandages that swathed his head.

Drunks reeled down the street. Women in kimonos leaned from their windows to hail the riotous townsmen. Raucous hoots, and shrill yippees were punctuated by the blasts of pistols pointed skyward, the clattering hoofs of ponies ridden hell bent by late arrivals. And in a corner of the plaza a crew of Mexicans toiled at the barbecue pit.

Grimes hid his shotgun in the dark alley which ran between the general store and the city hall. Then he set out to find Glass Eye Regan. After peeping in through the side doors of several saloons, he noticed that the crowd was shifting from the bars toward the street. Their destination was the plaza, whose broad expanse was now reddened by the leaping flames of a bon fire.

A rostrum had been erected at the farther end of the square. The crowd was gathering about it, yelling and hooting as three men ascended from the rear and came toward the railing. Grimes recognized the mayor and the postmaster. The third was Glass Eye Regan. He had the silver trophy.

The champion was going to present the cup to Timber Creek. In return, he was going to get the keys to the city. And that final injustice made Grimes change his plan, then and there. Shooting it out with the treacherous winner was just a personal matter. The public spirited thing to do was to seize the trophy, and carry it back to Aztec Hill.

"Ladies and gents," began the mayor, raising his hand. "As a fittin' climax tuh this glorious victory—"

But Grimes was not waiting for the speech. He had already sized up the lay of the land. He dashed hell bent to get his horse, and also the shotgun which he had brought to lend a touch of poetic justice to his encounter with Glass Eye.

Once in the saddle, he looped around, approaching the rostrum from the rear. Glass Eye and the postmaster occupied chairs. The mayor was in the midst of his oration, pausing at times to spit and wipe his mustache with a red bandanna. He concluded, "And now we craves a few words from the hero of the evening. Git on yore hind legs, Glass Eye, or hold yore peace forever."

But the champion's bow froze, and so did the applause that greeted him. Grimes, head and shoulders visible above the rostrum, leveled his shotgun and shouted, "Fork over that there trophy, or I'm blowin' the guts outen the three of you. Stay clost together an' edge toward me, easy-like."

The double barreled gun that menaced the trio likewise quelled the front ranks of the crowd. They knew that at the first hostile move a hail of slugs would sweep the champion from the platform.

"Yuh kain't take my trophy," Glass Eye protested. "Anyhow, it ain't worth much, unless yore name's engraved on it."

"Turn around, slow," Grimes commanded.

Glass Eye obeyed. He recognized the man with the gun. The silver cup dropped from his hand to the floor. He quavered, "Honest tuh Gawd, I didn't aim fer yore gun tuh bust. I was jest fixing tuh play a prattical joke?"

Beyond the rostrum, the crowd was muttering and beginning to mill around. Men were slipping from the further edge of the gathering and darting into the shadows. The mayor gulped and said, "What's this here yore talkin' about? Whut prattical joke?"

"Y'all out there, stand fast," Grimes yelled, "or these gents catch hell. Glass Eye ain't had a chanct to fix this here gun so's it'd blow up." Then, to the champion, "Gimme that cup, now."

He spurred his horse to make a quarter turn. Gun barrel resting across his left forearm, he still commanded the three on the platform. His left hand snatched the trophy. That was what the crowd was waiting for.

A pistol crackled, and then another. Lead whizzed past Grimes. He had his hands full, and his horse bolted. The trio on the rostrum howled and flattened to the floor. That saved them; for Grimes, unable to steady his wobbling weapon, jerked both triggers.

The recoil tore the gun from his grasp. The double charge of shot pelted the crowd that was surging from his left. Smoke obscured him for an instant. That gave him a chance to recover. He booted his horse, and still clutching the handle of the cup, he twisted in the saddle and brought his Colt into play.

Glass Eye Regan was on his knees, clawing at his holster. Grimes' Colt jumped, and the champion slumped face down. The confusion of the crowd was what saved the invader. Men got in each other's way, and those in front were still too stunned to make the most of a galloping target.

Before the concentrated population of Timber Creek could spread to cut off Grimes' retreat, he was clearing the city limits; and drunken marksmanship had not a chance at that range.

Grimes, galloping back toward Aztec Hill, saw no chance of redeeming himself, or of inducing Hickman to approve to loan to Jane's father. There was no regaining the money which the town had lost. All that he could do was deliver the cup, tell his story, and shake a hock.

* * * *

A light glowed in the front room of Hickman's house. A saddled horse was at the hitching post, but in the darkness, Grimes paid no attention to the beast. It made little difference who was calling on the banker. He tramped down the gravel walk; but before he reached the verandah steps he heard a woman's hysterical entreaties.

"What in tunket *she* doing here?" he muttered, ascending the steps and approaching the window. "Reckon I didn't tie her very good."

"But you've got to go after him!" Kitty Baxter was saying. "You've got to stop him. He's gone to Timber Creek to kill Glass Eye Regan. He can't do that in a hostile town."

Grimes peeped past the edge of the drawn shade. Kitty, disheveled and hastily dressed, caught the banker's good arm. Hickman shook his head, and jerked clear of her grasp. He grumbled, "Ef Grimes is loco enough to try to finish Glass Eye in his home town, that's his lookout."

"But it's on account of that contest not being fair."

"Huh?" He turned, caught her by the shoulder. "How come?"

"Oh—" She twisted her handkerchief, looked down at her feet.

"Speak up!" Hickman demanded.

"I can't."

"Ef yuh can't, then I ain't asking no one tuh Timber Creek tuh stop that young fool from getting a hideful of lead. Why'd he go? What's he know? How come, it warn't fair?"

Kitty looked up. Her hands opened and closed for a moment. Then she desperately blurted, "I was crazy about Simon, and I was jealous. When Glass Eye Regan told me how to fix up shotgun cartridges so Simon'd lose, I went and done it."

"Why—what—gol dang yore hide—yuh mean—?"

Hickman was choking. Kitty slowly backed into a corner. Grimes bounded to the door and yanked it open. "I didn't reckon yo'd learn what happened," he began, offering the banker the bullet nicked trophy. "But now that you do, you needn't bother to save me from a posse."

240

He wiped a trickle of blood from his cheek. Red smudged his vest. But Grimes grinned and went on, "I popped Glass Rye, an' if he didn't die sudden-like, I low he'll confess. He was startin' to when I cut loose."

"Simon—" Kitty swayed dizzily, then clung to him with one arm as she anxiously dabbled the blood from his face. "You were hit. Oh, it's my fault—will you ever forgive me—?"

"Yuh gol blasted trouble-maker!" Hickman stormed.

"Look-ee here, Mistah Hickman," Grimes went on, "I risked my head twict account of this silver trophy. Onct trying to win it, an' onct gettin it back."

But his plea was interrupted. He had no chance to argue that Hickman was morally obligated to make the loan to Jane's father. Jane herself bounded out of the hall. She closed in on Kitty with both claws.

The sudden onslaught landed the tearful brunette on the sofa. For a moment there was a flailing of legs, a rending of cloth. Both combatants were in tatters as they thumped to the floor, still searching and plying their nails.

Hickman's eyes widened as the ladies peeled each other down to bare essentials. He was fascinated, but he did not want anyone to know it. "Simon," he growled, "I'm crippled. Git them shameless hussies outen here afore—afore—gosh a-mighty!"

He stood there, gaping. Kitty's skirt was now hobbling her ankles.

"Git them out yo'self." He did not want to see any more of Kitty, and he wanted to mount up and ride before he met Jane's accusing eye. "If y'all reckon I ain't had enough embarrassing situations, yo' plumb crazy. You got yo' dang cup, and I'm through with this fool."

Then Jane emerged from the tangle, and with most of Kitty's upper garments trailing from her grasp. She dropped the tattered silk and overtook Grimes at the door. She flung both arms about him and cried, "I don't care if you are crazy about her—or if she's wild about you—"

Her eyes were gleaming, and the flush on her cheeks slowly spread to throat and bosom. Grimes gulped, pointed at Kitty, and said, "Tain't exactly her, nohow. I'm jest quitting the law."

"Simon, yuh jughead," Hickman interposed, "I done told Miss Jane that being as how yuh tried yore damndest, and it warn't yore fault that gun blowed up, I'd loan her old man the man anyway, when she come in this evening tuh axe me to give him another chanct."

"Huh?" Grimes whirled. "Yo' mean that?"

"Of course he does," Jane cut in, breathlessly. "Of course you'll stay, won't you, darling? Even if you do have too many kissing clients."

"The way yo' put it, honey," he answered, "I reckon I keep on being a attorney."

When Hickman saw the clinch that followed, he coughed and turned to help Kitty reorganize her scattered odds and ends. Grimes grinned, brushed back his cowlick, and said, "Now that they ain't no one lookin', y'all get set for a sure nuff kiss..."

SHE HERDED HIM AROUND

Originally published in *Spicy Western Stories*, Feb. 1941.

Scowling, the boy from Georgia stamped out of his hotel room and down the hall. A straw colored cowlick reached to his china blue eyes; he was lean and long, and a black frock coat hung from his shoulders. He stopped at the door next to his own, tapped with a ham-sized fist, and barged in without waiting for an answer.

"Ain't no woman on Earth can herd me around," he began.

The girl sitting in the rocker let out a yeep and cried, "Simon, you might wait to find out if I was dressed."

She bounded to her feet and held a red silk dress in front of her to cover the most conspicuous bare spots.

Simon Bolivar Grimes stuttered, "Dang it, Elma, how'd I know you'd be plumb...ah...uncovered-like?"

He backed toward the door, but the dark haired girl said, "Might as well stay, if there's anything you've missed, I'd love to know what it is."

She turned her back and proved her point. There was a fluff of chiffon about her hips; it didn't reach very low in one direction or high in the other. Her back and shoulders had a creamy richness. She was plump and shapely; her legs were sleek, and her garters made luscious indentations. Just a single graceful move, and the red dress was slipping over her head and sinking down to her hips. A pat, and it rustled past her knees and cut off his view of her calves, which tapered down to dainty ankles.

"How'd I know?" Grimes repeated.

"I guess you wouldn't." Elma sighed, then winced. "Ouch!" She picked a needle from the red dress. "Never occurred to you I'd have to patch the only dress I have. And you're as ragged as I am, after riding a hundred miles in a frock coat!"

A frown again tightened Grimes' coffin-shaped face. "Look here, Elma, ain't no woman on Earth can herd me around. I am damn-blasted if I aim to be a cowpuncher just account you got a notion I'm too dumb to reckonize gold if I stumbled over it."

"Simon, darling, I don't mean you're stupid. I mean, you just don't know a thing about mining. Anyway, mining towns are poison, and miners are the lousiest ruffians."

"Huh! When I found you, you was hustling drinks in a dance hall!"

Elma slapped him with both hands before he could dodge. "Yes, and I got you out of jail, I got you the horse you escaped on, and you were a small town lawyer when I found you, you long-legged idiot!"

She began crying and clung to him. "Simon, mining towns are poison! Claim jumpers shot my dad. Anyway, your uncle's a cattleman, if you weren't so stubborn you and me could get a start with him."

"Aw, honey—" She was close enough now for him to be delightfully aware of her generous curves, and she snuggled closer; but the Grimes stubbornness won out. "Look here, I ain't got more'n a couple hundred dollars, and my uncle'd mock me, coming back thattaway, after I busted outen that jail wheah that crooked Jedge Hillman flung me fo' contempt of court. I got to get myself some gold, and I'm a-going to."

She jerked back, wiped her eyes. "Simon Bolivar Grimes, you weren't too proud to have me smuggle saws into the jail!"

The boy from Georgia straightened up. He dug into his pocket and brought out a buckskin poke and emptied half the gold pieces on the dresser. "M'am, I am mighty sick of these here reminders." He looked at the heavy gold watch his grandpappy had given him just before he was hanged for shooting a revenue officer. "It is jest about time for the stage coach to get here. You kin keep both the hosses you got."

He turned to the hall. She snatched the coins and flung them. They hit the panel just as he closed the door behind him.

"Ain't no woman herding me around," he repeated. He knew he'd miss Elma, and he had to build up his courage.

Grimes stepped into his room and shouldered the saddle bags which contained his razor, a quart of whiskey, and a pair of field glasses. Then he went down the creaking stairs and stood in the doorway.

Cowpunchers yelled when, a few minutes later, the stage came clattering down the dusty main street. Hostlers brought out the new relay and took the sweating team to the stables. The driver leaped down, and so did the shotgun messenger who guarded the heavy box of gold coin. A blond girl stepped from the stage.

There was a seductive rustle of skirts, a coy flash of shapely legs; the slanting rays of the sun twinkled on the sheer silk of her hosiery. The sweetness of her perfume warmed Grimes' heart; he felt a little less bleak inside.

Grimes watched her walk into the stage station. She lifted her skirts a little and picked her way daintily across the dust and among the bottles and cigar butts that littered the dirt sidewalk; but she looked at home, for all her frilly garments and the little hat with the blue plume. Neither did she grimace when she entered the dingy dining room.

Grimes bought a ticket for Skull Gulch. He had barely stuffed a few ham sandwiches and a slab of apple pie into his coat pocket when it was time to board the coach. He held the door open for the fascinating stranger and then followed her to the coach; now that she had walked the cramps out of her legs, she needed no assistance.

Grimes looked up at the window at the end of the second floor hallway of the hotel. He caught a glimpse of Elma, and for a moment he felt like a skunk. Then he said to himself, "Ain't no woman kin herd me around."

He had half hoped she would fling her few odds and ends into her carpetbag and follow. But she had not, and it was too late to back down. Then the driver cracked the whip; the stage lurched forward, flinging the lovely blonde all over Grimes.

She had curves in the right places, even though her prim blouse hid them from the eye. The momentary pressure, the warm contact of her hand, the fragrance of her garments: they all made Grimes tingle down to his boots.

They were alone in the coach, but the girl might as well have been surrounded by a board fence. He could not get up his nerve to edge her into one corner and slip an arm about her; that puzzled Grimes, and fascinated him. She was sweet and friendly, and she wasn't stand-offish, but he kept his hands clear.

He said, after the exchange of names followed the untangling of accidentally scrambled limbs, "Miss Anne, I knowed you belonged out here, the minute I seen you picking yo' way, calm and placid-like into that there station. Me, I'm a miner, but I usta practice law. I'm aiming to make a pile fo' myself at Skull Gulch."

Anne Parsell made a gesture of dismay. "Why, Simon, that's the murderingest town in Arizona."

"I reckon it ain't too wild," he answered and hitched about a little, for the .45s in his leather-lined hip pockets were a nuisance. Now that he was through being a lawyer, he'd wear his guns on belts again. "Anyways, a fellow can face a few risks for a saddlebag full of nuggets."

* * * *

She laughed merrily. "Well, they do say gold is where you find it. You know, there's the New Golconda, where I live, in Broken Axe. For years, it's been completely played out. And do you know, now they're taking ore out of it so rich they don't let the miners leave the mine, or else they'd fill their boots with nuggets whenever they headed for town."

Grimes sat up straight. "Miss Anne, mebbe I been a mite hasty about Skull Gulch. Reckon I oughta go to Broken Axe instead."

"You won't get rich on miner's pay. Since you've practiced law, why don't you work in dad's bank?"

"Yo' pappy own a bank?"

"No, he's only president of it. Brad Thorman owns a bit of stock, and he wants to marry me, but he's old as the hills. I wouldn't be surprised if he's thirty-five."

* * * *

It was dark now, and above the clatter of the stage, Grimes heard the yip-yip of a coyote, and the answering howl of another. Anne's profile was exquisite in the gloom. The noise made conversation lag. She sat up, lovely and straight; but finally, as the hours wore on, her lovely head nodded.

She leaned against the arm rest. She gasped, murmured an apology as a jolt flung her against Grimes, but she did not take her head from his shoulder. She pillowed her blond curls against the black frock coat, and Grimes said to himself, "Jest like a dang-blasted angel, gosh, she's beautiful..."

To hell with Skull Gulch! He was going to Broken Axe. He hoped Elma wouldn't follow him to Skull Gulch, it'd be too bad, going so far out of her way.

Grimes must have been dozing, for the screech of brakes startled him. Then there was a shot. Anne cried, "Good Lord, a hold-up!" Men yelled, rocks clattered down the moonlit slope of the pass. The guard cut loose with his carbine, and then a volley raked the coach.

The driver was trying to swing clear of boulders heaped in the trail. Grimes caught Anne by the shoulder and thrust her to the floor. "You scrunch down, honey," he yelled and drew his .45s.

She cried, "Simon, you'll get killed—oh!"

Two slugs had zinged from bolts inside the coach. Grimes leaned out the window. Four men were pelting down the slope. Their horses struck fire from the rocks. Their guns blazed. The driver was whipping the team, sawing the lines, weaving in and out among the boulders, trying to get back on the trail. Grimes fired. A man slumped over in his saddle, then rolled off; his horse galloped with the others.

Then the messenger lurched from his post.

The lead team piled up. A horse screamed. Grimes yelled, "Cut them loose, I'll hold these here bastards!"

The driver answered, and Grimes' Colt blazed again.

The nearest road agent doubled up, clutched for support, and thumped to the ground. Grimes shouted to Anne, "Honey, get out on the other side, get outen here and hide yo'self afore you git a stray bullet."

And then a hammer blow knocked the breath out of Grimes. He had many times before now felt the paralyzing smash of a bullet, but this was different. He could not feel a thing from his collarbone to his knees; the moonlight blurred and blackened.

He never did know how long it was before he heard Anne cry, "Oh, he's not hurt at all, really."

The driver, head bandaged, knelt beside her, with a lantern. Grimes sat up. "M'am, what in tunket you mean I ain't hurt none?"

"Why, the bullet hit the big gold watch in your vest pocket."

"They busted that heirloom," he muttered, looking at the wreckage. "If ever I ketch that sculpin, I'm staking him out on an ant-hill. How's the hosses?"

"One kilt, I had to shoot t'other whilst Miss Anne was looking for bullet holes in your gizzard. And they got the gold."

Anne recoiled. "They got the gold? Oh, good Lord."

Grimes hoisted himself to the seat and leaned back against the bullet-riddled upholstery. "Huh! Tain't yo' gold, is it?"

* * * *

At the next town, Ojo Caliente, the driver got a lead team; but Anne refused to go on.

"Simon," she said, "you've got to see a doctor, you got an awful wallop, watch or no watch. And I'm going to stop over to see that you're taken care of."

Once the coach was on its way, Grimes muttered, "Shucks, nothing wrong with me, here I am letting a woman herd me around again."

Before he reached the head of the hotel stairs, he did think his gizzard had been knocked out of place; but he told the doctor, "Ain't nothing wrong with me, get me a quart of liquor and a cigar."

* * * *

It was perhaps an hour or two before dawn when he awoke, a gun in each hand, and sweat pouring down his cheeks. He looked around, realized that he had been dreaming of a second hold-up, and took another swig of rye.

Then he heard the sobbing next door; Anne was crying, tossing restlessly. It was all plain through the thin partition. He got up, put on his boots and coat, and tapped at her door. When she answered, he said, "Honey, it's jest me. I done heard you weeping like yo' little heart's busted wide open."

"Oh, just a minute—" There was a flurry of bare feet, the scratch of a match; then, "Come in, Simon, I'm so worried."

She wore a filmy robe over a lace-paneled gown; the two garments together wouldn't have been enough to wad a shotgun. Her hair was shimmering gold in the light of the smoky lamp. For all her reddened eyes, Anne was the loveliest creature he had ever seen; through the frail garments he could just distinguish the shadowy roundnesses of her slim figure.

He caught her in his arms, gritted his teeth for a moment, then let himself down into the rocker.

"It's that robbery," she said, snuggling against his shoulder.

"Huh. Tain't yo' money."

"But the loss will hurt dad's bank, there may be a run on it."

"Shucks, ain't the stage company responsible?"

She shook her bead. "The bank owns the stage line."

Grimes stroked the golden hair, slipped an arm about Anne, and kissed her. She did not protest, and before he could marvel at that, she was clinging to him, murmuring, "Simon, when you were half conscious from trying to defend me from the road agents, you said the sweetest things."

That kiss inspired Grimes. "Honey, all the more reason fo' not working in yo' pappy's bank, and going to the New Golconda instead. I'll give him the gold, and I wont ask fo' my money until the bank's earnt enough to stand the loss of the robbery."

"Simon, darling, miners just get pay."

Grimes chuckled. "Not me. I'm a-filling my boots with nuggets every shift I work. They ain't keeping me locked up at any mine!"

"Oh, but that'd be stealing."

"Huh. Tain't neither. It's downright stingy, expecting a fellow to dig and drill and blast all day long, and then holler if he stuffs a couple nuggets into his pockets. Did the owner of the New Golconda put the gold into the ground in the fust place? You jest hush up, honey, I'm saving yo' pappy's bank if I have to high-grade two-three mines."

Anne didn't have an answer. Then he was kissing her until she couldn't say anything for a while. At last Grimes said, "That there light's too dang glaring..." He got up and blew it out. When he got back to the warm white shape in the gloom, he went on, "Who'd you say owns the New Golconda?"

"Brand Thorman."

"Huh. He's the gent that thinks he'll marry you!"

* * * *

It was dawn when Anne said, "Simon, you better go back to your room, folks might start talking."

He wrote a letter, telling Elma he was not going to Skull Gulch; but he did not tell her what his destination was. No woman was going to herd him around...

When the following stage brought Grimes and Anne to Broken Axe, the town turned out. The marshal and half a dozen cowpunchers surrounded Grimes and Anne, demanding a first-hand account of the vain but valiant defense of the coach. Anne's father, Jim Parsell, joined the crowd. He was a tall, ruddy man with a blond mustache. He wore boots and store clothes and a battered Stetson jammed down on shaggy white hair.

"Simon," he said, "I done heard all about it, and I'd sure like to have you be chief counsel for this here bank."

Grimes answered, "If it's jest the same to you, suh, I'm plumb sick of law and I'd ruther work in the New Golconda mine."

Anne said, "Dad, why don't you ask Brand, Simon was defending his interest, too. It was bank money."

"Well, I reckon I could, if Simon insists."

And then a dark man with a close-cropped mustache came up. His thumbs were hooked in his green satin vest; a good looking fellow, except for his gimlet eyes and too-hearty smile.

Anne said, "Hello, Brand, Dad and I would like for you to give Simon a job in your mine."

Brand Thorman cocked his head and eyed Grimes from dusty boots to bullet-riddled hat. "So you're Simon Bolivar Grimes, the Texas gunslick, eh? Nice work, smoking out two road agents."

"Huh? What's that?" Grimes scowled; he didn't like the man. "I ain't no gunslick."

Thorman chuckled. "No offense, Simon, no offense. And I'm sorry, but I don't need any more miners, I've got plenty." He lifted his hat, "Goodbye, Anne."

Grimes watched him mount up the slim-legged palomino in front of the Thorman House Bar. Then Anne's father said, "Simon, let's liquor up a bit and see if I can talk you into working for me."

Anne cut in, "I wish you could persuade him, dad."

Though Grimes stepped into the Thorman House Bar, he was still determined not to have any woman herd him around.

After two or three quick ones, he said, "Lookee here, Mistah Parsell, you got to get me into that mine, I'm plumb set on mining, I allus craved to learn the business." He omitted any mention of his plans for pocketing nuggets; he sensed that rugged Jim Parsell would have the same childish ideas that Anne had. "Though mebbe I ought to help the sheriff run down them robbers that ruined my grandpappy's watch."

Jim Parsell's craggy face tightened. "I'd sure love to see them dancing on the business end of a riata. Forty thousand bucks, and if the news gets out how hard we're hit, no telling what'll happen."

* * * *

The following morning, cattlemen came driving into Broken Axe, supposedly to buy groceries; but each one went to the bank and drew out cash. Grimes watched Jim Parsell through the fly-specked windows; the tall rancher was saying to each depositor, "Your *dinero's* safe, neighbor. But if you drag it down, you might get held up, same as the stage."

Parsell was sweating. Some depositors did return most of the money they had drawn, but some got stubborn. It was touch and go, all day.

Grimes was impatiently waiting for night. He and Anne were driving out on the mesa. She was bringing a lemon pie, some cushions, and a Navajo rug. Anne would pass by the hotel to pick him up.

Brand Thorman drove down the street in a buckboard and pulled up in front of Cy Daley's General Mercantile, Hay, Grain & Feed Store. He did not notice Grimes, and Grimes barely noticed him; the passengers sitting on boxes set on the wagon bed accounted for that last.

There were two Mexican girls built like Percheron mares, three chemical blondes, and a redhead. They were painted up like a carnival parade, their perfume drowned the main street's odor of stale beer and horses, and their low-cut dresses made Grimes gape.

The redhead said, "See anything you ain't seen before, dearie?"

Grimes answered, "Not yet, m'am, but if that there wagon hits any bumps, there's jest no telling."

She laughed and patted the deeply cut yoke of her dress, just by way of checking up. One of the Mexican girls said, "*Señor*, you are too fonny!"

"Where you all ladies going, to a picnic or suthin?"

"Picnic?" A blonde turned to her nearest neighbor. "Sure, and he thinks it's a picnic, up there at the mine."

Then a little gray man with a blue apron came out of the store carrying a case of whiskey. Brand Thorman followed, a case on his shoulder. Grimes asked the girl nearest the tailgate, "Gosh, m'am, is that there liquor for the miners?"

"Miners get thirsty, don't they? Listen, dearie, come up to see me Friday night, I live right next to the post office."

Thorman took the reins and cracked the whip. The cargo of girls and whiskey rolled down the street. Grimes said to Cy Daley, "That gent sure treats his miners mighty nice."

The storekeeper said, "Finding nuggets the size of steers, he can damn well afford to! It beats all, bub, the luck of some folks. Mine's been given up fer years, and Brand snoops around and finds the lost vein."

Grimes watched the dust cloud rising from the desert. As he went to the hotel to wait for Anne, he said to himself, "No dang wonder these gals holler when a fellow aims to work in the mines. Some of them ladies was right pert looking, too."

He ate a steak and four eggs and half a dried-apple pie. But thinking of Elma took the edge from his appetite.

"After all," he said to himself, "she's got them two hosses, and I gave her half of my roll. No, I ain't being herded around by no woman."

It was dark now, but he sat there, trying to devise an approach to the problem of getting a job from a man who did not want more employees. Finally he brightened up: "If Thorman don't break all the likker out at once, which he wont, supposing I snuck in and opened a case? Them miners ain't going to know their own names fo' a week."

* * * *

When Anne Parsell drove up in her father's buggy, Grimes took the reins, and flicked the high-stepping bay's rump. "Sure a scrumptious night, honey."

Anne sighed, leaned back against his shoulder.

Well out on the mesa, Grimes pulled up at a *tinaja* whose slow ooze of water filled a small rocky basin just enough for the grass that covered the thin soil for a few yards about the basin. He spread out the Navajo rug, and Anne snuggled beside him, in the lee of the boulder that sheltered them from the cool wind.

The silence finally made him look up from the girl in his arms, for all that she clung to him, lips eager and misty eyes veiled by drooping lashes. "Gosh, honey, I could almost grab them stars and put 'em in your hair."

She sighed ecstatically. "You're so poetic, Simon." And then, needing both arms, Grimes was unable to reach for the stars...

The way it ended, he forgot all about the chicken sandwiches and the lemon pie until Anne exclaimed, "Oh, it's getting late, we ought to get back to town before everyone turns out for the westbound stage."

He helped her to her feet, sighed regretfully, and then became practical. "Better let me brush the burrs offen your skirt, honey."

There weren't any to speak of, but it was nice work.

On the way back to town, Grimes asked, "Why in tunket don't Thorman put up gold brick and save your pappy's bank?"

"He's offered to, if I'll marry him."

"That old buzzard, I bet he's dang near forty. Your pap can't make you marry Thorman, can he?"

"Oh, it's not a case of *forcing* me to, Simon. But dad's worked so hard with that bank. He's carried so many ranchers through bad years. I just can't let him fail now. I'd be letting all our friends down."

Grimes flicked the whip. "Look here. Suppose you and me cut up so scandalous that Thorman'd not want to marry you, and then maybe your pappy could deal with him reasonable."

Her eyes brightened. "That would be fun, darling." But the smile faded quickly, and she let go his hand. "Only Thorman'd kill you. No, that's not the way—oh, hurry! Here comes the stage!"

He plied the whip. The bay stretched his long legs. The buggy bounced and careened over the rough road; but for all his gallant effort, the stage beat Jim Parsell's trotter. And when Grimes pulled up, all of Broken Axe had turned out.

Grimes gave Anne the reins. "Shucks, mebbe we coulda made it through the arroyo instead of to town, I musta been absent-minded."

"I'm afraid not," Anne said, "without going miles and miles around."

Even so, the late return might have been inconspicuous, but for one passenger who had stepped out of the stage. In another moment, she would have been in the hotel. As it was, she stood there under the lights at the door. Elma Austen had followed Grimes.

She saw him, and she saw his blond companion. She dropped her carpetbag and darted toward the buggy. Grimes leaped to the street and said, "Anne, you hurry—"

The crowd, however, blocked her way, but it did not block Elma. She said, "You jailbird, maybe you think I didn't see this blonde bait get on the coach with you! Maybe you thought I'd not hear of that robbery and know where you'd gone?"

She bounded to the step of the buggy and said to Anne, "If you think you can take advantage of this long-legged idiot, you're crazy! Not after I got him out of jail."

Grimes caught Elma's shoulder. "Look here," he stuttered, "you can't talk thattaway, this lady's totally respectful, she's a banker's daughter." That did not soothe Elma a bit. "Banker? Oh, you low-down coyote, you fortune hunter, after all I've done for you!"

She smacked Anne. Grimes, trying to drag her from the buggy step, tore Elma's red dress to the waist, and Elma turned out a good display. A crowd of cowpunchers cheered.

Then Anne took a hand. Two hands, in fact: both full of brunette hair. Elma's feet slipped. The buggy step was too narrow for footwork. That threw Grimes off balance. Anne could not let go in time, and Elma would not: the pair of lovelies landed between the buggy wheels and on top of Grimes.

"Grab that there hoss!" he yelled, "and git these gals offen me!"

He was submerged in a flurry of legs, skirts, tattered outer and under garments. But someone did grab the bridle, and the wheels did not mar either girl's curves.

Grimes dragged Anne clear. Elma came up clawing. Before he could shake her until her teeth rattled, Anne was driving away with a Navajo rug about her shoulders to keep the breeze from her bare spots. Her chin was in the air. She did not say good-night.

"I barely get you loose from a judge's daughter," Elma stormed, "when you get tangled up with a banker's high-nosed baggage!"

"Her nose ain't all that's high," Grimes retorted and stalked away. Broken Axe had become complicated. He would have left on that very stage, but no woman was going to herd him around.

* * * *

In the morning, be got a livery nag and rode out toward the buttes whose gold was making Brand Thorman rich. He reasoned, "Now that Anne ain't got no use for me, Thorman won't be refusing me a job outa spite."

Gold he had come for, and gold he was getting.

Presently, he heard the wheeze of a steam engine, the pounding of the ten-stamp mill. But he could not see any miners. There were no ore cars coming out of the black tunnel to feed the mill; no ore cars took useless rock to the dump. All Grimes knew about mining could have been written on a postage stamp, but even so, he felt that there should have been more activity than that thump-thump-wheeze.

He might never have thought of ore cars had he not seen three of them on the rusting rails, up there along the butte's eroded side.

Then there was activity aplenty. That puff of vapor from the engine house might have been steam, but just on the off chance, Grimes piled out of the saddle. Two seconds later, a slug buzzed past. He heard the rumble of the gun. As he clawed dirt, he muttered, "Either that coyote's shooting a cannon, or they jest fired a blast in the mine."

A second shot kept Grimes from taking his horse to a sheltering dip. The animal toppled over, kicking. A third shot from the buffalo gun drove the rider scrambling for cover. He pitched and rolled. Then, minutes later, he took off his hat, held it well to one side, and cautiously crept toward the lip.

A .55 caliber slug drilled the Stetson. He tried to crawl in the opposite direction to reach an arroyo that seamed the mesa. A slug fanned his ear. Grimes' Colts were outranged by a good 600 yards. He was bottled up. He could not get at the canteen hooked on the saddle.

The sun was beating down. Horn toads raced among the hot rocks. Grimes' mouth became dry; his lips cracked in the searing wind. He began to doubt that anyone could get a job at the New Golconda.

At hourly intervals during the blasting afternoon, Grimes tried to creep to the arroyo. The final attempt cured him. Another quarter inch, and he'd have had both lungs torn out by a 550 grain slug. Brand Thorman wanted to make sure that snoopers didn't return with reports on the lay of the land.

The sun was low, and Grimes was fairly perishing of thirst. Little whirlwinds blinded him with dust and burrs. The whole mesa danced crazily. He took some mesquite sticks, tore his shirt into strings; he peeled out of his coat and pants.

"I'm getting into that mine if it takes till Judgement Day," he mumbled as he set to work. "Mebbe I ain't working there, but I'm getting a look, and I'm getting a nugget."

He made a dummy of mesquite branches tied together. He dressed it and put his hat on the dummy. Then, crawling on his belly, he caught a wooden "ankle" in each hand and made the scarecrow simulate cautious peeping.

No one fired. He wondered if the watcher was looking. He tried again, making the dummy pop up once more, a little nearer the point where a man might make a dash for the arroyo's protection. Grimes reasoned that a man who had baked in that deadly heat all day would not have patience to wait until dark; he might be too crazy with the heat. Indeed, Grimes was practically that, or he would have let well enough alone.

Once more he managed to put his double up to spying.

The dummy jerked. An ounce slug had smacked it between the shoulders. A big puff of dust rose. Grimes lay there, flat on his face, the scarecrow just ahead of him. From the mine, it must have looked like that final, perfect shot. Mirage and sunset haze had kept the sniper from seeing that he had plugged a dummy.

* * * *

Patiently, Grimes waited for darkness. Then he went to his dead horse to get his canteen. The hot water tasted better than any beer. Once in the arroyo, he headed upgrade, toward the now silent stamp mill. Lights gleamed in the buildings. As he came nearer, he could hear voices; there was laughter, some feminine, some masculine, and all drunken. A foghorn voice bawled.

"Three gals came down from Canada,
Drinking rum and wine,
The subject of conversation was,
Your hair ain't as red as mine—"

It was the chorus that shocked Grimes. He muttered, "They sure weren't ladies," and picked his way up the grade. Soon he was at the narrow-gauge line for ore cars.

He got a look through a crack in the nearest shack. Four miners were paralyzed, one was nodding, and one was bawling another verse of the song. The second case of whiskey was open, and the half dozen girls had most of their garments scattered all over the tangle of bottles and tin plates and pack saddles. One was doing a dance that fascinated Grimes.

"Gosh, I never knowed a gal could wobble in so many places at once."

The nodding miner prodded her hip with a cigarette butt. She cried, *"Chinga'o borrego!"* and smacked his mustache. He toppled over. The song went on. So did Grimes. But the life of a miner sure did have its high spots.

The other lighted shack was new. The lumber had not yet turned gray in the blistering sun. The narrow-gauge tracks ran right into the building; it had apparently been whacked up with no regard to ore cars. That was odd. But not half as odd as what went on in the large room.

There were three-decked bunks, horse gear, a sheet iron stove. Three men sat on packing cases; Brand Thorman sat on a solid oaken chest with a shattered lock whose express company seals still hung from wires. The fifth man knelt before a little crucible under which there was a charcoal fire; sparks flew as he pumped goatskin bellows and sweated in the red glare.

There was a box of black sand in which ingots cooled; there was a depression in the sand, ready for the next crucible of melted gold. The man with the bellows said, "Dump in a bit more, Brand."

Thorman straightened up, took a double handful of coins out of the chest, and dumped them into the crucible. By then Grimes understood the whole game. One of the gang was familiar; he had taken part in the stage robbery.

No wonder Thorman kept his gang of miners dead drunk and did not want strangers prowling around! The miners and the stamp mill were to fool the natives of Broken Axe. The mine was a fake; a hideout for bandits to melt down stolen coin and palm it off as gold from a lost lode. Thorman was sinking the bank and then offering to ante in enough to save Jim Parsell, marry Anne, and also get control of the bank. Simple as pouring sand out of a boot!

These men were sober and armed. Even for a surprise party, five to one was too much to bite off. Grimes retreated up the rusty tracks. Fifty yards upgrade, he came to an ore car. He released the brake and heaved to free the rusty axle. It squealed. The car began to roll. Grimes vaulted into the steel shell. Creaking and groaning, the car picked up speed.

The clump and clatter warned the gang a little too soon. Two men dashed out, guns blazing. Slugs zinged from the sides of the car. Grimes rose, a Colt in each hand. Light from inside the house silhouetted the gunners. One doubled up and rolled down the grade. The other stumbled.

Brand Thorman's buffalo gun cut loose from the window. Grimes, however, was already ducking. The next instant, the car ploughed into the cabin. A lantern smashed. The crucible and furnace tipped over. It was the oaken chest that derailed the ore car. Guns laced the murky glare. Slugs smacked and screamed; Grimes came up shooting, but two men escaped.

Horses clattered down the grade. The wrecked cabin began to blaze. The drunken miner and one of the Mexican girls still sang, *"Three gals came down from Canada, drinking rum and wine..."*

Brand Thorman and one accomplice had escaped. Grimes thrust his guns into his leather-lined hip pockets and bounded toward the tunnel where the horses had been stabled. He lost time catching a saddled nag; the fugitives had stampeded the dead men's animals. When he set out, he could no longer hear the pounding of hooves across the mesa. But he quirted a dead man's mount toward Broken Axe.

Thorman couldn't leave Broken Axe. Thorman could scarcely suspect the identity of the snooper; neither could he double back to recover the unmelted coins from the blazing shack. So Grimes galloped on.

*   *   *   *

He dismounted in front of the Thorman House Bar. None of the horses at the hitching rack were blowing or sweating. He was sure that Brand Thorman had come down a side alley and gone either to some bar or to his quarters in the hotel he owned. Grimes poked his head into several saloons and decided, "He'd go to his room and pertend he's been in all evening. Fust find him, then find his hoss."

Grimes bounded up the narrow stairs to the second floor. "Mistah Thorman," he yelled drunkenly, "if you think yo're marrying Anne Parsell, yo're crazy—yo're crazy, you sidewinder, you ain't fit for Anne!"

There was no action from any hall door. But men in the lobby heard the bawling challenge. Someone shouted, "Brand'll shoot your gizzard out, kid! You better go home to bed."

Grimes repeated the challenge, then answered the men below: "I'll be any dirty name if I back down, he ain't marrying my gal!"

Just then two doors opened; one at his left, near the head of the stairs; the other at the further end of the hall. Elma came dashing out of the nearer door. She wore a transparent nightgown, and her dark hair was streaming. "If you're that crazy about her," she cried, "go ahead and good luck, you jughead!"

Brand Thorman stamped into the hall. His boots were dusty, and he saw the dust on Grimes' boots, the alkali and rust and dirt on the frock coat; he saw, and his face changed. He understood.

254

Elma screamed, "Simon, watch it!"

But Grimes was already whirling from that lovely distraction. Thorman's guns were clearing leather when the kid from Georgia cut loose. No one, Thorman least of all, believed that any man could get a Colt from a hip pocket and clear of a long frock coat in time to win the exchange.

But Thorman learned. His own shot went wild, just as Grimes' Colt bucked a second time and knocked a second jet of dust from Thorman's green vest. The big man spun, his knees buckled, and he fell face forward; his smoking gun skated down the hall.

Elma clawed her breast. Her gown was soggy, blood-soaked. Before Grimes could catch her, she caught the door jamb, missed, then slumped to the floor.

"Simon—you fool—I told you—mining towns—are poison—did he get you —?" She shivered, held to him with one arm. When he supported her in the crook of his elbow, she smiled. "Kiss me, Simon, you idiot—it's been fun— herding you around—"

The men who came pounding up the stairs checked up short. One said, "Hell, the pore gal's been shot, get a doctor."

"Shot, hell!" Grimes choked. "She's dead, and so is that son of a—!"

* * * *

He was right. Later that night, he rode to Jim Parsell's house with the marshal and told of Thorman's trick to palm off stolen coin as gold from a high grade mine. Anne came out, wide eyed, and laid a soft hand on his arm.

"Simon, darling," she said, "I'm so sorry about that poor girl. And I'm not angry about the way...the way she called my hand. You saved us all, Simon, and—"

Grimes kissed her, then gently thrust her from him. He said to Anne, and to Jim Parsell, and to the marshal: "Folks, you all been mighty nice, but I'm leaving tonight. I'm going back to my uncle's spread, like Elma wanted me to—" He choked, blinked, then jammed his hat on and ran down the front steps. As he stumbled toward town, he muttered, "Damn it, I wish I'd let her herd me around."

DRINK OR DRAW

Originally published in *Speed Western Stories*, Dec. 1943.

Weariness made Simon Bolivar Grimes' coffin-shaped face seem longer than ever. Spitting alkali dust, he muttered, "Another dang sign, DRINK RED QUILL BOURBON. Gosh, I wisht I was a hoss, they don't git thirsty for nothing but water."

Mile after mile along the wagon trail to Stinking Springs, Red Quill billboards had tantalized him by suggesting a bar, a free lunch counter, hard likker, and cool beer.

Some distance ahead, a freight wagon lumbered along. Instinctively, the kid from Georgia had sized up the country, a habit which had often kept him from being bushwhacked, and thus he noted a twinkle in the clump of post oak at the crest of a knoll. It was as though binoculars mirrored the blazing sun. Someone was spying on travelers.

The Stinking Springs region was the orneriest in Texas. Simon had a poke of gold pieces, the proceeds of the sale of some cow critters. If he were robbed, Uncle Jason would whale him with a wagon spoke; he'd claim that Grimes had spent the money on women and liquor.

"Dunno what in tunket else a man'd spend money for," Grimes grumbled as he pulled over to the whiskey sign.

Though the country was too open for ambush, nevertheless he wanted a look-see, so he peered through a knothole. "Ain't noticed me, they're still studying the wagon," he decided as the flickering continued.

He had brought Uncle Jason's binoculars in his saddle bags. Grimes had barely focused the powerful glasses for a bit of counter-espionage when two riders came pelting out of the clump of post oak, their guns blazing.

The wagon pulled up. The men dismounted. They tore into the tarpaulin at the back, exposing a cargo of barrels. A sharp faced man came toward them from the wagon. He was unarmed, and he made gestures, as if begging them to be reasonable.

One of the raiders smacked him with a pistol barrel, knocking him down.

The taller of the pair, who had a brace and bitt, began drilling at the keg. By now Grimes had read the lettering on the head: OLD VICKERY BOURBON, NELSON COUNTY, KENTUCKY.

Then a girl, apparently having remained on the driver's seat until indignation overcame her alarm, came racing toward the tail gate. She was blond, golden blond like a palomino filly. She bounded toward the man with the brace and bitt, and caught his arm.

He spat, grinned, thrust her aside. She recovered and smacked him. The other yanked her away; she tripped, landing asprawl in a puddle of whiskey. Liquor drenched her blouse and skirt.

Whatever was behind this insane business of letting whiskey run into the dust, Grimes decided that when people began slapping old men and girls, it was time to investigate. He mounted up and raced for the wagon. And then came the final horror: one of the ruffians touched a match to the whiskey, and flames began to lick the tarpaulin.

At the sound of his approach, the two whirled about, but seeing just one rider, they hooked their thumbs on their belts and waited. And when Grimes dismounted, they began to grin.

He looked as if he were about to fall over his own feet. Tall, gangling, with a straw colored cowlick reaching down to his china-blue eye, he did not look any too bright.

"What in tarnation you mean, burning good liquor?" he demanded. "And mauling that there lady?"

They chuckled tolerantly. The one with the brace and bitt explained, "Ain't allowed to haul nothing into Stinking Springs but Red Quill, bub. That's Colonel Delevan's orders. And we carry them out."

The other was rolling a smoke, and his amusement at Grimes was competing with his interest in the blonde, who wept in futile fury as she straightened her drenched garments. The old man, still dazed, was struggling to his feet. And all this was too much for Grimes.

"Hist 'em!" he commanded and went for his guns.

The man with the brace and bitt yelled. The other dropped his Durham and slapped leather. He was quick, but his Colt had not half cleared the holster when Grimes drilled him between the eyes.

Though the man with the brace and bitt made good time, his first shot went wild; and then, shifting, Grimes sprayed him with lead. He jerked one more shot, kicking up rocks. He lurched, fell across his gun.

The girl's scream made Grimes whirl: "Oh, they hit dad!"

The old man was clutching his side. "Ain't nothing, Melba, never you mind me, you help this young feller put out the fire."

Then he sat down.

* * * *

So Grimes and Melba got blankets and whipped out the flames. That done, she gave him strips torn from her skirt, so that he could stop the flow of whiskey while he whittled plugs.

The old freighter said, "I'm mighty grateful, son. I'm Amos Hanford, and this here is my daughter, Melba. Baby, you get the jug for this gent, don't you fuss with me, I ain't more'n scratched."

257

Grimes started to protest, but Hanford's glance silenced him. As the girl hurried to the front of the wagon, the freighter said, "I don't feel none too spry, but it's no use scaring her. I can turn around and go back to Cold Deck instead of trying to get to a doctor in Stinking Springs; I'd probably get murdered there."

"Not if I go with you," Grimes countered.

"Bub, I never seen a draw like yourn and never heard of any like it," Hanford countered. "Fust one gets it betwixt the eyes, and the second musta had most of his heart shot out with them three slugs. But whilst you're watching me, who'd watch the whiskey?"

"Gosh, that's right," Grimes agreed.

Melba came back with the jug. Grimes hoisted a long one. "Is this here what you got in them kegs?"

"It is. You have jest drunk OLD VICKERY," Hanford said proudly. "The finest bourbon made at Bourbon Springs, Kentucky, ever since 1833. Drink up, suh!"

Grimes hoisted another. Melba, who had impulsively put an arm around his shoulders, became more beautiful than ever. Her voice sounded like angels playing harps, and even the landscape was no longer repulsive. "This is sure larruping whiskey," Grimes said, and wiped his lips. "Anywhere but a downright warped and perverted town, it'd be welcomed with—"

And then, he saw that Hanford had fooled him as well as Melba. Grimes caught the old man just in time. "Honey, it looks like that chaw of tobacco he stuffed into that wound ain't plugging it enough."

"Oh, why did you have to start shooting?" she cried, panic again gripping her. "I'd rather lose all the liquor in the world—"

Grimes tipped the jug and gave Hanford a swig.

"M'am, they was banging away at me, and it is downright unreasonable, blaming me for someone else's bad shooting. If you can prod them oxen, I'll make your pappy comfortable and do what I can."

"Oh, what can *you* do?"

"He's jest weak, he'll come outen it. And as soon as your pappy's took care of, I'm going to run Red Quill and Colonel Delevan out of that ornery town, and when I'm through, they'll be drinking Old Vickery in every bar in Stinking Springs."

"Baby," Hanford said to his daughter, "I'm all right, and Simon looks like the man that can do it."

CHAPTER II
Recipe 309

Stinking Springs got its name from the hot sulphur spring which made the air reek with a rotten-egg bouquet; and the town itself, a sprawl of frame shacks and adobes centering about a plaza, looked pretty much like it smelled.

258

Grimes dismounted at the Cozy Corner Saloon, which was between the Eldo-
rado Hotel and Wing Lee's Restaurant.

Bellying up to the bar, he called for whiskey. The sour-faced barkeep set out
a bottle of Red Quill. The stuff made Grimes choke and cough. "Gosh, this
here tastes like soldering acid and sheep dip, ain't you got any good liquor?"

"Son," the professor retorted, "there ain't no other kind sold in this man's
town. Lookee here, bad liquor makes you shiver like a dog swallering peach
seeds; this here just sort of chokes you a bit."

The half dozen cowpokes who were watching looked as if this was an old
and amusing story to them. One said, "Stranger, it ain't no use bellyaching
about Red Quill. Mrs. Hopkins, she's a widow-woman, and the daughter of the
Injun fighter that saved the hull dang settlement from the Comanches, and all
she's got to live on is dividends from Red Quill shares, and there ain't a man in
town low enough to drink any other kind of likker."

This was bad. While one might outpoint Colonel Delevan, the widowed
daughter of a local hero was something else. Grimes bought a round for the
house and went out, muttering, "Hell, they are all heroes in this town, I'd ruther
fight a passel of Comanches than a bottle of that rotgut." Once on the boardwalk, he decided to head for Wing Lee's; the only civilized person in Stinking
Springs would be the Chinaman. And then he saw that even this ornery town
had its good points.

A redheaded girl was stepping out of Lem Bigg's General Store with an
armful of packages cuddled against her bosom. She was an exquisite creature,
slim-legged as a race horse; she wore silk stockings and store clothes. The
group of small boys who sat on the curbing playing stud poker and chewing tobacco quit their game and stopped cursing. They chorused, "Evening, Mis'
Hopkins."

The smile and voice which acknowledged the greeting were smooth and
lovely, and as heartwarming as Old Vickery. For a moment, Grimes forgot that
Doreen Hopkins, the Red Quill heiress, was a stumbling block in the pathway
of good liquor.

She tick-tacked along on high heels which flattered her trim ankles, but a
knothole in the tricky boardwalk played the devil with her alluring footgear.
She snagged a heel. Her stride broke, and her ankle twisted.

Grimes lunged. Eggs poured from one of the paper bags, but he got an armful of the widow, and managed to keep her clear of the uncooked omelette and
coffee on the boards.

Regretfully, he let her slide to her feet as he straightened up. Then, as she
clung to him for a moment to steady herself, he asked, "You ain't sprained your
ankle, I hope?"

"Thanks, no!" After the full impact of dazzling smile and greenish gray
eyes, he helped her salvage the groceries and stow them in the rubber-tired
buggy. Doreen waved, smiled, drove down the dusty street. No dang wonder
that Colonel Delevan was looking out for her interests!

Grimes stepped into Wing Lee's restaurant, ordered a steak, six eggs, and a slab of apple pie, and settled down to studying it out. Finally he asked, "Wing, can you get me a couple empty whiskey bottles with the labels washed off?"

"Catchee quick," the pigtailed proprietor said, and shuffled to the rear.

* * * *

Darkness had fallen. After wiping the egg from his chin, Grimes went to the hitching rack, and got his jug. Then, back in the restaurant, he said, "Look here, folks tell me that all Chinamen are honest fellows."

"Thass light, Clistian Chinaman, watchee want now?"

Grimes stepped into the kitchen. As he filled the bottles, whose Red Quill labels had been soaked off, he said, "You keep what's left in the jug, don't tell no one, and I'll give you five bucks."

"My savvee plenty, Missee Glime. Allee-time, lynch whiskey sell-man, allee time thlow blicks in my window. Town no damn good."

Wing chuckled gleefully. Grimes demanded, "What in tunket is so funny about getting bricks flung through your window?"

"I gettee even, I spit in coffee."

"Someone oughta spit in their whiskey. Wing, have a drink."

He offered one of the quarts. The Chinaman poured a shot into a tiny teacup, and downed it. "Vellee nice. You take dlink, Missee Glime. *Ng ka pay*, China whiskey."

He dug out a stone jug and poured a shot of reddish and syrupy liquor. The stuff tasted like kerosene and orange shellac. It was almost as bad as Red Quill. But Grimes, having met the only civilized man in Stinking Springs, downed it and said, "Mighty good."

Wing wagged his head. "You velly nice man. Evly-one else thlowee locks when I give *Ng ka pay*."

"How long ago was this?"

"Mebbe-so five, ten yeah."

That was odd. Today, they drank something worse and didn't even blink.

"Wing, who hauls whiskey to town? Where do they keep it? Who dishes it out to the saloons?"

"Wagon tlain bling-ee Led Quill. Keep-ee in big house by jail. Ev-ly-body catch-ee whiskey flom Colonel Delevan."

"How about Mrs. Hopkins?"

"Velly nice lady. Colonel Delevan fix-ee all business, him savvee plenty."

Grimes went back to the Cozy Corner Saloon, after taking his horse to the livery stable. The same bunch of cowpunchers were playing poker in the corner. They dropped their cards, and eyed him as he went to the bar.

Grimes said, "Belly up, gents! I'm buying!"

There was a whoop and a jingle of spurs. The sour-faced professor set out glasses and Red Quill.

Grimes pulled a quart from his hip pocket. "Gents," he said, and slapped a gold piece on the bar, "I'm buying the local likker. Only, I am gal-danged if I can drink the stuff, try some of this."

He filled the glasses with Old Vickery.

The cowpunchers blinked, eyed each other; one said, "Stranger, you're violating a local ordinance, Colonel Delevan had the mayor pass a law agin foreign liquor."

"Ain't I paid for Red Quill? Ain't I doing right by the widder-woman?"

"Pardner, that's gospel."

They thrust out their grimy paws to grab the glasses.

The swinging doors slammed open. A stern voice shook the house: "Drop that, right now!"

Two men had entered. The foremost wore a star. He had a sawed off shotgun leveled at the group. The man beside him was tall, distinguished; slouch hat, frock coat, a pique vest, and flowing tie; drooping mustaches, and a neatly trimmed beard, an Imperial, perfectly tailored. And just for emphasis, he had a Colt .45 pointed at Grimes. He looked as if he could shoot.

Grimes demanded, "What's this, suh, breaking into some sociable drinking?"

"I am Colonel Delevan," the man in the frock coat answered. "And my companion with the shotgun is Mr. Frost, the marshal. Selling liquor—without a license—"

"I am giving it away."

The colonel fingered his silky beard. "Ha! That also is in violation of a city ordinance. Giving or selling, or causing to be given away or sold, without first having it tested for wholesomeness and purity, is a violation of the law. Mr. Frost, be pleased to seize the evidence. Young man—"

Grimes shouted, "This here is good whiskey, the finest dang whiskey I ever drunk, that Red Quill is sheepdip, it's poison, it ain't fit for human consumption!"

"If you were not a beardless boy," the colonel retorted, "I would challenge you to a duel. Mrs. Hopkins, the daughter of a local hero, sponsors Red Quill."

Mr. Frost seized the bottle of Old Vickery. Grimes saw no chance of shooting it out; and as Amos Hanford had observed, shooting a customer doesn't improve sales.

* * * *

Late that night, Grimes decided to get to the bottom of things. If everything else failed, he'd set the Red Quill warehouse afire.

"Arson," he told himself, "is genrully agin' the law, but this here is an extenuating circumstance, every time you take a drink of that stuff, it's committing arson on your gizzard."

Wing's description made it easy for him to find the warehouse. The place was of adobe, thick walled, with small windows high up and barred. Ceiling beams projected far out and supported the eaves whose overhang kept the rains from cutting into the adobe. Grimes had brought his lariat; it was simple enough, roping the end of a ceiling beam. Then, in the gloom at the rear of the adobe, he went up, hand over hand, and in a moment, he was on the roof.

As he had expected, this was of clay tamped over bundles of cottonwood saplings which had been laid athwart the massive ceiling beams. Such a roof, unless constantly maintained, deteriorates, and this one had been neglected; thus Grimes had less work than he had anticipated. He found a patch of bare saplings and very quickly worked them right and left, until he could, being lean and lanky, wriggle through.

His lariat, let down into the whiskey-scented darkness, was as good as a portable stairway. In a moment, Grimes was down in the stockroom.

He struck a match, lighted a candle stump, and with hat and bandanna, shaded the flame. Along the wall furthest from the door was a row of barrels which were marked "proof spirits." On a table was a plane, some paint, and a stencil which read, "RED QUILL BOURBON." There were several empties, freshly stenciled. But what most interested Grimes was the cabinet in the corner.

There he found a bucket of stewed prunes, some one-pound plugs of chewing tobacco, and a jug of wine vinegar. Also, there was a pail of beef blood. Hanging from a nail was a paper bound book entitled, AMERICAN BARTENDER'S GUIDE. A glance at this last item confirmed his suspicions; he read, "To one hundred gallons of proof spirit, add four ounces of pear oil, two ounces of pelargonic ether, thirteen drachms oil of wintergreen, and one gallon of wine vinegar; color with burnt sugar."

But what prodded Grimes to a high fury was *"Recipe 309; Bead for Liquor. For every ten gallons of spirit, add forty drops sulphuric acid and sixty drops of olive oil previously mixed in a glass vessel."*

"There ain't no Red Quill Distillery," he said to himself. "There ain't any likker hauled to Stinking Springs. That sculpin makes it right here, outen chemicals and acids."

Such being the case, how could the daughter of a local hero be dependent on dividends from Red Quill shares? Instead of setting the warehouse afire, it would be far better to expose the fraud and drive Red Quill forever from the market.

CHAPTER III
A Risk To Be Taken

There was a lot of excitement in Stinking Springs when two horses came into town without riders. Grimes, going from bar to bar, drank Red Quill and listened to the news. Dusty and Pecos, gunslingers protecting the whiskey market, had heard that a rash freighter was heading for Stinking Springs, and they had gone to meet him.

And now this.

Most of the population galloped out to investigate. They found, after chasing away the buzzards, enough odds and ends to identify beyond any doubt the remains of Dusty and Pecos.

Thereafter, when Colonel Delevan appeared in public, he had Buckshot Frost at his heels. Grimes, barging into a saloon, caught a snatch of conversation: "That long lanky galoot that don't look like he had sense enough to come in outen the rain..."

Silence. Dripping silence. Then the boys began whooping it up again. They could not believe that he had cut down the two gunslingers, and yet, there was something odd about it all. So Grimes began to cat-walk about town. People were wondering about his protests on the whiskey question.

Stinking Springs got another sensation when a shapely blonde came driving down the main street in a rattling buggy. She looked sweet and helpless. Her somber mourning accented the pallor of her face and the pale gilt of her lovely hair. Grimes, sitting with the hotel lobby wall at his back, heard her say to the cowpoke who carried her carpetbag, "Thank you so much! Never mind the things in the buggy, it's just a sewing machine, would you mind taking the rig to the livery stable?"

She signed the register. Then, to the clerk, "Oh, what is that *horrible* smell?" Grimes chimed in, "M'am, that there is Red Quill Bourbon."

The girl was Melba Hanford. Her dainty nose rose a degree or two, and she sniffed. The clerk said, "M'am, that there is the hot sulphur spring, it ain't bad when you get used to it."

* * * *

The hours dragged. Grimes watched Melba come down the stairs and sweep past him, head high. He watched her return from the restaurant. He heard the muttered speculations of the cowpunchers who lounged on the board walk.

"Widder-woman... Sure looks like a lady...proud as a queen...hell no, she ain't fixing to work in the dance hall, not that gal..."

* * * *

That night, Grimes went to bed with his boots on. But the real novelty was that he did not sleep. He was on edge, alert, and at the first faint scratch at the panel, he was on his feet. Just for luck, he had a gun ready.

Melba edged in when he opened the door. "Simon, it's the craziest thing, I nearly died when I came to town, with everyone eyeing me."

"How's your pappy?"

"He'll pull through, though I hated to leave him. What have you found out?"

Once Melba had found the settee in the darkness, he seated himself on the floor at her feet. "Honey, it's thissaway—"

He told her everything and concluded, "The hull dang town's against us. I'd figgered a gal like you might have a chance pertending you was a orphan or

263

widder, but that there Doreen Hopkins is mighty purty for a old woman dang nigh thirty; these jaspers worship the ground she walks on, account her pappy, and I jest don't know what to do next."

"You mean, if you did prove that Red Quill is just chemicals and acids, you'd be casting reflections on a hero's daughter, and that would not help us?"

"Correct, honey." Grimes sighed gustily. "But there's sumthin' salty about it all. That Mis' Hopkins looks like a honest woman. She don't look like the kind that'd have cowpunchers drinking sheep dip and soldering acid and sechlike. This here Red Quill musta once been fitten to drink, account they nearly lynched Wing Lee for offering them *ng ka pay* on Chinese New Year. And this Colonel Delevan, you call on him, tearfullike, and whilst he's listening to you sobbing, I'll sort of make a *pasear* around the house, he's a bachelor."

* * * *

The following evening, Grimes lurked in the shelter of a weeping willow until Melba drove up to Colonel Delevan's big white house. He came from cover when the colonel went to admit his lovely visitor.

"Good evening, m'am. What is your pleasure, Miss Hanford? You had scarcely arrived in town when I took the liberty of ah…inquiring at the hotel."

"You're very kind, colonel. I hardly know where to begin—"

Grimes crept to the window. Delevan was stamping down the hallway and bawling, "You, Tomas! Paca! Where are you?"

The only answer was echoes; then, returning, he said to Melba, "I had hoped to have one of the servants offer you refreshments, m'am, but the scoundrels have, so to speak, folded their tents like the Arabs. But I make a very tolerable mint julep."

Grimes grinned. Delevan had merely made a loud show of assuring Melba that they could have a cozy chat. And when he went to the rear to prepare juleps, Grimes tapped gently at the window, and whispered, "Do your best, and if he gits familiar, I'll pistol-whip him."

Delevan lost surprisingly little time in coming back with a silver bowl and tall glasses.

Melba said, hesitantly, "Colonel, I hope I don't seem rude, but I don't drink strong liquor. I might take a sip of Madeira, though I really shouldn't—" She dabbed her eyes with a lace edged handkerchief. "Not so soon—after—poor father's death."

As he poured Bourbon and added sprigs of mint to garnish his tall glass, Delevan said solicitously, "M'am, it was all too evident from your mourning—ahem, if you'll forgive my saying so, it is most becoming—you remind me of the late Mrs. Delevan, when her distinguished father passed away."

He sighed gustily. "I am a very lonesome man and have been for many years now. Pray accept my heartfelt sympathy, m'am, for I also have been bereaved."

The man was magnetic. Grimes' trigger finger began to itch. He said to himself, "That goat-bearded sculp-in's got a routine for widder-women and orphans, I 'low he ain't ever asked Mis' Hopkins to marry him, not with them notions for preying on bereaved gals."

The colonel was on the sofa beside Melba. He barely touched her further shoulder with his fingertips; he was waiting for her grief to get out of control before he offered consolation.

"You're so kind, colonel. I almost hate to bring up a matter of business—"

"Consider me your servant, m'am."

"It's about—*whiskey*."

"Whiskey, m'am?"

The lovely blonde head inclined in a nod. "My poor father, practically ruined by railroad competition, was freighting a number of barrels of OLD VICKERY BOURBON into new territory, and—and—"

Her voice broke. He patted her shoulder. Melba went on, "Bandits—road agents—held us up. There were two of them—I begged him not to resist—but he fought like a lion—he killed them both—but his wounds—he succumbed, and here I am, trying to sell—that whiskey—and I've been told—that nothing but Red Quill is allowed in Stinking Springs.

"They gave me to understand, Colonel Delevan, that you are a stockholder in the Red Quill distillery, and that this ban on other liquors is to—well—protect your interests."

She eyed him reproachfully; but the colonel's glance did not waver. "M'am, I have been put into a false position. Pray let me convince you. The truth is, I am protecting the interests of a widow, the daughter of that gallant hero, the late Cyrus Barlow."

Melba rose. "Colonel Delevan, it is not gallant to put the blame on a widow!"

The colonel's face became red. "Madam, I have been put in a false light! I shall challenge the dastard who put me in such false light! Pray let me convince you."

The colonel stalked out, and in a moment came back with a tin box which he unlocked. He took from it various papers, and began, "M'am, this should convince you that years ago, as a gesture of gratitude, I conveyed to Mrs. Hopkins' gallant father every share of my Red Quill whiskey stock."

"I know so little about business—" Melba wavered, her knees buckled; she would have fallen had he not caught her. "Oh—I'm sorry—I'm dizzy—I think I'm about to faint—"

The colonel scooped her up in his arms. "Let me make you comfortable in the late Mrs. Delevan's room—there are some smelling salts—"

Melba protested feebly, but the masterful colonel insisted that nothing was too much trouble. And he had barely started up the stairs when Grimes tiptoed into the living room.

Melba's voice filtered down from the upper darkness: "Oh, colonel, I'm so confused and worried and lonely... I don't know whom to believe... I'll be all right in a moment—"

Grimes scooped up the papers. The first one seemed to bear out Delevan's contention, but as he riffled his way through the file, Grimes found a letter of earlier date, on the stationery of the Red Quill Distilleries. The colonel's thousand shares were to be assessed $5 each, and in return he would get one thousand new shares. Grimes muttered, "Participating perferred, gosh it sounds worsen the time Uncle Jason got hornswoggled outen that mine in Arizony."

Another paper: a notice of bankruptcy, dated a year after the assessment. Grimes, listening to the murmuring upstairs, was assured that Melba was holding her own. Delevan, while a scheming scoundrel, was in his own way a gentleman. And so Grimes hurried out to make a move which neither he nor Melba had planned.

There wasn't and there had not been any Red Quill whiskey for some years, except in Stinking Springs. Bit by bit, Delevan had cut the stock of Bourbon, so that the local cowpunchers had gradually become accustomed to rotgut bearing the label of a once drinkable brand. And he had used Doreen Hopkins as a front.

Exposing Doreen as a crook would be tough work. It might end in an all around shooting scrape which would not help the sale of Old Vickery. But Grimes had to risk it.

CHAPTER IV
Challenge!

When Doreen Hopkins came to the door, the lamplight put a flame-gold halo about her red hair; it played tricks with her white robe, which had been made out of an embroidered Chinese shawl.

"I rarely have visitors—if I'd been expecting you—"

"M'am, you look scrumptious thatta-way. And if you ain't too busy with your embroidering, I'd admire to talk business with you."

He thumped a buckskin poke of gold pieces into the heap of embroidery silk. "It's about your pappy's Red Quill shares. The Old Vickery Distillery craves to buy your interest and good will."

"It's paid such splendid dividends, I'd have to consult Colonel Delevan. He's advised me ever since father died."

"How many shares you got?"

She shrugged. "Good heaven, I don't know! But wait a moment."

When she returned, she had a thousand-share certificate made out in her father's name. The date was prior to the dates of the letters announcing the assessments. Grimes, scrutinizing the late hero's name, saw what only a keen eye could have noted: there had been an erasure, and *Cyrus Barlow* had been written, letters widely spaced, in the space once occupied by, as a good guess, *Worthington Delevan*.

"M'am, when'd you know your pappy had it?"

"Colonel Delevan found it among father's papers, after the estate was settled. I guess it hadn't paid dividends for some time, but soon after the colonel found it, I began getting checks, in my own name, he said he'd written the company that I'd inherited the stock."

Grimes picked up the poke of gold. "Thank you kindly, m'am, but that there certificate ain't wuth the paper it's printed on."

"How can you say that?" she flared up, "when the dividends have kept me in comfort? I'd never believed you to be a slicker, trying to cheat a widow out of her legacy, trying to tell me it's worthless, so I'd accept an absurd offer."

"Ma'am," he persisted, "there ain't no distillery, it's jest a fraud Colonel Delevan's worked up to palm off pizen likker on poor, honest cowpunchers, keeping good whiskey like Old Vickery out of town. I come here to see you account of a orphan lady whose pappy was shot down by gunslingers the colonel sent out to keep him from bringing honest Bourbon into Stinking Springs. If you got any conscience, let it guide you, m'am."

"You wait till I get dressed, I'll see if you dare repeat that statement to Colonel Delevan!"

That was just what Grimes wanted. Catching Colonel Delevan consoling Melba would drive a wedge into Doreen's trust and admiration. Hearing Melba's story of her father's death would finish the job.

"That there stock is wuthless," he repeated.

"It's been keeping me in comfort!"

"What you mean is, Colonel Delevan's been keeping you in comfort," Grimes retorted.

"You dare say such a thing!"

She slapped him, one-two-three. And as he recoiled before her stinging blows, he tried to amplify the statement she had interrupted. "M'am, what I meant—"

* * * *

Then the door slammed open. Colonel Delevan, with several peculiar and long scratches on his handsome face, stamped into the room. "I heard my name bandied about, and fortunately I did not enter until I heard the atrocious reflection you cast on Mrs. Hopkins! Please stand aside, m'am, do not sully your hands, I'll shoot him down like a dog!"

Grimes yelled, "Go for your guns when this lady's outen the way. Or keep your hands in sight whilst I tell you what I was aiming to say when she started slapping my teeth loose!"

"That vicious slander can't be explained! Doreen—"

Then Doreen, who now clung to Grimes with both arms, cried over her shoulder, "Colonel Delevan, I am surprised that you would want a gun fight in my house! Need I remind you of the light in which that would put me?"

Delevan bowed. "M'am, my indignation made me forget myself. Mr. Grimes, if you have any manhood left, you will not precipitate a shooting array in this house."

"I'm agreeable."

Flushed and breathless, Doreen broke away.

Grimes went on, "M'am, what I was starting to say wasn't a reflection on you, if'n I'd said all of it."

"Silence!" the colonel thundered. "My seconds will wait on you. We shall arrange this so that I can demand satisfaction, and without any slurs on a lady's name. Your remarks, made in several bars, casting aspersions on the integrity of Red Quill Bourbon, are ample cause. Good evening, sir."

* * * *

On his return to the hotel, Melba was waiting for Grimes in the doorway of her room. "I couldn't help it, darling," she said, "but I simply had to claw him crosseyed, the old reprobate!"

"And then he come over to the widder-woman's house, and we had words."

Melba's eyes narrowed. "Simon, someone has been clawing *your* face," she said coldly. "Am I to understand that you were making love to that middle-aged creature."

"Honey, when I kiss 'em, they don't kick and claw."

Melba rose. "You do take things for granted! I didn't claw or slap you, did I, which makes me—oh, get out! You and your fool ideas, putting me in such a humiliating position."

She flung herself face down on the sofa and began to sob. When he patted her hair, she cried, "Get out, or I'll scream!"

So he got.

* * * *

He was ready to shake the dust of Stinking Springs from his boots. "Every dang time I open my mouth, I put my foot in it," he muttered, and he stamped his way down the hall. "The gent that said silence is golden was speaking gospel."

After having risked his life in a gun fight, after having defied an entire town, he'd been misunderstood by the very girl he was trying to help. And with an impending challenge, he could not run out.

That challenge would settle everything. Smoking out the colonel would only confirm Doreen's grudge; Delevan's cronies would continue making Red Quill using the lovely widow as a front. One remark with an unintended double-meaning had killed his chance of appealing to the widow's better nature. Then he remembered the bottle of Old Vickery which the marshal had seized for test-ing. He went down the backstairs and down the alley.

Half an hour afterward, when he had finished the rounds of the saloons, he went to the jailhouse, where the turnkey asked, "What you looking for?"

"Back up, pappy! I know jest where to find what I want."

He walked to the door marked "Town Marshal" and kicked it open.

Frost jumped up. His sawed off shotgun was well out of reach. In one hand, he had the confiscated bottle, and judging from the level, he had been testing it. "Marshal, that there's my likker, get your hooks offen it."

Frost went for his belt gun; but the gesture froze before it was half completed. He was looking into the muzzle of Grimes' .45, and it was entirely beyond his imagining how such a thing could have happened. His color changed, and he raised his hands.

"Bub," he stuttered, "that jest wasn't possible."

Grimes replaced the gun, and with a move little slower than his draw. "Marshal," he said softly, "what you seen don't prove I can hit anything when I come out smoking, does it?"

"I ain't craving proof. Lookee here; your name's Grimes?"

"I ain't denying it."

"I mean Simon Bolivar Grimes."

"I ain't saying I am, I ain't saying I ain't."

"Help yourself to the whiskey."

Grimes reached for the bottle. Edging about as a guard against surprises from the doorway, he took a quick snort. The gaping turnkey, who had seen the draw, made no effort at trickery.

"This here," Grimes said, as he lowered the quart, "ain't been tampered with. How you like it?"

"It's sorta nice."

"Get busy and drink."

The marshal took a shot.

"When I say drink, I mean, drink deep."

Another hefty one.

"Take more."

"Bub, Colonel Delevan told me to save him some."

"Drink or draw!"

Gurgle-gurgle-gurgle. Finally Frost said, still gulping, "Uh—um—I'll get plumb plastered, hogging it down thissaway, and I'm a lawman, it ain't right —"

"Come up," Grimes commanded, "with a drink or with a gun."

There was still an ounce left when the marshal fell forward on his face. Grimes handed the remainder to the turnkey. "Down it!" he commanded.

"I ain't a drinking man, I ain't touched a drop since—"

"Since how long?"

"Nigh unto seven year. When I start, I jest can't stop, I dassent, so I took a pledge."

"You ain't teched a drop for seven years? *Drink up!*"

Tremblingly, the turnkey obeyed. He licked his lips. He hitched his pants. He cocked his hat at a rakish angle.

"You went and done it! Now I'm a-going on a bender, I'll be staying drunk for three-four weeks, and gosh, it's going to be fun!"

"How'd it taste?"

"Finest Bourbon I ever wrapped around my tonsils, and I been drinking, man and boy, for thirty year afore I took a pledge."

He headed for the door.

"Where you going?"

"Aiming to get dead-drunk quick as I can."

"You ain't going to like it, not if you ain't used to Red Quill," Grimes solemnly promised.

He went from bar to bar to size things up before he forced some group of cowpunchers to drink Old Vickery. This would be his revenge, and let the results be what they might; since Melba had turned against him, nothing mattered.

* * * *

Presently, he stepped into a place just as the turnkey, already roaring and stuttering, staggered to the street. Grimes could feel a difference between the guarded looks which now searched him and the open stares of only an hour previous.

The turnkey, it seemed, had babbled between drinks. When the tin piano's jangle stopped, and the silence caught some speaker off guard, he heard, from a far corner, the voice of a man who had an instant earlier been talking against the jangling music: "—I'm betting he kilt Pecos and Dusty."

Two men marched in, shoulder to shoulder. Both were hard cases. Their eyes restlessly covered the entire saloon; though in home territory, instinct kept them on guard. One said, "Mr. Grimes, we are speaking direct to you for Colonel Delevan. Being as how you're a stranger, you ain't got seconds to repersent you."

"That's right, gents, I repersent myself."

The spokesman went on, "The colonel challenges you to a duel and wants to know whether you aim to fight, or get hoss-whipped outa town account of saying Red Quill ain't fit for man or beast."

Grimes set his quart bottle on the bar. "My compliments to Colonel Delevan, and say that I am tickled silly to fight. And is he game to let me pick the weapins?"

"On hoss or on foot, shooting or cutting. What style do you take?"

The whispered debates as to whether this was or was not the original Grimes had ceased. The answer seemed very loud: "Gents, tell the colonel that it'll be drink and shoot."

"What's that? You aiming to be funny?"

"That's up to the colonel. What I aim is a duel like Clay Allison fit with Wild Bill Hickok. I know the old marshal can explain."

"Drink-and-shoot," they muttered, still puzzled.

"Speaking of drinking," Grimes went on, "this here bottle is the only one in town with likker in it that's fitten to drink. Belly-up, gents."

270

"We ain't drinking with anyone that's insulted the—uh—tastes of Stinking Springs."

"You are drinking," Grimes asserted, "or I'll be taking my own answer to the colonel."

He held his hands well away from his sides. "Take your choice, gents, grab that bottle or slap leather."

The two exchanged a side glance. One said, "Slim, this fool is asking for trouble, and if we give it to him, there won't be anyone for the colonel to duel with."

* * * *

Slim went stubborn. He sidestepped toward the bar. "You suit yourself, Top Rail."

And Top Rail crossed from his pardner's right to get the bottle, passing in front of him. He was in no position to draw, and Slim was blocked. They had backed down, and they had covered themselves by saying that they had to save the victim for the colonel.

Or so it seemed to the cowpunchers in the corner, until guns blazed.

Slim, sidestepping from the bar as his pardner moved toward it, had drawn during the split second in which he was masked; but during that same shred of time, Grimes had gone for his .45s. They smoked and bucked as he advanced on the gun slicks.

Slim stumbled, tried to level his weapon again, but a third slug knocked him down. And Top Rail, whirling when he sensed that something had gone wrong with the whipsaw play, barely reached his holster.

His vest jerked three times from impacts before he doubled up and dropped in a heap against the brass rail.

Grimes turned in his cloud of smoke and faced the customers. "Gents, two agin one, and they aimed to whipsaw me. Anyone here see it any other way?" There was no answer. "Being as how Colonel Delevan's fust second and second second ain't talkin', I'd admire to have someone tell him we'll fight a drink-and-shoot duel, unless he's leaving town."

He picked up the bottle, took a swig, set it down. "That there is real Bourbon, it ain't Red Quill rotgut. Help yourselves, gents."

Then he went to Wing Lee's restaurant. Half-emptied plates showed how the sound of gunfire had cleared the counter. And Wing Lee's face showed that he was not surprised to see that Grimes, while waiting for half a dozen scrambled eggs, jacked expended cartridges first from one Colt, and then the other.

The Chinaman said, "You gettee flee glub, Missee Glime."

"Slim and Top Rail used to throw rocks at you?"

"You savvee plenty."

Grimes could not positively assume that the dueling colonel, unable to back down in issuing his challenge, had planned for his seconds to settle the matter, yet the whipsaw trick which the gun slicks had attempted did indicate that the turnkey's account of Grimes' dealing with the marshal had left its marks on the town.

Whether Melba deserved it or not, old man Hanford deserved a break. Grimes was going to make one final attempt to pave the way for honest whiskey in general, and Old Vickery in particular. He said to Wing, "I'm giving a barbecue the day of the duel. You fix everything. Exactly like I tell you."

"Me savvee plenty," the Chinaman answered, and Grimes settled down to explaining.

CHAPTER V
Doctored

For the next three days, Grimes camped on the open range. Some thought he was taking precautions against being bushwhacked before the duel; others, hearing the pistol blasts, checked up with field glasses, said that he was practicing his draw and popping the heads from quail and rattlesnakes.

But his campfire, each night, assured the curious town that he had not run out. And then Stinking Springs became interested in the Chinaman's preparation for a barbecue out in the plaza.

When Grimes rode back to town, Melba pushed her way through the crowd which lined one edge of the plaza, and ran to meet him as he dismounted.

"Simon," she cried, catching him with both arms. "I was worried to death, thinking you'd be dry-gulched."

"Honey," he answered, "I was purty sure they wouldn't, account they wanted to see a drink-and-shoot duel."

"But that fire!"

He whispered, "That there was so the Chinaman could find me."

The marshal advanced to the center of the plaza and began, "His Honor, the Mayor, asks me to announce to all and sundry that this here drink-and-shoot duel concerns itself entirely with the aspersions Simon Bolivar Grimes has cast on the good name of Red Quill Bourbon, and that Colonel Delevan is defending the liquor he has sponsored. And anyone claiming a lady is involved is a liar and a skunk. Is that clear?"

A shout of assent answered him.

He went on, "Colonel Delevan, you got anything to say?"

The colonel bowed ceremoniously, raised his hat, and answered, "Suh, I am ready to defend my honor."

"Mr. Grimes, you got any statements?"

"I'm buying a keg of Red Quill for the public. Jest to show I ain't got any hard feelings. Instead of each one drinking outen his own bottle, me and the colonel share the same keg."

The colonel's handsome face tightened a little. "I cannot drink with a man I am about to meet on the field of honor."

Grimes grinned amiably. "Colonel, you can make that right by giving me back half of what I paid out for the keg. Thataway, we are both contributing alike to the cheer of our feller citizens. Me, I got some Old Vickery, but I'm meeting you half way, taking your brand. Or mebbe them bottles in that basket your hired man has got ain't got Red Quill in 'em?"

The colonel had no argument left. The marshal cut in, "If you gents are ready, get to your posts."

Grimes and the colonel marched toward each other, arms folded, until they were within three paces of each other, with a whitewash line separating them. Two cowpunchers rolled the little keg to the line and drove in a spigot, then gave the combatants tin cups. The marshal went on, "Ladies and gents! This here duel is a test of skill and endurance. Once I pass the sidelines, taking away the empty cups, they can draw without warning, any time till I come back with a fresh drink, and then all shooting's cut until I get over the side line again. The idee is, who can shoot the straightest when he's drunk the mostest."

The only one who paid no attention was Wing Lee. He shuffled about the barbecue pit and monkeyed with a pot of sauce.

Grimes raised his drink, and when the marshal had backed away, he said, "Colonel Delevan, your good health, suh! Beef blood, prune juice, plug terbaccer, chemicals, and acids."

The colonel gulped his cup, shuddered, lowered it, glanced about him. Grimes, lips barely moving, said, "Your choice, colonel. Drink or draw?"

"Fill them up, marshal!" Delevan demanded, loud and strong.

* * * *

Silence ringed the square. Then, in the dusty and deserted main street, they heard the turnkey whooping it up.

"Gimme more likker! Put rattlesnakes and trantlers in it, I want it hot and strong! *Wheeeee!*"

After seven years, he was making up for lost time.

Grimes whispered, "Colonel, this here ain't what you use in your juleps. You know what they'll do if I ever tell 'em what you put in them barrels?"

Delevan did not answer. Straight as a ramrod, he accepted his cup of Red Quill. Each eyeing the other over the rim, they downed their poison.

"Suh, you can't stand this here likker much longer, and if you fall on your face, I'm telling 'em why."

The colonel raised his voice. "That was delicious, marshal. Fill them up again."

Arms folded, they faced each other; once the marshal crossed the sideline, each had the option of a quick draw, or else waiting until the other had faced another jolt of forty-rod.

Grimes' cargo of Red Quill was raising ructions. He was beginning to wonder how long he could endure his own contest. He had no qualms about his gunnery. As long as he stayed on his feet, his trigger finger would work by instinct. But winning an exchange of lead, shooting down the widow's sponsor would gain him and the Hanfords nothing at all, for the town would forgive the dead and coddle the Indian fighter's daughter.

Gun to gun, he had the colonel bluffed. It had worked just too well. Delevan would not draw, and if Grimes was the first to collapse, the duel was lost.

Already, the plaza began to weave a little. Grimes was sweating from the effort to keep his attention focused against the instant when he could make his play.

Finally, he caught the first sign of the colonel's wavering, and Grimes risked letting himself go a little. He sagged, his legs went wobbly.

Delevan's draw, considering all, was very good. But Grimes' was better.

His gun blazed as it cleared the holster. The slug smashed against the cylinder of Delevan's heavy Colt, and lead fragments tore his hand. The weapon was useless, and so were the gunner's fingers. And then Grimes yelled through the smoke, "Knock 'er loose!"

The Chinaman swung the axe with which he had been chopping fuel for the pot of sauce. The whiskey barrel's hoops burst. They had been filled almost to the breaking point the night before the duel. Wing Lee had seen to that.

Grimes pointed at the scattered staves. When the crowd saw what came out on the flood of liquor, they howled, "Putting trantlers and rattlesnakes in it!"

The colonel saw and turned a sickly pea-green. He doubled up. Doreen Hopkins rushed from the sidelines and cried, "Oh, you scoundrel, poisoning all these people! I'd rather starve than take dividends for such filthy liquor!"

Delevan was too sick to protest, and the shock of a bullet-torn hand did not help him. Doreen clawed and slapped him, ripped his flowing tie and his fine shirt. "I hope they lynch you—putting snakes and tarantulas into their liquor, just to make more profit!"

There was talk of lynching, but Grimes and the marshal won Delevan a chance to get to his house to pack up for a trip. And then Grimes went to get the bottles of whiskey which Melba had concealed in her rig.

"Drink up, gents; it's this lady's treat. Old Vickery, the best dang Bourbon ever come outen Kentucky, and no chemicals and acids in it. Jest repeal that ordinance, and her pappy'll haul in a wagonload of it."

Outraged citizens smashed all the other barrels of Red Quill. And an hour later, when Grimes and Melba drove back toward Cold Deck to tell old man Hanford the news, the blonde pillowed her head on his shoulder and asked, "Simon, how did you stand it, knowing Wing Lee had put rattlers and tarantulas into every barrel in the warehouse?"

She shuddered. He drew in the reins, and his arm closed about her.

"Honey, when I was in Arizony, I et rattlers. They ain't bad when you get used to the idee, and the trantlers was some Wing Lee made up outen black darning cotton, they sure looked good enough to turn the colonel's stomach more inside out than if'n I'd shot him there."

SHORT-CUT TO HELL

Originally published in *Six-Gun Western*, April 1950.

CHAPTER I
"Lock him up, Sheriff!"

Pete Barlow, sitting among the emigrants of the Red Fork Company, watched firelight play on the tanned faces of the men and on the canvas covers of wagons. Barlow, not yet discharged from the army, was conspicuous in his uniform, but no one noticed him. No one noticed anyone or anything but Kirby Swift, second in command of the emigrant wagon train.

The sodbusters, squatting in a half circle, had the same look Barlow had noted at political meetings when a spellbinder tricked his hearers into agreement, not because he spoke sense, but because he wished them to agree. Horace Parker, with the wheat colored beard and grave face and kindly eyes was still captain of the emigrant company, but his flashy *segundo*, Kirby Swift, had stolen command. Tall and swarthy and good looking, he filled the eyes. He had a daredevil swagger even when standing still. The tilt of his head, the set of his shoulders, the roving glance convinced the others that they could be like him simply by agreeing with him. He had them all wishing they were Kirby Swifts, admired by all men, and eyed fondly by all women.

Parker, trying to regain the attention he had lost, got to his feet and began, "All in favor of hauling out at dawn—"

Kirby Swift broke in, "Well, now, gentlemen, when do *you* think we want to haul out?"

The interruption was bravado, small boy showoff, and outright rudeness both to the speaker and the speaker's office, yet the younger men and some of the older ones chuckled appreciatively as though they had heard rare wit and brilliance. But Barlow, who had a snootful, got up to speak his own piece.

He was tall, and coffin faced, and lanky; a good soldier, yet he did not look it. Though carrying himself well, there was nonetheless a suggestion of awkwardness and self consciousness in his posture and manner. He did not have presence, and he was setting himself against a man who did.

"Mr. Parker," he began, gesturing with an oversized hand.

"Sit down, soldier!" they shouted. "Sit down!"

But Barlow's earnest face and voice encouraged the outpointed emigrant captain. "Yes, Pete? What is it?"

Kirby Swift remained standing. He gave his admirers a meaningful glance. Barlow's ears got red from knowing that half the company regarded him with derision and contempt, of a good humored sort simply because Swift wanted them to. Barlow cleared his throat, which seemed funny enough to get a fresh crop of grins.

"Mr. Parker, everything is done by vote. That's the way the articles were written up, and that's what we signed for. These here men all voted the other night to take a week more to finish refitting wagons and swapping for better oxen and horses, and then having a short shakedown run. They voted thattaway because it was good sense. It is just as good sense tonight!"

"What you say is true enough, Pete, but the majority—"

"We're hauling out in the morning!" they chorused, drowning the captain's words. The meeting broke up without formality of adjournment. The presiding officer stood there, no one giving him heed. Women appeared from among the wagons. Banjos plink-plank-plonked, and someone began to sing, *"Oh Susanna!"* Herd guards quit their posts to come in for fun and coffee. No one would do any thieving right at the outskirts of Kearneyville, they reasoned.

Above all the jollity, Swift called, "Stick to your tin horn army, soldier! Wait for your discharge, or haul out in the morning like a man and let 'em whistle for you!"

One of Swift's admirers began to count, "ONE two three four, *hup! hup!* One two three four—"

Barlow, not marching to cadence, measured his man as he made for him: for Swift, not the mocker. The instant the final springy stride brought him within reach, he popped Swift, one-two. The *segundo*, amazed and caught off guard by the agility of an awkward looking man, went glassy-eyed before he got his hands up. He had been knocked so stiff that he toppled like a tree, instead of lurching to his knees.

"Next man up?" Barlow invited.

Nobody came up.

"You silly sons," he went on, quietly, "taking off before you are ready to march is a fine way to commit suicide."

He turned and shoulder-brushed the pack as he cleared their front. Once in the shadows beyond the wavering firelight, he looked back to see if he could find Sally Clayton among the dancers; but before he could spot the girl on whose account he had planned to become an emigrant, Horace Parker came toward him.

"Pete, it isn't as bad as it seems to you. Everyone is naturally interested in getting to Red Fork ahead of other companies that are forming. To get our first choice of land is really necessary."

Barlow shrugged; he had not the heart to attack Parker's attempt to salvage a little self respect by accepting Swift's reasoning. "If Sally hadn't become so attached to you and Mrs. Parker during the time you folks have been camping and resting at this jumping off place, I'd tell her to call it off, and stay here, and to hell with the money we paid in."

There was nothing but kindness in Parker's voice as he countered, "Do you really think you could talk her into backing out now? She's got her heart all set on taking up land, having a home of her own. She's been waiting on you for quite some while to get out of the army so she could marry you."

"She and I, getting two adjacent homesteads! Now I am marking time while army red tape unwinds. I am as good as out, only I can't jump the gun. That *segundo* of yours, that loud mouthed show-off, has been playing up to her, talking big, till I guess I couldn't get in a word edgewise any more."

"Oh, shucks, Pete! He simply has to get all the women admiring him, there's so many of 'em that each one is safe enough."

"What I aimed to say," Barlow went on, with rising resentment coming into his voice, "is that this sudden vote to rush things is Swift's personal dirty trick to get me to get desperate and desert, and get myself into a heap of trouble, or else sit here while he's playing up to Sally. I've used up all my spare cash, mainly blackjack winnings, to get my discharge by purchase. Unless I stole a horse, to overtake you people when I do get out, I'd be hanging around here waiting for another company to arrive and take off. That foxy devil had it all figured out. He'll stake a claim alongside hers. And you've played into his hands, Mr. Parker!"

"*That's* why you hit him. It wasn't his mocking the army."

"Oh, all right," Barlow exclaimed, helplessly; he could not begrudge this good hearted man the chance to forget his humiliation. "But you see where it has left me."

"Pete, you don't need to buy or steal a horse, nor desert either. Take my mare, Alezan. Even if we have a week or ten day's head start, you can overtake us in no time at all. Come on, I'll get her now and you can saddle up."

Alezan was a Morgan, fast and durable; whether she was worth five hundred or a thousand dollars depended largely on how Parker felt at the time someone made him an offer. The colonel at the fort would give his right eye for such a mount. But Barlow said, "You're mighty kind, only I'll talk to Sally first."

"Very well, Pete, I'll be saddling Alezan."

Before Barlow could protest at being waited on by a man old enough to be his father, Parker was making for the picket line. Then, while Barlow still looked about him, a woman said from the darkness of the captain's wagon, "He's doing the best he can for us, darling."

The whitish blur in the darkness of the wagon cover was Sally. He extended his arms, caught her, and after holding her close for a long moment, he set her on her feet. They stood there in the half light, clinging to each other as though they had been separated for days and weeks, rather than hours.

She was well shaped, solid, squarish of hip and shoulder, yet graceful. The smile of her upturned face was whole hearted; her nostrils had an eager flare, and the eyes, slightly prominent, radiated friendliness to all the world, though now they had an especial warmth and glow.

"Don't worry, Pete," she murmured, when their kiss finally ended. "That good looking fellow hasn't impressed me with anything except the travelling salesman show-off manner that was just part of the day's work, back in that hashery in St. Louis!"

They ignored the dancers, and set out for the willows of the creek which ran past the wagon park. There, watching the moon rise, Barlow tried to persuade her to withdraw from the Red Fork Company.

"Parker's a fine man, but not tough enough to be captain of anything. Those fools might of a sudden vote for something to land the whole kit and caboodle in the worst kind of trouble!"

"Oh, don't be such a worrier! Kiss me and quit frowning!"

The moon was high and the shadows short when at last they went slowly for the camp. Alezan was tied to the wheel of Parker's wagon. Before Barlow boosted Sally to the tail gate, she whispered, "Think of me at reveille, darling. I'll be up and moving by the time you hear first call..."

On his return to Kearneyville, Barlow left Alezan at the livery-stable, and said to the sleepy hostler, "Don't skimp on the oats! I'm coming in every day to look at her and see how's she's doing."

He was good as his word. He learned the following evening that Alezan liked ginger snaps and rock candy. He was engrossed in getting acquainted with the mount that would shorten his race when a man called from the corral fence, "Wait, it gives an apple, for nothing."

The speaker had just let go the handles of a pushcart on the side of which was lettered in red, EPSTEIN WILL FIX IT. His nose, broad and curved and lordly, combined with sagging jowls to give solidity to a tanned and deeply lined face. The twinkle of his eyes suggested that his slogan was justified. He raised his Stetson, and with red bandanna mopped his high forehead. Except for a fringe of crisp hair to hedge his ears, he was gleaming bald.

"Where is it?" Barlow demanded. "If it's free, I'm buying. Otherwise, you dicker with the mare!"

Epstein, dug under the tarpaulin which partly hid a tin smith's kit, a cobbler's kit, and a clutter of gear and merchandise. In addition to peddling odds and ends, the pushcart man repaired and patched his way from town to town. He got out a withered crab apple, which he offered Alezan.

Barlow nodded appreciatively, and joshed, "So you're a one man covered wagon, eh?"

"No, this outfit is the cart before the horse. What time is it?"

Barlow glanced at his size sixteen watch. "Six five, exactly."

"You need a chain, with a fob, for that beautiful time piece." He produced both articles from his cart. "As good as new. Solid gold. Fourteen carats, and I guarantee it. Just what you need when you put on civilian clothes."

"How the hell you know that's what I'm going to do?"

"I was leaving the Red Fork Company yesterday, where I fixed things, and that young lady of yours, she told me. You didn't see me when you came up and I left, you had something else on your mind."

"I sure did! But look here—maybe I'd better sell you the watch, I have more time than money."

* * * *

They ended by agreeing to have a beer, and not talk business until the following evening. Epstein, it seemed, would spend another week or so, working out of Kearneyville, and going to the farms and cattle ranches which surrounded the jumping off place. "Every time I sell, it means I got to buy," Epstein compromised, amiably. "And every time I buy, it means, I got to sell some time. You see how it is? No matter which way, I am bound to lose, so I don't care what is your choice, as long as it gives a little business."

After an interminable week, the final mile of red tape was cut, and Barlow, at last wearing civilian clothes, rode from the post with a supply troop teamster. The sun was low when they reached town. He had to fight the crackbrained urge to mount up and ride, if only for the remaining hour or two of daylight.

At the livery corral, he paused to look around for Epstein; but the pushcart man had not yet returned to park at his accustomed spot.

"Can't haul out without telling Saul I'm not buying and not selling," Barlow said, and decided to cure his restlessness by taking a sentimental ride to the now deserted flats, and the spot where he and Sally had sat beneath the willows.

Barlow had just done saddling Alezan when the hostler came in, trailing after the two purposeful men who loomed up in the doorway of the stable. One was a leathery, saturnine fellow with deep set eyes, deeply lined face, and drooping moustaches; judging by boots and vest and hat, a cattleman. The other was Lem Craven, the deputy sheriff who had only a few days previous taken over because of the illness of the town marshal.

"That's the mare, Craven! And that's the thief!"

"You sure, Lathrop?"

Lathrop snorted. "Arrest him, man! Now! Course I'm sure! Why do you suppose I swore out a warrant?"

And Barlow was helpless. Even if he had been the sort ready to shoot it out with a lawman, he would not, could not have risked Alezan's stopping a stray bullet. Neither could he submit to arrest, and spend weeks, perhaps months in the hoosgow before clearing himself of the unjust charge. Freedom, and without gunplay, looked like a hopeless proposition: the two were loaded for bear.

CHAPTER II
Ambush

Lathrop, who looked as if he'd take his own grandmother's scalp for a one peso bounty, must have put up a convincing yarn, whether he himself did or did not believe it. Craven, reputed to be pretty much on the level, was probably playing it as it looked.

Barlow said, "Running a man in for stealing a horse is pretty serious business, sheriff. Reach into the saddle bags and you'll find my discharge papers, I just done got out of uniform, after serving most of a hitch out at the fort. I've had this horse stabled here for over a week, open and above board. Taking me in and locking me up for Lord knows how long, whilst I am proving legally what anyone out to the fort can tell you and a lot of folks in town here will back up, is downright unjust."

"Mmmmm…where'd you get that mare?"

"From a sodbuster, Simon Parker. Captain of the Red Fork Company."

Craven smiled crookedly. "And it's mighty handy, those emigrants being way to hell and gone on the road from here. Got a bill of sale?"

"Parker loaned me the horse to overtake the wagons. Sheriff, who's named in the warrant? I'm Pete Barlow and you can prove it a dozen times over."

"It's thissaway," the law man answered. "The writ is for one Jawn Doe. It's for the repossessing of such and such a hoss from the hands of party or parties described irregardless of name."

Lathrop, Barlow now knew, had been foxy. Whoever the man was, he was gunning for Alezan, who could not speak for herself, claiming to have traced or trailed her; in so doing, he had neatly forestalled Barlow's proving that he, Barlow, could not have been traced to Kearneyville, since he had been in and about town all the while. Yet Barlow persisted by repeating, "I can prove who I am, and where I've been for weeks, months, a couple years."

He looked and sounded doleful, futilely indignant. And Lathrop on that account overstepped himself a shade more than he realized.

"Don't make a damn bit of difference who you are, you got stolen property in your possession. And I got witnesses to prove that there animal is mine."

"That's the point of the process," Craven said. "It is receiving stolen property. Serious as doing the outright thieving yourself. Too dang much of it going on, fellows saying they didn't know a hoss or a cow critter was stolen. Nobody'd buy or sell a valuable animal like this'n, without there being a bill of sale. You come along and if you can prove you didn't knowingly and willfully and maliciously and intentionally receive a stolen critter, you won't be fined or strung up or sent to the pen or nothing."

This was entirely on the level. Craven was merely trying to do his duty and he was getting impatient. Barlow, having worked up to within arm's reach of a saving play, felt like a cat walking on eggs. If he fumbled in trying to bait Lathrop, the man might catch on, and the trick would then kick back.

"Look here, sheriff," Barlow said, with a show of despair that was all too easy to feign, "it's up to him to prove this is his animal—it's not up to me. I'm no thief."

"That's for the jedge, I'm not a-trying this case."

And then, from the doorway, another county was heard from. Epstein, chain and fob temptingly displayed, stepped into view and said, "Hey, wait, I am giving you a special price. Or I sell it somewhere else!"

The lift and quirk of Epstein's left eyebrow told Barlow that the pushcart man had been dallying outside long enough to have learned what was going on.

"They claim I stole this mare, Saul! Where I'm going, I won't need watches and chains, time won't mean a thing unless I round up a good lawyer. You take my watch and find me one, in case I'm locked up."

Epstein regarded Lathrop with an ingratiating smile. He turned on him with the chain and fob. "See how nice it looks across the vest front. Prosperous with dignity—"

"For hell's sweet sake, get out, I'm busy."

"Officer, the man is busy." Epstein's face changed; he backed off. He eyed Lathrop, and then Barlow, and as though with growing recognition of something significant or important. "Sheriff, I been travelling. Every place I go, I pick up wanted posters. You wait, I get them. If you got a wanted man here, we split the reward—"

He darted for the door, agile as a lizard, all the while chattering about wanted men he had met in his travels. And Barlow noted Lathrop's change of expression, a flicker of uneasiness. This was Barlow's moment, and he challenged, boldly, "Lathrop, if that's your horse, give the sheriff a close description."

"He's done given it, for the writ," the lawman cut in.

But Barlow, interrupted, "Describe her teeth. What's odd about them, or is there anything odd?"

"Shucks, they're just like any five-year-old's teeth," Lathrop declared.

Outside, Epstein was muttering in a voice that would carry across a parade ground, "No, this ain't him—hmmm—but with the moustache shaved—hey, sheriff, how would Mr. Lathrop look with a shave?"

"She's a seven year old!" Barlow countered. "Claims he owns the animal, don't know her age. Never seen her teeth. Me, I've seen 'em, every one of, know 'em by heart. Sheriff, you take a look and see who's right."

Craven turned to open Alezan's mouth for a look at the disputed teeth. Epstein came in, waving a fistful of posters and dodgers. "That's the man! That's the man!"

Lathrop turned; Barlow whipped the Peacemaker from his hip and clouted him. Buffaloed, the man dropped to his knees and clawed the stable floor. And Barlow, pocketing his gun, said to the lawman, "She's got tusks—look and see! Ain't one mare in a thousand got tusks in back of her mouth like a stallion or gelding, but this one has, and that coyote couldn't think of a thing to say excepting about how old she is from her teeth."

"By gravy, she sure has tusks!" Craven muttered, and then, turning, "Hey, what's this?"

281

"Good Lord must've struck him with lightning, for a liar," Barlow said, shaking his head as though perplexed by the sight of Lathrop lying face down and mumbling. "Fact is, she's a four year old. This dirty son didn't guess any too bad, he must've looked her over pretty close, but he skimped the job. If you'd owned her, you'd for sure have known she had tusks."

Epstein came in with a dodger. He masked the lower part of the face, looked at Jed Lathrop's back, looked at the sheriff, and said, as-though crestfallen, "No, this ain't right around the eyes, this ain't the same jail bird, sheriff." He sighed. "And it gives no reward for us to split."

"Mebbe not! But if this son ain't out of town by noon tomorrow, I'm throwing him in the pokey jest to wait till I can find out where he is wanted, if any. Huh! Didn't know she has *tusks*!"

Jed Lathrop was now scrambling to his knees. Craven repeated his advice about getting out of town. And as the man lurched from the stable, Craven added, "And that goes for your witnesses, too!"

When the law man left, Barlow let out a long sigh. "Saul, if you hadn't had that stinker so worried, I couldn't've clipped him, I'd've had to shoot it out, and then there'd been the devil to pay. What the blazes are you, toting reward notices? Pinkerton?"

"Man hunting ain't my business. But a fellow pushing a cart gets into lonesome places, and he meets all kinds of people—and I lose enough money, without being held up."

Barlow chuckled, "I bet you do!"

Epstein grinned and raised his hat. "But so far," he said, stroking his gleaming bald head, "I ain't been scalped. You leaving now? All saddled up?"

"Just restless, aiming to ride a bit, so I'll sleep better."

"When I was your age, I wouldn't sleep a wink either, with a race starting in the morning to catch up with such a nice young lady. If you won't sell me your watch, maybe you will buy a wedding ring—I got a brand new one—wait, I show you!"

Long before dawn, Barlow was in the saddle; and when the sun reddened the mesquite dotted plain and outlined the iron-purple crags on the horizon, he picked up the ruts left by emigrant wagons. A couple of hours later, he came to the first camp site, which had taken the slow moving oxen a full day to reach. And Alezan stretched her legs, eating up the miles.

Well past midafternoon, a gentle climb led to a low summit, one side of which was topped by a rocky wall. He had no more than entered the pass when he glimpsed the next water hole.

The trail swung left, down a narrow valley which for a stretch had grass and a few stunted poplars. Bit by bit, the higher ridges blocked out the wind which had been peppering him with sand. He rode into sweltering calm. Ocatillas, thumb-thick stalks armed with spines half an inch long, found root in the tumbled rocks of a slope which supported no other growth. Each had a crest of red blossoms.

Barlow looked up and about him from force of habit. The scent of water made Alezan perk up her ears. Out of the oven, and into the coolness—

Then he noted the stirring of one ocatilla somewhat ahead and well up the wall. The lowering sun's glare put him at a disadvantage: but that motion, where every thing else was dead still, warned Barlow, and a deceptive patch of shadow seemed to shift a bit.

There was little enough warning, yet Alezan, sensitive to the moods of which her rider himself was not fully conscious, snorted and made a skittish move. Smoke blossomed from the rocks. Instead of drilling Barlow, the bullet ploughed through the saddle skirt. Coming from a considerable height above him, the angle was such that the slug no more than raked a furrow in the horse's hide. She reared, and Barlow, half out of the saddle already, and reaching for his carbine, was piled to the rocks.

Alezan clattered away. Barlow, paralyzed by the fall, rolled helplessly until an outcropping checked him. He was still exposed, with hardly enough cover to protect a jackrabbit. A man came up from cover, rifle in hand.

Barlow, recovering a little from the crash, got his Colt. He steadied it. The man stepped down out of the worst glare. Barlow fired. The lurker recoiled, stumbled, and lurched downgrade several strides. He won the shelter of a rock and shot again, just as Barlow cut loose.

The two blasts were simultaneous. Lead screamed and whined. Barlow, however, did not hear the ricochet of his own, or of his enemy's shot. The glancing slug had dug a long gash which girdled his head. The impact, though cushioned somewhat by the Stetson, nonetheless knocked him out as from a hammer blow, so that he slumped, rolled over his limp gun hand, and across the weapon which had dropped from it.

* * * *

The bitter chill of dawn aroused him to thirst and pain. The early light, treacherous lavender gray, found him wondering how he had come to be in a draw, where small pools reached out from beneath the overhang of a dry creek bed. Bit by bit, he recollected the ambush, and realized that as though sleep walking, he had crawled back to the trail from which he had been shot and apparently left for dead. And his enemy had not made such a gross mistake after all.

Before starting on his half-conscious stumbling, Barlow had holstered his pistol. He still had his hat. It was well jammed down over the inflamed furrow left by the bullet. He knelt to drink and to bathe his eyes. He fell face down in the shallow water. The drenching shocked him to alertness for a moment.

After tying a piece of shirt tail over the eye injured by chunks of flying rock, he set out to overtake the wagon train, though the easier task of returning to Kearneyville would have been far too much for his strength. The valley soon became a blast furnace. A glimmering of sense told him to turn back toward the water he had left behind. Still out of his head, and getting more so, he worked his way to the emigrant camp site.

He found among the scattered rubbish a sack from which he shook more than a handful of cornmeal. This he put into one of the tin cans lying about. Presently, he had a mess of mush cooking.

Elsewhere, he found a bottle and cork. A gob of mush, a quart of water, and the rest depended on his boots. One trouble with a fancy horse: someone was always ready to steal it.

Barlow moved as in a nightmare. Though making back for Kearneyville, to get a fresh start, he seemed also to be hunting Sally. Every so often, he found her, and talked to her. Most of the time she ignored him, as though she did not hear his voice, or feel the hand which reached for her. And what made it worse, Sally seemed always to be a phantom which would not fill his arms.

Coyotes yip-yipped, and for a change, they howled eerily. Barlow baked, and then he froze. Sleeping and waking became one continuous confusion. The cornmeal and the water were gone. Buzzards, after long circling, now settled to perch on mesquite and scrubby acacia. Barlow had come within sight of a *tinaja*, one of the water holes at which the emigrants had camped, when he dropped. It was dusk when someone shook him.

"Drink only a drop now. Later, it gives soup."

And presently, Saul Epstein handed Barlow some jerked beef broth. "I left the morning you did," the pushcart man explained, "only later. And when I saw the buzzards coming down, I went past the *tinaja* and here you are. Now I will patch you up where you been shot."

"Buy my watch, so I can get myself some sort of critter back in Kearneyville," Barlow proposed.

But Epstein wagged his head and countered, "In the morning, that is something to talk about. Not now!"

CHAPTER III
One-Man Covered Wagon

When, after days of hoofing, Barlow finally sighted the dust of the emigrant train, he and Epstein followed in its wake until dusk. Then, leaving his companion well beyond the sight of the herd guards, he left him and made for the fires which outlined the wagon tops.

Once or twice as Barlow picked his way about the fringe of the camp, a man or woman spoke a civil word of greeting, as to a fellow emigrant not individually recognized in the darkness. For a moment, it was all unreal, doing what he had done so many times before, wandering about in delirium to find Sally. Of a sudden, his being in camp became the foremost wonder of his life, so that he could not believe that it had happened. He choked and his eyes swam, and he leaned against a wagon wheel as though mortally tired, or very drunk.

284

Then his eyes focused and his ears heard: and there she was, close at hand. "Sally," he said, quietly. "I had trouble on the way, but I made it."

There was enough reflected firelight to show how little her face changed; it was as though she had known to the minute when he would arrive, and had never doubted that he would rejoin her. "Oh, Pete, I've missed you!" She did not raise her voice, or cry out in gladness, lest the others hear and intrude. "What happened?"

Then they were in each other's arms, and for awhile, neither spoke. Finally, he repeated, "Trouble on the way. Had to walk most of it."

She took his hand, and they went toward the fire where the captain sat. "Mr. Parker, look what I found!"

Horace Parker got to his feet. "Well, Pete! Where've you been?"

Barlow was busy watching Kirby Swift's face. He did not expect the *segundo* to join the others who welcomed him, though largely out of curiosity and by way of following the captain's example. To nearly every one of the emigrants, Barlow was a stranger whose brief appearance in Kearneyville had been a triviality in a long succession of important events. Meanwhile, Sally had become one of the group: and to the young fellows who had had an eye on her, the newcomer was an intruder.

Barlow said, directly to Parker but to the others as well, "I took good care of your Alezan, boarded her well, and came from the post each evening to see she was getting her oats. The way she ate up the miles the first days was a sight!" He raised his hat. "Right up till a .45 scratched her, and she reared up just as I was fixing to pile out of the saddle for some skirmishing. This here crease in my head is the second shot the bushwhacker fired, and it saved my life. Knocked me out, and the skunk figured no need coming to finish me off. When I come to, I had a piece of walking to do, and I've done it."

"What'd you eat?" one demanded, having apparently estimated the days it would take a man afoot to overtake lumbering oxen.

"Shucks, that was simple! Snared quail at the tinajas, and rattlesnake is mighty tasty when you're hungry."

The women insisted on getting him leftovers from supper, but Barlow shook his head. "Fellow shouldn't over-eat, when he isn't used to rich living. Captain, you set me to whatever chores you've a mind to in the morning." He dug into his pockets. "Here's my watch, and here's what money I've got left. I'll make up the balance I owe you for losing Alezan, one way or another, soon as I see my chance."

"Talk about that when we get to Red Fork, Pete. Right now, you rest up, you look all fagged out and peaked."

He sat down, with Sally beside him, and drank coffee, and smoked. Later, when by common consent and weariness, the harmonica player quit competing with the banjo, and the emigrants made for their shake-downs, Barlow laid a hand on Sally's arm and whispered, "You wait outside for me a minute."

He stood aside until Swift was apart from his admiring crowd. Barlow, accosting him, said in a matter of fact tone, "You and I had trouble. Not from the way you and your sidekicks mocked me, but because it looked as if you'd undermined me. Between here and Red Fork I am obligated to get along with you, and you have to get along with me. When we get to where we're going, there is plenty of time to square our accounts if you think you've got something against me. That fair?"

"I don't bear you any personal grudge for the blow, though it was a dirty one and without warning," Swift answered. "But striking me, the *segundo*, isn't a personal matter—it was pretty nearly as bad as hitting Mr. Parker. We're the law and the leaders."

"We weren't on the march, that evening. Anyway you've not lost any respect, judging from the way your cronies hang on every word you say. You and I can keep peace till further orders, but your boon companions may not feel that way toward me. I want you to call them off before they start anything."

"Meaning," Swift demanded wrathfully, "I need them to take my part?"

"I'll say you must've needed someone to do your dirty work! I've not said it to anyone else, and I won't, because I can not prove it. But till my dying day, I'll be sure you fixed it to have Jed Lathrop try to have me arrested for a horse thief, so I'd lie rotting in jail till Sally lost hope for keeps."

"Didn't you tell everyone you were shot at?"

"I noticed you looked funny when I told that part of it. The part you had not aimed to have done. I pistol whipped Lathrop after I made him out a liar. And that's the man who laid for me with a gun. Who else would be lurking in that pass, with no stage, no freight, nothing expected? How would that man know way ahead of time I'd be passing through, excepting he'd been in cahoots with you?"

"You dare start any such story," Swift began.

Barlow cut in, "My story sort of proves itself, don't it? But you keep your boot lickers off of me, and I'll save you the trouble of trying to live down a story that'll prove itself. I'll work with you as long as you are *segundo*. Turn my offer down and take your chances on what will happen."

Without waiting for an answer, he went to join Sally. Once they had spread a blanket beneath the Parker wagon, and wedged their backs against the spokes of a wheel, she said, "There's a lot you've not told me, Pete. Don't tell me there wasn't more to it."

"You hush up, honey. This is kissing time, not talking time."

In the morning, Barlow set to work yoking and hitching oxen. Swift, riding one of Parker's fancy horses, made a grand figure as he bossed the job. The lead position, being dust free, was a prize which went by rotation, but before the train got rolling, the captain had to settle a wrangle as to whose turn it was to lead. The loser showed his spirit by refusing to fall in at the rear. He swung out and found his own track, alongside the train.

* * * *

Within the hour, a dozen other wagons had pulled out, each bullwhacker bent on dodging dust. When a dry wash was to be crossed, there was a scramble of those from right and left trying to cut in ahead of those still keeping in column. Barlow, trudging along with his bull whip, figured that Saul Epstein had easier going.

Toward sunset, there was a rush to be first at the water hole. The pool got all fouled and trampled. Later, Barlow said to Sally, "See what I mean? Fretting and wearing themselves out, running their animals extra miles that get them nowhere, and ending up with less time for the critters to graze—this outfit's not going to Red Fork, it is bound plumb to hell in a hand basket!"

"Is that why you were looking back, all day?"

He was not aware he had done anything of the sort, but he answered, "Sure, looking at you, or trying to."

"But often it wasn't in my direction. It was right back-trail."

"I deserted afore I got my discharge, and I'm nervous account they may be sending after me."

"Don't you expect me to believe that! What *are* you expecting to put-over on us?"

"Being shot from ambush leaves a fellow skittish," he answered, and realized that whatsover obscure reason he might have, he was undoubtedly expecting more trouble from Lathrop.

And then it was time for supper. Barlow, joining up with his mess group, was just getting his portion of stewed dried peaches when one of his messmates exclaimed, "Well, can you beat that! One man covered wagon."

Saul Epstein had overtaken the emigrants. Several, remembering him from his tinkering, back in Kearneyville, greeted him and made room. But Barlow, aside from bidding him good evening, was casual as though they had never before met. He figured now that however much his pondering on Lathrop's skullduggery had kept him looking over his shoulder, he had actually been anxious for Epstein to overtake and join the train, as they had arranged.

"If something is wrong," the newcomer announced, "Epstein will fix it. Young man, you need some good half soles, you are pretty nearly barefooted, and I give you a special price."

CHAPTER IV
Redheaded Peril

Like most of the girls and younger women, Laura Frazer tramped along, picking up brush for the evening fire. She contrived every so often to fall in step with Barlow as he drove Rafe Ainsley's oxen. For all her apron-load of fuel, Laura managed to slip a couple of molasses cookies into his hand; and for a few strides, the curve of her hip brushed eloquently against him.

287

The redheaded girl was slender enough, yet the wind driven calico of her dress clung close enough to make it plain that she was full breasted in a dainty way. She smiled from the shadow of her sunbonnet, and went on, leaving a promise behind her, and an invitation. She went on, easily outpacing the lumbering oxen, and still having time to stoop and pick up brush. Each glimpse of momentarily bared legs fascinated Barlow, mainly because of the smile and the promise she had left with him. He became riled with himself because it became increasingly difficult to keep his eyes and his mind off of Laura, who was by no means the only attractive and well shaped wench the wagon train offered. He did not want to think of her. Sally was plenty for any man to think of, the most exciting female critter he'd ever kissed or looked at: and he resented his response to Laura.

He resented it because he began to feel awkward whenever he came within reaching distance of Sally. He began studying Sally of an evening, studying her face and her voice and her eyes, looking for her to reveal her awareness of his thoughts, and of the redhead's attentions. And when he could find nothing of the sort, he was more than ever disturbed, for he felt then that Sally must know and was concealing, pretending to ignore the matter.

Standing guard at night was different from watching cattle bedded down; oxen ordinarily were not spooky. The purpose of the guard was to keep a lookout for varmints, human or four legged, so when Laura found Barlow sitting on a blanket near the edge of the *tinaja*, one night, she did not interfere with his duties by joining him.

"I couldn't sleep," she murmured. "I thought I screamed, but I couldn't have, else someone'd have awakened—oooh, it's chilly, Pete, let me have a corner of your blanket. I should've brought my coat."

"What was the nightmare about, Indians or renegades?"

Laura shivered. "Just afraid, afraid of *something*. Dark, dangerous, all bad, but you don't know *what* it is."

A coyote howled. "That's maybe what gave you the creeps?"

She drew some of the blanket over her shoulders and snuggled up cozily. Until that moment, Barlow had been wondering how soon he could get rid of her; but the first light touch made him fear that she would leave way too soon. Knees drawn up, she hugged them with her arms. Her legs gleamed in the moonlight; and then, after unclasping her hands and stretching her feet out before her, she hitched about to get the bunched up skirt back to her ankles. In this, she succeeded: but the shift of weight threw her closer to Barlow.

Before he could even think of what he wanted to do, he had done it; he had the armful he had craved. After a moment of feeling her yield to his arms, the two were mouth to mouth, and he could not have let go. She would not have let him, even if he had had the will.

"Oh... I shouldn't stay here," she murmured, finally. "There'll be someone coming to take your place on watch."

He drew her closer. "Won't be for awhile yet. I'll hear him."

288

"Pete—you're driving me crazy—you're killing me—"

But she pressed nearer, to hasten the fatality. And then, startled, she tried to get away, and might have, except that he could not so suddenly release her.

"Pete—oh—*let go!* Someone—"

The smell of fresh coffee shocked him. The chill that gripped Barlow cracked his embrace. A stick, a bit of brush snapped, and then Sally was so near them that Laura, scrambling to her feet, barely missed lurching against the newcomer.

"I thought you'd like some coffee," Sally said, with only a little tremor in her voice. "I didn't mean—I didn't know you had company already."

Barlow's horse snorted, whinnied. Barlow turned to face the dark shape looming up not far from Sally. It was Kirby Swift. He said, "What's all this lollygagging? You girls better go back to bed, this fellow's here to keep watch!"

Barlow took a step toward the *segundo*. "You sneaking son!"

Sally interposed. "Don't blame Kirby. It's his job to keep an eye on things." She set the coffee down. "Don't forget to bring the pot back, Pete," she said, and took the *segundo's* arm. "I think I should get back to my wagon."

Confusion made Barlow stand fast as Sally and the *segundo* blended into shadow, and he heard him say to her, "With you stirring around, I got to wondering. Half aroused me, you know how it is when you hear something and you're not quite awake, I wasn't snooping."

"Oh, I know you weren't, Kirby."

Being at once fighting mad, embarrassed, and wholly in the wrong, as far as appearances were concerned, kept Barlow from any action at all. After a long moment, he again became aware of Laura. Timidly, she laid a hand on his arm. "Pete, I'm sorry! Don't hold this against me. He didn't hear *me* stirring around."

Unreasoning hatred of this shapely redheaded girl who penitently awaited his outburst grappled with helplessness, and the certainty that he could never explain how impulse and attraction had pulled him off balance against his will. He felt desolate and abandoned as ever he had during those hours of wandering in the delirium of wounds and exhaustion. He remembered that dreadful futile groping, and turned to Laura now as something real and solid.

"Sit down for a spell," he said. "We're both in the wrong."

He reached for the coffee pot and emptied it to the ground.

For some minutes, Laura sat in silence. "I ought to be leaving." She twisted her hand free. "Don't keep me here, not after the trouble I've made you."

"It wasn't your fault."

"When you are sure you mean that, you'll come looking for me."

She kissed him lightly, and got up to make for camp. After a single step, Barlow stopped short, instead of detaining her.

While he could have, he did not wish to, and this puzzled him. Laura came close to being the prize package of the entire party. Her parents were solid folks. Barlow liked them both, they had not followed the common reasoning that only the shiftless and the worthless ever enlisted in peace times in the army. And when, after the relief man came to take his place, Barlow headed for his blankets, he still could not figure out why Laura's promise had been poor consolation.

Early in the morning, Barlow found time for a word with Epstein, who had just finished lashing the tarpaulin over his pushcart.

"Morning, Saul! Aim to swallow dust another day?"

"The more I see this outfit, the more I know it gives yet some more to be fixed. And for business, a man can eat dust."

"You're expecting something to go wrong."

"You don't see buzzards making circles, do you?"

"Look-ee here, Saul! Did you ever answer a question in your life, even once, instead of asking another question?"

Epstein grinned. "Maybe you didn't notice, but that's a habit you've got, and just now, you did it."

Barlow cursed in good humored exasperation. "Well, it's nice having you tag along, whatever your notion is."

"Now let me tell you something. That redhead is going to make trouble for you."

* * * *

All day, Sally avoided Barlow without being conspicuous about it; and in a similar easy way, she and Swift exchanged words during halts, or as he rode alongside her wagon when she took a spell from walking.

People were eyeing Barlow. He could feel their glances. He knew that the story of the previous night's encounter had spread. Horace Parker, riding up for a few words, stuck strictly to business, yet acted as though he had come to offer advice and had thought better of it.

Toward mid-afternoon, Swift returned from his usual scouting trip, and said that the next watering place was little more than a puddle. That evening, the rush for advantage was all the worse because of the warning. Barlow, doing his best to control his animals, got his thanks by having Laura's father, Walt Frazer, cut slantwise across his way. Old man Ainsley, for whom Barlow was driving, let out an indignant screech and snatched the bull whip.

Ainsley cracked the whip. The thirsty leaders responded. Where the most skillful whacking would not move them from their slow pace during the day's march, the sodbuster's lash now got them running. Barlow tore the whip from the owner's hands. He easily outran the peevish oldster. But he did not, and could hardly have made the leaders swerve in time to avoid the Frazer team.

There was a tangle of harness, a clash of horns, a grinding and smashing as wagon hubs locked and the vehicles came to a halt.

Frazer loomed up in the dust. "You young whelp! First my daughter and now my team!" He slashed at Barlow, giving him a whip cut which for all its clumsiness bit and tore, "You've had this coming, you no-account son! You—"

But now Barlow was inside the reach of the whip. He dropped his own. The blow and the reviling were the final touch to set him off. He danced in and knocked the farmer staggering backward. He gave him no chance for defense or recovery. He shook off the awkward blows and bored home with smashing jabs that shocked and cut. In a flash, he had Frazer out on his feet, bleeding, stumbling drunkenly, hands drooping.

Barlow hewed him again. He went with him, keeping him upright with blows until the man crumpled and lay a sodden bloody heap in the dust; and then Barlow stood over him, gasping, "Get up and fight, you dirty mouthed skunk! I've had enough of you!"

Parker and Swift came up with a dozen other scowling emigrants; sweaty, tired, angry at the whole world, and muttering about Laura. Parker said, "You've half killed him! Loomis—Christy—get those bulls untangled. Barlow, get away, we'll tend to this."

And, then Laura came up, wide eyed, to Barlow. "Don't worry, Pete," she said, laying a hand on his arm. "Dad's awfully hot tempered, though you'd never suspect it."

CHAPTER V
Kangaroo Court

They held a trial that night according to the by-laws of the Red Fork Company: and when Barlow saw the faces of those whose vote would convict and sentence him, he knew that a plea of self defense would do no good at all. Too many young men hated him because of Laura; and every family man, particularly if he had an unattached daughter, was against him. There was not a word said about the meeting of Laura and Barlow, the previous night, but the very way in which the men assembled about the fire avoided all reference to Laura or any other woman made it clear that the story of kisses stolen by moonlight had spread to every family.

Sally had confided in someone…

Laura had talked…

Swift had made the most of it…

And as Barlow heard Parker, who presided as a matter of course, read the paragraph on "brawlings and affrays," he was betting that Kirby Swift had got things going; just as Swift, coming up from behind, had covered him with a gun and had disarmed him.

Laura's father was, after all, a decent and right minded man; and when Barlow saw the terribly battered face, he was ashamed, and so much so that he could not resent his having appeared without a bandage. The light made his closed eyes and slashed features look far worse than they actually were. Parker was grave and troubled. Swift did his best to look that way, but could not make a go of it. This was his meat.

"I was trying to keep my team from fouling up with his," Barlow said, when they gave him his chance. "Trying to obey orders, not rushing for the water."

"That's right," affirmed the owner of the team.

"And he cut me with his bull whip," Barlow concluded.

"And you damn near beat him to death, a man old enough to be your father," several summed up at once. "What're the laws?"

Parker read, hastily skimming until he came to, "…shall be flogged; or expelled from the party, with or without refund of what monies he has paid in, according to the merits of the case, which will be decided by vote… Gentlemen, understand that that is what *may* be done. It does not have to be done. There is provision for a fine assessed by the group."

"Fines, my eye!" one shouted. And another, "Whale him within an inch of his life!"

Parker rapped on the barrel head for order. Order was restored long enough for there to be a sentence, by acclaim and not by vote, of one hundred lashes. The hostile faces made it plain that the penalty would be as final as hanging, except not as quick. Parker got up to protest. He was shouted down, until Swift restored order. In another moment, Barlow would be tied up to a wagon wheel.

When a soldier was flogged, the post surgeon stood by to supervise the punishment, and there was also an officer;—remote, aloof, neither for nor against the culprit. Here there was a mob.

Barlow demanded, "Give me a word while I can talk," and when this was granted, he went on, "Let Mr. Frazer do the flogging. He has the grievance. None of you have."

A mutter of approval greeted this logical quirk of justice. Swift, however, could endure nothing which impaired his vengeance. He loomed up more as the man actually in command, and before Parker had a chance for a word, Swift took charge.

"This is not a matter of revenge at all. It is a matter of law and order. Is that not right, Mr. Parker?"

Calling deferentially on the captain established more than ever that Swift, the polite man, was also the important man. But the moment Parker agreed with words which in form could not be disputed, Barlow snatched at his next risky chance.

"Swift, you're not captain, but you are the law around here. So you take the whip. Then it won't be personal at all. It won't be a man getting even because he likes Mr. Frazer."

"Lay it on good!" Swift's admirers chorused. "You got the heft, Kirby, you can peel him!"

Barlow, unrestrained, held his hands out before him, and took a step toward Swift, and a second. Looking the man full in the eye, he said, "The harder you hit, the bigger name you'll make. Your bunkies expect a lot of you."

Barlow's voice was soft. He cocked his head a little, and his eyes became pointed; a small, twisted smile, almost as of triumph, prodded the *segundo* with its mockery. It was almost as if Barlow had actually said "The harder you hit, the more surely you are through with Sally. You'll be showing yourself up for a skunk!"

And Swift's face changed. Those watching him shifted and choked back exclamations. They had understood, as clearly as if Sally's name had actually been spoken.

Parker took heart. He cleared his throat. "This has gone too far. This—"

"Let him be," Barlow broke in quietly. "He has to finish me this chance. He is afraid to meet me man to man, at Red Fork. He knows he's going to meet me. On horse or on foot. With guns or knives. Here's his chance of being sure to win."

"Fight him now, Kirby!" someone shouted.

"Silence! Quit this!" Parker protested.

"Oh, shut up! Shut up, Cap'n!"

And then a stranger intervened, Epstein, parking his cart at the fringe of the crowd, spoke up. "Vait, this ain't constitutional. It ain't right, making a man defend himself. He didn't have counsel to advise him. You didn't do it American style."

"It's all in the bag!" Swift retorted, eager for a change of subject. "Plain as the nose on your face, and he didn't need a lawyer, we heard him out."

The quip about noses got a splendid guffaw, and restored Swift's power. Epstein rubbed his nose, and grinned quizzically, playing up to the laugh. Then he declared, "The sentence is wrong." He faced them for a moment, standing as though about to review a regiment; he stood so that the width of his shoulders could counter-balance his paunch. The firelight exaggerated the deep lines of his face, the sag of his jowls. He was no longer funny; he was no longer a man offering bargains; and the nose, broad and lordly, had ceased to be amusing.

Epstein took off his hat. For a moment, he held them with pose and gesture. Then he grinned, inviting them all into his confidence and his generosity.

"You wait, I show you something!" He got a solid, black covered book, well worn and well thumbed, from his push cart. He opened it and read a few lines which not a man of them could understand. "That means in English," he interpreted, "that the Good Lord don't allow more than forty stripes on a man at one whipping."

Swift flared up, "Oh, to hell with that! What's a Yiddish bible count around here—we're Christians!"

Epstein smiled benevolently. During a scene stealing pause, his deep set eyes twinkled, catching and holding the eye of this one and that. "What I read is written in your Bible, my friend. In your own. In the fifth book, chapter twenty-five, second and third line. Mine is just like yours. What I got is the first edition, that's all."

Several chuckled appreciatively. Parker said, "Epstein's right. And there's hardly a man of you here who isn't familiar with the Scriptures. Forty lashes —"

And then Swift saw his chance to regain the lost hold. The darkness of his wrath faded, and he shouted triumphantly, "This Daniel coming to judgment is exactly what we need! I am not doing the flogging, and I am not meeting this loud mouth for a knife or gun fight. It'd look like spite-work, account he and I had words, back in Kearneyville. Get a whip, and let Epstein do the job!"

"Let Epstein fix it!" several cried, thoroughly enjoying the big fellow's neat twist. "Do it good, Saul, or we get our money back. We'll take it out of your hide if you don't do it good!"

"Hey, vait a minute!" Epstein protested. "You ain't heard everything—"

"Go shove your book, we've heard enough!"

Half a dozen sodbusters swooped in on Barlow, to hustle him to a wagon wheel. Others crowded forward with cords and bull whips. They swept Epstein from his cart and took him with them in their rush. By the time Barlow was jammed up against the wheel and secured, his shirt had been torn from him.

"Eye, wye, wye!" Epstein muttered, and mopped his forehead, when the pressure eased off. "This ain't right, I tell you."

The butt of a bull whip was thrust into his hand. He shoved it aside. "That ain't for whipping a min, it iss for an ox. I won't do it. A cat with nine tails, yes, but not this here."

Swift pulled the Peacemaker he had taken from Barlow at the time of arrest. "Listen, pushcart man! You're getting to work and doing as you're told, understand? You talked him out of sixty lashes, so you are damn well going to give him the forty he still has coming."

Epstein's eyes bulged perceptibly. He shrank from the pistol as though it had been a rattlesnake ready to strike; and he cringed as he took the whip and edged away, and toward Barlow.

"Pete, I can't help it. I won't make it too easy, I won't make it too hard. It is better I do it instead of somebody else. Anyway, I got to. He pulled a gun. He's still pointing it at me, he won't put it in his pocket."

"Go ahead, Saul!" Barlow said. "Get it over!" He added, in a whisper, which none but the executioner could hear, "I can take forty good ones, and the harder you hit now, the better I'll do when I cut his guts out and wrap 'em around his neck!"

Epstein backed away. He gestured for space, and he got it. He flexed the long whip, fingered the lash, hefted the grip. He seemed less apprehensive about Swift's revolver. After all, it was no longer dead center on him.

"Someone count, so I don't give him too many."

He unleashed the whip. The bitter cold hiss and explosive smack of the lash made Barlow wonder why he had been able to flinch, when he should have been slashed to the verge of paralysis. Hot iron seemed to have been streaked across his back; he could feel that, but no weight or shock at all. He heard the involuntary gasp of the spectators.

"One!" Epstein called.

Again, the hiss and blast. The man was a fancy performer. All bite, sting, welt, but no tearing and shredding of the flesh; nor that feeling of having one's ribs collapsed and one's breath knocked out as though forever, the way the army's "cat" did the job for a chronic trouble maker.

"Two!" Epstein announced.

What followed perplexed Barlow. A man cried out in pain and bewilderment. "Don't move!" Epstein commanded. "It is loaded."

Then the peddler was beside Barlow. A knife flashed, and the haft was thrust into his liberated hand. When he turned about, he understood: Epstein, whip in one hand, and an enormous Smith & Wesson .44 in the other, stood there like a lion tamer. He commanded the close packed crescent of spectators. He had bunched them up with his neat handling of the whip—and he had with his third blow slashed Swift's gun hand instead of Barlow's back.

Epstein made the whip ripple like a living snake. The Colt he had torn from Swift's grip engaged in the lash. Epstein drew the weapon right up to his feet.

"Take it, Pete," he said. "Two heads are better than one." Then, to the sod-buster, "Instead of the other thirty-eight lashes, it gives exile instead. We are going to Red Fork, faster than an ox."

Barlow quickly reached to the ground and scooped up the gun.

CHAPTER VI
Gold for Dead Men

The following day, Epstein parked his cart at a tiny spring far off the emigrant route. "We got no oxen to graze," he explained, "so it gives a shortcut to Red Fork for a one man covered wagon."

Barlow, having taken his turn, was ready to drop. Pushing a cart took skill as well as beef. "Be damned!" he muttered, as he helped make camp. "How do you stand up to it?" And then, as they hunkered down to bake sourdough with chunks of bacon in it, he went on, "I hate like snakes to run out this way on Sally."

"There you are wrong. This gives her time to get good and sore at Mr. Swift. People always get sore at what is closest to them. And when we get to Red Fork first, you and I pick out the best homesteads for you and her. Maybe I even stake one in my own name, even if I won't work it. A fellow is crazy, killing himself with farming!"

They tramped on, each day's march covering half as much again as even a well managed ox train. Looking back from a high crest, could see not even the dust of the emigrants.

Toward noon, four dusty riders hailed them. They were leather faced, unshaven, and heavily armed. They had the wary eyes of scouts, which was what they proved to be. They were trailing horse thieves, and they'd get and forthwith hang them, if they had to go all the way to Mexico to do it. Satisfied that neither Barlow nor Epstein had information, they spoke of doings far west, in the Red Fork country.

"Some bad Injuns snuck off the reservation," the spokesman said. "Raising sand with emigrant trains, freighters, and such like. But now the army's patrolling the route and probably driving the varmints off this way. You all better watch your hair."

With that, the four rode on. Ahead, barren ridges loomed up. The way, though clear, became harder. There were stretches of black lava flow. It had thin spots which concealed blowholes big enough to swallow a wagon. More and more, this shortcut became country which demanded a good piece of knowing. Long windrows of tumbled fragments looked as if hundreds of cars of coal had been dumped. The trail wound in and out among these.

"Over there," Epstein announced, near sundown, "it gives a basin your hat can hide. If you don't know where it is, you go thirsty for a whole day."

When they rounded a ridge, they saw that two men had already made camp near a tiny basin which had scarcely a trace of green growth to betray its presence. The pair had burros. Prospecting gear made up most of the packs laid out on the ground. Epstein hailed them, and in a moment, the bearded desert rats were plying the newcomers with questions.

Grover and Phelan they called themselves, and they were gold-drunk. They had to talk. Any audience would do. They showed ore specimens. "Rich as all git out," they babbled. "From the Muleshoe Mountains, yonder." Grover handed Barlow a chunk. "Scads of it! A ring-tailed heller of a lode. Free milling ore—"

The threads and flakes of wheat colored metal spoke for themselves. This had not the glitter of fool's gold; it had the mellowness of the real article. "Looks good, Saul," Barlow observed, and handed him the specimen. "Too bad it isn't pushcart country over yonder."

Phelan cried out, "The devil it ain't! This canyon here, this draw betwixt the lava, it leads right into the Muleshoe Canyon, and that's lousy with float."

Epstein's hand and voice shook as he surrendered the sample. "It gives a town there before you know it. Eye, wye, wye! I can get a load of bargains in Yuma and come back in time for the first business. Come now, Pete, we got no time to lose!"

The prospectors stared. "Gosh, man, you loco? Figuring on trading when you can stake a claim?"

"We're running short of grub," Barlow contended.

Epstein filled the canteens. "It gives another hour of daylight, hurry up, Pete, no time to lose."

Once they were on their way, Barlow said, "I got your play so strong I could taste it. What was wrong with the outfit?"

"With those fellows, something smells. I been in plenty camps. Some prospecting men don't talk even to burros, some talk like magpies and drunks. But there ain't any ore like that in these parts. And that ain't the only lie they told. Some of the fresh sign is horses. And the burros' hoofs and the men's boots don't look right for the kind of country they say they been working."

Once darkness fell, they camped in a swale. It was not until after supper that Barlow's uneasiness came to a point, and he said, abruptly, "Saul, a fake gold strike would be enough to drive sodbusters crazy as coots, particularly with a fellow like Swift. He'd get his crowd to head this way, a far piece from the route the army is watching."

Epstein let out a long breath. "I been waiting to see if you caught on by yourself. What do we do?"

"I aim to sneak back for a look-see and listen. Find out what those jiggers are really thinking. If there is sure enough dirty work, I'll risk going back to warn Horace Parker, and take my chances on what I get."

"What do I do?"

"I'd admire to meet anyone who ever figured out what *you* are fixing to do!"

"Most of the time I don't know it myself until I do it," Epstein admitted. "But better I wait to see how it goes with you."

Barlow accordingly set out along the back-trail. The silhouette of the lava ridge against the stars guided him. He did not slow down until he could smell the mesquite root fire of the prospectors. Wind whine and the incessant spatter of driven sand made a curtain of sound to mask his approach. The subdued glow of embers warned him that he was within sight of his goal. On working his way closer, he decided that the pair had decamped.

The ash filming the coals suggested that the two had left soon after he and Epstein had moved on. He wondered if they had aimed to bushwhack him and Saul. While this was an uncomfortable thought, he realized that his companion would hardly be caught napping. "Having us go yonder, instead of on our way," he reasoned, "couldn't do 'em a bit of good unless they knew we'd meet someone up the draw who'd keep us from coming back."

The moon's first glow was reaching into the draw whose general direction was toward the distant Muleshoe Mountains. He worked his way along an earth bottom which before long began to dip from its first steady rise. As he rounded a bend, he smelled horses and tobacco. There were men lounging about a small fire in a sheltered alcove.

The dim light gave him glimpses of hobbled horses. There seemed to be no lookouts. There was no reason for any, in this corner of desolation. Thinking of the four scouts who hunted horse thieves, Barlow asked himself whether these he now saw were the crowd the quartet had been looking for.

As the fire flared up, he saw many more horses, further up the draw, than the men in sight could possibly need. And then he recognized Horace Parker's mare. Alezan stood out like a torch light procession among the bangtails and scrubs of the remuda. The man who had bushwhacked Barlow in the pass outside of Kearneyville was now sitting in on a game involving fake prospectors and a fake gold strike. There was far more to this than Barlow could possibly figure for the moment.

One thing however was certain: he had to recapture Alezan. Doing so would not only cancel a debt, but would lend weight to his words when he rejoined the wagon train and outlined his suspicions to Horace Parker.

He considered half a dozen plans which would have a chance if he went back to get Epstein. He ended by rejecting them all. It took only one man to steal a horse. He remained in hiding, shifting at times when moonlight invaded the shadows of the rocks which sheltered him. He watched the strangers spread their blankets. And he kept his eye on Alezan…

* * * *

The approach was infinitely harder than the act. He was shaky, sweating, and dry-mouthed when he left, leading the mare and shouldering saddle gear. He had fed her rock candy and ginger snaps during the week she was stabled in Kearneyville, and she remembered him. She made no disturbance at all on being taken from her companions.

Once Barlow told Epstein what he had done and learned, he muffled Alezan's hoofs with pieces of blanket. The peddler said, "Don't worry about me. Lots of times, I have walked by moonlight. And if someone trails you to this camp, they won't go further after me. Not even Epstein can carry a horse in a pushcart."

"When'll I be seeing you?"

"Maybe at Red Fork. Maybe somewhere else. If I knew, wouldn't I say so?"

When, after hard riding, Barlow finally saw the dust of the emigrant train, it was, as he had feared, far off the guarded route, and making for the shortcut which he and Epstein had taken. He came down from the ridge; which ran parallel to the train's direction, and rode so as to approach it from the rear. He overtook the caravan when halted for a rest.

Despite the dust which masked him, the men Barlow accosted recognized him, but were too astonished for speech.

"Where's Parker?" he demanded. "Where's Swift?"

Mounted as well as armed, Barlow carried more weight than he had as a bullwhacker; and that in a large measure he controlled the fate of all these people added something to his presence. The man he addressed lost countenance, and instead of saying, "Try looking for them!" he answered, "Up toward the head, last time I seen him."

He wore his gun strapped low. He tested the way it sat in the holster. Whatever happened, they'd not catch him off guard again. When he recognized the captain among a group waiting their turn at a water barrel, he reined in, and deliberately eyed them until one looked up as though he had felt the impact of the stare. Barlow saw the expression of recognition, but ignored the man, and said, "Mr. Parker, I am here to pay a debt. If you can control these knuckleheads of yours, I'll dismount and give you your horse. If you can not keep them in order, I'll be riding on, while you're busy tending to some burials you'll be having on your hands. I'd like to hear your choice, sir."

298

Parker whirled. "Pete! Where did you come from? By George, that is Alezan!" He came, forward, hand extended. "If there's any trouble, the horse is yours for keeps. Get down, I'm glad to see you!"

Voice and handclasp made it plain that Parker spoke from the heart. At least half the others were embarrassed, rather than angry at seeing the man they had intended to flog within an inch of his life. Women were drawing nearer, but holding their distance.

Dismounting, Barlow flashed a glance that sought Sally, but he saw only Laura, whose eyes widened in the shade of her bonnet.

"Sound, and none the worse," Barlow said, slapping the mare's shoulder. "But what's the idea, being so far off the track?"

Parker looked embarrassed, and fingered his beard. "Prospectors with rich ore. We voted to—"

"The hell you voted! You mean Swift's loud mouth and a handful of hotheads hounded the rest of you into it. I bet you've got ore specimens they gave you."

"Yes," Parker answered, and sounded nettled. "Here it is."

One of the men growled, "Gun or no gun, you can't run—"

Barlow turned on the man. "Reach, or shut up! I remember your loud mouth at my trial." Then, addressing all: "That gold strike is a fake. Get back on the track quick as you can. The army is patrolling it. Indians and renegades are on the prowl. You're being baited into a trap, somewhere ahead, where you'll be easy meat."

Parker interposed, "Calm down, all of you! Swift is out scouting, beyond the next ridge. Barlow, I'm beholden to you for coming back with my mare, but that does not entitle you to throw the entire party into an uproar. You others, you listen to me—you are not going to bring up the difficulty Barlow had with Frazer. He's recovered, and that business is at an end. Now go about your own business, all of you."

Barlow, seeing their expressions as they obeyed, was sure that Parker's leadership was not strong enough to enforce more than a temporary and partial obedience. "Where's Sally?" he asked the captain. "If it weren't for her, and my debt to you, I'd've let the whole kit and caboodle of you go to hell and the quicker, the better!"

Parker smiled indulgently. "No, Pete, you would not. Quite aside from the women and children who'd suffer, you would not let your anger keep you from warning us. Sally's riding in Higgins' wagon, up toward the head of the train. It's been wearisome walking. Even the oxen are footsore."

Unthinking, Barlow led Alezan with him, and Parker let him. It was as though both men sensed that he might need a horse at hand if gold crazed emigrants flared up against his story. Barlow found Sally nested among the household goods in the wagon.

"Oh, Pete!" she cried, as he vaulted over the tailgate and with one swoop caught her in his arms. "Darling, I knew you were all right with Saul, but I was worried—I felt terrible, not going with you, then and there."

"You hush up, honey. Three couldn't've made it."

"I was silly, all upset about—well, it didn't occur to me that maybe you hadn't been able to do anything about it, the way she came out there, that night."

He shrugged. "I wasn't kicking and screaming." And after that honest admission, he told her what he and Epstein had learned, and what they suspected.

When she had heard it all, Sally said, "You're right. Kirby did all he could to start that gold rush that none of the older heads wanted. Though we'd not learned of Indians on the loose. Kirby threatened to divide the company, and pull out with all his friends. That was what made Mr. Barker give in."

"This time," Barlow declared, "the party does divide if it has to, even if only you and me have sense enough to keep off any shortcut to hell." He cocked his head. "That's Kirby they're hailing now. He's come back from scouting out the pass, I bet."

Barlow moved over to clear the tail gate. Sally caught him by the arm. "There'll be trouble for sure, Pete. Wait for things to cool down," she pleaded. "I know you're not afraid of him. It's just that he may be more sensible if he doesn't have to face you."

"He'll know I'm back."

"But that's not the same as facing you and getting riled and feeling that he has to show off, then and there."

Barlow shrugged. "He'll keep, all right."

Sally tugged at the edge of the wagon cover, so that they could peep out and toward the head of the halted train. Swift and another who trailed after him rode down the line. The two dismounted to talk to Parker, who had succeeded in getting the others back to their chore of checking up on the rawhide shoes they had laced about the hoofs of the oxen.

"Good camp over the ridge," Swift was reporting. "Plenty water and forage."

And then Swift's companion came into Barlow's field of vision. With a quick move, he broke away from Sally. "There's a man I want to talk to, and right now! What's he doing here?"

"Oh, that's one of a posse looking for horse thieves. He joined us about the time prospectors met us."

"Whatever his go-by is this time," Barlow told her, "that's Jed Lathrop, the stinker that tried to have me jailed in Kearneyville."

He cleared the tailgate, and taking Alezan by the curb chains, he led off for the three who discussed the road ahead.

CHAPTER VII

Epstein Does It With Mirrors

Anger and triumph made Barlow light headed and reckless, so that he spoke, instead of drawing to shoot it out on sight. Lathrop recognized the mare before he did Barlow. His first glimpse of Alezan prodded him to action. He was slapping leather before Barlow had fairly challenged him. His haste, however, made him fumble. Lathrop's first shot went wild.

Barlow made up for lost time. He did better, though not well enough. His pistol blast came a split second after Lathrop, but instead of drilling him dead center, he raked the man's forearm for half its length, and knocked dust from his shirt. Lathrop tried to shift the weapon to his left hand, but missed, and it dropped to the ground. Barlow, cheated of his chance to finish the fellow, closed in to pistol-whip him to shreds.

Parker, who had been blocking Swift's sight of Barlow, leaped clear. Swift reached for his gun and shouted. Barlow whirled, and before the *segundo's* weapon could clear leather.

"Hold it!" Barlow warned.

From behind him came a scream. Alezan bolted. A woman flung herself against Barlow, snatching his arm. She hung her weight from him, tangling her legs with his until he staggered off balance and came near lurching to his knees. It was Laura, the red headed trouble maker. She cried; "Don't you dare, you dirty son! You—"

Swift could not shoot. Laura blocked his line of fire. He stood there, gun in hand and nothing to do with it. But this was only for a moment.

Sally, coming up with a shotgun she had snatched from the wagon, had the muzzle trained on Swift, and without menacing anyone else. "Drop your gun, Kirby," she said in a quiet, deadly voice. "Get your redhead away, or she can have you in two pieces."

Swift obeyed. Sally's voice had made him turn ash grey. He let the weapon fall, not even daring keep it long enough to holster it. He took Laura by the shoulders, and stuttered, "It's all right, you let go of him, it's all right."

Barlow yelled, "Stop that—Stop him! Damn it, let go of me! Stop him!"

Laura still clawed and kicked until he broke away. Blind with fury, he blazed away at Lathrop, who had taken advantage of the fracas to mount up and ride. The fugitive, un-hit, swerved between teams of restive oxen. Barlow had to lower his gun.

He lost time catching Alezan. When he was in the saddle to make a race of it, Parker snatched the reins.

"We need you here, Pete! I can't have you riding off and plunging into an ambush."

"That brute he's riding is fast," Barlow grumbled. "Too far off already to do anything with a rifle." He dismounted, and returned Swift's look of surly defiance. "You're right, Mr. Parker. I'd better stay here and make it clear what your *segundo* has been doing.

"You, Swift! You listen and if you let out one word till I'm through, I'll shoot you in your tracks, no matter if you're not heeled! You don't deserve a white man's chance; so I'm keeping your gun. You made it up with Lathrop to have me jailed for stealing Alezan. I ended by getting her from a crew of thieves in the hills yonder, right where you and Lathrop aimed to lead us.

"He didn't dare ride her into camp because he knew she'd be recognized! He came here figuring he was sure he'd killed me, a long piece back. Now have you got something to say before you get a taste of what you aimed to give me?"

"I didn't know," Swift, began gropingly. "I didn't believe Lathrop had bush-whacked you after you left Kearneyville."

Somehow, the man was convincing; but Barlow tore into him, pressing the accusation: "When Lathrop and the prospectors 'accidentally' tangled with this company, you knew him for a coyote who'd connive to have a man jailed— have me jailed, so you could have Sally all to yourself. You took the word of a skunk like that and gulped the gold rush story."

"I've got a stake in this company," Swift protested. "Do you suppose I'd knowingly risk my own money, animals, everything?"

Parker looked at those who had gathered round. "I don't think he would, Pete. I think he's guilty of no more than poor judgment in dealing with a man he knew was low enough to try to jail an innocent man. We'll vote on it tonight."

"Vote on what?" Swift demanded, voice cracking with apprehension.

"Electing another *segundo*. You're through with show off tricks, shining up to all the women folks, and making the young fellows imitate you and back your every play. We are backtracking right now. The by-laws say we organized to settle at Red Fork, and to Red Fork is where we are going."

Parker paused. He saw that for the first time, he was actually leader, instead of captain in name only. But his justifiable satisfaction hardly outlasted the deep breath which expanded his chest. One of the sodbusters shouted, "Maybe we're bound for Red Fork, but we'll get to hell first! Look yonder, riding out of the pass. They knowed we'd not be crazy enough to go further, so they're com-ing to get us."

Barlow looked and saw the riders on the skyline. He wondered whether it was insensate wrath that made them strike at once, or whether it was fear that the emigrants would send for help, or in one way or another survive to tell what had happened, and who had menaced them. As he looked, he wondered also at the peculiar blinding flash which winked from the heights of a further ridge. But getting the wagons into a circle, with the animals inside, was far more im-portant than speculating as to the enemy's motives, or what caused the queer flickering so far away.

Most of the riders proved to be Apaches. They wore the levis issued by the Indian agent of the reservation they had quit; they had their heads bound, tur-banwise, with red calico. Judging from the whine and spat of bullets they poured into the wagon train as they rode in a circle about it, they had plenty of ammunition. But there were white renegades, worse than any Indian, in the howling pack.

The sodbusters had firearms enough: shotguns and rifles; powder and ball and caps, and cartridges for the breech loaders and the few repeaters in the train, but by no means enough for a siege such as this promised to be. They had come fixed for pot hunting, and not for battle. Even though they had reckoned on the possibility of trouble, none had had any idea of how much powder could be burned in a short time.

Barlow, crouching behind a wagon wheel, picked a renegade, and leveled his Winchester. He taught that one the advantage of riding Indian style, protected by his horse. But that one effective shot set the emigrants off on a wild burst firing. Barlow quit squinting through the dust for a glimpse of Jed Lathrop and got up to find Parker.

"Make 'em quit wasting powder," he demanded. "They're doing nothing but keep the varmints away till we're out of ammunition."

A .60 caliber buffalo gun bellowed. The emigrants howled in triumph, seeing man and beast drilled with a single slug; the animal had been knocked stem winding, lifted and flung. Barlow raced over to the marksman. "Hold it a spell! You've got every pot-head in the crowd trying to do the same with buckshot and bird-shot. Let 'em get close, and then hose 'em!"

The emigrants' fire tapered off. Those who lost their heads and let a good target tempt them, or those who were plainly defiant, served their purpose. Barlow said to Parker, "Might as well let them be. If we all quit shooting, those devils'd think we aimed to do the very thing we are going to do—let 'em have it from close range. Now with a dribble of shots, it looks like we're hard up for powder."

They busied themselves with the wounded. Women were tearing up sheets for bandages. A child went out beyond the barricade of wagons, enjoying all the fun. A man shouted, and would have gone out to get the little fellow, had not Barlow laid him out with a well planted fist.

"We need that man for fighting," he told those who cried out against him.

A woman did run out. She was riddled by bullets. The child came back, slugs kicking up dust about him. He was unharmed.

"Pete," the captain began, hoarsely, "you can't—"

"We're fighting a war. She's done for anyway."

The circle of riders suddenly closed in. Lead spatted through wagon tops. Lead thumped into wagon beds, and zinged from bolts and hubs. Animals in the center of the barricade were hit. Horses fought their hobbles.

"Hold it!" Barlow shouted. "Hold it till buckshot will count!"

Sally, bedraggled and grimy and scratched by flying splinters, came up beside him with a cap and ball Colt and a double barreled derringer. "I'll hand you these when you need them," she said.

And she went with him to crouch behind sandbags he had filled. The emigrant volley was ragged, yet a dozen riders were knocked out. The charge broke. Bullets drove the enemy off until Parker made the sodbusters quit firing.

During the confusion, and with dust rising high, Barlow darted from cover and scooped the wounded woman from the ground. He walked back with her. She lived long enough for a word with her husband, who had recovered from Barlow's blow.

"Now you're fit to fight," Barlow told the man, "and you have plenty to fight about."

Then Kirby Swift came up. "Pete," he said, grinning painfully, as he wiped blood from his face, "you called me a grandstand player. Look at *you*."

"Saved a man for when we needed him."

"I'm beating you with a better play." He turned to Parker, who had just come up. "Horace, if we run them off once more like we just did, there's a chance for a man to ride out through all the dust and get away without being noticed—they'll be too confused for a second or two to notice who's who. A man with a fast horse could get word to the army patrols. Give me Alezan. Better than having those devils get her."

Parker eyed Barlow questioningly.

Barlow answered, slowly, "Kirby's entitled to this chance. Providing our folks don't misunderstand and think he's joining the enemy. That'd make them throw up the sponge."

Kirby Swift's face whitened beneath the dust. "I earned that one. They might think I was going to tell Jed Lathrop we can't hold much longer. But if they didn't believe I meant well, they'd've settled me before now, wouldn't they?"

"Get ready to ride," Parker told him. And when Swift left to saddle Alezan, Parker said, "Pete, did you have to pour it on him that way?"

"The dig might help him get through." He looked at the sun, all red through dust. "Maybe he'd better wait till dusk."

"If they know a man got through," Parker objected, "they'll start worrying and might pull out. Indians don't usually close in by night."

"That's right," Barlow admitted. "Though you can't tell what they'll do with white renegades working with them."

Parker went to talk to Swift.

Before Barlow could learn the decision the captain and Swift had made, the enemy was closing in again. Again, the defenders held their fire: but the Apaches had a surprise. They were not yet close enough to get the deadly raking that awaited them when they wheeled; and those among them armed with bows loosed a flight of blazing arrows.

The flaming shafts dotted the wagon sides and covers. Wind whipped the dry wood and dry canvas to fierce burning.

Covered by musketry, Barlow and others tore and slashed at the wagon covers, while, some fought the blaze with water soaked gunny sacks. Parker was busy trying to keep this one and that from wasting water on wagons ignited beyond saving.

Gusts of smoke rose high, and then, wind driven, flattened out to blanket the earth, and hide whatever the enemy might next do.

The sodbusters manhandled two wagons which were too well ablaze to be saved. This kept the fire from spreading to those which had been put out. Then came a wild yell, and a whip crack.

Kirby Swift, stampeding some twenty oxen, followed them through the gap. Crazed by excitement, they raced for the enemy, who was closing in again, this time through a wall of smoke. As he rode, Swift threw away his bullwhip and went on with a pistol in each hand. The stampede crashed headlong into the ranks of the converging Apaches. Swift followed through.

Buckshot and pistol ball broke the charge. The next rush, however, would settle things; Smoke and dust covered the field. There was no telling what had happened to Swift, but Barlow said to Sally, as they shared a dipper of water, "He could have got through; Pass the word along that he did get through! All we have to do is keep holding till help gets here! Tell 'em!"

He gave her a squeeze and then a shove, and turned to encourage those who looked as though they knew themselves good as done for. He caught a sodbuster and his woman crouching in the shelter of two water barrels. They had an old revolver. The way they looked at it and each other made Barlow step up, snatch the weapon, and slap them with the flat of his hand.

"Stand up and fight till you can't be taken alive! What do you mean, you fools, fixing to waste cartridges on each other? Kill those devils out there instead!"

The two stared at him, half defiant, half ashamed. Then the haggard woman's face changed. "We're good as dead already!" she cried, hysterically; "Hear the trumpets and music! You hear it, Asa?"

Barlow's thought was, *"He couldn't have found help so soon."* Then he caught the thin, far off sound, and yanked the woman to her feet. "Angels, my eye! That's a cavalry trumpet sounding off!"

Either the wind shifted, or else the troop had come up out an arroyo that had choked the sound, for in a moment the call swelled, loud and fierce. There would be a charge—but not by renegades and Apaches.

The sodbusters heard, and shouted crazily. They helped speed the departing enemy. Barlow, resting a long barreled .45-90 on a sack of grain, unseated riders as far as he could hit them.

There was far off firing; but a squad of troopers led by a corporal came toward the wagons to take charge until the main party had done its work.

"Hell, no," the noncom answered in reply to Barlow's question, "we didn't get any messenger. The skipper'll tell you, maybe, when he comes in. It was funny business. What outfit were you in?"

And answering that question led to other things which kept them busy until the corporal cocked his head and remarked, "Sounding recall. Show's over. Hey, where you going?"

"Someone I hope got knocked over. Renegade by the name of Lathrop. I'm going out to make sure."

"No, you're not! The skipper sent us to see no 'dead' Injuns came to life and raised sand whilst he was chasing those that ran out. You stay put."

"OK, corporal. But there's something else I want to find out."

"It'll keep. Another scalp you're hankering for?"

"I did, right up till a little while ago. Now I feel different about that jigger."

When he had told about Kirby Swift, the noncom shrugged. "One man couldn't've got this whole outfit off the track if the captain'd been worth a second hand chew of tobacco. It's everyone's fault, not just the showoff's—well—what's *that*?"

A pushcart was coming up out of a swale. A longish bundle was lashed over the tarpaulin. "That's Epstein," Barlow said. "And for once, he didn't get around to fixing things."

But Barlow was wrong. Epstein's odd cargo was Kirby Swift, and his two emptied Colts. Far behind him, a familiar horse loomed up: Alezan, apparently none of the worse. Epstein called, "Pete, it gives something back there I didn't take the scalp from. It belongs to Swift."

"Jed Lathrop?"

Epstein nodded. "He had a pistol, and from that far, you wouldn't be pulling a pistol for using against these wagons. They shot each other up, Lathrop and Swift. What happened?"

"All of a sudden, Swift ran hog wild. Whether he meant to ride for help, or just had a hunch he'd get square with the skunk that led him into trouble, no-body'll ever know."

And then, when the cavalry troop came to the wagons, Barlow got the answer to the remaining riddle. Epstein dug into his cart and produced four small, framed mirrors. "Some of my bargains," he said. "From a high spot I could see far off with the spy glasses. So with the mirrors I made signals. Like the army heliograph. General Crook used to use them, and I bet the captain here caught the flashes and read my bad spelling."

Later, when the dead had been buried and the camp set in order, Sally came from one of the wagons and joined Barlow and Epstein. Her eyes were gleaming, and tears still trickled down her cheeks.

As she clung to Barlow's arm, she said, "I've been with Laura Frazer. She's all broken up about Kirby. Poor thing, she was playing up to you just to make him jealous. Anyway—thinking of how she and Kirby have been parted for-ever—"

Words choked in her throat. Barlow carried on, saying, "What Sally means is, she doesn't want to wait another day or hour. With all your handiness with scriptures, you don't happen to be a rabbi? That'd make it legal."

Epstein sighed regretfully. "Look at me, do I have a beard? I ain't even a justice of the peace." He pounced for his cart, and as he rummaged, he said over his shoulder, "But I got a nice ring, brand new, solid gold, just the right size—I give you a bargain and it ain't far to Red Fork and preachers."

DESERT JUDGMENT

Originally published in *Six-Gun Western*, Oct. 1950.

The pushcart parked in the lot opposite the Jefferson House, the only hotel in Poplar Junction, was crammed with every sort of gear for making good the slogan: Epstein Will Fix It, in big letters on both sides.

At the moment, Saul Epstein was plying his razor at the horse trough. Finished, he crossed over to the Antler Bar, to see what news he could pick up about a boom in Panamint.

The first person he ran into was Ben Hurley. He was blowing the froth off his beer and his angular face bore no sign of the beating he had taken when a run had cleaned him out of his Silver Bend National Bank. No one could have suspected that he had just sold every acre of land and every steer to pay off his depositors.

"Yep! I'm makin' a new start," Hurley was saying.

"Aim to drive freight clear across the Amargosa to Panamint. It can be done, and save that long haul from here to Frisco, then over the Mojave Desert." Epstein sidled up, a glass in his hand. "Prosit Ben! I'm doing some freighting to Panamint by the Nevada backdoor myself!" Hurley turned, surprised. "Saul! Where in hell did you come from?"

"When's your first haul, Ben?"

"Any day now. Mostly provisions. What me and Wiley, here, don't eat we'll sell."

"Got room to haul some freight for me?"

"Plenty—and that makes you my first bona-fide customer." He turned to the weather-beaten man at his elbow. "OK, Wiley—the jugheads are at the stable and the provisions at Hoskins' General Store. Get them stowed."

Epstein chuckled. "Just to make it interesting, I'll race you to Panamint."

"That's a bet." Wagging his hand at Epstein, Hurley walked out. But once alone his fierce animation quit him. His thoughts went back to the day after the bank failure, when he had faced Emily Crawford.

On his advice, she had bought into the bank. Like other stockholders, she had been forced to make good. Everyone had been flattened except Lucky Ballard, who a month before had sold his shares to invest in a cattle outfit in Arizona. That was the rub—competitors in all things, Hurley and Ballard had been courting Emily.

"Honey," Hurley had said, "saying I'll make good might sound like big talk. But I see a fresh start, the way I got my first break—skinning mules."

Though the well-shaped blonde was tall, she had to look up to meet his eyes. She forgot the bank disaster. Then, as he caught her in his arms, she said more than she had intended. "Don't go yet—"

The catch in her voice, the misting of her eyes, and the ardor of her lips told him this was his moment, and that he had won an advantage over Lucky Ballard.

This had been in Silver Bend, a month ago. Raising a grubstake had been harder than Hurley had realized. Meanwhile, Lucky Ballard would be on the job, smoothly sorry for a girl who had left her home and lived in a boarding house.

No one had known until after the bank failure that Ballard had gotten out. There had been nothing wrong with the bank; but one night when the vault was packed with cash and securities it had been blown open. Even so, it might have survived, had not the depositors stampeded.

He had all this in mind, and it drew his attention inward as he stepped into the lobby of the Jefferson House.

Drawn into himself, Hurley was not prepared to meet the couple leaving the dining room.

The girl had not put on her gloves. A diamond gleamed from her left hand. She was flushed and gay. Looking past the pair, Hurley saw the champagne bottle in the cooler beside the table they had just left.

The girl was Emily Crawford. From the grey tailored suit, Hurley judged she was traveling. The man was Lucky Ballard.

"Well, Ben!"

Ignoring the man, Hurley snatched the hand Emily had tried to draw from sight. His glance flickered toward the ring, then back to her face. "Not your honeymoon, anyway!" He thrust her aside. Caught off balance, she came near plopping into a chair, but missed. She landed in a tangle on the floor.

Hurley, swinging toward Ballard, had gone for his gun. Ballard clawed for his hip pocket. Hurley, only now aware that he had unintentionally floored a woman was gripped by the urge to pick her up. The conflict within him cost him his advantage.

Ballard's gun was the first to come into sight.

And then Saul Epstein, who had followed Hurley, made a darting lunge, catching Hurley just above the knees, knocking him down and pitching him against Ballard before his gun could rise into action.

A shot smashed into the pigeonholes behind the desk. The other raked the floor.

The marshal and his deputy ran out of the bar off the lobby. "That mule skinner again! Sam, help me haul this jigger to the hoosegow."

Epstein said, "Listen, officer, nobody was hurt. You can't put him in the calaboose."

"The hell I can't!"

"Well, I'll go his bail. He's got freight to haul."

"That's up to the judge," the marshal spat, "If he gets off, he'd best haul freight out of this man's town!"

Epstein waved as Hurley overtook him at the outskirts of Poplar Junction. Whip cracking, Hurley's voice boomed as he cursed the jugheads and the eighteen-foot wagon rolled on.

The second day out, Epstein got his chance to whittle down Hurley's lead. There were arroyos, which a freighter could not cross. There were dry-lake beds—a hard crust of salt and soda, with a foundation of muck—into which a wagon would sink to the brake blocks. Epstein played the shortcuts as he made for the Amargosa Desert.

Lips cracked, eyes reddened by alkali dust, Epstein tramped along. Then the air became oppressive, the sky bronze-colored. An unnatural dusk darkened the desert. An icy wind whined across the flats. Raindrops, the size of grapes, plopped down, foretelling the rage of Nature that was poised in the skies overhead.

Epstein first was tempted by the gully ahead. The undercut bank offered shelter. Instead, he got under his cart. The rain came down, drenching, blinding, choking.

The dry wash became ankle-deep in water. Some moments later, a six-foot wall of water came down the channel. It was as though a dam had burst.

Abruptly, the downpour stopped. The sun came out, blazing. Already, the mill race was subsiding as Epstein's garments steamed in the sun.

Soon he crossed over on dry bottom. Toward sunset, Epstein came to the wagon and the dry camp.

HURLEY said, "Wiley fell off. Wheel crushed him, but he may live."

"The buzzards say he won't. Let me look."

The peddler knelt beside Wiley, and shook his head. "There is nothing left to fix."

The man died within the hour. After they had buried him under a cairn of rocks, Epstein asked, "He was drinking?"

Hurley cursed bitterly. "I busted the bottle and told him I'd bust his head, but he had another one."

"You need a helper with the mules."

"That's what I've been thinking."

"Then hitch my wagon on behind, and I will take the job."

"It's a deal, Saul!"

The following day they paralleled the mountains. That evening, while getting camp gear from the wagon, Epstein found a case of whiskey cached among the canned goods.

"Maybe," said Epstein, in announcing his discovery, "Wiley was going to do some private trading in Panamint."

"Where the devil'd he get the price of a whole case? Old man Hoskins might trust him for a tin dipper of red eye from the barrel, but never for a case. There's something salty in this deal! Some one aimed to cold-deck me."

Epstein followed the hint and found a sales slip from the general store. It was a duplicate receipted by J. Wiley. But the goods had been sold to Lee Ballard.

A hail from the darkness startled the two. A man, weaving and lurching, stumbled into the circle of light. His clothes were bedraggled and torn. Bloodshot eyes stared from a taut face. He carried a satchel which he would not relinquish, even when Epstein caught him by the elbow to help him make the final step beside the fire. "Water!" he croaked.

"Here is coffee. Wait, I will get some grub."

"Not now. There are others. All in. I chased your firelight. They're all played out. You've got to help us."

Epstein said, "What happened, where do you come from, on foot?"

"The stage from Poplar Junction was caught in a draw. We've been walking ever since. Lot of the road was washed out. Got lost, and then saw this fire. Take us to Poplar Junction, or to the nearest town in the other direction. I'll pay you well."

"Who the hell are you, hiring an outfit so free and easy?" asked Hurley, who had been studying the man.

"Jubal Garlock."

"You could be the Governor of Nevada, for all I care. We're bound for Panamint. Ride with us, or walk to wherever you please."

Garlock got up, stiffly and painfully. "I'll go tell the others there's grub and water, anyway."

He had scarcely gone beyond the circle of light when a woman exclaimed, "Oooh! That coffee smells good!"

And the first of the group to take shape at the fringe of the firelight was Emily Crawford. She had slashed her tailored skirt to knee length. A piece of the garment had been used to make an outlandish sunbonnet. Other pieces were bound to her feet.

Hurley recognized her before she recognized him, since the fire dazzled her eyes. He took a step to meet Emily. She recoiled, and the face of the man following her changed. Hurley had command of the situation.

"Lucky Ballard!" he said, with an ironic bow. "But I'm kind of lucky myself, seeing you and Emily so soon after some one butted in on our talk."

Ballard stopped short. His hands made jerky motions, as though he could not decide whether to raise them or reach for a gun.

And then Epstein came over from the wagon. "Meals at all hours," he pattered, amiably. "Anything you want, ask for it—it gives bacon and biscuits and canned peaches."

Smiling, Hurley said, "Set down folks. I was only mocking you a bit. Saul, give them coffee, it's better'n water, for folks plumb fagged out and all a-thirst!"

Epstein obeyed. Hurley came after him with a bottle. "Take a dollop in your coffee, Lucky. You, too, Garlock." He regarded the label and displayed it to his guests. "Best in the West, Lucky. Got a whole case of it, barring a couple bottles. Wiley drunk 'afore he fell under the wheels and killed himself. Yes, Sir, old man Hoskins does carry good case whiskey."

Ballard managed to keep his face immobile. Garlock, who had not spoken since his return reached out with his pannikin'. And as he drank, he kept a caressing hand on the satchel.

Hurley was breaking out blankets when Ballard said, "Ben, personal differences can wait on a better time. Carry us to the road and the nearest town. I'll see you don't lose out."

"I'm going to Panamint. Ride with me, or walk your way."

"Oh, Ben!" Emily cried. "You can't do that! It'll be a couple of days before they miss the stage. They're likely to find just enough wreckage to make it seem none of us lived through it."

"I said, you can ride to Panamint."

"My God!" Ballard exclaimed, indignantly. "You can't make a woman face that."

"When Saul came up, just as Wiley died, account of some one giving him a case of whiskey," Hurley said, remorselessly, "I knew I'd get a sign that meant, shove on. Now with you two moving in on me, I know it's all the more a sign. It's Big Medicine—it's desert judgment—and I can't back down." He dug the charge slip out of his pocket. "The whiskey was on you, Lucky. Now—see what I mean?"

"But—but—Emily—!"

Emily interposed. "Ben, Lucky was heading South, to look at his property. I was going to visit relatives in Yuma. I am sorry you jumped at conclusions, but I can understand. And you needn't carry on with what happened in the hotel. We all understand. Let's just forget it."

* * * *

In the morning, Hurley acted as though there had been no dispute the previous night. "All aboard!" he shouted, as he climbed to the driver's seat. Epstein, after helping Emily, took his station toward the rear of the load. The cargo, well stowed, shifted hardly at all, but Emily, perched precariously and muffled in a blanket, lost her balance. In trying to check herself, she landed in Epstein's arms. Then, as though at a signal, Ballard pounced forward, while Garlock turned toward the back.

"Take it easy, Saul," Garlock said from behind his short barreled revolver. "Let Emily take that gun you got stuffed under your shirt."

Epstein pretended to be a good deal more scared than he was. "I don't want trouble," he stuttered. "Watch out—it's loaded."

Up front, Ballard had a pistol against Hurley's back. "Pull up, Ben! You're covered."

Hurley obeyed. "What's all this monkey work?"

"You're going to take us to town," Ballard answered. "I'll take your gun first."

Disarmed, Hurley faced about, hands shoulder high. "Can any of you skin mules?" he asked, leaning forward, chin outthrust, brows beetling. His hands seemed about to reach out and slap down. Epstein broke out in a sweat lest Hurley try the fatal trick of making a swipe at Ballard's weapon.

"Can you skin mules?" Hurley repeated.

"Yes," Ballard answered, "even though I didn't get my start that way."

"She's all yours, then." Hurley clambered down. "I'm whipped."

"What do you think you're doing?" Ballard demanded, warily.

Then Epstein spoke up. "I'm going with him. I got to get my cart loose. Do you have to keep my pistol?"

Epstein unlashed the vehicle. He picked up gun and cartridges Garlock dropped. "All right, Ben," he said, cheerfully. "Panamint or bust. We're on our way!"

Hurley wheeled about. "There's not a drop of water in tank or barrel. While you pounded your ears last night, I gave every jughead all he could drink. You can backtrack and follow my wheel tracks, but nary a drop of water for three days. The nearest water is toward the mountains yonder. A spring hidden so's you could die of thirst within a hundred yards of it and never know it was there. Pull down on me, and you're shooting yourself out of your last chance of a drink till you find it in hell. Let's go, Saul!"

Epstein bent to the push-bar of his cart. Stretching his legs in a long, swinging stride.

Hurley set the pace.

A pistol whacked.

Hurley swung along as though he had heard neither report nor the zip of the wild bullet, but Epstein, looking back, saw that Garlock was grappling to disarm Ballard.

When this was done, Garlock raised his voice. "You win, Hurley! He lost his head for a second. Come back, and take over."

Hurley turned, grinning. "Bring me all the hand guns." And once they were back at the wagon, he said, "Saul, they didn't even look to see if I was a-bluffing. Show 'em!"

The tank and barrel were dry.

By the time Hurley reached the promised spring, his passengers had learned a few things about thirst.

Toward the end of the day's drive up the ravine, they came to another spring, small but sweet. On the cliffs were marked figures that looked like a schoolboy's attempt at drawing men and animals. Epstein studied these and turned and eyed Hurley. Since they stood well apart from the others, he risked a single word: "Indians."

Hurley nodded. Both scanned the cliffs and the bare suggestion of trail which snaked along toward the rim-rock.

Hurley announced, without any mention of Indian sign, "We're shoving on as long as we can see. Drink up, and we'll make for the open. We have no time to lose." Ballard was becoming more and more uneasy, which was odd, since he had not noticed the drawings on the cliff. He had been too busy squinting at the upper slopes of the mountains. Epstein baited him by getting his binoculars and saying, "Here, have a good look."

Ballard snatched at the glasses. He muttered something about the kinds of ore indicated by the bands of green which streaked the slopes.

* * * *

Well out on the mesa. Hurley pulled up to make camp. He said, "Just to be sociable, everybody gets his shooting iron. Whoever craves to drive back is welcome. Saul and I can hoof it from here to Panamint. We've answered the question whether wagons can get through with freight. Saul—get out some of that whiskey Lucky sent with us—we'll have a drink to good fellowship."

Before dusk closed in, Epstein picked a spot, somewhat apart from camp, close enough for him to be handy, yet not in the middle of things. Issuing guns and whiskey had been a taunt and he feared Hurley was pushing his luck too far.

After supper, Hurley and Epstein decided to stand watch, each taking a four hour trick.

"Saul, which'll you have?"

"I'll take the second. What do I watch out for—passengers or Indians? You've been rubbing it in on Ballard. If you are looking for a showdown, you will win a gun fight but lose the girl."

"Mmm...you're right. What do you make of Garlock?"

Epstein shrugged. "What does Emily say about him?"

"He is some kind of engineer, studying irrigation and reclaiming land for sodbusters."

"I'm moving my cart over by those rocks, so I can watch the camp and the mules, too," Epstein said sagely. "The way things are, I'll need four eyes to see in all directions at once."

* * * *

When voices awakened Epstein, the moon was spreading its glow across the mesa. He saw Emily, blanket about her shoulders, going with Hurley toward a small outcropping.

Emily was saying, "Ben, do quit trying to get my mind off the track! What more is there to what you were going to say?"

314

Hurley drew a deep breath. "Maybe Lucky told you the truth when he said he was strictly on the level, staking Wiley to a case of whiskey to sell in Panamint. Maybe he didn't aim to undermine me the way it looks he did. But look at it all—everything!

"I once heard a fellow say every man, woman, and child has an angel tagging along, watching him. Well, it's been as if some critter with wings big enough to cast a shadow over half of creation has been riding herd on the whole pack and passel of us."

"All of us?"

"Sure! Look back at all the freak things. Saul running into me in town, and being able to give me a lift when lacking Wiley. And you three, wandering around half loco from thirst, finding my camp which wouldn't've been there at that time, excepting Lucky had staked Wiley to whiskey. That's how it came to me, that night, to give the mules every drop of water."

"Condemning us to this trip!"

"No! But I'm facing judgment with the rest of you. Couldn't I've shot it out with him 'afore now?"

"You couldn't force a fight with a man you've taken into your camp. Can't you understand—this ring is not an engagement ring. He didn't give it to me, it's family jewelry. And where else'd I keep a ring but on my finger? I know you think Lucky was just too lucky, selling out of that bank when he did—but you'd've done the same, if you'd had a sudden opening in a good land investment. But you suspect him as though he'd made the bank crash!"

"Honey, that's why I stick to the one thing that does show up clear—this here is a desert judgment to answer things. If I knew he'd been fixing and planning to sink me, I'd have shot it out."

Emily, despite herself, was impressed, yet she said, "You've not accounted for Jubal Garlock. Your dark angel, your desert angel must've had some reason for putting him into this!"

He shrugged off the hollow-hearted mockery, knowing why she offered it. "Betwixt here and Panamint, that'll be answered."

She bounced to her feet. Then Ballard broke in on the two. Epstein knew he had to do something quickly. He moved, cat-quick, and silently.

For such close range, the shooting light was perfect. Ballard made his move.

There was a hiss, a blast, a cry of pain. "Don't shoot!" Epstein shouted, but only after his whip had paralyzed Ballard's gun hand and disarmed him. Then Hurley pounced and clouted him, dropping him in his tracks. Emily cried out, as though there had been an exchange of shots.

The whine of the wind, combined with the dry rustle of sand blown against his sheltering rock made a curtain of sound which might have soaked up the less regular noises of the night, had Epstein not been so thoroughly at home in the desert. Presently, a mule snorted, making a sound which put Epstein more on edge. After some moments, he noted motion in the solid shadow. There was a dim glint of metal at a mule's forefeet. Some one was cutting the hobbles. Epstein was certain only of one thing—an Indian was at work.

Epstein drew his gun. Then the show opened as though at a signal, before Epstein fired his first shot. From his right a flight of blazing arrows thudded into the side of the wagon. Simultaneously, arrows with flaming heads raked the browsing mules.

Epstein's gun roared. The prowler jerked upright, then fell, kicking and clawing. The mules with fiery arrows sticking in their hides stampeded. Then the raiders turned on Epstein.

Several had muskets. Epstein's sheltering buttress of rock stopped a dozen arrows and several bullets. He let out a yell, and lurched into full view, to lie there, exposed.

* * * *

Seeing Epstein apparently finished, the Indians checked their rush. One said in paleface English, "Watch out for the other one."

His advice came too late. From beneath the wagon came the whack of a Winchester. The marauders scattered. The muzzle loader boomed again. Epstein, popping up from an unexpected quarter, had drawn the attention of the raiders long enough to give Hurley and the others a chance to gather their wits and fight back.

The wagon sides, tinder dry, began to burn from blazing arrows. Jubal Garlock, who was sleeping on the cargo, grabbed a blanket to swing down at the flames.

"Keep down, Jubal!" Ballard shouted, and Hurley called, "I'll slosh it with water! Keep down!"

Taking heart, the raiders made a rush. Emily screamed a warning. Epstein saw his chance to come into action. He took the enemy from the rear, now that they were bunched up and silhouetted by the blaze they had started. When his gun was empty, the show had ended: the survivors raced after the animals they had stampeded.

Once the fire was out, Epstein learned that while Hurley and Ballard had suffered only scratches, Garlock had been nailed with an arrow, and drilled by a bullet.

Once they got Garlock down from the wagon, Hurley demanded, "Saul, you can doctor a fellow. Get busy!"

"For bullets, I can't probe. But that arrow is so near through that if I drive it on, while he is unconscious, and cut off the head, I can pull the shaft out."

As Epstein set to work by the light of the lantern, Ballard demanded, "Let's round up enough mules to pull the wagon without cargo."

"Keep your shirt on, Lucky! Mules are as good eating meat as anything else, and them Injuns'd fight to the last man to keep 'em!"

Epstein, meanwhile, lost little time. He had the arrowhead cut off and the shaft withdrawn before Jubal Garlock regained consciousness. Then he said, "I have some laudanum for cholera medicine. It will keep him resting easy."

No one had thought of getting a look at any of the fallen raiders. As far as Epstein knew, he was the only one who had heard the use of English. He paused when he came to those that had dropped when he had caught them from the rear and it was not until he came to his cart that he found the one who had crawled to the shelter of the outcropping. He had been winged. And that man was white.

Pistol drawn, Epstein knelt beside him and took the renegade's gun. "Who are you?" he asked. "Why do you run with Indians? I've seen you in Poplar Junction. Or maybe in Silver Bend. Who set you on this job with Indians?"

The man cursed. Epstein cocked his pistol. "Two things I can do. First, what a man deserves for running with Indians, I can fix it for you. Or I can give you something for the pain. And put some rocks on you when you are done so the coyotes won't scatter your bones." He hefted the big S&W, and resumed, "Not with a bullet. Just with a good pistol whipping—"

"Ballard, the dirty son! He said—only two—only two—" The man choked and went limp. The face relaxed.

Epstein shrugged. "So? I scared him to death. He don't need a pain killer."

Now Epstein knew why Ballard had been afraid: having sent a renegade to get Indians to ambush Hurley, the man naturally had shrunk from going into the trap. His proposal to trail the mule-stealers suggested he hoped to deal with his accomplices, and get back enough animals to get him out of his own snare.

When Epstein rejoined the others, he was wondering about Garlock's black bag; but they were wrangling about the best way out of their predicament. Hurley was saying, "The further we'd chase those varmints up into the piñons, the more advantage they'd have on us. And getting Garlock to Panamint comes first. This poker-faced jigger from nowhere got shot and riddled, fighting in the open, whilst the rest of us scrunched down behind cover. So we're hoofing, and toting him in Saul's wagon, to give him his chance."

Epstein gave Emily the bottle of laudanum. "He will soon be conscious. Give him a spoonful, no more."

Then Epstein got Garlock's keys and hunted for the satchel. The shifting of the cargo had locked it among the boxes, so he could not release it except after prying with a pick-axe handle. He opened the bag, and when he saw the sheaves of currency and Government bonds, he said to himself, "No wonder he fought the fire to keep this from burning when he couldn't get it out."

After locking the bag, he got down the shadowed side of the wagon. The water tank had been bullet-riddled. The barrel had been nearly emptied to fight the fire. But both canteens were full.

Hurley said, "With nothing but water and a bit of grub to tote, I can move twice as fast as when we're shoving the cart. Let me hoof it to Panamint, and hire one of those carry-alls with fast horses. You can wait here, if water holds out, or you can head south. If I can gain no more'n a day, it's worth the gamble.

Garlock drew the Injuns' fire and sort of saved our hides, and I owe him any chance I can win for him by gaining time."

He stuffed his pockets with jerked beef and slung a canteen from his shoulder. "Head due south," he repeated. "You'll cut the wagon track from Bakersfield or else I'll be meeting you with fast-stepping horses."

Toward evening, Garlock began muttering and mumbling.

"Saul, hadn't you better give him some more laudanum?" Ballard asked.

"If it gets on your nerves hearing him, get away and I'll sit out your turn."

"No, no, that's not it!"

Whereupon Epstein went to grab dead mesquite for the fire. When he had stacked up a heap, he let Emily help cook supper. "What do you want?" he asked her. "Wait here, where the water is not so good, or move on, and gain a day that way? If you sleep till moonrise, can you walk another stretch, like we've already covered?"

"Walk it or drop from trying," she answered, smiling away her weariness.

"Then we move tonight. Hey, Lucky! Supper is ready."

Ballard ate as though swallowing blotting paper. Finally Epstein asked, "How is the patient?"

"Resting. But I'm afraid he'll be hard to handle when the fever gets bad. He's got something on his mind."

"Right now, you better get some rest before we move on. I'll watch."

* * * *

When the night chill bit into Epstein's bones so deeply he quit cat-napping, he knew it was time to strike out. After throwing wood on the coals, he shouted, "Coffee! Wake up!"

Emily answered. Ballard did not. The blankets he had kicked aside were a dozen yards from the small circle of camp activity. Snatching a blazing brand, Epstein went over to the undisturbed ground—and saw footprints leading north.

When Emily joined him, Epstein said, "Lucky went back the way we came."

"But why, Saul? Good lord, why?"

Instead of answering, Saul said, "Hold the light," and went to kneel beside Garlock. He raised the man's eyelids, looked at the pupils, and asked, "How much laudanum did you give him?"

"Saul, you know I didn't give him any."

"Somebody did. The pupils of the eyes—they are like pin points, see? And the pale lips."

"Do you suppose Lucky made a mistake, and then realized what he'd done, and then got scared?"

"If you made an honest mistake, would you run from Saul Epstein?"

"Oh, this is crazy, crazy, crazy! We can't go off and leave Lucky, so we'll have to wait now."

"Maybe that is why he went away, just to make us wait," Epstein said. "You go back to sleep. But first, let me show you this man's watch. It is interesting. I looked at it some time ago. How do you read the initials on the case?"

"Why, J. G., of course—no, J. C. Maybe it's an heirloom."

"Let me open the back and show you. Here, see the engraving inside."

She read, "From the Directors of the First National Bank of Independence. Kansas, to Joash Carson, June 15, 1848-June 15, 1873. Well Done, Thou Good and Faithful Servant."

Epstein said, "Now, less than a year after he finished being a good and faithful teller or cashier he shows up in Nevada being an engineer. Is he making some kind of deal with Lucky?"

"I don't know. But if they did have any plans, I think Lucky ought to be on the look-out for crooked work."

"So? Now watch this." He reached inside his shirt and brought out a bundle wrapped in a red bandanna. Opening it, he displayed high denomination currency, United States bonds and other negotiable securities. "Count this. You are a witness that this is how much he had."

With trembling hands, she counted the gold certificates, and the bonds. She exclaimed, "There's over $200,000 here!"

"Keep it until we meet the law. You fix it up inside your dress, so it don't make bulges. Nobody must know, so there won't be trouble between Lucky and Ben. Don't tell anybody you've got it. No matter what happens."

* * * *

Shortly after dawn, Ballard stumbled into camp. He had Garlock's satchel. He asked, "How's Jubal? He muttered so much about his bag, I was afraid he'd get up while we were dozing and start back for it."

"That makes you a Good Samaritan," Epstein said. "But now we can't move on—not before you have rested." A few hours of rest, then Epstein aroused him, saying, "Time to shove."

They plodded through the blinding glare. Epstein would not halt until at last Emily protested, "Saul, Lucky is ready to drop."

They stopped. Epstein bent over Garlock.

"This man, whoever he was, has taken a shortcut. Pick up rocks, while I dig."

When he had dug a shallow trench, he took Garlock's watch, purse, keys and pistol, putting them in a compartment of his tool chest. After letting Garlock down into the trench and filling the grave, he reached for the pushbar, and they tramped on. Ballard cursed him. Epstein said, "Walking back was foolish. What good was a satchel to a dying man?"

After three more cruel hours, Emily clung to him. "Saul, I can't go another step."

Epstein picked her up bodily, and set her into the cart. "Then ride. And have a drink. The last, until I find water."

Ballard jerked along like a mechanical toy. When they got to a fringe of ironwood trees, he sprawled face down in the shade.

There was water. Epstein drew some from the pool.

* * * *

Later, while Ballard still lay in an exhaustion which made him seem lifeless, Hurley drove up with a carryall.

"Oh, Ben!" Emily cried, kissing him hungrily.

Ballard seemed half numbed by the fierce punishment. His eyes, however, were unnaturally bright. When he aroused himself, his words and gestures were jerky. Hurley listened to an account of what had happened and then asked, "Saul, what was that name in Garlock's watch?"

"Read it," Epstein answered, after getting the watch and the other things. "A bank man all his life until last year, and all of a sudden he becomes an engineer." As he spoke, Epstein dipped into the satchel and brought out a packet of hundred dollar gold certificates. "No wonder he worried. Here's more!"

Ballard came to life. "He said he was Garlock," the watch says he used to be Carson. What'll we do with his property?"

"We turn this over to the law," Epstein remarked.

"That's crazy!" Ballard flared. "Money is money, and nobody knows who this man really was. Ben, you and Emily were hurt badly in the bank crash. We can call this salvage. You're crazy not to do it! What the devil has Epstein got to say?"

Epstein gave him a biting glance. "Maybe the desert plays this cockeyed trick to give you back what, you lost."

"Saul," Hurley persisted, "you're entitled to a cut."

Epstein's eyes became more emphatic. "I want none. For you folks, maybe it is different. Anyway, I don't know the law, and I won't take chances."

"I'm not looking a gift hoss in the mouth!" Hurley declared "Dip in, Lucky!"

Ballard dug eagerly into the bag. His face changed when, clawing again, he came up with socks, a shirt, a necktie. Hurley exclaimed, as he eyed the pile, "Something like thirty thousand bucks! Nice divvy."

"Thirty thousand?" Ballard echoed, dazedly. "Nice divvy?"

Epstein said, "Ben, I'll tend to the horses. You sit down. You're winning again. Enjoy it."

He had the horses unhitched, and was busy grooming the long-legged sorrel when Ballard came up. The animals were some yards from camp, and Hurley and Emily were busy beside the fire.

Ballard said, in an ominous voice, "You're foxy, Epstein, pretending you wouldn't touch that money, and spouting that stuff about surrendering it to the law. You took most of it. Make a good story."

"What do you mean?" Epstein countered. "You walked to get the satchel. I didn't. If something is missing, you took it. Anyhow. How do you know some-

320

thing is missing?"

"He told me how much he had. There's $200,000 missing."

"I don't have it. And let me tell you something. I said, don't give him more laudanum, and you gave it. His eyes showed it. Hey, Ben! He says—"

But Hurley was too much interested in Emily to hear; and Ballard cut in, "You lying son, what's that you dropped over there?"

He gestured toward something on the ground, and went for his gun. Emily cried out. Ben, belatedly aroused, shouted, "Hold it!"

Guns blazed, one-two. Hurley, on his feet, lowered his weapon. Epstein looked through swirling smoke at Ballard, who was down and twitching.

A PAIR OF QUEENS

Originally appeared in *Romantic Western*, November 1938.

"You dirty coyote, that deck's stacked!" The snarling stranger went for his gun as he jerked to his feet, upsetting the table.

Dexter Blaine remained seated. He did not even drop his cards. One hand snaked to his spring clip holster, and the blast of his .45 shook the Bull's Head Saloon. The stranger stood there, gaping. It took him an instant to realize that a bullet had hammered the cylinder of his half drawn gun. The shock had paralyzed his hand.

Blaine wore a black frock coat, a figured silk vest, and a fine white shirt; but his thin face was tanned, and so were his hands. Nothing about him was soft but his voice. He drawled, "Stranger, you oughtn't to risk more than you can afford to lose."

Baldheaded Tim Higgins, owner of the saloon, caught the dazed fellow by the arm. "Shake a hock, afore I bust yuh with a bung starter. This yere's the only honest game in Tecolote."

New players came to match the cool Texan. Inwardly, Blaine was troubled. Ever since Smoke Radford had tried to induce him to run a crooked game—a straight one being unfair competition—out of town gun slicks had been coming in to accuse Blaine of cheating.

* * * *

Later, Blaine tapped at the back door of the Hoot Owl Restaurant. The girl who answered was fresh and lovely. Her copper gold hair was haloed by the lamplight whose warm glow picked out alluring reflections in the blue silken robe that outlined her lithe figure.

"You're early, Dex," Eve Hollis murmured in his ear as he held her close.

A straight flush could not change Blaine's expression, but Eve's exquisite curves made his heart hammer. And as he followed her to the rooms above the little restaurant she operated, his blood was warmed by her very nearness.

But when Blaine seated himself beside her on the cushion decorated divan, Eve evaded his ardent kiss. She protested, "You've been catching me half asleep. So this time I sat up waiting for you."

"Honey, I might of knowed you couldn't like me with your eyes open!" And Blaine caught her again in his arms.

Eve wriggled from his embrace. "Don't," she protested. "I have to tell you something. You've got to quit gambling. I heard about that fracas tonight. Oh, I know you're slick with a gun, but your luck's bound to change. Being a gambler's wife is bad enough, but a gambler's widow is worse."

"Why—what ya'll mean, honey?"

"I won't ever marry you, unless you quit." Her lips trembled, but her pert little chin was held high and firmly.

"Dawgone it all!" he protested, "I run an honest game. The highest court in Texas declared poker is a science, not a gamble."

"If you're so scientific," she countered, "I'll sell the Hoot Owl, and take your stake and mine and we'll raise cattle."

He considered for a long moment.

Eve clasped her hands behind her head and leaned back among the cushions. "Dex," she murmured, "we can be so happy, if you'll just quit."

"I'll think on it," he compromised; the first time he had made any concessions.

"Will you? *Really?*" Eager arms reached toward him, and splendor brightened in her long lashed eyes. Then, when that sultry kiss finally let Eve regain her breath, she gasped, "Silly! Don't be so impulsive and take so much for granted."

When Blaine slipped out of the back door of the restaurant into the moonlight, he still had not made any promises. Eve, however, had nearly converted him. He was still a little lightheaded from her kisses.

With an effort, he composed himself. Premonition flashed through his mind: "Could have been hit on the head with an ox yoke, and never had sense enough to duck."

And that was why he moved by instinct, a moment later. Reason would have failed him, and so would natural speed. There was a faint, metallic crunch, as of a rusty tin can getting the brunt of someone's shifting weight.

Blaine hurled himself for the rain water barrel that loomed up in the shadow of a 'dobe. Spurts of flame reached out from the spaces between fence pickets that lined the other side of the narrow street. Lead flattened against the thick wall.

His movement was so nearly simultaneous with the murderous fire that a familiar voice yelled, "Got the son of a—!"

"*Cuidado!*" warned his companion. "*Par amor de—*"

The Mexican was going to say, "For the love of God." But Satan or the saints heard the last word; certainly no man. Blaine's gun was in action. Though fence pickets enabled a man to see without being seen, they were extremely treacherous shelter.

Tin cans rattled under the convulsive drumming of a dying man's feet. The loud voiced man groaned. And Tecolote, aroused, began to shout and stir.

Blaine called from his shelter, "Stranger, will yo'all live and talk, or do I come a-shootin'?"

"All right, I give up." Heavy metal clattered among the rubbish. "Don't shoot."

Blaine could half discern the huddled figure behind the pickets. He was certain that from the fellow's posture he could not direct a second gun, even if he had one. That groan was not faked. The man was hard hit without a doubt.

In a moment, he had shouldered his way through the lead riddled pickets and was beside the two dry gulchers. One was dead. The one who still lived was the stranger who had accused Blaine of cheating. The gambler said, "Pardner, y'all played the fool twice in one night. But what have you got agin me?"

The hard case glared, slobbered bloody foam. Blaine went on, "Someone sent you. And that man's going to disown you, you pore fool."

There was no resentment in his voice. Blaine felt none. He was a fatalist; a gambler, that is. The stranger sensed this.

The street was a confusion of yelled queries and answers, now that the men of Tecolote had found and donned their boots. The participants of the three cornered battle were out of sight, and the noise masked their voices. "Speak up, pardner," Blaine persuaded. "Who sent you? Tell me, or…but blast it, I could of killed you already. I'd rather not."

That did it. The stranger began, "That dirty—skunk—told me—"

He choked, slumped back, completely finished.

Blaine called to the men in the street, but when help came, it was only to carry two dead men from the city clump. He explained, "I reckon these gents had a grudge." Since he had no proof, he did not mention Radford.

"Reckon," said the marshal, who had heard of the earlier encounter.

Then Blaine approached the heavy jawed man who had unerringly led the investigation to the vacant lot. He was the only one, beside Blaine, whose shirt was tucked inside his trouser waistband. The gambler smiled amiably and said, "Evenin', Mistah Radford. Was y'all a-settin' up late, or was you expectin' trouble, right in this heah corner of town?"

Smoke Radford wore a pair of guns, but he kept his hands away scrupulously from them. He chewed his trailing mustache for a moment, then said, very loudly, "Shucks, Blaine! I allus set up late, readin'."

"The straight game at the Bull's Haid," Blaine went on, "stays straight and keeps on furnishing unfair competition, Mistah Radford." Radford cleared his throat, then turned abruptly and went his way.

No man had ever run Blaine out of town, and no man would. But it would be tough, telling Eve that he could no longer consider quitting the gambling house in Tecolote. So Blaine evaded her eager queries each night, and kissed Eve to rapturous silence. But that would not last long. She'd surely corner him eventually.

* * * *

The game went on. Tough customers religiously avoided the Bull's Head. But one of the dance-hall girls began playing up to Blaine. Milly Graves was a redhead modeled after the Goddess of Liberty, except that her dress was less dignified and more revealing.

She was almost as tall as Blaine; her figure was intriguing, her ripe curves were enough to tempt any man. And whenever she had a chance, during a lull in the game, she leaned against Blaine, giving him a warm pressure and a gust of heady perfume.

One evening she stopped him in the alcove at the head of the stairs, snuggled close and invited, "Come on and have a drink, Dex."

He shook his head. "Sorry, M'am. Agin' the rules, trifling with house employees. I'm powerful sorry, Milly."

"Oh…silly!" She lifted full red lips to tempt him. "I just meant, have a drink while I'm changing. And meet me at my house."

Blaine smiled, more amiably than before. "Sounds mighty tempting, Milly. I'm sho' flattered." One arm went around her waist.

She noted the sharp glance that dropped to the fair skin below her throat. She leaned back from the waist, as Blaine raised his left hand, slowly. Milly expected a caress, a pat on the cheek at the very least, but she was mistaken.

One deft move plucked at the edge of her bodice. There was nothing caressing about the gesture that followed. Blaine extracted a lengthwise fold of new bills. As he flashed them before her eyes, he said, "Either you been picking someone's pockets, or Smoke Radford paid you to entertain me, with my guns out of reach."

He flipped the bills into her face, and went back to his table. She choked, then screamed at the half dozen cowpokes who were chortling and staring. "You low-down skunks, mind your own business!"

Blaine began avoiding Eve. Once he had shot it out with Smoke Radford, he could leave Tecolote; not before then. But despite the outward calm of his face, Blaine was shaken inside. His uncanny judgment of the cards began to waver. He lost oftener than he used to. And still he went on playing.

* * * *

Then Blaine's luck changed. A big, smooth-faced cattle man came all the way to Tecolote instead of getting his supplies at the town nearest his spread, the Rafter JG. Jason Gale was young, noisy, confident, and a shade drunker than a poker player should he.

His red face beamed like a harvest moon. Blaine said, "Pardner, this heah's a free country, but supposin' y'all come back tomorrow night."

Gale chuckled. "Deal 'em out! Yuh been losin' plenty, yuh'll lose tuh me ef I follows up!"

Blaine did not like it. Eve's lectures had been getting under his skin. Despite his stout defense of poker as a science, his philosophy had been shaken, just a bit. This yokel, not long from Ohio, had no business gambling recklessly.

Still, Blaine could not turn business away from the house. He played, and Gale foolishly backed hands he should have dropped.

Finally the ruddy face became drawn. Then it became gray. Gale was now painfully sober. His blue eyes were haggard, and sweat cropped out, trickled down his cheeks. He mopped his forehead with his bandanna, and grimly hunched forward in his chair.

At last he produced another poke, poured it on the table, and settled down to recoup. Poker, however, is very much a science. Hours later, the big fellow tottered out into the chilly gloom. Blaine shook his head.

"Poor devil, he couldn't afford that loss."

"Reckon not," admitted a bystander. "Reckon not. He was a-heading fer the county seat tuh make a payment on his notes er mo'gage, er suthin." When he saw Blaine's jaw tighten, he hastily added, "Shucks, Dex! No offense, a-tall. Wan't yore fault, Gale bein' a fool kid! It'll larn him suthin', the young booby owl!"

Blaine slowly rose. "Gents, the game's closing for tonight. Meet me tomorrow, and we'll court lady luck for a spell."

But Blame went to his own rooms. He realized more and more that Eve was right. Only, she would not understand; if he told her he had to stick until Smoke Radford came out in the open, she would be all the more insistent on his quitting.

* * * *

The next night, Blaine did not go to his table.

Instead, he waited for Eve to close her restaurant. They were sitting in the room overlooking the main street, and the silence became more awkward every moment.

"Dex," she finally said, "what's the matter?" Her eyes were wide and blue. In the moonlight, she was a sweet length of white and gold. Her legs gleamed, long and lovely and silken, and the curve of breast and throat were glorified in the night's glamour.

Blaine drew her to him and said, "Honey, I been thinking a lot."

"About Smoke Radford?"

He nodded. "I cain't let him run me out of Tecolote!"

Her lips tightened. She sighed. "Well… I understand that, darling. But isn't principle above pride?"

"Blast it!" he flared, "that's what this is. Principle. You women jest cain't understand matters of principle, a-tall."

Eve forced a laugh, but the smile that lingered was real. "Dex, I love you an awful lot. You know that. Couldn't you please me in just this one thing?"

She might have won, had it not been for the sudden shouting in the street, the clattering of hoofs. Blaine stepped to the window. Eve, right on his heels, snuggled close beside him when she reached the window sill.

A man lay face down, and crosswise in the saddle. The sheriff and a deputy rode with the dead. They stopped in the full glare of the lights that blazed from the saloon just across the street. The yellow glow brought out every stark detail when they dragged the corpse from the horse. First the coroner, then Boot Hill...

The rumble of voices gave enough clear bits to tell Blaine the story. The bullet riddled man was Jason Gale. To recoup his losses, he had set out to rob a stage coach.

Worst of all, Eve understood. Blaine's exclamation, coupled with the gossip she had heard as she fed the town at her lunch counter, made only a few words necessary. Her voice was bitter. "Poker's a science! Dex, you can't kiss me silly any more, and make me forget like you've been doing."

"Why—honey—now, listen," he protested.

She evaded his arms. Head flung back, she went on, "Being a gambler's wife or widow, no! Quit me, or quit gambling."

"Blast it! Listen, I didn't cheat Gale. It was a fair game. By God, Smoke Radford can't run me out of town."

"So your pride means more than I do?"

He tried to wheedle her into reason. For a moment, she relaxed in his arms; her eyes misted, and her breath came in quick, short gasps as he drew her closer, kissed her into submission. Then she cried out as though in physical pain and said, "Don't touch me—don't—I won't—*you* murdered that poor fellow! *Don't!*"

Her stinging slap made him blink. She turned and ran into the adjoining room, and flung herself face down on the bed. Dimly, he could see the silken sheen of her lovely legs. But Blaine knew that he had lost out. He slowly went down to the street.

* * * *

Blaine knew his cards better than he did women. It never occurred to him that Eve was hurt because he placed her second to his pride. He staved well away from the restaurant, convinced that she despised him.

Radford went about with a contented expression on his blue-jowled face. Blaine, despite his well founded suspicions, could not force a quarrel; not after Eve had called him a slayer by proxy, and a card slick who won tolerance by his gun skill. Though they were estranged, the lean Texan still wanted to avoid justifying her charges.

Smoke Radford had his plans; they formed when he saw that Blaine and Eve were avoiding each other. Though their quarrel had been private, everyone in Tecolote knew that she had from the beginning wanted him to stop gambling.

Eating his own smoke was giving Blaine spiritual indigestion. He never drank while at work, but he began taking a bottle home with him. The rumor spread, and Radford liked it. He enjoyed it even more when after a separation of two weeks, Eve and Blaine accidentally met at the post office steps.

Either could have spoken, but neither did. Eve went home with her head high and chin up, but once in her room, she did some private weeping. Blaine just sent for an extra bottle that night. If that's the way she felt, to the devil with her.

And then fate brought a splendid creature to the Bull's Head Saloon; though none of the boys used any such high-faluting terms. They said, "Jeehosaphat! That gal's built like a brick silo, an' purty as a picture."

Both counts were true, and Viola's shoes were danced to tatters her first night as a dancehall girl. Her red smile and sultry eyes and blue black hair marked her among the bleached blondes. Instead of a gown that was low on top and high at the bottom, she featured coy concealment.

Her black lace dress gave tantalizing hints of the beauty beneath. Her dainty feet and fine ankles slyly suggested the sleekness of legs hidden from view, except when her skirt clung to their curves for an indiscreet moment. But most alluring of all was that promise of fire smoldering behind a dark screen.

"Where she come from?" wondered Blaine, turning from his vacant table.

"You orta know better," reproved Tim Higgins. "Did I ever axe you any impertinent questions when you come to Tecolote?"

Blaine nodded. "Uh-uh. Seein's believin', I reckon."

Tim winked, jabbed a stubby forefinger into the gambler's ribs. "Shucks, Dex! Yo're the only gentlemun in town, and she's a lady. Refineder an' all get out. Don't tell me you cain't dance!"

Baldheaded Tim felt that getting a new interest in life would keep Blaine from living on a diet of Bull Durham and Old Crow.

The gambler smiled bleakly. He understood the old fellow's solicitude. There might be something in that idea, too. Those sleek hips and that proud, firm carriage didn't make a lady; but the way she refrained from flaunting her curves did. Viola, he sensed, was another of those women whom fortune had hammered down in the world, yet without shaking her quality.

"You mustn't neglect your cards, Mr. Blaine," she smiled, slipping into his arms when he asked her to dance.

Blaine tossed a gold piece to the keys of old Pablo's piano. The cowpokes yelled to the fiddler, "Twist 'er tail, 'Doro!"

"Drown me in a rain bar'l ef that lanky galoot cain't dance!" Tim Higgins rubbed his hands together. "That's jest the female critter to straighten him out!"

Blaine had the same idea. An armful of Viola told him that she had none of the dancehall girl's tawdry tricks. Once, sitting close to a light, he noted a faint, unmistakable depression that encircled a finger. She had recently removed a wedding ring.

* * * *

But that was no subject for queries. Later, in Viola's room at the Antler Hotel, there were too many other things to ask her. The kind of things one can ask without being inquisitive…

"Why… I hardly know you," she said. Though the reproof was whimsical, rather than indignant. "Just because I dance at the Bull's Head—"

Viola no longer wore the baffling black gown, but her chiffon robe was scarcely less a riddle.

And the long, splendid line from hip to knee brought Blaine's heart to his throat. Even if not to blot Eve from his memory, he would admire this gorgeous creature who smiled at him from the lounge.

He evaded her futile white hands, and for a moment, she was pressed against him, warm and throbbing. That instant of abandon ended in a lithe move that left his arms empty. All he had won was the taste of rouge, a momentary glimpsed beauty exposed when her evading motion parted her chiffon gown for an instant.

"Please don't—" She was soft voiced and serious until her smile blossomed in a promise, and she added, "I feel so strange in Tecolote. Later—"

She was a lady, so he let it go at that. If "later" didn't mean "soon," he might as well go back to school and start all over.

* * * *

That night, Blaine ignored his bottle.

Regardless of the outcome, he had at least burned his bridges behind him. Only the hotel clerk had seen him enter and leave, but all Tecolote would know by noon. Since there could now be no reconciliation with Eve, Blaine was no longer wavering. Nothing could induce him to back down from his principles. He was his own man again.

The next day, Eve had taken down the "For Sale" sign that had decorated the window of her restaurant. But that meant nothing to Blaine, other than that the jig was up. Which he knew without any signs!

A week passed. Each night Viola evaded him. He began to slip out of the back door of the hotel, to avoid letting the town know how early he left her. But the pursuit stimulated him, and his game improved.

One night he found her with her face buried in a pillow. Her bare shoulders shook convulsively. He knelt beside her and said, "Honey, what's wrong? Someone get familiar—was it that polecat, Smoke Radford?"

Viola sat up, raised somber eyes, blinked away her tears, and cried, "Oh, it's a crazy world—crazy—*crazy*!"

"Why—sweetheart—" He didn't know what to make of that, so he supported her with one arm, stroked her sleek, trailing hair. "You look sad-like."

"My Lord—" She checked herself, then fiercely caught his arms and demanded, "Kiss me, Dex—kiss me from now to sunrise—then leave town!"

Women were all more or less crazy, he reckoned. First Eve, now Viola, teched in the head, babbling about leaving town. Might as well kiss her for a spell. But Blaine lost the initiative. Viola was clinging to him in a possessing frenzy that inflamed him too much for any thought as to its reasons, or why she made him promise to leave Tecolote the following day. Naturally, he promised her anything. He was a bit too dizzy not to.

* * * *

When they met again, at the Bull's Head, they maintained the pose of formal courtesy, suitable between a gentleman gambler and a prima donna whom the cowpunchers did not paw. If she was surprised at seeing him still in Tecolote, she gave no sign; though he wondered at the strange light in her eyes.

"Po' gal's a widow," he reasoned. "Broodin' over someone. Lonesome, and made fo' love, and last night just didn't somehow seem *exactly* right…"

That piece of feminine psychology worked out, Blaine dismissed the eyes that had become windows into hell. The cards whirred and hissed in his supple grip, and he invited, "Gents, fickle lady luck is honing to be played with tonight, and there's no limit except your stack!"

Once, Blaine felt a probing stare. He turned, just in time to see Viola regarding him. The motion of her swiftly dropping hand told him that it had just left her bosom. This night's gown was cut lower.

He had an uncomfortable moment as he deliberately turned his back and resumed the deal. Maybe she *was* a mite teched in the head. Maybe that was a derringer concealed in her bodice. But Blaine could not be a gambler without being a fatalist, so he went on helping four poker players court the fickle goddess.

One of them was a stranger with a well notched gun. He had a mean eye, a chronic sneer, whether winning or losing. And the losses predominated. Blaine felt it coming. The name, Presidio Jack, was vaguely familiar; so also was that lantern jaw and jutting nose.

Blaine had seen his picture. Probably the thousand dollar reward offered in the Big Bend country had been withdrawn. Nobody in New Mexico would risk trying to collect it. That was an old story, but it was worth remembering that Presidio Jack was left handed.

Just a mental note. It was Blaine's business to know his customers. That was why the highest court in Texas had declared poker a science.

Jack scarcely picked up his cards when he slammed them down, growling, "Marked, by God! No—wonder I'm losing!"

His right hand stayed with the cards. He did not rise. But his left hand had started with his right. He was betting on an early draw. And he was quick, deadly swift.

His only mistake was in not knowing that a good gambler studies his customers. Blaine slumped to the planks, just as lead and flame swept over the table. The other three players fell backward over their chairs.

Blaine fired from the floor. The shot kicked Presidio Jack's stomach into his lungs. He piled over in a heap, lay there with his left hand convulsively groping for the gun he had dropped.

He found it. Girls and men, thinking him dead, were crowded about the table. They did not realize how dying fury drove him; that someone would die with him. But Blaine knew his customer. On his feet now, his eyes flickered right and left; he saw women's soft curves that a wild slug would riddle.

He saw, scarcely understanding, a white hand flicker toward the table. That woman was in danger. Blaine had no choice. He fired again, and Presidio Jack's forehead became a horrible blot. His gun dropped, uncocked. Blaine was sick. Those curious fools crowding about him did not even now realize how death had narrowly missed one or more of them.

The Bull's Head was an uproar. Smoke Radford had come in from the street, but he did not join in the incredulous cry, "Must of been crazy, sayin' them cards is marked."

Radford boomed, "Try lookin' at the cards. That'll tell."

That was fair. Someone snatched the deck from the table. A dozen men squinted at the pasteboards. Tim Higgins, face white with wrath, announced, "By gravey—they is marked!"

Blaine could scarcely understand. Both guns were out; the only logic to answer the muttering that swelled across the hall. Radford was grinning. The marshal had appeared. He said, "Dex, I ain't sayin' yuh doctored them cards, but thar they be. Slick work, too."

"Are yo'all referring to Presidio Jack's heart failure?"

The marshal shrugged. "Even with slick cards, self-defense is self-defense, I reckon."

Tim Higgins cut in, "Yo're givin' a honest place a bad name, Dex."

Blaine smiled bleakly. "Your next house man won't be a lily, Tim." He turned to Radford and said, "Nice work, Smoke. But I ain't leaving town. Now that the Bull's Head ain't bein' injured by my actions any more, you and me are shootin' on sight, starting sunrise.

"*Smoke?* Smokin' out folks by proxy. Dudes, old men, boys, and gents with their backs turned. Want it now, or sunrise?"

He holstered his guns, so that his enemy could get an even start. But Smoke Radford declined the invitation to draw. He said, "Yo're all het up, Blaine. I'm ignorin' hot words, but onless yuh eats 'em by sunrise, yuh better come a-shootin'."

Blaine put his gold pieces into a long buckskin pouch. He wondered where Viola was. None of the other girls had left. He shook his head, and as he went down the street, he said, "It's crazy. Why'd she put a crooked deck in place of a honest one?"

He had no fear of ambush. Smoke Radford would not dare fire from cover; not after the challenge that had been offered and accepted before witnesses. Tecolote would not stand for that.

Blaine however knew that he'd have to face trick work. He had won too often. A man's luck changed, sooner or later. Gunnery, like poker, is a science in which there are slips. A strange urge moved him toward Eve's rooms. He was fatalist enough not to be chilled at the prospect of sudden death, but before that happened, he wanted a final word with Eve. He knew now that he had never ceased loving her; that he perhaps never would.

He met her at her own back door. She started, recognized him, resolutely turned her back. He caught her shoulder and said, "Ain't what you think it is —"

"I know," she bitterly retorted. "Want to play on my sympathy! As if I didn't know you can blow Smoke Radford and all his crooks to ribbons! You—you fool! You silly conceited jackass! That girl—Viola—she's Jason Gale's widow!"

"How do you know?"

"None of your business!" she choked. "I know. Now go ahead and make love to her. You killed her stupid young husband, beating him at poker."

She slammed the door in his face. Blaine retraced his steps. Sheer wrath left Eve no chance to dissimulate. Moreover, he had to believe her. That explained Viola's strange actions; she must have planted the crooked deck, so that Presidio Jack, who by an unforeseen slip had just failed to kill Blaine with an early draw, would have had ample justification for firing without warning.

Without that marked deck, such a shot would have been murder. It all pointed to Radford, who had seen other gunslicks fail. So he had worked on Viola Gale's loyalty, set her to work seeking vengeance.

Blaine digested that, and suddenly, all Eve's influence combined to hit him a single blow. Gambling was a rotten business. He had killed three men; skunks, all of them, but nonetheless, men. His honest play had made a young numbskull's celebration end in a fatal robbery.

With a wife like Viola, no wonder Jason Gale turned to crime rather than telling her he could not meet his notes.

Only Blaine remained aloof, unwounded in body. Gambling, he now saw, was all that Eve had said. And staying to kill Smoke Radford would prove it beyond any doubt. He now felt, somehow, that he surely would kill Smoke.

"Ain't worth it. Feuds and enemies are one thing. Making a routine of it is suthin' else," he told himself.

He stalked into the Antler Hotel. The clerk's eyes widened. He said, "Mis' Viola's done left, sudden-like. She said she was fixing to go to Jason Gale's spread. Dangnation, who'd of believed she was his wife? Thought him a stranger, genrully allus going tuh B'ar Gulch fer vittles—hey, whar y'all going to, now?"

"To give her my gambling money!" Blaine was too weary to resent the direct question.

* * * *

Blaine rode through what remained of the night, and all day long he continued his ride. He made no attempt at trailing Viola. He was no tracker, but he could inquire his way to the Rafter JG.

That evening he approached the ranchhouse. He heard neither horses nor cowpunchers. The Ratter JG must have fallen flat, since Jason's death.

He entered the silent house. Viola was there, but she did not hear him until he was almost at her side. She jerked upright from the sofa. Her reddened eyes widened, and fear made her oblivious of the fact that the kimono she wore was hardly adequate for receiving visitors.

"Go ahead," she challenged. "I planted that deck to protect Presidio and I wanted him to kill you."

"I ain't aiming to hurt you, Vi," he said, seating himself beside her. "I just learned who you are." He laid the heavy pouch of gold pieces on her knee. "I ain't insulting you by paying for Jason's death. But it's all I can do. I shuffled my last deck of cards."

For a long moment their eyes clashed. Her body was frozen ivory in the failing light. Suddenly she cried out, flung her arms about him.

"I know you didn't cheat Jason. Not after doing this. Dex, darling—that evening in my room—I was falling in love with you—and hating myself for it —and for what I'd promised to do. I didn't know—will you—"

She was going to say *forgive*, but his kiss smothered the word. And her hungry mouth told him how love and vengeance had battled that night...

The moon rose, glorifying her loveliness. The glow in her dark eyes was no longer somber; but for all the sweetness of her ardent mouth, there was bitterness in Blaine's heart. Finding himself had cost him Eve's devotion. Yet the reward of pride and stubbornness was warm and throbbing in his arms...

Hoofbeats brought the lovers apart. Blaine was on his feet, pistol ready, just as the door burst open. A rifle barrel gleamed.

"Hold it!" he snapped, before he saw the woman's silhouette.

"Dex!" It was Eve, and she recoiled, seeing Viola's beauty in the patch of glow the moon cast through the window. Then she said, "It's not on her account I'm here—I don't blame you—I expect that—"

She thrust the Winchester carbine into his hands, reached into her sagging blouse, bringing out two boxes of cartridges. Before Blaine or Viola could find their voices, Eve went on, "Radford knows where you are. He heard it. Like I did. He knows that if you and Viola get together, his rotten plan'll be exposed, and he'll be run out of town. So—"

"There'll be a dozen hard cases with him," Eve panted.

Viola picked up the old .45. It was loaded. Blaine said, "Eve, I thought you was plumb through with me."

"Men are the dumbest critters! You, Viola! Light a lamp—"

"Lamp?" echoed Blaine.

"Do as I say! A dozen are against us."

Eve had arrived with no more than minutes to spare. Horses with muffled hoofs came up like ghosts. Men dismounted, many yards away, crept from shadow to shadow. The Rafter JG ranchhouse was silent, but a lamp glowed in a bedroom window.

"Thar they be!" muttered Smoke Radford. He licked his lips as he saw Viola's body silhouetted against a shade. He knelt, drew a Colt. "Ain't no use rushin' 'em. He'll be passin' by, any second."

"Better you git closter, Smoke," someone advised.

They hung back. A shot from the dark was safer than rushing Dexter Blaine. His past record made them cautious. And Radford had a private score to settle. He had promised Viola vengeance for a price, but she had fled instead of waiting...

He crept ahead. A wheelbarrow, out in the middle of the yard, was his goal. Its shadow would conceal him, if the lovers did find time to glance out the window. But he cursed between clenched teeth when he heard Viola sighing, "Oh... Dexter...*darling*—"

What followed froze him to the heart. A cold voice said, "Fire at will, Smoke. I warned you!"

Dexter Blaine was not kissing a woman to ecstasy. He was rounding the corner of the house. Radford yelled. His shot went wild. Blaine fired, just once. As Smoke Radford sprawled in a heap, a Winchester began crackling from the other corner of the house.

The ruffians fled, howling. They did not stop to think that Eve Hollis would be a very poor shot, even in daylight. The death of their chief, and Blaine's searching fire combined to send them away in panic.

A few moments later, Dexter Blaine faced the two women. He would rather have looked smoking guns in the eye. He did not know what to say. So he blurted out, "Eve, I quit gambling. And I gave Viola every cent I made at it. To —uh—to—make it really quitting."

Eve said, "I'll tell you how I knew who she was. I went to her room to claw her eyes out. And I found some letters."

The widow laughed softly. "Dexter, don't be afraid to tell me. I know where your heart is." She picked up the buckskin pouch. "You two will need that. I'm going back east."

Eve shook her head, caught Blaine's hand. "We won't need it. We're in the restaurant business. With a clean start." She watched Blaine gulp, redden now that he had time to think of the close embrace the blond girl's sudden arrival had interrupted. Eve laughed in sweet malice and went on, "We'll call it the Royal Flush! Just for old times sake, you know. Don't be silly! I'll look the other way while you kiss her goodbye."

But as Dexter Blaine rode back to Tecolote with Eve Hollis, he could not help but think that if the Hoot Owl Restaurant was going to change its name, it should be called Pair of Queens.

YOU CAN'T FIGHT A WOMAN

Originally published in *Speed Adventure Stories*, Nov. 1943.

"Slim—don't!" the red haired girl protested. Her voice was tremulous, and her eyes were misty in the moonlight. "I've got to get home before dad gets back from town. He'd kill me if he knew—"

Reluctantly, Slim Crane let Madge slip from his arms. For a moment, he watched her pat her disheveled hair into shape, and smooth out the blouse that a close embrace had pulled all awry.

"Shucks, honey," he answered, broad month twisting ruefully, "what do you low *my* old man'd do if he knew about *me*, sneaking away like this!"

Madge's sigh, and the way she laced her fingers behind her finely poised head as she leaned back against the rock that sheltered them brought pert young curves into charming relief as her blouse drew taut.

Slim watched the play of moonlight accentuate her beauty. He abstractedly ran his fingertips over his thumb, as though still trying the texture of a fine fabric. He was thinking, "Gosh...she's wearin' silk...an' she smells nicer every time..."

Madge Daley in gingham was fascinating enough to make him a traitor to every cow country tradition. As she slowly rose and smoothed out her rumpled skirt, he caught her hand. "Honey—I don't think my dad's going to have time to cut your bob-wire fences again, not fo' a spell, no-how."

A frown puckered her smooth brow. They had not until this moment mentioned the feud that forced them to meet on the sly. Then her eyes brightened. "Oh—Slim! You mean, he's getting reasonable?"

Slim Crane loved Madge enough to swallow the unintended jab. "No, dang it! There's a passel of skunks beefing our critters. Killin' 'em and hauling 'em off."

"And that," Madge said, a sly bit of malice creeping into her voice, "is even worse than a nester putting a fence about his lawful property?"

"Aw, blazes, honey!" He tried to be grim, but he simply could not, so he tried to laugh it off. "You and your pappy don't understand nothing. Look-ee here. My dad and his'n, afore him, fit the Injuns to get this yere country. They starved, froze, kilt varmints and Mexicans and brought cow critters into this corner of what used to be forsaken hell. Now a bunch of galoots in Washington pass laws, giving nesters the rights to settle down, put fences aroun' the water holes our critters need—"

"But Slim, darling." She sadly shook her head. "Your cows aren't hungry and they're not thirsty!"

"Makes no difference!" He stubbornly shook his tow head. "Fust drought that comes along, the Diamond C critters won't have a thing to drink except whar your pappy's squatted."

"He's not a squatter!" she flared. "He's a homesteader!"

"I don't give a tarnation damn!" He snatched his hat and jammed it on his head. "Between homesteaders and this new passel of varmints that's beefing our critters and selling 'em in Paso del Norte, we'll git shoved to the wall."

"Why—you—you—putting my father in the same class with beef thieves!" She slapped him, and it sounded like a pistol shot. "Thieves, are we! You listen here, Slim Crane! Your father, the pig headed old fossil, he's a thief! Tearing down a mile of barbed wire that cost dad every cent he made—"

"Made outen hogging our water hole!"

But Madge was in the saddle, galloping recklessly from the grove toward the section that Herb Daley, lawfully enough, had "proved up." Crane, just as sore, mounted his blue roan, and growled, "Gol dang my hide, she's a snake, like all them nesters! Thief, huh?"

But as he rode, he had more and more difficulty in keeping his rage white hot. He could not forget those stolen moments when Madge looked up, lashes drooping and lips half parted for a kiss; he could not forget how a runaway team had flung her into his arms, that day before he knew that she was the daughter of the first nester to come to Arroyo Rojo.

For the next few days, he tended strictly to business, scouting around the vast Diamond C spread, ready for a clash with beef thieves. The coming of the railroad to Paso Del Norte had started a boom; hundreds of pilgrims, gamblers, dance-hall women, business men and railroad contractors had poured into town, and all the newcomers needed steak—principally, it seemed, from the Diamond C herd.

Brand inspectors, supposedly, were scrutinizing each hide at the slaughter-houses, checking them against bills of sale. But the inspectors were either drunk, blind, or bribed. And old man Crane was madder than a hornet. His line riders had made no progress. Thus Slim's father was in the saddle, stalking thieves as he once had tracked down marauding Comanches.

"Way I figger it out," the old man said, pointing, "is that they're fixing to turn a trick over yonder. Judgin' from old wagon tracks, and the lay of the land, it's got to be."

"Why'n't y'all put our riders over there, then?"

Crane spat, shook his grizzled head. "Son," he said, patting the stock of "Jezebel", his buffalo gun, "when I tends to varmints, I tends to 'em. Jails ain't wuth a damn! Less company, the better. Now, you ride over that-away, up through that gulch."

Stealthily, with muffled hoofs and curb chain to silence his advance, Slim went up the gulch. The full moon cast black shadows, but in the open, the shooting would be good, if it came to that. He hoped it wouldn't. It had been bad enough when Madge's dad had just missed stopping a hatful of .45s, that day when the first fence had been destroyed.

He rather wondered why Madge had continued meeting him. She probably reckoned he'd saved her life, or something. Then, because he'd indirectly called her old man a thief, she'd gone hog wild. Women are sure as hell funny critters.

When Slim heard vague sounds some distance ahead he crept forward on foot, his Winchester ready. If he got the drop on them, a killing might be avoided. His father would not shoot unarmed men, not even thieves. The old man liked to startle them into going for a gun, which was pretty nearly always fatal—for the other fellow.

Slim wondered if his dad's skill was what it had been, thirty years ago. A man couldn't keep that up forever. Not even a good one. He was vaguely worried. A premonition urged him to hurry, and to hell with noise.

A wagon was just discernible in the shadows of a grove, out there in the open. The very silence was ominous. Slim squatted, straining his eyes to outwit the treacherous blend of shadow and blue-white glare. A twig crackled. Someone whispered, "There's the old son of a—! Yonder—"

The thunderous boom of a buffalo gun cut into that. A horse screamed, wood splintered, and wagon tires rattled over the rocky outcropping as the team bolted.

Then Slim went wild. It would take the old man just a split second to shove another cartridge into "Jezebel", but three rifles were crackling, and Crane, enraged by his bad shot, was roaring more loudly than his .60 caliber gun.

Slim raked the flame-stabbed shadows with his Winchester. A man yelled. The kid's gun jammed. He drew his Colt and charged, cursing as he fired.

The silence in his father's quarter froze him. They'd killed him! A man broke from the shadows. He doubled up, cut down by a pair of slugs. Then Jezebel's blast drowned every other sound.

The old man bobbed up from cover, a .45 in each hand. But two men escaped his wrath. They reached their saddle mounts, and galloped hell bent. When father and son met at the overturned wagon, they found only one raider, his own blood mingled with that of three butchered beeves.

"Had ye worried, heh?" old man Crane chuckled.

"Gosh, pap, you sure did!" Slim was shaking all over.

Then he felt sick. His mouth sagged, and the gun fell from his hands. His father, striking a match, was kneeling beside the dead man, and sombrely shaking his head. "By God," he mourned, "I shore *am* gittin' old. Wan't old Jezebel that got this jasper, after all. Yes, sir, I'm shore gittin' old, when all I kin hit is a pore, helpless hoss." He looked up, sharply. "Whut in tunket? Ain't you never seen blood afore!"

"Ug—uh—" Slim choked, gulped. His face was gray green in the moon glow. "That's—um—that's the—nester. Herb Daley—"

"Mighty nice, son." The old man rubbed his hands together. "Smoking out a double action varmint. Though it's too bad, him having a daughter."

He scrutinized the wagon and the horses. He was saying, "Brands blotted out, so's they kain't be traced. 'Tain't Daley's rig."

Slim went to get his horse. When he returned, he said, "I been thinking mebbe I could go to Paso del Norte and find out who's behind this crooked stuff. It's a cinch Daley ain't the head man, and we didn't ketch no one to question."

"By gravey!" This after a moment of pondering. "That's right. Arter daylight, when I kin study the sign, I'll tell you what size jasper to look fer, and what kind of hosses they was riding."

That would be an open book to an old scout. Slim nodded, then said, "Pappy, why'n't you tell the sheriff and the coroner you done this yourself? Thattaway, won't nobody suspect me, if anyone hears I'm going to Paso del Norte. Being as these yere are your critters, on your spread, ain't no one going to as much as axe you a cross question."

Old man Crane straightened up. He appreciated modesty in a young squirt. "They allus lowed you was a easy going jasper and none too dang smart, nohow." He slapped his thigh, chuckled. "I allus looked dumb too, when I was your age. Which fooled a lot of folks. You go right now, and I'll write you to Paso del Norte, telling you what all I larned."

That helped. "Good God," the kid told himself, later that night, "I'd ruther be shot than face Madge. And onct I help pappy outen this mess, I ain't never coming back."

Then his face hardened, and looked older, years older, than it had an hour ago. Even if Madge never learned he had fired the fatal shot, she'd still hate him for his father's sake...

* * * *

All the hard cases in the southwest had come to Paso del Norte. Longhaired trappers in buckskin, frock coated gamblers, waddies in faded levis, all busy with their own pursuits; and none, as far as Slim Crane could tell, with an eye for him.

As the sun dipped lower, Slim saw the women who had flocked to town. They leaned from windows, beckoning and smiling; they lounged in doorways, clad only in kimonos whose thin fabric and loosely gathered folds seconded the wearer's brazen invitation.

Somewhere in hell roaring Paso del Norte, Crane expected to get a direct lead to the beef thieves. His father had mailed him descriptions of the fugitives who had survived the melee at the Diamond C. Hoof-prints, bits of hair rubbed off on trees, human hair in the sweatband of a hat lost in flight; boot prints, and the length of strides, all these built up the picture. A short, heavy man whose feet were cramped by new, tight boots, had ridden a *grullo*; a long legged, red haired man with a slight limp had escaped on a strawberry roan with one defective shoe.

From one saloon to the next, Slim hunted the pair. Appealing to the law was useless. The beef contractors, the railroad builders, the slaughter house operators were hand in hand. Unless he found overwhelming evidence, he had not a chance.

The only way was to catch the thieves with Diamond C hides in their possession. That would justify cutting them down in their tracks; a frontier jury would acquit him.

"And to hell with the jedge and his whereas-nevertheless-buts!" Slim told himself, as back prudently planted against the wall in the corner, his biting glance covered the smoke filled barroom.

One thing Slim had not overlooked; though leaving Arroyo Rojo by night, he could not hope to have reached Paso del Norte unheralded. Two fugitives had ridden ahead of him. Thus, his back was to a wall.

Slim watched the dancers whirling about the rough-hewn floor, and the girls who hustled drinks to the tables along the further wall. They were trim wenches, fresh and shapely; too subtle to wear short skirts. Slim had seen that type in the saloons of Arroyo Rojo, and they seemed downright indecent. But these girls stirred his blood.

Before Slim realized it, he drew a slow, deep breath. The glass in his fingers spilled little drops of whiskey. He shook his head, as if to clear it of dizziness. When a blonde girl with hair that was more silver than yellow came lithely toward him, he could not avoid her glance. Nor did he want to, when he smelled her perfume and heard her voice.

She seemed almost shy, like Madge, the first time they met by moonlight, and she nervously fingered a concha on his vest.

"I wonder if you'd not take a table, over there." She gestured. "We could drink together." She looked up, and hesitancy blossomed into a smile. "Wouldn't it be fun, pretending we're old friends? I'm...well...a newcomer, and it's awfully hard, playing up to these tough customers. I never realized it would be like this."

A tall man with a drooping black mustache stood in the corner, arms folded. He nodded as he watched her accost Slim. This was the proprietor. The girl flashed him a glance as Slim followed her.

Then he saw a red haired man, long legged and limping a little. Slim remembered his father's description. He wondered if the cowpuncher had a strawberry roan outside.

"Listen, Sally," he whispered, as they approached the table in the corner, "I'm waiting for a fellow, and I can't see much, from here."

A waiter was bringing the drinks Sally had ordered before leaving the bar. One glass, Slim realized, would be cold tea, but he didn't care.

The tall redhead's face went sour, then black when his glance shifted toward Sally. The blonde shrank, caught Slim's arm. Her hip would have brushed him, but for the holster tied to his thigh.

The redhead moved swiftly, despite his game leg. He spat and wrathfully said, "Well, you towhaired tramp, I guess he's handsome, huh?"

Slim did not want to quarrel and make himself conspicuous; his job was to follow the lame man, "Now, look-ee here, pardner." He raised his left hand in a placating gesture; Sally still clung to his right arm. "That ain't no way to talk to a lady."

"Please do go away, Randy," Sally implored.

Between them, they only managed to get him hostile.

"Why, you long legged son of a—"

The music had stopped, and Randy's voice filled the entire place. Sally cried out, and Slim thrust her away from him. That move was enough to start Randy for his gun.

He was quick, but he delayed a little, to give Slim a chance to get shed of Sally. This was from over-confidence, and the desire to make it clear that he had not drawn first. His face made that all very plain; Slim knew that this man had moved in for a kill.

So did everyone else. Men were scrambling, and girls were diving for cover.

Randy's eyes suddenly bugged out, and his jaw sagged. That was when Slim snapped, "Drop it, you polecat!"

The gun in his left hand enforced that. Randy, too intent on timing the kid's right hand reach for the holster at his right hip, had missed the Colt which Crane had flashed from the waist band of his pants.

Randy's smoke pole chunked to the sawdust, Men and women began breathing again, murmuring; it seemed almost funny, that surprised gunner's gaping mouth and popping eyes.

But what followed capped a good start. As he holstered his Colt, Slim closed in with his free fist. Randy was cold on his feet, and he had no time to lower his hands to defend himself. He crumpled, cracked his head on a cuspidor, and lay there, not even kicking.

The spectators shook their heads. A bouncer said, "Shucks, Randy won't know his own name fer a couple days." This was as they hauled him to the rear, his scalp deeply gashed.

Slim said to Sally, "M'am, I'm pow'ful sorry, but I can't tarry and drink with you."

He went to the street. A strawberry roan was hitched at the rack. By the saloon lights, he could plainly see the hoof prints: half the near front shoe was missing.

"That gent was fixing to kill me," Slim reasoned, and with certainty. "But ain't nobody around here that's got ground for thinking I know it."

Randy's studied attempt to make Slim draw first indicated that the law was biting into this tough town's hide. Self-defense had to be pretty clearly proved. So, as he headed for his hotel, he chuckled and said to himself, "Nothing to do now but see I don't get myself shot in the back. And whilst Mistah Randy is trying to recollect what his right name is, there's a chanct of finding his pardner."

Once in his room, he thrust his gun under his pillow, and began unbuckling his spurs. He was thinking, "Mebbe if I fixed myself up like a Mexican, I'd have a better chanct of sneaking up on Randy's pardner."

Winning a few gunfights would not expose the chief of the cattle thieves; that would only block the trail. He sat there, thinking it over; he recollected that Sally knew Randy by name…

A furtive tapping at the door brought him to his feet before he removed his boots. A feminine voice whispered, "It's me. Sally."

He let her in, and replaced his gun when he saw she was alone.

"Oh, I'm in a terrible predicament," she breathlessly began, a hand on his arm.

Sally still wore her blue satin gown. Lamplight reached down into her low cut bodice to model the loveliest curves. A backward move as his boot closed the door behind her. She let go his arm when he offered her the only chair in the room. When he seated himself on the bed, Sally resumed, "I've been robbed—I mean, someone went through my room—over at the Buckhead Saloon—I'd just saved up enough to pay my fare home—"

"Ma'am, I sure would admire to help you." Slim was touched by her distress, "But I'm dang nigh busted. If ten bucks'd help—"

"Oh, but it's worse than that!" She buried her face in her hands, and her white shoulders for a moment were shaken by sobs. As Slim seated himself on the arm of the chair and stroked her head, Sally went on, "I married a man—who advertised—he was a wealthy rancher—"

"What? A gal like you, looking for matrumonyal advertising jaspers? That jest ain't reasonable."

"But I lived in Cross Plains. Everyone that amounted to anything left town, except those that got killed in feuds."

He began to catch the point: a lovely girl, one of the many extra women in a town depopulated by adventure and the interminable quarrels of the post oak country, had snapped at the first prospect.

"Uh—what's wrong with your—um…mail order husband?"

"He's a drunken bum. He's one-eyed, and positively filthy! Most of the time, he's in jail. I told him I'd pay his fine and give him a hundred dollars in cash if he'd promise to leave town and never look at me again!"

Slim, touched to the heart, tried to offer a consoling arm. The chair nearly upset, and in the scramble, Sally ended on his knee. She clung to him, curled up in his arms like a kitten. "Gol dang it, m'am," he gasped, "in another second, I'll be busting right out crying myself. But where in tunket I can get the money—onless mebbe I win myself a reward—" He was thinking fast. "For nailing rustlers or road agents or something."

"Oh, you're wonderful!" Her generous kiss made him realize he had really discovered something. "Slim, if you can just keep an eye on things and protect me until I can save up some more money—"

Sally was built to arouse protective instincts, and her voice encouraged such emotions. That sufficed to start a reckless exchange of kisses; and the fact that her father's thievery and violent death had erected an impassable barrier between Madge and Slim clinched things... He turned the lamp low.

But Slim was surprised when the door slammed open, and Sally screamed, clawed herself out of his arms. "Oh, my God! That's him!"

One of the men revealed by the hall light was the proprietor of the Buckhead Saloon. Slim scarcely more than noted his black mustache and twisted mouth and craggy jaw. It was the drunk at the threshold who held his attention.

So this was Sally's husband, strangely released from jail? A chinless, one-eyed beanpole whose weak mouth twitched and slobbered tobacco juice as he screeched, "You dirty—Sally, you lousy stinking—!"

Sally cried, "Look out, he'll shoot," and flung herself clear across the room, legs for a moment twinkling as she vanished in a flurry of silken slip and streaming blonde hair.

But Slim hardly heard that. A fellow hears nothing when a .45 is weaving into line with his gizzard. The drunk lurched a pace. Slim had no time to debate. His hand came from beneath the pillow. The drunk was slow and fumbling. Sally's boss made a move toward his hip.

Slim cut loose, and the room shuddered from the rolling blasts of his Colt. The drunk's hammer thumb slipped, and he dropped with a cold gun. Men were tramping and shouting down the hall. They had been attracted by the two who had barged through the lobby, hunting trouble.

Sally's boss did not shoot or even draw. But a deputy marshal was advancing behind drawn guns. Slim knew that that hard bitten specimen would never back down; they'd kill each other.

"Hist 'em, bub!" His icy eyes covered everything; the dead man, the disheveled girl who came from cover, crying out that it was not Slim's fault. "Mebbe 'twarn't his fault, defending hisself," the law allowed. "But smoking out a gent that's pertecting the sanctity of his home is downright murder, m'am, and yo're a disgrace to yore sex, yuh shameless hussy. Mr. Kenyon bails the pore feller outen jail, and look whut you was doing!"

Sally's boss was smiling contentedly, and stroking his mustache. That told Slim a lot. The blonde had not deliberately betrayed him; she had been no more than a cog in the machine. And the marshal was bona fide; also he was stubborn in his notions on a husband's rights.

It looked like a hanging. At the very best, more years in the *juzgado* than any man could endure. Sally was paper white, wide eyed; she made inarticulate sounds as she swayed, uncertain on her feet. Slim wondered when she would collapse, or burst out with insane laughter.

The marshal was coming forward, one gun now holstered, so that he could search his prisoner. There was no help for this. Slim saw a man approach Sally's boss, Burt Kenyon.

Kenyon started, cursed, whirled from the scene. That brief distraction left Slim wondering what had happened. A gun blast shook him. Flame from the marshal's Colt set his shirt afire. Glass had spattered. Kerosene fumes thickened the air. The lawman was buckling at the knees.

Slim could not put these details into their natural sequence. Things had happened too quickly, and he was already in motion. Sally was slamming the door, bolting it, screaming, "Run, darling! Before he gets on his feet!"

She had snatched the lamp from its bracket and smashed it across the marshal's head. Slim picked up his gun and bolted for the window. Men were yelling in the hall. Sally cried, "They can't hang me for this! Run, you fool!"

The door was splintering. The bolt was yielding.

* * * *

Slim landed in the alley. They could not do much or anything to a woman who had become hysterical. Sally's laughter was clear above the uproar in his room. And before the alarm could spread, he was forking his unsaddled horse.

He was well out of Paso del Norte before a posse combed the town. But Slim Crane's mission was blown all to hell. Whether a warrant would follow him was another question. He'd better talk it over with his father. That urge drove him toward Arroyo Rojo, the town he had resolved to quit. And quit it he would; he'd get a fresh horse, some money, and his dad's blessing, then head for New Mexico before Madge could ever curse him for being in on her father's death.

As he rode, he wondered what news had startled Burt Kenyon.

Then, hearing hoof beats far behind him, he had no further time for thought. How in tunket could a posse have picked the trail so surely and quickly! With his start, that was all wrong.

Someone might have guessed his next move. Certainly, his identity must have been blazoned all over Paso del Norte.

Slim, however, outwitted his pursuers. His horse, unburdened by a saddle, carried less weight. So he gained for a while, then doubled back; from cover, he watched them swoop past him.

"Dang funny, only four of 'em!" He shook his head, frowned. "And that damn' sure of where I'm going, they ain't bothering to track me!"

He mulled that over. He could not get the full significance. However, his best guess led him toward home, though along a short cut. It was a toss up whether he'd get there before or after the posse. Still, that really made little difference, so that they did not meet.

"Just as long as I can put a bug in pappy's ear. If Kenyon ain't in the beef business, I'm a polecat's uncle!"

When he reached the Diamond C spread, after swinging wide of Arroyo Rojo, it lacked less than an hour of dawn. The cook was not stirring about, nor was anyone snoring in the bunkhouse. Slim guessed that the riders, including his father, were out patrolling the range. That made it bad. He did not know whether to go out to find them, or stay and wait.

A horse whinnied. Even in the gloom, Slim could plainly enough discern the silvery mane and tail of a *palomino* at the hitching post; and the Diamond C had no animal of that coloring in its entire string. Then he noted the glow of light from a side window. Something was dead wrong. Whoever the stranger might be, there should have been some sound of conversation, and dominated by his father's voice.

But Slim's unwary approach had given warning. As a window rattled up, he flung himself from his mount and landed behind the grindstone. A woman cried, "Stay right where you are, or I'll shoot!"

Madge Daley was at the sill, ready to slide to the ground and get to her *palomino*; though only Slim would have recognized her in the shadows that blotted out all but the white blur of face and throat. It seemed that the desire to escape without recognition had spurred her to that desperate outburst; her voice was tense and tremulous.

She was the last person on earth he wanted to see. He wondered whether, vengeance bent, she had come to assassinate his father. Finally, he contrived to croak, "Madge—what the blazes—what you doing here?"

"Slim!" She choked, and there was a metallic gleam as she lowered a pistol. "Good God, I thought—I've got to get out of here before your father gets back —don't ever tell anyone—dad would kill me!"

She was scarcely coherent. Slim vaulted to the sill. "Get back in. I'm alone. What's wrong?"

For a moment she clung to him, trembling and groping for words. Then she tugged at his arm, urging him to the lighted room. She said, "Slim, I'm so ashamed. I don't know what to say. But that—" She gestured toward the table, "That'll prove—but don't ever tell dad!"

She did not seem to know her father was dead. He regarded her disheveled hair, the torn blouse that trailed in tatters, exposing a good deal more than she realized. But as she hid her face on his shoulder, Slim's eyes popped out of his head.

On the table were bills of sale, which he recognized from their legal appearance. There were a dozen squares of rawhide, cut from as many freshly peeled hides. Each piece had the Diamond C brand!

"When we quarreled that night," she went on, haltingly, "I was furious. But the next night—oh, I hate to say it, but I learned that dad was beefing your cattle. To get even for that fence you cut. And for good measure—well, I realized why he'd bought me so many nice things, so suddenly. So I left, Wednesday night. To steal evidence, in Paso del Norte. I tricked a watchman there, and—"

She flushed, grimaced wryly. But Slim didn't notice that. He was too busy with his thoughts. While her father faced fatal bullets on the Diamond C, Madge had been in Paso del Norte, on the prowl. Slim demanded, "You mean you was fixing to sell your own pappy to the law! Why—" He thrust her from him. "Why—you damned low-down—"

"Slim, don't look at me that way! Don't you understand, I came to throw this stuff in through a window. But no one was in. So I put it here, where he'd find it. There's nothing against father, only against Burt Kenyon. A politician, beef contractor, saloon owner."

"Oh." Slim understood. "Trying to save your pappy, huh!"

"More than that! Trying to get him out of crookedness and revenge. I'd begun to see the cattleman's side of it."

Then Slim's misery returned a hundredfold. Madge was honest to the core, and brave as they made them. And he had killed her father. He didn't know what to say or do. Even if it never leaked out, he could not face her. The glow in her eyes burned him when she went on, "You and I can make peace between our parents, can't we, Slim? I hated you for what you said, but it set me thinking."

"Sit down, honey," he muttered, sinking into a chair.

"I can't. I've got to get home to dad. I'll lie out of it, somehow, so he won't suspect, right away, what I did."

"I'll ride with you." Slim could not evade the issue, or let her go to an empty cabin, to wait until the news reached her. "I got—uh—a heap—to tell you."

She regarded his drawn face. She sensed something was dreadfully wrong, and apprehension gripped her. "Slim, what is it? Tell me now. Right here!"

But Slim had no chance to explain. A rifle blast and the shattering of glass were sounds prolonged by Madge's scream. His side went numb. He did not realize that the distortion of the pane had spoiled the marksman's aim. Other slugs thudded against the heavy walls, and sprayed the room with flying splinters.

As he went for his .45, Madge snatched a poker and swept the lamp from the table. It crashed in the fireplace. She smothered the blazing kerosene with cushions from the lounge. Slim steadied his pistol barrel on the sill to squeeze lead at the tongues of flame that spurted from the woodpile and from the corner of the barn.

When the fusillade slowed down to futile sniping, Madge crept to Slim's side and said, "We can slip out the other side. There's only four shooting at us."

"We can't," he muttered. "They got my hoss and yourn. It's too close to dawn, anyway. We'd not get far."

A man shouted from the murky shadows, "Throw out those papers, and we'll go away."

Slim leveled the Winchester Madge had located. As he did so, he thought, "Gawd, if I had dad's buffler gun, I'd bust hell outen the grindstone that son is hiding behind." He fired, heard the futile whine of a ricochet slug, then a mocking laugh.

"Don't be silly, you young fool. Throw out the bills of sale. We know exactly what she stole. We trailed her, and you."

"Come in and get 'em," Slim challenged, wrathful at having ridden into a trap. The enemy had craftily lurked to learn the entire sense of that baffling alliance they thought it was.

There was a furtive stirring outside, but gloom still protected the besiegers. Slim did not realize what was in the wind until he smelled burning hay. Flames first yellowed, then reddened the gaping door of the barn.

Dry as it was, it would go up like gunpowder. Worse than that, the first gray of dawn brightened the open ground. If he or Madge tried to make a break on foot, they would be hunted down.

The barn was smartly ablaze. Choking fumes billowed in through the broken window. Gusts of furnace heat lashed the besieged. At any moment, Slim expected the shingles to catch afire over his head. And the flames would now expose him, whichever direction he tried for flight.

"Honey," he choked, catching her hand, "you try slipping out yonder whilst I go out, shooting, tother way. You got a chanct!"

"I won't," she said. "It's my father's fault all this is happening. If you're killed, I'll feel like a murderer, and he'll be one!"

That whipped Slim to desperation. He caught her shoulder, shook her violently. "You damn little fool, get out! Your pappy's dead. I shot him the night you was in Paso del Norte. I didn't know 'twas him that was beefing our critters, but I kilt him!"

Horror widened her eyes. He repeated, "I kilt him. Now git out; you got no call to stick with me. Git, you fool, I'm going out a-shooting!"

He had found and loaded a second .45. Gun in each hand, he bounded toward the side furthest from the fire. He had thrust the evidence in his shirt. Grimly he saw that his death would still nail Kenyon. The'd not search his riddled carcass; they'd assume the evidence had gone up in smoke. But when the old man found him, they'd be sunk, the bastards!

Though four men had circled to await his break, regardless of direction, he still caught them momentarily off guard. His long legs seemed to cover yards at a stretch as he zigzagged, ducked, guns blazing for an instant, then silent during another bound. The enemy fired as they concentrated to cut off his flight.

Lead whipped past him. One of the raiders jerked back, and lurched into the open. Then Slim caught a glimpse of big Burt Kenyon. He shifted, spraying lead. He missed, and a hammer impact from the other flank made him spin, numb and helpless; his guns would not work any more.

Kenyon shouted, "Where's the girl? You, Hubbell! Doran!"

"Watch it!" someone howled above the roaring flames.

Kenyon ducked. Somewhere, Madge screamed, but no one heard. Pounding hoofs shook the ground. Slim, recovering a little, saw two riders charging hell bent. His old man and Whitey Harris, a cowpuncher, had been attracted by the flames. They could not have distinguished pistol shots from the crackle of blazing wood, tinder-dry.

They were riding into a trap. Slim tried to yell, tried to shoot. God, wouldn't they see it was more than just a fire!

Kenyon, thinking Slim finished, was turning his fire on old man Crane. Hubbell's gun was dancing. The two riders piled from their saddles, pulling iron as they dropped; but the roll of the ground was their only cover. The raiders' slugs kicked up spurts of dust. Answering fire whistled over Slim's head; the buffalo gun was roaring.

Then Slim cocked his gun with his teeth. He yelled a challenge, and as Kenyon jerked up, the kid's .45 did its work. And the smack of a Winchester, tying into the roar of the Colt, cleared the deck.

Madge, coming out of the house, flung the rifle on the ground.

"It was empty," she cried, "and I fumbled the shells till the last second. Why didn't you wait?"

Slim, staggering toward his father, hailed Whitey Harris. The cowpuncher, wounded by that first volley, was clawing a red splash on his chest.

"We seen the blaze," he choked.

Madge caught him as he sagged. He thrust her aside.

"Look to Dad Crane, he's damn neart finished."

Slim knew that, even before Whitey spoke. The old man forced a grin, tried to speak, then slumped in a heap. Madge, now at Slim's side, caught his arm.

"Are you hurt bad? What can I do?"

The kid's drawn face twitched.

"Fix Whitey. I just got a rib knocked loose and my shoulder drilled. And what the hell you doing here? I told you—I told you what I'd gone and done. Get out, I can't stand looking at you. You know what I done!"

"I know." Her lovely face was pained and weary. Tears gleamed in her eyes, and cut white paths through the dust and smoke stain of her cheeks. She shook her head, very slowly. "First I couldn't believe you. Then I went wild, but when I got the gun loaded—Slim, I couldn't hate you enough, so I fired at them, instead."

"Uh—what!" He couldn't believe all the implications.

"No," she solemnly went on. "All this, tonight, is what my father's pardners led him into, using his resentment for their own gains. Look what you've lost —from *our* fault—"

Slim scratched his battered head. "Honey, you forgiving me, you mean!"

"You didn't do it on purpose, and he was in the wrong. You and I can't carry on a feud. We've no relatives to keep it up."

Something told Slim that some day she could smile at him, and that she would. His own grief left him too numb for hatreds, and perhaps she felt that way, too.

"Honey," he finally said, "you can't fight a woman, so the feud's off, if you see things thataway. Orphants ought to stick together."

www.ingramcontent.com/pod-product-compliance
Lightning Source LLC
Chambersburg PA
CBHW032235010726
47494CB00002B/501